KNIGHTS
OF THE
CROSS

ALIEN ARRIVAL

M/F
MCDOUGAL FICTION

KNIGHTS

OF THE

CROSS

ALIEN ARRIVAL

BY
CHRISTOPHER J. ANDUHA

Published by:

McDougal Fiction
a label of McDougal & Associates
18896 Greenwell Springs Road
Greenwell Springs, LA 70739
www.thepublishedword.com

ISBN 978-1-950398-39-3

Printed on demand in the U.S., the U.K. and Australia
For Worldwide Distribution

DEDICATION

To my father, Ralph DeLuccio, who passed away at the end of 2021.

To my daughter, Miriam Anduha: When you were in your mother's womb, I started writing this book so that you would remember to reach for your dreams and never give up.

Finally, I would like to dedicate this book to my Lord and Savior, Jesus Christ, Who is the Author of my faith and Who helped me to be the author of this book.

ACKNOWLEDGEMENTS

I would like to thank my wife, Julie, for her love and support during the writing and editing of this book. Julie, you were the spark that helped me, not only to start, but also to finish this book. Whenever I got stuck, you helped me figure a way out and through, so that I could finish it.

CONTENTS

CHAPTER 1

ENCOUNTERS

FROM DEEP IN SPACE, a portal opens to our solar system, and from it comes a massive starship that is ten miles wide and thirty miles long. It is followed by a fleet of eleven other ships, each five miles wide and fifteen miles long. Within these starships exist beings called Psystructs, a blend of different alien species that have been merged with cybernetics, increasing their speed and power and granting them psychic abilities. These forms made it easy to intimidate, dominate and execute their mission of galactic domination. Their purpose is to strip planets of their resources and to expand their forces within each galaxy, so that they may establish their grip over every living being.

As the portal closes, the Psystructs' fleet stops near the rings of Saturn and activates their cloaking technology, to keep them from being discovered. Now, aboard one of the other starships, they begin to prepare one of their scout ships to explore their newest target—Earth.

The Psystruct scout general known as Sadoom makes his way toward the hangar, and with each step there's a thunderous echo that can be heard throughout the corridor. When Sadoom arrives in the hanger, he goes to the scout Squad Leader named Brykar, and as he turns to face him, Brykar bows before him, saying, "We are nearly ready to depart, General Sadoom. What are your orders?"

Looking squarely at Brykar, General Sadoom replies, "Your orders, Brykar, are to head to the planet known as Earth and research their defenses, although I do not expect the earthlings to be a problem. However, at this point, we have no way of knowing if they have been warned about us. Just remember: your mission is to test, observe and report. But if, for some reason, their defenses prove to be too powerful for you, I want you to let me know as soon as possible, so that we may send additional forces."

"Yes, General," Brykar replies. "I will do as you order."

Brykar stands to his feet and enters the ship. As his crew prepares for launch, he says, "This should be interesting!"

Sadoom, standing nearby, tells Brykar, "The Earth has minimal resources and isn't of any value to us, but we must do as ordered."

Suddenly a mysterious voice is heard. "Sadoom, the Earth has great value, for it is the only planet that possesses a rare material that could be used against us. If we can get this rare element, we can ensure our rule and make sure that no one will ever be able to challenge us again."

With this, Sadoom falls to his knees and says, "Forgive me, master. I will not doubt you."

Rising, Sadoom exits the hanger, and as he does so, the doors close, and the scout ship departs for Earth.

MEANWHILE, ON EARTH, a large group of students have arrived at the Grand Canyon for a class trip. As the students exit their buses, some of them are excited, while others seemingly could care less. As the students and teachers gather, the teacher in charge starts to speak. "May I have your attention, please. As you all know, each of you are to document what you learn about the canyon and then prepare a report. Also, each group will have two opportunities to document, once in the morning and once in the afternoon, before we leave."

He then begins to announce who will be in each group. Although most of the students listen, a young man named Brad trips one of his classmates, Joseph, and Joseph falls to the ground. Some of the students begin to laugh. One of the teachers sees Joseph getting up and says, "Joseph, please be more careful."

Once all the rules have been explained, the students are divided into five groups of twelve, and each group is given an hour to examine the canyon.

ABOUT FIVE HOURS LATER, the students have some free time. Joseph decides to spend some time away from the group. He is a Puerto Rican male, about five feet eight inches in height, with a muscular build. He has long jet-black hair that he keeps in a ponytail and is wearing a white polo shirt (a bit dusty from his earlier fall), a pair of blue jeans and boots.

He notices a cliff overlooking the buses and decides that would be a good place to enjoy some solitude. As he makes his way up the path to the cliff, Brad follows him, and this is noticed by several other students.

The first of the students to notice this is Janet, a black girl who is the student body president. Janet is five feet six inches tall. In addition to being the student body president, Janet is also captain of the volleyball team. Today she is wearing a pair of red jeans shorts, a pink blouse and hiking boots.

Max is the next to follow, and he is a Korean boy, five feet eleven inches tall, and is wearing a gold colored polo shirt with blue jeans and hiking boots.

Maggie watches them as they go up the path, and then decides that she wants to follow them too. Maggie is a Chinese female. Five feet five inches tall, Maggie is captain of the cheerleading squad. This particular day she is dressed in a silver sleeveless shirt with green shorts.

Looking up from his tablet, Desmond, or Des as everyone calls him, watches as the others go up the path and decides to investigate what all the excitement is about. He is a black male, five feet, ten inches tall, and is wearing a grey polo shirt and brown cargo shorts.

Just as Des goes up the path, Jessica, a Puerto Rican female, who is the girl most girls want to be, the one all the guys dream about, also decides to follow the growing crowd. She is wearing an aqua blouse and a blue skirt.

Then Tasha, another Puerto Rican female notices Jessica and the others going up the path and decides to see what's going on. She's wearing black shorts with a yellow T-shirt.

Tasha catches John's eye, as she heads up the path, and John, a Chinese male, who is wearing a loose fitting T-shirt with some blue jeans, follows them as well.

Wearing a white top with a silver skirt, Britney, a black female, notices the students going up the path and walks toward it herself.

As Britney starts up the path, Eric, a white male, wearing a silver shirt and black jeans, starts to follow her.

Sally, a white female, is wearing a pair of rose-gold shorts and a matching top. As the others head up the path, she follows them.

ONCE JOSEPH REACHES THE TOP of the cliff, he walks toward a large rock near the edge, but before he can begin to enjoy the solitude, Brad approaches him. When he reaches Joseph, Brad shouts "Did you have a nice trip, loser?" He was mocking Joseph.

Not amused, Joseph replies, "Back off, Brad! I don't feel like dealing with your nonsense today."

"Don't treat me like I'm beneath you, retard," Brad says. "In fact, the last time I checked, I run this school." It is clear that he is trying to show Joseph that he is superior.

"That may be true," Joseph replies, "but we're not at school. And out here, you're like me ... just a guy—nothin' more, nothin' less."

With that, Brad runs toward Joseph and grabs him, lifting him off his feet. As he does so, he is yelling, "Who do you think you are?"

Suddenly, the other students arrive and see what is going on, and when they do, Brad turns, allowing Joseph to slip from his grasp, and the two begin to square off. Joseph takes his glasses off, as if to challenge Brad. "Great!" he says, "Now we have an audience."

"Let them watch!" Brad shouts. "It'll be the same as before."

"That's what you think, Brad," Joseph countered. "This time I won't hold back." And he and Brad prepare to face off for what they can only hope will be their final showdown.

BEFORE THE TWO CAN ACTUALLY EXCHANGE BLOWS, they hear a loud explosion. Breaking off their fighting stance, they look to see where the sound came from and see that their school buses have been destroyed. "Oh great! There goes our ride," Joseph says sarcastically. Turning to Brad, he continues, "As much as I love our pow wows, this will have to wait."

All of the students rush to the edge of the cliff. Joseph's best friend, Max, asks, "What just happened?" Turning to his friend, Joseph replies, "Let's see ... Brad's a jerk, and all three of our buses were just blown up. Need I say more?"

"We can see that," Max concurred, "but how were the buses blown up is the question?"

Janet, pulling closer to them out of curiosity asks, "Who would want to blow up a bus?"

Des, peering down at a crater left by the blast, replies, "Judging by the crater where the buses were, who (or whatever) is powerful. Chances are it's not human."

"Des, are you serious saying that aliens did this?" asks Max.

Jessica chimes in, "Hey, Des, this isn't one of your sci-fi books."

But as the smoke clears, the students begin to focus on what has caused their buses to be blown up, and they are left in utter shock. Before them, lowering itself slowly to the earth, is some sort of alien craft.

SOON AFTER THE STRANGE CRAFT HAS LANDED, the students watch as Brykar exits. Next, they see alien soldiers exiting the ship as well. Unknown to them, these soldiers are known as Psydrones. They are the foot soldiers of the Psystructs, Brykar says to them, "Fan out and destroy any humans in the area."

As the Psydrones disperse, their first victims become the students' teachers hiding nearby and their remaining classmates. They are all viciously killed by the Psydrones as the students on the ledge watch.

John whispers, "I guess Des was right. These things aren't human."

Brad says, "If these things aren't human, then how do we stop them?" He has forgotten his anger with Joseph for the moment.

Suddenly a figure emerges and begins fighting the Psydrones. Sally says, "Who is that guy? And look at him trash those freaks. Hey, Janet, do you think he might be cute underneath that mask?"

Janet shouts back, "Sally! Are you serious?"

Britney utters what could pass for a chuckle, "Unfortunately, when it comes to guys, she's always serious."

Tasha asks, "Is it really safe to stay here while those things fight it out?"

Eric answers, "Right now, our best bet is to stay put, unless you want to fight those things yourself."

Maggie says, "Guys, we may have to fight after all. Check it out." They all turn to see where she is pointing and see behind them, a huge hole opening up, and four Psydrones begin to emerge from it. In an instant, they all get to their feet and scatter.

AS THE TEENS SCATTER, they split into four groups of three, each group being chased by one of the Psydrones. The first Psydrone chases after Joseph,

Janet and Max. They run for their lives and find a rock slide to duck behind. Joseph whispers to the others, "Okay, this is getting old. I say we fight." Turning to Max, he says, "Are you with me, Bro?"

Before Max can reply, Janet says, "Hey boys, don't forget about me. I want in as well."

Max says, " The lady has a point."

Joseph raises up a little to see how far away the Psydrone is, and as he does, the alien creature spots him and begins to fire in the direction of the teens.

"What just happened?" Max asked.

"Nothing much," Joseph replied. "He just spotted me is all."

Shaking his head, Max looks at him and says, "I thought the point was seeing where he is, not giving away our position, making us a target."

Janet looks at the two of them sternly and says, "We can worry about who is to blame later. Right now we need to deal with these things, so which one of you guys has a plan?"

Joseph answers first. "Actually, I do," he says. "First, I'll throw a rock behind that thing. Once it turns around, Max, I want you to knock it off its feet. And Janet, after its down, I want you to finish it off."

Even as the two of them nod in agreement, the blasts are getting closer. Joseph quickly grabs a rock the size of a tennis ball and throws it. It lands just as he had planned, behind the Psydrone, and this causes the creature to turn around and look behind. Just then, Max charges at the Psydrone and slides underneath him, knocking him off of his feet.

As the Psydrone falls to the ground, Janet runs toward him. Then she leaps into the air, so that as she lands, she strikes the Psydrone on the head with her heel, knocking him unconscious.

Joseph is right behind her and he grabs the blaster the Psydrone had been using. It was unlike anything they had ever seen. "Looks like Des was right for once," Joseph decides.

Relieved, the other students chuckle a little as they make their way to where they could rejoin their friends.

WHEN THAT FIRST PSYDRONE SETS OUT in pursuit of Joseph, Max and Janet, another chases Brad, Desmond and Jessica. This Psydrone is using what looks like a type of sword. Fortunately, the students are able to run fast and then quickly find a good hiding place.

"Listen," Brad says, "I'll hold him off, and you two run for it."

"Not on your life," Des answers. "As much as I don't like you, I have a better idea and one where we all walk out of here." He then pulls from his pocket some rocks he has found, which, on impact will create a dust cloud. He tells the others, "Once I throw these, we need to rush him while he is distracted."

"That's not a bad idea for a dork," Brad says, chuckling.

"I'm gonna pretend I didn't hear that," says Des, shaking his head.

Jessica adds, "Could you boys finish this macho contest when our lives are not in danger?"

Des throws his rocks at the Psydrone, and when they hit, a dust cloud begins to form. The three students take advantage of the moment and attack, knocking the Psydrone into a wall and leaving him unconscious.

SALLY, BRITNEY AND TASHA ARE ALSO TRYING TO ESCAPE the Psydrone that is after them, when suddenly Britney falls to the ground. As the Psydrone approaches, Tasha also runs toward Britney, calling to Sally to keep running. As Tasha races toward Britney, she can see that the Psydrone will get there first. Then, without warning, Britney grabs a handful of dust and throws it at the Psydrone's face, blinding him for a moment. While the creature is dazed, Tasha grabs a metal rod and throws it to Britney.

"Thanks Tasha," Britney says, "I needed that." She swings the rod at the Psydrones' feet, and, as he falls to the ground, Sally turns and charges toward him, leaping so that when she lands, she strikes the Psydrone in the chest, leaving him unconscious.

JOHN, MAGGIE AND ERIC ALSO HAVE THEIR HANDS FULL with the Psydrone after them. When they come to an open area, John says, "What are we gonna do? We can't hide here."

Eric answers, "No kidding! We don't even have weapons to fight with."

Maggie doesn't agree, "You boys may not have weapons, but a girl is always prepared," and she pulls the strap off of her pocketbook and throws the pocketbook. When he blasts it, the powder from her makeup creates a cloud of dust. Panicked, the Psydrone fires wildly, but Maggie uses the strap from her pocketbook to snag his blaster. She then turns it on him, so when it fires, the Psydrone is vaporized.

AFTER SUCCESSFULLY BEATING THEIR RESPECTIVE PSYDRONES, the teens are able to reunite and try to catch their breath and figure out what to do next. They don't have long to think about it because no sooner have they found each other and reunited, than they turn and see Brykar standing there in front of them.

Seeing him up close for the first time is a shock. His entire body looks midnight blue in color, but it is made of metal. His face is covered by a mask, except for his mouth. As he walks toward them, they notice that in one moment his hands looked like swords, and the next moment they change back to resemble hands again.

Walking toward them, Brykar says, "Interesting! Not bad for children!"

Brad steps up and says, "Who are you calling children?"

Joseph pulls him back, and says, "Now is not the time to anger this alien with an army." He turns to Brykar and asks, "Who are you and what do you want?"

"My name is Brykar," the alien answers, "and what I want is to claim this planet for my master. Now prepare to die, children." He turns and speaks to the Psydrones that are with him, "Prepare to fire."

Then, suddenly, the figure they had seen earlier stands before them, and, as the Psydrones fire at them, the figure and the teens all vanish.

"Who was that?" Brykar says, "and where did he go?" Realizing he would have to find out later, he adds, "Never mind! I'll deal with that later. Now, prepare the ship."

THE PSYDRONES BEGIN THE PROCESS OF CONVERTING THEIR SHIP into their new Earth headquarters. Once the conversion is complete, the ship/headquarters then descends into the ground and begins converting the ground around it to suit their needs.

MEANWHILE THE MYSTERIOUS WARRIOR AND THE TEENS EMERGE in his secret base. After getting their bearings, Brad says to the strange man, "Okay, mystery man, time for you to speak up and tell us what is going on here?"

Annoyed, Des says, "Brad, can you please not anger the dude who just saved us from those things."

Joseph then steps forward and says, "Des is right, Brad, we all want answers, but first let's show some gratitude to our host."

With his back to them, the mystery man then turns and takes off his helmet. When he turns to them, they are surprised to see that he looks human. He says, "My name is Manuel, and welcome to my home and your new base."

A little taken aback, Joseph says, "What do you mean our base?"

Manuel then disengages the armor he's wearing and says, "The creatures that attacked your bus are known as Psystructs, and they are a race of cybernetic telepaths who go from planet to planet enslaving the people and using the conquered planet for the resources they need. I was chosen to be one of the guardians of this planet should anything threaten this world. However, my role as guardian is changing, for you twelve have been chosen to carry on as the protectors of this world."

Jessica then says, "That's great and all, but we barely were able to defeat those things. How are we going to protect the entire planet?"

Manuel answers, "Look before you."

As they look, the teens see twelve circles. He continues, "Step forward, and you will be given the power and the weapons necessary to protect your world and fend off this invasion."

"Not to be a wet blanket," Maggie says, "but who said we even want to be a part of this at all?"

Not phased by her remark, Manuel answers, "I understand that some of you may not want this. However, I'm asking you to help save your world from destruction. Will you help me?"

Joseph steps forward and says, "I can't and won't speak for my friends and classmates, but I can speak for myself. I will join you in your cause to save our world."

Brad says, "If you're going, I'm going too. I can't let you get all the glory."

Max shakes his head, thinking, "Why did Joe have to be the first to step forward?" He says, "Hey, Joe, where you go, I go. Besides, someone's gotta help you keep Brad in line." The two of them chuckle.

Janet then steps forward and says, "Boys, boys, boys! Instead of trying to fill your macho egos, how about we look at the bigger picture? If we don't stop these things now, we might not have a home to return to. To protect our world, I will also join the fight."

Des now steps forward and says "This is going to be interesting."

Eric adds, "If I'm gonna die, it may as well be to save the world."

John also steps up and says, "Yo, Eric, I got your back, Bud."

"Great!" Eric says. "Now we're both dead men."

"Speak for yourself, Bud," John says. "I'm coming to ensure that we both make it home."

Now Tasha steps forward and says, "I don't like this idea, but I do agree that we need to make sure we have a home to return to."

Sally then says, "I'm tired of running, and I agree it's time to fight back," and she too steps forward.

Britney turns to Jessica and Maggie, saying, "They're right. If we're the only ones who can stop this, then we need to step up," and she too steps forward.

Jessica says, "Okay, I'm in."

Maggie says, "Same here," and the two girls step forward together.

Manuel then says, "Now, it's time for the selection process."

Joseph says, "What selection process? I thought we were all chosen."

Manuel answers, "You were all chosen to defend your world. However, the selection process I speak of is to determine which powers you will receive." Suddenly the lights on the circles begin flashing in different colors, and, as the teens look to each other to figure out what is going on, the circles stop flashing, and each teen is suddenly enveloped in a beam of light.

Manuel then says, "Brad, the Armor of Fire has chosen you to be the Fire Knight.

"Des, the Armor of Earth has chosen you to be known as the Earth Knight.

"Maggie, the Armor of Wind has chosen you to be known as the Wind Knight.

"Jessica, the Armor of Water has chosen you to be known as the Aqua Knight.

"Britney, the Armor of Lightning has chosen you to be known as the Bolt Knight.

"Eric, the Armor of Shadow has chosen you to be the Shadow Knight.

"John, the Armor of Light has chosen you to be the Light Knight.

"Tasha, the Armor of the Beast has chosen you to be the Beast Knight.

"Sally, the Armor of Hope has chosen you to be the Hope Knight.

"Max, the Armor of Faith has chosen you to be the Faith Knight.

"Janet, the Armor of Love has chosen you to be the Love Knight.

"Joseph, the Armor of the Cross has chosen you to be the Cross Knight. And, Joseph, with these gifts comes the mantle of leadership. All of you will now be forever known as the Knights of the Cross."

Even as Manuel is speaking, an armor begins covering their bodies. It is harder than steel, and yet as flexible as cloth. Once they are completely covered in the armor, the guys receive helmets, while the girls receive masks. Their hair is now covered in the same metal.

WHEN THE LIGHTS SUDDENLY DISAPPEAR, so does the armor they were wearing and Joseph says, "What's going on?"

Manuel answers, "The armor has bonded with you so that whenever you need it, all you have to do is call on it. As you will notice, each of you now has a crest on your forearm. In order to activate the armor, just raise your arm to the sky and repeat this oath, and you will be transformed:

As days of darkness near, and people run in fear,
From they who prey on the weak, and silence those who speak,
We will take to the sky with courage and battle cry.
To protect the world from loss, I am a Knight of the Cross!

"After that, all you need to say, in order to transform, is which knight you are."

Joseph then steps forward and repeats the oath, and once he says it, he shouts, "Cross Knight," and he is immediately transformed in the armor of the Cross Knight. As his friends watch him being transformed, they are both shocked and amazed. But then, each of them steps forward and does the same. And just as Joseph has been transformed, they, too are transformed. Each of them is amazed at the power he or she now possesses.

Manuel then says, "There's much each of you will discover about your powers and yourselves. If you need to engage Brykar and his forces, the armor you now possess will guide you."

"But what if we need to contact you?" asks Brad.

Smiling, Manuel answers, "When you need me, I'll be there. Now go and face this new enemy."

With that, the teens vanish from the base, and Manuel turns to an unknown figure behind him and says, " It is done, my Lord. I have chosen the twelve as you have commanded."

The figure answers, "Well done, my son. Be sure to guide them, for there will be many tests for them."

THE TEENS ARRIVE BACK AT THE SPOT where they last saw Brykar. They look at the wreckage of the buses and pause a moment to remember their classmates and teachers. However, before they can mourn over their teachers and friends, they are spotted by Brykar and the Psydrones, and Brykar says, "I don't know who you are, but this world will be ours."

Joseph responds, "That's what you think. Knights, mobilize!" With that, the Knights take up their battle positions and prepare to face Brykar and his forces.

Brykar sends five Psydrones to attack each of them, and the first one they go after is Brad. As they surround him, he wonders what he can do since Manuel never them exactly how to use their power. At that moment, Brad hears Manuel's voice and is wondering where it's coming from. Manuel is saying, "Brad, I'm speaking with all of you telepathically. Do not be worried about how to use your powers. Although each of your powers is limited to a specific type, they are controlled by your thoughts, giving you limitless ways to use those powers."

The Psydrones now begin firing blasts at Brad. He throws both hands up in order to block them, and suddenly a shield of flame appears engulfing the blasts. The Psydrones look on in surprise, as Brad crosses both arms and extends both hands, releasing a fire from his hands which knocks the Psydrones down and scorches their weapons and armor.

As Des watches Brad use his powers, he understands what Manuel was saying. He says, "Get behind me. I have an idea."

The others reluctantly get behind Des. He extends his hands toward the Psydrones, and they start to sink into the ground.

"Nice work, Des," Joseph says. "How did you do that?"

"I got the idea from Brad," Des answers, "and from what Manuel said. He said we are limited to our power types. For example, my power is of the earth, so all I have to do is envision the ground beneath them becoming quicksand, and it happens."

"Amazing!" Joseph says, "Great work! Now, let's get down to business. Knights of the Cross, attack!"

Hearing this, Brykar chuckles and says, "Not so fast, Knights of the Cross. You have succeeded in defeating a few Psydrones, but this is only the beginning."

Suddenly, in a flash, Brykar and his Psydrones all vanish. The teens are left looking on in shock. Maggie says, "What just happened?"

BRYKAR AND HIS PSYDRONES ARRIVE at their base, and one of the Psydrones asks, "Why did we retreat so suddenly?"

Brykar chuckles and says, "I thought this planet's defenses were very weak! These 'knights' will make the conquest of this planet sweeter. There's something familiar about them and their powers. Anyway, I had us return here because I have a special treat for them. Now, get me two transtanks, and we'll see how these 'knights' fare against them."

The Psydrone does as Brykar has said, getting two transtanks fueled. Once they are ready, Brykar selects two Psydrones to pilot each transtank and sends them to the surface. Brykar then links to a satellite above the earth and uses it to watch the movements of the knights as they talk among themselves about what just happened.

Joseph says, "That was way too easy!"

Brad says, "I bet they realized how strong we are and decided to end their conquest."

Des shakes his head and says, "I really doubt that they came all this way to quit after one fight."

Suddenly, the ground under them begins to shake. As they all wonder what's going on, Des uses his powers to see what's causing the tremor. He say, "Everyone scatter! Two very large objects are coming toward us."

The teens scatter as the transtanks emerge. Brykar speaks through one of the transtanks and says, "Knights of the Cross, if you think I'm that easily beaten, you are dumber than I expected. These are my transtanks, and they will finish what my Psydrones began."

Des kneels down and touches the ground, and as he does so, he is able to tell just how large the transtanks are. He says, "Guys, we have a problem. These transtanks are a mile wide and one and a half miles long."

Max says, "Great! As if things weren't bad enough. Now, does anybody know how we can take these things down."

"I think I have an idea," Joseph says. "Des, do you think you could open up two giant holes beneath those things?"

Des answers, "That shouldn't be an issue."

Joseph continues, "Brad, I need you to focus all your power on both of those transtanks." Joseph is formulating his plan. "Jessica," he says, "after Brad unleashes his powers on those tanks, I need you to fill those pits with water. And, finally, Britney, once the tanks are covered, I need you to electrify the water." He is hoping that this plan will work.

"That's a pretty good idea," Des says, "and it might just be crazy enough to work." The others look puzzled.

Joseph is thinking to himself, "I wish you could see what I'm seeing." Suddenly, they all begin to see Joseph's plan and to understand what he's thinking.

Des takes his position and, as the transtanks move toward them, he has the ground open up beneath both tanks, leaving them both in deep pits. At the same time, Brad is firing two streams of fire at them. After several minutes of this, he breaks off his attack and tells everyone to scatter. Joseph and the others wonder what's going on, but Brad says, "Just keep watching."

SUDDENLY THE TANKS BECOME AIRBORNE. When they return to the ground, they begin to transform, forming two giant robots that then head for the teens. Maggie says, "Great! Our problems just got bigger."

Joseph looks toward the transtanks. As they begin to fire, he leaps in front of them, and his body forms a cross, creating a shield to protect his friends. As the transtanks bombard this shield, Max says, "We've got to stop these things now! Does anybody have any ideas?"

Des answers, "If we can get in close and attack the joints of the transtanks, we may be able to force them back to tanks."

Max adds, "Not bad! But we still need a way to take the tanks out."

Max turns and looks at Joseph, noticing that he can't keep this up much longer. He says, "We're out of time. Everybody move!"

Once they're out of the way, Joseph moves himself, and the shield disappears. The tanks' blasts hit the mountainside and vaporize it. The teens look on in shock. How had Joseph's shield been able to withstand such an onslaught.

Now Joseph regroups with them, saying, "So, have you figured out how we can stop those things? Max, we've figured a way to stop their robot forms, just not the tanks." When no one else offers anything, he adds, "Well, let's take these things out, and we can worry about that later."

As the others rush toward the transtanks, Max goes to Joseph and says, "Are you okay, Bro?"

"I'm good," Joseph answered, "just thinking about how we can beat those things." Joseph then focuses on Des, Maggie, Brad, Jessica and Britney and telepathically tells them to focus their powers into their weapons. That should give them enough power to take out the joints of each of the tanks. They all nod in agreement, and the selected warriors charge toward the transtanks.

Once they are within striking distance, Des opens up another hole underneath the transtanks, so that, as they sink in, the knights can target the shoulder joints. But, as they do this, the arms of the transtanks don't break off as expected. Surprised, the young warriors continue their attack.

Then, telepathically, Joseph says, "Everyone pull back!"

Brad responds by asking, "Why do we need to pull back? If we keep attacking we'll wear them down."

"Brad," Joseph responds, "if we keep attacking we may wear them down, but we need to take them out before they reach a populated area."

"You're right about that," Brad answers, "so, what do we do?"

"I'm not really sure," Joseph says. He is wishing they could tear those tanks apart. Then he says, "Britney, I need you to hit both of the transtanks with a massive negative charge. Can you do that?"

"I'm not sure," she answers, "but I'll try."

"Des," Joseph says next, "we're only going to get one shot at this. After they're hit with the charge, they should be completely magnetized for a brief period. When that happens, I need you tear them like tissue paper."

Des chuckles and says, "That might just be crazy enough to work."

Britney now raises both hands and brings a massive surge of lightning that magnetizes both transtanks. Then Des uses his ability to rip both transtanks in half, forcing the Psydrones to retreat.

AFTER THE TEENS ARE SURE THE PSYDRONES ARE GONE, they examine the wreckage and are amazed by how advanced it is. Joseph comments, "Des, can you open a big enough tunnel to where Manuel is so that we can bring this stuff back with us? It might just come in handy."

Before they can do that, the wreckage is gone and Manuel tells them, "Don't be alarmed! I have teleported the wreckage to the base. It's next to the research facility, so that you can examine it to see how this may aid you in the future."

"That's good and everything," Des says, "but are we sure this thing doesn't have some kind of tracker in it. If it does, we may be in trouble."

"I'm very familiar with this tech," Manuel assures them. "Before I teleported it, I teleported the tracking components into the sun."

Joseph responds, "All right, let's get back to the base and figure out where to go from here."

CHAPTER 2

FIREFIGHT: FLAME OF FURY

AS THE TEENS RETURN TO THE HIDDEN BASE where Manuel is, he says to them, "You have done well. However, the war has just begun."

"Yeah!" Des responds, "these dudes are intense."

Joseph asks Des, "How long would it take for you to see what we can do with that wreckage?"

"I'm not sure," Des answers tentatively, "I would say maybe a couple of months." He knows that working with this alien tech will be a challenge for him.

Manuel says, "I may have a way to shorten the length of time it would take for you to understand it all. Follow me." He takes them to a room next to the research facility. As they enter, they are all amazed. Manuel says, "Welcome to the Kinetic Neural Interface Giving Heightened Technical Skills, also known as the KNIGHTS machine. With this machine, we will be able to increase all of your technical skills beyond anything you've ever known and allow you to understand the Psystructs' tech in days as opposed to the months it normally would have taken. So, the question is: who wants to go first?"

"Has it ever been tested on humans?" Joseph asks cautiously.

"No," Manuel says, "it hasn't."

Des begins to step forward, but Joseph says, "No, Des! I'll go first, to make sure it's safe."

Watching Joseph do this frustrates Brad. He says, "Forget the both of you. I'm going first." And, with that, he leaps through the doorway of the machine.

As Brad enters, the machine starts up, and Joseph tries to go in after him. "It's too late," Max says, holding Joseph back, "we'll have to wait and see what happens."

AFTER ABOUT TWENTY MINUTES IN THE MACHINE Brad emerges. Frustrated, Joseph says to him, "Why did you do that? You could have died."

"But I'm alive aren't I, you dork?" Brad shouts back.

Manuel interrupts them, saying, "Brad, take this." He gives him a disassembled blaster taken from one of the Psystructs. "Reassemble this." At first, Brad is puzzled, but after a few minutes, he is able to reassemble the blaster and also to improve on its original design.

"How long do the effects of the machine last?" Joseph then asks.

"The effects of the machine," Manuel answers, "are permanent. However, it doesn't alter your personality. It only ingrains the knowledge and understanding in building and repairing equipment."

"I've gotta try this," Des say excitedly, as he rushes into the machine. As he enters the doorway, he feels the surge of energy enveloping him and his mind. Once the process is over, he emerges from the machine. Even more excited, he says, "That was amazing! Now, let's see what I can do with this tech." He then races through the door to the research facility. As he enters the room, he sees a control panel with a massive screen. At first, he is in awe of the alien tech. However, his awe is short lived, as he quickly accesses the alien computer so that they can utilize the transtank wreckage.

Des begins to have the transtank wreckage scanned and, as he does, he notices that the circuitry is far more complex than he at first imagined. But, thanks to the KNIGHTS machine, it is now easy for him to understand.

WHILE EXAMINING THE CIRCUITRY, DES NOTICES that there seem to be a number of different codes, and he starts decrypting them. He then turns to everyone and says, "This is gonna take a while, so you guys might want to go relax."

Angry, Brad steps forward and shouts, "Don't tell us what to do, you nerd."

Before Des can respond, Joseph says, "Back off, Brad! We're all on the same side here. There's no need for this."

"Ohhh, our fearless leader decides to speak now," shouts Brad sarcastically as he squares off with Joseph.

Joseph says, "You don't want to do this, Brad. Whatever issue you have with me, you'd better deal with it."

Brad grabs Joseph and says, "What are you gonna do if I don't?"

Watching what is occurring, Janet, concerned for Joseph, shouts, "Brad, stop this!"

Enraged, he shouts at Janet, "Stay out of this, you little trick. First, I'll deal with him, and then I'll deal with you."

Now Joseph grabs Brad's arm, twists it and slams him to the ground. He says, "Enough, Brad! This has to stop!"

As Joseph holds Brad there, Manuel says, "If you two wish to fight, we do have a training area where you can work this out."

Smiling, Joseph replies, "I'm game, Brad! What about you?" Brad chuckles in agreement.

All of them follow Manuel out to the training area, with the exception of Des and Jessica. Then Janet pulls Joseph aside and says with concern, "Are you really going through with this?"

Joseph looks at her and says, "I have to. If I don't, we don't stand a chance."

Manuel and the other teens enter the control room for the training area and he has Brad and Joseph stand on two discs. Then Manuel presses a button on the console, and the two are teleported to the training area below. Manuel then says, "In this training area, you can learn and develop your powers. So, when you two are ready, begin."

"Get ready," Brad snarls, "cause, you are gonna pay for all you've done."

"We'll see about that, Brad," says Joseph with a bit of excitement, as he takes his stance.

Brad then charges at Joseph. He sticks out his arm as if he had a sword in his hand, and suddenly a blade of flame forms from his hand.

Joseph holds his position as Brad charges. But, as Brad swings the flame blade, Joseph leaps over him and kicks Brad in the back. The others watch in amazement at this, and, puzzled, Max asks, "What's going on? How is he able to access his flame power in human form?" Manuel explains that their powers can be used in both Knight and human form.

Max then asks, "How can he fight against that?"

Manuel turns and points to Joseph, who is able to dodge Brad's attacks. They are all shocked to see that Joseph has a similar blade, except that his blade is blue and made of pure energy.

As Brad continues to attack him furiously, Joseph smiles as he begins to taunt Brad: "Is that the best you can do? If so, you're not gonna win this fight!"

Brad forms a new blade in his other hand and continues his assault on Joseph, but Joseph manages to block and evade his attacks. As the others watch, Max notices something about the way Joseph is fighting, Noticing Max's expression, Janet is curious. She asks, "What is it, Max? What do you see?"

"That's just it," Max says. "All I'm seeing Joe do is either block or evade, but no attack. It's almost as if …" Max suddenly realizes what Joseph is doing and, with excitement, shouts, "Now I get it!"

Puzzled, Janet asks, "Get what?"

Max then turns to everyone and says, "Joseph never intended on fighting Brad." As the others wonder what Max is talking about, he points to Joseph and Brad and says, "Look at Joseph. The entire fight he's been taunting Brad and dodging his attacks."

Already knowing this, Maggie snickers and replies, "Wow! Captain Obvious, we really wouldn't have guessed that!"

Max says, "Look closer." As they do, they notice that Brad is becoming tired. Max continues, "Joseph intended to get him to tire himself out, similar to a matador in a bullfight."

IN THE TRAINING AREA, JOSEPH CONTINUES to taunt Brad and dodge each attack. Finally, Brad's sword disappears. He says, "What have you done to me?"

"I haven't done anything to you, Brad," Joseph answers. "In fact, you did this to yourself. When I first saw your flame blade emerge, it gave me an idea of how to win this fight. Without oxygen, a flame has no power, so I knew that if I could get you to tire yourself out, you wouldn't be able to fight."

Shocked, Brad stands there looking at Joseph, wondering why he has done this. Joseph continues, "Brad, I did this because you are part of the team, and we need you." Joseph then turns and walks out of the Training Room through the main doors. Brad falls to the flood unconscious.

Manuel sends the others to get Brad to the infirmary.

Brittaly asks, "Does anyone know what Brad's deal with Joseph is? I mean, what did Joseph do that made Brad so mad? Everyone shakes their head.

A FEW HOURS LATER BRAD AWAKES and sees everyone gathered around him. Even Joseph is there. When Brad sees him, he shouts angrily, "Get out of here, you glory hog!" Without realizing it, he throws a fire blast at the wall next to Joseph. Frustrated, Joseph turns and walks out again, and Brad leaps out of his bed to follow him.

John, annoyed, grabs him and asks, "What's your problem, dude?"

"He's my problem," Brad shouts, still exhausted from his fight with Joseph. "Ever since he showed up, my life has been screwed up?"

Maggie was puzzled. "Brad," she said, "last time I checked, Joseph just transferred to our school less than a year ago."

Brad says, "That's just it! I've known him for longer than that. The truth is ..."

Before Brad can finish his statement, Des contacts them through the base's com system and says, "I've found something interesting you might want to see. In fact, it's something you definitely *need* to see." So Manuel and the knights head to where Des is.

When they arrive, John asks, "Okay, Des, what is it that we need to see?"

Before Des informs them about his discovery, he asks, "Where are Joseph and Brad?"

Max answers, "Brad is still tired from the fight, and Joseph disappeared somewhere."

Suddenly Joseph enters and replies, "I'm here."

Des then begins to explain that while scanning the metal of the transtanks, he found that they were made from a metal known as psychromium. The puzzling thing, he says, is that this is not a metal that has ever been seen on earth before. In fact, psychromium is at least a thousand times harder than titanium but can be as flexible as cloth. Turning to the computer, Des says, "I also found this while scanning the transtanks." On the screen appear different vehicles. Des resumes his explanation, "I'm not sure how, but each of these vehicles and weapons are incomplete. After looking at the transtanks, I believe we can use their parts to complete them. Also, while the scan was being done, I noticed that a lot of the circuitry used on the transtanks is like what we have here. Although we would be better off utilizing the psychromium metal, not the circuitry."

"Is that it, Des?" asks Joseph, still bothered by what has happened between him and Brad and wondering how he can lead a team that is so divided. Des nods, and Joseph leaves the research facility.

AS JOSEPH GOES OUT THE DOOR, MANUEL FOLLOWS HIM and asks, "Are you okay?"

With his back to Manuel, a frustrated Joseph answers, "Not really! How am I supposed to lead a team when there are so many dividing factors. I mean, I knew Brad was going to be a pain, but I never thought it would be this bad."

"I've been meaning to ask you about that," Manuel says. "Why did you choose not to fight him in the training area?"

"I don't know for sure," Joseph offered, still unsure of himself. "But now that I think about it, maybe I did it because if we're on the same team, we shouldn't be fighting with each other."

"Come with me," Manuel says. As the two walk through the base, they come to the library. As they enter it, Manuel pulls a book from the shelf and hands it to Joseph. At first, Joseph is stunned because the book Manuel has given him is written in a language he doesn't understand. However, as he continues to look at the book, the words suddenly transform into English. Shocked, he asks, "What's going on?"

"Simply put," Manual answers, "now that you have activated your powers, you have gained much more than simple destructive power. Each of your armors comes equipped with a translator unit that allows you to speak and read in any language used throughout the galaxy — both in human and armored form. What I have given you is an ancient text from the first world the Psystructs conquered. It possesses the key to stopping them, but until now, it has been locked. Now that your powers have unlocked this box, you and your team must discover its secrets and save your world."

Shocked, Joseph replies, "Why are you so sure we will be able to discover its secrets?"

Chuckling, Manuel answers, "Open the book, and you will see why?"

Joseph opens the book, and there on the very first page is the oath they recited to unlock their powers. Stunned, he asks, "Manuel, have you ever seen this before?"

Manuel looks at the page and replies, "No, I've never seen this before, and it is strange that this would be on the first page. Still, it wouldn't hurt to see what could be learned from this."

JOSEPH RELUCTANTLY TAKES THE BOOK, and as he does, he feels a surge. Suddenly he sees Brykar and his team behind him. They are encased in an amber-like substance and trapped. Even more startling is the fact that he sees himself alone before Brykar.

Then, just as quickly, the vision fades, and Joseph is back with Manuel, who asks him, "Is everything okay?"

"Yeah," Joseph says, "I'll be good. I just have a lot to think about."

Manuel points to a desk and says, "If you would like to stay here and read, the library is at your disposal." Manuel then turns and leaves.

BRAD, IS UP NOW AND WALKING AROUND. He sees Max, who says, "Hey, Brad, have you seen Joseph? I can't find him anywhere?"

"No I haven't," Brad answers, "and if you do see him, let him know this is not over!"

The others hear the commotion and John shouts, "Dude, you need to get a grip. This obsession is really getting old. I mean, we all know you don't like him, but right now we need to be a team, in order to save the world. So, this pettiness needs to stop now."

Max responds, "You're wasting your breath. Brad's not gonna let this go. And do you all wanna know why? It's because Brad and Joseph are ..."

Before Max can finish, Brad screams in anger, "Don't you dare tell them, Max! Don't you say another word!"

Max steps toward Brad and says, "No, Brad, I am *not* going to stand down. They need to know that you and Joseph are brothers!"

The others are shocked to hear this, and Janet chimes in, "Yes, they are, and because of how you treat him is why I dumped you, Brad. Still, John is right. We have to work together, and so this has to stop."

Enraged by this, Brad says, "Fine! I'm out of here!" Suddenly Brad is covered by flames and disappears in a cloud of smoke.

As the others watch and wonder what happened, Manuel walks in. "Don't be alarmed," he says, "what he has just done is known as Fireport. It allows a person to travel anywhere by simply tapping into their elemental powers."

Max asks, "Can we all do that?"

"Yes," Manuel answers, "along with discovering new abilities and powers."

Brad now finds himself outside where the bus was destroyed, and as he walks around, he thinks to himself, "How dare they do that! How dare Joseph, Max and Janet embarrass me like that! Who do they think they are?"

Brad suddenly stops, and a voice calls to him, "Why are you angry? And why has your face fallen? If you do well, will you not be accepted? And if you do not do well, sin is crouching at the door. Its desire is for you, but you must rule over it.[1]

Puzzled and shocked, Brad asks, "Who are you?"

The voice speaks again and says, "I'm known by many names, but you can call me Justice. Brad, I know you are angry, and I know you are hurting. When you need someone to be there for you, I will be here."

"Where is *here*?" asks a puzzled Brad, looking around.

Justice then says, "If you want to see me, close your eyes and focus on my voice."

As Brad does this, he sees a flame. As he focuses on Justice's voice, the flame begins to take the shape of a female made of fire. The female speaks, "Brad, I am a part of you, and I hate to see you hurting. Since you donned the armor, I've seen all your joy and sorrow. I'm here to help you, and right now I know you are angry with Joseph. I know the secret things that only you know."

"How could you possibly know my secrets?" asks Brad, still in shock that Justice seems to know him so well.

"Brad, I was there when Joseph's father married your mother. I was there when he disappeared, leaving Joseph with you and your mom. I know the times you cried yourself to sleep because it seemed that Joseph always got more attention than you. I know these things because of the link I share with you as a Knight of the Cross."

SUDDENLY THE GROUND BEGINS TO SHAKE, bringing Brad's attention back to the immediate area. He notices a cave-like structure emerging from the ground several hundred feet below him and watches as Psydrones exit it, carrying what looks to be a rocket. He watches them set up the rocket and wonders what they are setting it up for. Once it is set up, Brykar walks toward the machine, and Brad decides to take this moment to strike and transforms into the Fire Knight before anyone can see him.

Brad steps into the open and begins hurling a fury of fireballs at Brykar and his soldiers. As they are hit, Brykar and the Psydrones are thrown to the ground. As the Psydrones scramble to get up, Brykar realizes that one of the

Knights of the Cross is nearby. He stands and says, "I know where you are! Come out and face me if you dare?"

Seeing Brad move slightly, Brykar fires a blast in his direction, knocking Brad to the ground. As Brad gets up, he starts to think: "This may not have been the best idea."

Then Justice asks him, "Are you okay?"

"Yeah," Brad replies, "I just didn't expect the blast to be that strong."

"Don't you think you should call for backup?" inquires Justice.

Quickly Brad says, "No, don't call them. I started this, and I'll finish it." Now Brad has both his flame blades in his hands, just as when he fought Joseph, and he suddenly jumps off the cliff. Just as a swimmer would dive from a diving board, he puts his hands in front of him and begins to spin, creating what looks like a drill of fire.

When Brykar sees this, he begins to blast at it, with no effect, and when Brad hits the ground, the flame is gone. He emerges from the smoke and immediately engages Brykar in combat, using slashing strikes toward Brykar's head and torso.

BRAD QUICKLY REALIZES HE MAY BE OUTMATCHED, since Brykar has managed to dodge most of his attacks. Brykar then strikes him in the chest, knocking him to the ground. As Brad lies there, Brykar walks toward him and shouts, "You can't beat me, earthworm! As you can see, I am your better in every way, and you have no chance against me!"

Brad is starting to think Brykar was right, when Justice appears to him and says, "Brad, don't listen to him. Yes, you are impulsive, but you are also brave. Don't let your anger drive you, or it will consume you. Instead, let your desire to protect be the fuel for your fire, and you'll be able to win this."

Brad begins to see visions of Joseph and starts to realize that his anger toward him is misplaced. Brykar raises his sword to strike, but suddenly the ground beneath him moves backward. When it stops, Brad stands to see the other knights, as they rush to his side.

"How did you find me?" he asks.

"It wasn't hard," Des replies sarcastically, "subtlety is not your strong suit."

Now Brad realizes that despite their differences, they are a team and they have his back—especially Joseph, who prepares to square off against Brykar. Brad says to him, "Hold up! This is something I need to do. Let me finish this."

Joseph backs away and whispers, "Take him down hard, Bro!"

Brad turns and whispers back, "No doubt. And forgive me." He then walks toward Brykar and shouts, "Let's try this again."

Chuckling, Brykar says, "It's your funeral." Thinking it will be as the last time, Brykar stands awaiting Brad's first strike, but Brad remembers what Justice had said. In his heart, he says, "I will not be angry any longer. I forgive Joseph's dad, my dad, my mom, Joseph and myself."

In that moment, Brad rushes toward Brykar and thinks about everyone who depends on him and says in his heart, "I will not lose this time!" When he reaches Brykar, he fireports, leaving Brykar puzzled.

Then Brykar feels something hit him and knocks him to the floor. He says, "Impressive! But you will not get a second chance," and he charges at Brad. But Brad jumps up, then fireports, and as Brykar searches for him, Brad is falling from high above. Brykar sees him and runs from his spot, and Brad fireports again, so that as Brykar stops, he will hit him with the speed and velocity of a falling object. And it works. When Brad hits him, Brykar is sent flying to the floor.

Surprisingly, Brykar rises and says, "Not bad, earthworm, but that barely scratched me. Now I will give you a taste of my power!" Brad looks intently at Brykar and notices that there is not a scratch on him and wonders how this could be after an attack like that.

Des begins to communicate with all of them telepathically and says, "Brad, I know the reason there is no scratch."

"So, what's the reason, Des?" Brad responds.

"The reason there is no scratch on him is because the metal of his armor can only be damaged by the same type of metal or something stronger," Des conveyed.

Suddenly Brad shouts, "Firebird Battle Armor, engage," and suddenly he is engulfed by flames and is given two gauntlets that are now on his arms and a new chestplate. Next, a double-sided sword appears. As he takes hold of it, the flame disappears.

Brykar says, "Interesting! Too bad your new toys won't help you." He then charges toward Brad, who again strikes Brykar. Although he falls to the ground, there seems to be no damage done. Shocked, Brad wonders what is going on.

JOSEPH REALIZES THAT SOMETHING IS WEIRD and, telepathically, says, "Brad, we need to figure out why we can't beat this guy. Are you able to launch another attack?"

"I think so," Brad responds.

Joseph then reaches out to Des and says, "Scan this fight, and after that we need to vanish fast." Des and the others agree.

Brad holds his sword and walks toward Brykar. He then throws his sword up and charges toward Brykar, who braces himself to repel the attack. When Brad stops, a fireport portal opens up behind Brykar and Brad's blade rushes from it and pierces Brykar, causing a massive explosion.

While Des scans the battle and the smoke clears, Brykar emerges from the dust unharmed. Joseph now says, "Everyone fall back!" He fires a bright blast from his palm, temporarily blinding Brykar, and they make their way back to their base.

As Brykar's sight slowly begins to return, he says, "Well played, knights, but this is far from over." And he returns to his ship.

CHAPTER 3

FIREFIGHT: FLAME OF JUSTICE

AFTER THE KNIGHTS HAVE RETURNED TO THEIR BASE, Brad says, "First off, I want to thank you guys for coming out to save me, especially when I didn't deserve it. Joseph, I'm really sorry about how I've treated you. I let my anger and rage blind me, making me think you were my enemy."

Although they are all puzzled, Joseph is the one to speak now. "Brad … , not that I'm complaining about your attitude change, but what exactly caused this change in you?"

"Before I encountered Brykar out there," Brad says, "I was talking with someone named Justice. She is apparently linked to our powers."

As Brad says this, Justice suddenly appears in their midst. This time, however, Justice has taken on a female form and not the form of the flame Brad met her as. She is dressed in a long gown and has long, blue wavy hair. She laughs and says, "Forgive my sudden appearance. Brad, if you don't recognize me as we first met, what you see now is my true form. When you are in the field and you need guidance, I will be there, but you will see me in the form of your power. My role, as you fight the Psystructs and their Psydrones, is to guide you and to comfort you when you are hurting and lost. As you know, this is a war, and the Psystructs will not hesitate to use their psychic powers on you. But I can help guard you against their psychic powers."

"Why haven't the Psystructs used their psychic powers on us already?" Joseph asks.

Justice replies, "They haven't used their psychic powers yet because you have not yet posed a real threat to them."

Britney then speaks up, "Talk about brutally honest."

Justice continues, "I will help you all to unlock the secrets of your powers so that you will be able to end the rule of the Psystructs and save your world."

Then Manuel enters the room and says, "I see you've introduced yourself, my dear Justice."

She smiles and says, "Yes, Manuel, I have been explaining to them my role and explaining that they are not yet fully ready to face the Psystructs."

Des steps up and says, "Justice, I hate to disagree with you, but I have been working on a way to even the odds, and I'd like you all to follow me to the workshop."

As they head to the workshop, Brad asks the others, "Do you know what he's up to?"

Joseph replies, "I have no idea"

Once the knights have entered the workshop, Des turns to them and says, "After we defeated the transtanks, I've been studying their armor and the metal used to make them, which has been quite fascinating. Now, as I told you before, the transtanks are made of a metal called psychromium. Using the blueprints I found on this system, I should be able to finish these designs using the metal from the transtanks. Also, the armor that bonded with us, I have found, cannot only absorb metal to make it stronger; it can also improve on the metal adsorbed."

"Des, get to the point," Max says.

"Fine," Des answers. "Simply put, if we touch the psychromium, our armor will become just as strong ... if not stronger."

Manuel and Justice look at each other. Manuel asks, "Are you sure this is safe, Des?"

"To be honest," Des confesses, "I'm not sure. However, after the battle Brad just had, we can use all the help we can get. For now, what I can do is use the psychromium to make weapons that will allow us to stand a chance against Brykar and his forces."

"Hey Des," Joseph interjects, "before you start working on those new weapons for us, I think it would be good if we go over the data from that last battle, so we have an idea of what we're really up against. Everyone else, I would suggest that we train so we are ready for the next battle."

Now Maggie asks, "While we are training, what are you going to be doing Joseph?"

Annoyed at the way she asked this, Joseph replies, "I'll be in the library, trying to find more information on the Psystructs and why they are here. I have a feeling that they are looking for something, and it may just be what we need to defeat them for good."

"All right, everyone, let's head to the Training Room and prepare for the next battle," Max says and he walks toward Maggie and the others who now head to the Training Room.

AS JOSEPH WALKS DOWN THE HALL TO THE LIBRARY, Brad comes rushing up behind him and says, "Joe, wait up." Joseph turns around, and as Brad catches up, he notices something different and says, "What's up?"

When Joseph shrugs, Brad continues, "I know we talked briefly in the field, but I need to make sure you understand that I'm sorry for how I've treated you. I was so angry because I felt Mom loved you more than me and that you had become this 'star' at school. I felt the best way to handle it was through bullying you. I realize now that I've been a jerk and that I should have been a better brother rather than your tormentor. I just want you know that no matter what, I'm going to do everything it takes to make amends for everything I've done."

Surprised by this confession, Joseph answers, "Thanks, Brad, and I accept your apology. Also, there's no need to try to make up for it, cause I know you are sincere. I'm just surprised by the sudden change of heart."

Brad goes on to explain that before he found Brykar, he was having a heart to heart talk with Justice, who helped him to see what he was doing and that, instead of being angry with Joseph, Brad should have been there for him.

While listening to Brad's story, Joseph begins to understand what Justice was talking about.

Moments later, Des uses the comms throughout the base and says, "Everyone get to the lab quick. I've found out what's going on."

Upon hearing this announcement, everyone heads to the lab.

IN THE LAB, THEY ALL SEE DES REPLAYING THE FOOTAGE from the last battle. Brad asks him, "So, what did you find out, Des?"

Surprised, Des replies, "Well, after reviewing the footage, I see that Brad did more damage than we first thought to Brykar ... or at least what we thought was Brykar."

Puzzled by this answer, Joseph asks, "What do you mean, Des?"

Des pulls up two images of Brykar and says, "These are two scans that I did of Brykar. The one on the left was done when we first met him, and the second was done during the fight with Brad." He pauses a moment, and then continues. "Now, if you look closely, the images are identical ... at least until you run the scans through the DNA processor and find this." Now Des points to the screen and shows that the DNA from the fight with Brad was completely different. Des then pulls up a skeletal scan of the two Brykars, and everyone can see that the one on the left has a skeleton, but the second does not. "As you can see," Des says, "the Brykar on the right has no skeleton. This is because the Brykar Brad fought is not the real Brykar, but rather, a creature that looks like Brykar.

After pausing a moment, he continues, "Also, after examining the last fight, I found that just before Brad attempted to deliver the final blow, the fake Brykar created a clone that would take the force of the blast, making it look like the attack had no effect."

Joseph was intrigued by what he had just seen. "Interesting!" he says, and he tries to think how they might defeat such a creature.

Des continues, "I also noticed that after the clone was created, the original creature was dazed for a moment. That is when we must strike in order to defeat this creature."

Max chimed in, "Good idea! Does anybody have an idea on how to do it? I mean, it's not like he's just gonna stand there and let us. Not to mention, when the explosion is created, even with our armor, it's difficult to see."

Brad steps forward now and says, "I have an idea. Everyone meet me in the Training Room." As they head for the training room, they wonder what Brad's mysterious plan could be.

WHEN THEY ARE ALL GATHERED IN THE TRAINING ROOM, Brad says, "While Des was talking, I was thinking about how I fireported, and I just thought about how I wanted to get out of there fast. Then I thought, 'What if I used that same focus to create a temporary clone that could distract this creature long enough, so that when he does let the clone die, I can be there to finish him off before he can recover.' "

Des chuckles and says, "That's an interesting theory, Brad, but let's see if you can pull it off."

Brad has everyone stand back, and as he concentrates, flames begin to flow from his body, and a figure starts to form. Suddenly the form vanishes and Brad falls to his knees and says, "Looks like this is going to be harder than I thought."

"Yes it is," Des replies, "however, it's a good idea, and I think we should all try to master this ability, as it will be useful in the future."

MEANWHILE, BACK IN THE PSYSTRUCT CRAFT, BRYKAR STANDS AWAITING the report from the last battle with the Knights of the Cross. Someone enters looking like him and says "I've returned, my Master."

Enraged, Brykar rushes over to him and strikes him, saying, "Don't you dare ever speak to me while looking like me! Do I make myself clear?"

Deadly Double (the creatures true name) then takes on his true form, a being made of a blue liquid metal, able to take any form, allowing him to be able to clone himself or whomever he is impersonating at the moment. He resumes his position and says "Forgive me, Master."

Brykar stands threateningly before him and says, "What do you have to report, Deadly Double? Are those so-called 'heroes' vaporized yet?"

Kneeling now, Deadly Double says, "No, my Master, they are not yet vaporized. They will be soon though. I promise you that!"

Continuing in his threatening voice, Brykar demands, "Then why are you even here? Your task was to simply test the limits of their powers and then destroy them!"

"Master," Deadly Double replies, "that is what I have done."

"Then why do they still live?" Brykar insists.

"Before I could vaporize them," Daily Double explains, "they used my explosion to cover their escape. Be assured, Master, I will destroy them."

"Well," barks Brykar, "if you do not destroy them, I will destroy you. Do I make myself clear?"

Deadly Double looks up meekly. "Yes, Master, I will do as you command." As Deadly Double starts to leave the chamber, Brykar says to him, "This time, when you face them do not forget to start the uplink, so I can see for myself who and what we are up against."

"Yes, Master," Deadly Double responds, "I shall do as you command."

BRYKAR WALKS OVER TO THE COMPUTER closest to him and pulls up the video from when he first encountered the Knights of the Cross and starts reviewing it. He feels there is something familiar about them, but before he can fully examine the footage, Sadoom contacts him telepathically and asks, "What do you have to report, Brykar?"

Brykar responds, "We have arrived on earth and are in the process of testing their defenses. So far, we have encountered some resistance, but it will be neutralized shortly."

Puzzled by this, Sadoom says, "What kind of resistance?"

"They call themselves the Knights of the Cross," Brykar reports, "and there is something familiar about them. I can't put my finger on it exactly yet. So far, they have proven to be no real threat, but as standard protocol demands, I am testing their powers so we know what type of invasion force we will need to defeat them."

"Very well," Sadoom says, "keep me informed, Brykar." He pauses, then adds, "I look forward to when you have more to report."

ONCE THEIR PSYCHIC CONNECTION HAS ENDED, Brykar goes back to the computer and begins to locate an earthling identity that he can control and use to manipulate the earthlings to learn more about their defenses. Soon, his search turns up the perfect candidate—Secretary of Homeland Security, Alexander Marks. Brykar then walks over to his command chair. As he sits down, he begins to search psychically for Alexander Marks, and once he finds him, he implants in him the suggestion that he return home early in order to enjoy his family. It works.

As Alexander Marks drives home, Brykar begins to probe his mind, in order to learn if there are more heroes like the Knights of the Cross. Quickly he discovers that there are no known heroes like them. However, Brykar does discover that the earth's defenses are minimal.

WHEN ALEXANDER ARRIVES HOME and exits his car, Brykar then has him teleported to his craft, using his psychic powers to keep Alexander in a trance-like state. Brykar stands near Alexander, places his hand on Alexander's head, and creates a psychic link that will allow him to control the man no matter where he is. Brykar then plants the suggestion that Alex searches for people with special powers or abilities. He wants him to discover who the Knight of the Cross are and treat them as his number one threat.

Moments later, Brykar teleports Alexander back home, as if nothing has happened. As Alexander enters his house, he greets his wife with a hug and she informs him that the last time she heard from their daughter, she was enjoying a class trip she was on.

THE KNIGHTS OF THE CROSS ARE STILL TRYING TO LEARN how to create their doubles. While Joseph is in the library, trying to learn more about the Psystructs and understand the vision he had, when Manuel comes in, asking him, "Is everything okay, Joseph?"

Joseph sighs and answers, "I'm fine, Manuel. I just wanted to have a look at the book you gave me. I feel that if I open it, I might find something to help us beat the Psystructs ... or at least understand these new powers."

Manuel nods, "I understand that, Joseph, but wouldn't it be best to be with the others, helping them to learn this cloning ability?" He is concerned for the young leader of the Knights.

Just then Joseph appears behind him and says, "That just it, I am."

Manuel turns to see two Josephs. "How long have you been able to do this?" he asks.

"When Brad suggested it," Joseph replies, "I tried it, and it happened instantly. so I left one clone stayed behind to help the others train, while I came here to do some research."

"I will say this, Joseph," Manual says, "the use you have made of your powers is impressive."

"But that's just it, Manuel," Joseph answered, "I don't really know what I'm doing with my powers. All I know is that when my friends are in danger, I leap, and what I'm thinking either happens or materializes in some way. It's honestly very frustrating."

Suddenly Joseph gets the feeling that the other Knights have created their clones too. Sensing this, Manuel asks, "How do you know?"

"Because I saw them do it. Apparently my powers work through my clones as well. Apparently, when I touched each of them while they focused on creating their clones, not only were they able to create them; they were able to create multiple clones."

JOSEPH AND MANUEL GO BACK TO THE TRAINING AREA. As they enter, Joseph notices that the clones of the other Knights have not been created yet. Joseph's clone returns to him, and he begins to touch each of the knights, as he had seen earlier. As he does this, their clones begin to appear. When he has finished, the other knights are amazed. "I wonder why it wasn't it working before?" someone asks.

"We can figure that out later," Joseph says, "right now we need to figure out how to use these clones to beat that thing posing as Brykar. So, does anybody have an idea?"

Des steps forward and says, "I have an idea. If Brad can force this creature to create a clone, then we can have a small window of opportunity before he can create another one. If the clone Brad creates can cause a distraction, it can destroy the creature's clone while Brad destroys the original one."

"Sounds like a solid plan," Max interjects. "So, does anybody know how to find the creature?"

Des answers, "I'm still working on that, but we should be able to find him soon."

Just then an alarm goes off and Jessica asks, "What's with the alarm?"

Des hits a button on a remote he's holding and says, "Sorry about that. Like I said, I was working on a way to track the creature, and I had set that alarm to alert us when any of the Psystructs come to the surface."

"Annoying but impressive!" Jessica comments.

Maggie adds, "I know we need to beat this thing, but has anybody thought about what will happen if we don't return to our parents?"

Britney chimes in, "She has a good point. I mean, do we even know how long these clones will last?"

"You all raise valid questions," Manuel says. "I wish had the answers about the clones, but each of you has the ability to port to whereever you need to go."

"Still," Eric interjects sarcastically, "how will we explain where we've been? It not like we can say 'We were chased by aliens and were hiding.' They would lock us up just on that alone."

John agrees. "I hate to agree with Eric," he says, "but we do need a better cover story than we were just wandering around."

Des says, "I had a chance to examine the area where the bus blew up and found a cave where we could all have been thrown. There's enough wreckage there that it would make it seem possible that we were all thrown in there when the bus exploded."

Des's gauntlet starts to glow. As he looks at it, he sees a rescue team heading for where their bus was. He says, "Ohhh great! The rescue team should be here in thirty minutes. We need to get to that cave asap."

Tasha adds, "Does anybody have an idea of how we're going to be able to stop this clone creature and be at the crash site before the rescue workers get there?"

Before anyone can answer, Des's alarm for the creature goes off again, and he says, "We may have just lucked out?"

"What do you mean?" Joseph asks.

"Simply put," Des replies, "the rescue team is headed to where our bus was, and is about to collide with that clone creature."

In his sarcastic way, Max asks, "How is that luck? There's no way they stand a chance against the creature?"

"True," Des agrees, "but if we save the rescue crew from this creature, that could let them know we were able to rescue the students who survived the wreckage as well." He laughs at the irony of it all.

Now Joseph chimes in, "It might just work, but I think it would be good if half of us go to fight, while the others stay behind to be found, to add more proof to this story. So, for now, Brad, Des, Maggie, Jessica, Britney and I will go and fight this thing. The rest of you need to get to that cave, so the rescue crews can find you."

Before anyone can agree or disagree with Joseph's plan, he shouts, "Crossport!" and instantly the members of the team he has named that were to go to the cave are transported there, and the other team members are transported to within sight of the rescue team.

SUDDENLY THE CREATURE SLAMS THE GROUND, causing it to break apart and making the rescue team's vehicles unable to move. Brad says, "This is our chance," and flies toward Brykar's clone.

Joseph points to Des and says, "Go help the rescue team, and I'll give Brad some backup." Des looks at Joseph and asks, "Are you sure?"

"I'll be fine, Joseph answers. "Now, go help those people. Knights of the Cross, let's light the night!"

AS THE OTHER KNIGHTS GO TO HELP THE RESCUE TEAM, Joseph wonders how he will keep up with Brad. Manuel tells him that the armor they are wearing is a bio metal that can grow or change according to the user's will. He adds, "In short, Joseph, if you wanna fly, you can have the wings to fly."

Joseph suddenly imagines metallic wings forming on his back, and he leaps into the sky, heading after Brad.

WITHIN MINUTES, JOSEPH CATCHES UP TO BRAD. He says, "Brad, do you even have a plan on how you are going to beat this thing?"

Turning, Brad sees Joseph's wings and says "What the … ? Where did those wings come from?"

Chuckling, Joseph says, "I'll tell you later. Let's just beat this creep and join the others."

When the two knights see Deadly Double, they land and Brad says, "It's payback time, you duplicating doofus!"

Impressed that they had figured out that he isn't Brykar, Deadly Double switches on the video link-up and says, "Well then, since you found out my little trick, there's no need for me to pose as Brykar and no need for me to hold back!" Instantly, Deadly Double creates eleven clones and says to them, "Let's see how you handle this."

As the clones begin to rush Joseph and Brad, Joseph telepathically says, "Brad, I'll handle the clones. You need to find the original and destroy him."

Brad, replies, "Good idea! But how? There are too many clones for me to figure out which one is which."

As the clones reach Joseph, he uses his wings like a shield to block the clones from attacking him and Brad. The clones keep coming, but Joseph opens his wings, sending them flying. He remembers something Des said, that the more clones there are, the weaker the original will be.

Joseph then notices that one of them isn't attacking and informs Brad, who goes after that particular one. As the other clones rush to stop Brad, Joseph appears before them, and he is shouting, "What's your hurry, boys? This party just started!"

Joseph now draws his dual cross blades and begins attacking the clones, while Brad faces Deadly Double. Brad is saying, "As you can see, we are on to your tricks."

DEADLY DOUBLE ANSWERS, "Just because you've seen one of my tricks doesn't mean you've seen them all. By the way, before I destroy you, you should know my name is Deadly Double, and as it suggests, I do a killer imitation of anyone I choose." With that, he transforms himself to look like Brad.

In his transformed state, the double says, "Do I look familiar, Fire Knight?" "Just cause you *look* like me," Brad insists, "doesn't mean you *are* me," and he attacks Deadly Double with his swords. Somehow Deadly Double is able to evade each strike.

Now Deadly Double attacks Brad with a punch to the stomach, but Brad does a shoulder roll, escaping Deadly Double's attack and stands with his swords in hand, ready for battle.

As Deadly Double again attacks, Brad successfully blocks his attacks. Then Deadly sees an opening, catches Brad with a punch to the stomach, and Brad falls to his knees.

"You put up a good fight," Deadly Double says, "but it's time for you to die, Fire Knight." He raises his sword to finish Brad and swiftly brings it down, but Brad is able to swing his sword across and block it. As he dose this, he says, *"As the days of darkness surround ...."*

Deadly Double then swings his sword from another direction to attack, but again, Brad blocks that attack and continues, *"... and no heroes can be found."*

At this point, Brad struggles to his feet. As Deadly Double attempts to strike him down again, Brad block his blow, knocking Deadly Double off balance. As Brad does this, he continues to say, *"...While those descend and prey on the weak..."*

Desperate, Deadly Double creates one more clone, and the two of them attack together. Somehow he is able to block them both, as he continues to say, *"....who do not rise or dare to speak... ."*

The clone attacks Brad, knocking his sword into the air, Brad quickly grabs the clone by the arm, forcing him to drop his sword and punches him in the gut, destroying him. All the while, he is heard to say, *"...We will utter our heartfelt battle cry..."*

As his sword falls, Brad says, "*...as we raise our hands to the sky...*" Somehow he is able to catch his sword, and he now shouts, "*...To protect this world from loss, I am a Knight of the Cross.*"

Suddenly Brad is enveloped in flames, and he raises his sword and strikes the original Deadly Double with several slashes. When Brad is finished, Deadly Double is in pieces and his clones begin to disappear.

Seeing Brad standing over Deadly Double, Joseph walks over, looks at Deadly Double in pieces, and says, "That's definitely one way of getting cut. Come on! We need to get back to the others." The two knights hurry to link up with the rest of their team.

A SMALL LIGHT ON BRYKAR'S CHESt continues to blink, and on the other end, he watches the screen, thinking to himself, "These knights are smarter and stronger than I first gave them credit for. That is not a mistake I intend to repeat." He then transports the fragments of Deadly Double back to his ship, where he can be revived.

ONCE THE REMAINS OF DEADLY DOUBLE ARRIVE on the ship, Brykar has the Psydrones place them in the revival tube. Although it will take some time, Deadly Double will be back and even deadlier than before.

AT THE SAME TIME, JOSEPH AND BRAD ARRIVE to help the others with the rescue crew, only to find that the rescue crew is out of danger and about ready to head to where the destroyed buses were. Joseph tells Des and the others telepathically, "All of you head to the cave, and we will meet you there." Each of them replies and complies.

SUDDENLY THEY ARE ALL IN THE CAVE, and they begin to return to their human forms. They are tired and lay down, seemingly unconscious.

MOMENTS LATER THE RESCUE TEAM ARRIVES and begins to evaluate the wreckage. For a time, they stand there amazed, wondering what could have caused buses to blow up like that. Looking for survivors, some of the team notice the nearby cave, and there they find twelve of the missing students. They bring them out and begin to question them. One of the workers asks Max what happened.

"We had just gotten off the bus," Max says, "when suddenly we heard an explosion. When we woke up, we were in that cave you found us in." The rest have a similar story.

Eventually, the students are put in a vehicle to be taken back to where the rescue team is staying. On the way, Des asks Joseph, "How much longer do you think it will be before we can get back to the base? I mean, honestly, I don't expect Brykar to take Deadly Double's defeat lightly."

"I'm not sure, Des," Joseph replies, but if you have an idea, I would love to hear it!"

CHAPTER 4

STUBBORN AS STONE: A TIME TO REFRAIN

ON THEIR WAY TO THE HOTEL where the rescue team was staying, the Knights of the Cross try to face their dilemma. How are they going to get back to their base without being noticed, since they are in a moving vehicle? They soon realize that it would be easier to get back to the base from the hotel room than to try and travel in front of the rescue crew.

ABOUT AN HOUR LATER, the students are split into four groups and assigned heir hotel rooms. Joseph, Max and John are put in one room. Des, Eric and Brad are put into another. Maggie, Jessica and Janet are put into a different room, and Sally, Tasha and Britney are put into the final room.

WHEN THE GO TO THEIR RESPECTIVE ROOMS, the students notice that there are men in black suits standing guard outside the boys' rooms and women in black suits standing guard outside the girls' rooms. After a while, John opens the door, intending to grab something from a vending machine, and one of the men in black stops him. "For security reasons, no one's allowed to leave," he says. "If you need food, call room service, and it will be taken care of." He backs John into the room and shuts the door.

"Great!" John says. "We might as well be in prison. What do you guys think is going on?"

"If I didn't know any better," Max offers, "I would think that they're not buying our story. Also, judging by their gear, I would say these guys aren't going to be nice when asking more questions."

Chuckling in agreement, Joseph says, "This just might be the break we are looking for." He links everyone telepathically and says, "I have an idea on how we can get out of here. But we need to be quick. In a few minutes, we each need to go into the bathroom and generate one clone in our human form. We'll leave the clones in here while we port back to the base."

"Good idea!" says Des, "But, we don't know how long they will last."

"True," Max agrees, "but what choice do we have? I say let's do it."

The other's agree and get started creating their clones so they can port to their base. The plan seems to work.

ONCE THEY ALL ARRIVE AT THEIR BASE, Joseph says, "Des, see if you can find out how long those clones will last. The rest of us need to figure out who those guys in the suits are and what they want from us." Des rushes off to the lab to run some tests.

Jessica follows him and asks, "Would you like some help, Des?"

"Sure," Des replies, slightly puzzled, and goes on to the lab. Jessica follows him.

BACK IN THE MAIN ROOM, JOHN ASKS, "How do we even begin to find out who these guys are? I mean, if they are government, more than likely they are a secret branch with a whole different set of rules."

"Very true," Joseph agrees, "but I found something that might just help us." He takes them to the library. As they enter, they are surprised by all the books in the library.

JOHN SAYS, "SO IS THIS WHERE YOU DISAPPEAR to all the time?"

Joseph shows them twelve computers similar to the type they would use in school. He says to them, "Everyone, have a seat and let's find out exactly who we are dealing with."

"Isn't this dangerous?" Eric offers. "I mean, what if we find something and they try to trace the signal back here?"

Before Joseph can say anything, Manuel walks in and says, "Do not worry, my friends. These computer use a relay that bounces the signal so many times that even if they try to track it, it will appear that you are all in multiple locations at the same time."

"Wow, that's a relief," John says. "Now, let's figure out just who these guys are."

Maggie adds, "Great, but where do we start? In not like we can look up Black Suit Industries or something."

"Maggie," John says, "you are a genius! I know where we can start looking to find out why those guys are after us."

"John," Tasha replies sharply, "if you know something, spill it."

"Okay," John says, "it's an urban myth, but most of the time when suits like that show up, it is in response to aliens. As far as anyone knows, we haven't admitted to seeing any aliens, but I don't think they believe our story, and they're there to get the truth. Now let's see what we can find out." He begins searching the Internet for anything related to alien sightings and the suits.

Within a few moments, John finds a few blogs that talk about guys just like these, and they prove that his hunch was right. Nearly every blog he looks at mention black suits appearing when anyone has connections to an alien sighting or has gone missing. He scans for more blogs with any information, but finds that there just isn't much out there about these guys.

Eric says, "Honestly, I didn't think we would find much. It's just too bad we can't interrogate them and find out just what they want from us?"

"Well, maybe we can," Joseph retorted.

IN THE LAB, DES AND JESSICA ARE TRYING TO FIND OUT how long the clones will last. Des asks Jessica, "Could you create a clone for me that we can test?"

"Sure!" she says, and she creates a clone.

Des has the clone lie down, and he takes a needle and begins to lightly poke the clone. As he does, the clone responds to the pain, but so does Jessica. Des then says "This is interesting. We feel the same pain our clones do. Sorry about causing you pain, Jessica."

"That's okay," she says. "It had to be done."

Des uses a molecular scanner to scan the clone, and as he does, he says, "Amazing! According to this scanner, not only do the clones have an indefinite life span; it also appears that what they experience and learn will also become our knowledge, once they return to us."

"So, you didn't need to poke me, did you?" Jess asks.

"I'm sorry about that," he says. "Had I known it would hurt you, I wouldn't have done it."

"It's okay," she repeats. She is beginning to notice how very analytical and sometimes cold Des can be and yet he has a sensitive side.

Joseph calls them, Jessica has her clone return, and they head to the library.

AS THEY ENTER THE LIBRARY, DES IS ALSO AMAZED at how big it is.

"Des," Joseph says, "were you able to find out anything?"

"Yes," Des answers. Apparently, when we create our clones, we will feel any pain they feel, and they can last an indefinite amount of time. However, I still would not recommend using them for long periods of time ... unless, of course, the battle calls for it."

Jessica is surprised by this answer and asks, "Why, Des?"

"The reason we shouldn't use our clones for long periods of time," he says, "is because the longer they are out, the harder it will be for them to return. They will start to develop a will of their own."

"How do you know that,?" Joseph asks.

"Simply put," Des answers, "we are all strong willed, and I know that if we were to use them to fill in for us in our normal lives, eventually they would want to separate and have their own lives."

The others seemed to agree with this logic, and the consensus was that they would use the clones in battle only when it was necessary, to keep them secret.

"Okay," Joseph says, "the reason we had you come here is that I have an idea of how we can find out more intel on these guys in black."

"Let me guess," Des says. "You want our clones to be the ones to interrogate these guys, letting them think they've caught us, correct?" Chuckling, Joseph says, "Impressive as always, Des. Yes, that is my plan, but that's only the first step. Once they learn enough about these suits, half of us will go and rescue the clones. Then, once we are far enough, have them return to us and give us the information."

Des speaks: "That's actually a really good plan, Joseph. Now it's my turn to be impressed. Oh, and by the way, I also found that when we recall the clones any and all information they have obtained will become ours."

"Good," Joseph says. Then he asks, "Des, are you able to track our clones from your lab?"

"Of course," was Des' answer.

"Then let's find out who these guys are before they find out we know a lot more than we've let on," Joseph concludes.

THE STUDENTS BEGIN MAKING THEIR WAY to the lab. As they walk, Maggie, Sally, Tasha, Britney and Janet talk among themselves. They couldn't help but notice that Jessica has been following Des to the lab a lot and when Joseph called Des, she was right behind him. Sally now pulls Jessica aside, as the guys walk ahead. She asks, "So, Jessica, you've been spending a lot of time with Des the Dork lately. Does this mean the Prom Queen has traded the quarter back for a pocket-protector-wearing dork?"

"Back off Sally!" Jessica responds angrily. "Who I spend my time with is none of your business. Also, yes, I may have referred to him as Des the Dork, but he's one of the smartest guys here, and the only one who can understand this alien tech stuff fast enough. So, don't question my standards when you have none of your own and base your attraction to a guy solely on looks. Des may not seem to be the strongest fighter, but he has a strength of character I haven't seen from other guys. He can and does seem cold at times, but he can also be really sweet too."

Having overheard this exchange, Maggie smiles and says, "Sounds like you really like Des there, Jessica. Don't get me wrong. I'm not being sarcastic. I just think the way you described him just now is sweet and shows you care deeply about him."

Janet adds, "If you like him, Jess, you should tell him so."

"I know I should," Jessica answers, "but I'm not sure if he even likes me like that." For her, this was something new, being unsure for the first time about whether a boy liked her or not.

Tasha added, "I've known Des for a long time, and one thing I do know is that when he's around tech, he's like a kid in a candy store. He becomes incredibly focused. So, unless you say something, he's not going to know how you feel." Jessica nods that she understands.

Britney says, "We had better catch up with the guys before they notice we're not there." The other girls agree, and they make their way back to the guys.

AS THE GUYS WALK BACK TO THE LAB, John is asking, "Hey, Des, are you and Jessica a thing now?"

Shocked, "Des asks, "What do you mean?"

"Are you serious?" John says, so that only he and Des can hear. "Haven't you noticed that whenever you go to the lab, she's following you."

"To be honest," Des admitted, "I haven't really noticed. I've been too busy trying to understanding all this tech. Do you really think she likes me?"

"I've known Jessica for a long time," John says, "and although she is known as the Prom Queen, she does have high standards. She doesn't like just anybody. So, if she's been following you around, she may like you."

THEY ALL REACH THE LAB AT ABOUT THE SAME TIME. Des goes to the computer and pulls up the hotel and sees that all their clones are still in the rooms. "I'll watch the clones," he says. "Why don't you guys go to the Training Room and try out this new mode I found called Alpha Dog?"

The guys like the idea and off they go.

ONCE IN THE TRAINING ROOM, Brad was the first to try the new program, and he set it to Level 2. Suddenly, the doors along the walls open and robots called AIDS emerge. John asks Manuel what they are, and he explains that AIDS stands for Artificial Intelligent Drone System. The drones then begin attacking Brad. Using his Fire Blade in human form, he begins fighting the drones. The others notice that there is a scoring system.

BACK IN THE LAB, DES IS MONITORING THE CLONES, when Jessica walks over to him and says, "Des, can we talk for a bit."

Des nods, and Jessica begins, "Des, this is hard for me cause usually I can tell when guys like me. They usually fall for me instantly, but not you. In fact, you are a bit of a mystery to me. But I've really started to fall for you and have seen in you a strength I haven't seen in other guys."

Des gulps hard. "Wow!" he says. "I like you too, Jessica. I just didn't say anything before, because I am Des the Dork. I mean, honestly, I never thought I would even have a chance with you."

Smiling broadly, Jessica answers, "Before this, I might not have been attracted to you, but since this has happened, I've seen a strength I've never seen in you before—especially since you aren't a fighter like Joseph or Brad."

Chuckling, Des says "Hold it! You think I'm not as good a fighter as Brad or Joseph? Follow me." He sets an alarm to let them know when the clones are moved, and they go together to the Training Room.

IN THE TRAINING ROOM, BRAD HAS JUST FINISHED, and his score is 4,500, the average score for that level being just 2,500. Brad then returns to the Command Center for the Training Room, and Des says, "Let me have a go at it, guys. By the way, set it to Alpha Dog level 5." As Des goes into the training area, a scoreboard appears, and the top score is 10,000.

John says through the intercom, "Des, are you sure about this?"

"I'll be fine. Trust me," Des answers.

Just as the doors opened for Brad, they now open for Des, and he grabs two swords that appear before him. One of the AIDS begins to charge at Des, with weapons in hand. Des takes a step, blocking one of the weapons, allowing him to throw one of them into a group of AIDS, knocking them out of commission. The remaining AIDS continues their assault, and Des continues to block their attacks and turn them on each other.

Jessica and the others are surprised to see that he can fight at this level, with the exception of Joseph, who says, "To be honest, he's always been that good of a fighter. Before we became knights, I sparred with him a few times, and he's definitely a strong fighter."

Jessica thinks to herself, "This must be why he's doing this, to show me that he is a strong fighter."

The next wave of AIDS begins to emerge in the Training Room, and this group has laser weapons that they begin to fire on Des with. For his part, he grabs a nearby AIDS and uses it as a shield. While the newest wave attacks, he throws the drone, knocking several of the others out, and then he begins to use the swords, to deflect the laser blasts back at the drones, destroying their laser weapons.

Once the robots' weapons are disabled, the simulation ends. Everyone looks at the scoreboard and is amazed to see that Des has beat the high score with his 15,000.

Des exits the Training Room, but before he and Jessica can talk, the alarm he has sets goes off. Eric says, "Des, what's with the alarm?"

"That alarm," Des explains, was to alert me when the clones are moved from the rooms we were staying in." With that, they all rush to the lab.

WHEN THEY GET TO THE LAB, DES CHECKS THE COMPUTER and sees that the clones have just left the hotel. Joseph telepathically tells his clone, "I need you to find out as much as you can about these guys, and don't worry. We're tracking you, so that we can rescue you." Joseph's clone signals that he understands.

Joseph tells the others "All right, the clones know our plan, and only six of us are going to go, so as not to show all our cards. So, it's going to be Brad, Des, Jessica, Maggie, Britney and myself."

John protests mildly, "I don't like setting this one out, but I understand."

"All right, Knights of the Cross," Joseph commands, "let's light the night," and he and the other knights head out to follow the clones.

AT THE SAME TIME, THE CLONES ARE BEING LOADED into the back of two different vehicles. Joseph's clone telepathically tell the others that help is on the way. As they sit down in the trucks, a man dressed like the other suits appears on a screen, and Joseph's clone asks, "Who are you and what do you want with us?"

The man answers, "My name is Agent Martin, and you young people are being brought to my facility for questioning?"

John's clone stands and asks, "What do you mean by questioning? Why are we being brought to an unknown facility?"

"Now, young man, please sit down!" Agent Martin answers. "All will be revealed to you in time. And as for who we are, that is on a need-to-know basis. In regard to why you are being questioned, that part is simple: we believe that creatures of unknown origin destroyed your buses, teachers and classmates. We also believe that one of you may have noticed something that could be helpful to our investigation."

As Agent Martin is speaking, Joseph's clone notices a small logo on his jacket, with the initials ARC. He asks Agent Martin, "What does ARC stand for?"

AGENT MARTIN SHAKES HIS HEAD and says, "I'm sorry that you saw that, and because of that, you and your friends will become permanent residents at my facility." The clones can't believe this. Suddenly shackles appear binding their hands and feet.

Agent Martin adds, "Since you are all now going to be permanent residents at my facility, I will explain who we are. ARC, as it is named, stands for Alien Recovery and Capture. It is our job to keep watch on extraterrestrial threats and see how we can adopt their tech to suit our needs."

Eric now speaks up, "So, basically you watch for aliens, then steal their tech so that you wage war on other countries and kill how many more people?"

Chuckling, Agent Martin replies, "Well, that's a rather crude way of looking at it, but that does sum it up. For now, enjoy the ride, for this will be the last moment of freedom any of you will ever experience" With that, he cuts the communication.

Joseph's clone calls to him, letting him know the situation, and he informs his clone that they are following the trucks and will have them out soon. Des says, "Hey Joseph, do you have any ideas how we are going to get them out of there? It's not like they are in a wasteland; they're in the heart of the city. So how are we gonna rescue them without revealing our secret." Joseph begins to think it over and eventually says, "Des, I need you to use your powers and create a few small potholes to blow their tires. Once they've stopped, Brad, I need you to use your fire powers to lock the driver's and passenger side door and then break the lock on the back door, freeing the clones.

"Once they're free, Maggie, I need you to cause a small dust storm and then lift them up to us so we can get them out."

Des replies "Well, that sounds like a plan, but didn't you want to speak with the leader of the organization first?"

Joseph answers, "I do, but my clone let me know that he was never there and he cut off communications a short time ago. So, me talking to him will have to wait."

AS THEY CONTINUE TO FOLLOW THE TRUCKS, they notice they're passing a construction area. Joseph says "Des, do it now," and Des begins making his potholes, causing both vehicles to have flat tires. Then Brad uses his powers to seal the doors of both vehicles and break the locks. He then ports in both vehicles and breaks their chains, freeing their clones.

As the clones emerge from the truck, Maggie uses her power to lift the clones up high, out of sight, and the knights then have their clones return to them. Joseph says, "All right, everyone, let's head back and figure out our next move." With that, the knights head back to their base.

BRYKAR NOTICES THAT THE KNIGHTS ARE FLYING AWAY from the two vehicles and uses his computers to trace the signal back to Agent Martin. As it connects to Agent Martin's smartphone, Brykar says, "Hello, human."

Surprised, Agent Martin asks, "Who are you? And what are you? How did you get this number?"

Brykar replies, "My name is Brykar, and as for what I am, that is none of your concern."

As Brykar is talking to Agent Martin, he uses his psychic powers to learn about Martin's organization and then says, "I know you and your organization are alien hunters, and I am willing to share some of my technology with you, that is ... in exchange for some intel from you."

Agent Martin says, "That's an interesting idea. May I have some time to think about it?"

"You have three hours," Brykar says, "and I will call you back for your response."

With that, the phone cuts off. Agent Martin tries to trace the signal back, but he finds it to be impossible. He the uses the phone to call someone else. "We've made contact," he says, "and they've offered to share their tech with us in exchange for intel. However, the bad news is that we need to give them an answer when they call back three hours from now."

Agent Martin then listens as the person on the other end gives him instructions.

BACK ON BRYKAR'S SHIP, he is trying to determine which of the knights should be tested next. He chooses the Earth Knight, then walks through a corridor filled with some of the strongest warriors he was allowed to bring with him. He comes to a warrior known as the Scientific Samurai, a creature of great intellect and fighting skill. Suddenly, the eyes of the Scientific Samurai open,

Brykar slowly steps back, and the Scientific Samurai emerges from his tube where he has been kept kneeling before Brykar.

"I'm yours, Lord Brykar," he says. "How may I serve you?"

Chuckling, Brykar says "There are a group of knights who are protecting this world and who have become a thorn in my side. Still, I need to test their abilities, but there is one in particular I want you to test."

Brykar explains his plan to the Scientific Samurai, and once he has finished, Scientific Samurai disappears.

Now Brykar walks back to his chamber and contacts Sadoom. "Lord Sadoom," he says.

Sadoom, receiving the transmission, answers, "I'm here, Brykar. What do you have to report?"

"Lord Sadoom," Brykar continues, as he kneels before the hologram of Sadoom, "I have just recently made contact with the known alien hunters here and have struck a deal with them. I also know they intend to use our weapons to double-cross us. However they do not know it will all be in vain. Also, as you may recall, we have had some resistance from the local defenders here, who call themselves the Knights of the Cross. So far, they have defeated Deadly Double, but have allowed me to learn much of their abilities. Currently I'm sending the Scientific Samurai to test a different knight."

MEANWHILE THE KNIGHTS ARE ALMOST TO THEIR BASE, and Des notices that Joseph is unusually quiet and asks, "What's wrong, Joseph?"

"I just have a lot on my mind, Des," says Joseph.

Suddenly, they are all knocked out of the sky and onto the ground below. As they get up, they encounter what looks like a man of metal with the armor of a samurai and a lab coat without sleeves. Joseph asks, "Who are you?"

"My name is the Scientific Samurai," the creature before them answers, "and I shall be the one to eradicate you heroes."

Brad speaks up, "In your dreams, you galactic geek," and he charges the Scientific Samurai. The Scientific Samurai, taking an angle, strikes Brad in the back, then, grabbing him by the waist, throws him to the ground.

Now Maggie uses her wind powers to create a whip of wind and wraps it around the creatures waist, pulling him to her, so that she can strike him. But, when he reaches her, he twists so that he breaks free from her hold. Then, placing his palms on the ground, he pushes up, kicking her in the stomach and knocking her to the ground.

Britney throws lightning bolts toward him, but he draws his swords and uses them to redirect her lightning blasts back at the knights.

Joseph draws his swords and attacks, but the Scientific Samurai successfully blocks Joseph's attack. Impressed with Joseph's skill, the Scientific Samurai says, "You fight well, but I fight much better."

Now the Scientific Samurai twists his wrist so that he knocks Joseph's blades out of his hands. Then he kicks Joseph in the stomach and then in the head, knocking him to the floor.

Next, Jessica attacks, using her water power to try and freeze the creature. As he starts to freeze, he throws his sword up so that when it hits the ground, it drills down, causing molten lava to spew out from the ground, hitting his sword and hurling it into the air. Then he catches it. Before being frozen, the heat from the lava melts the ice. Before Jessica can react, he charges at her. As he is about to strike, he finds himself being knocked to the ground. Des is standing in front of Jessica, and he says, "Enough! If you want a real fight, try me."

The Scientific Samurai stands up and says, "Impressive! Too bad you won't live long enough to enjoy it."

Now Des charges the Scientific Samurai, drawing his sediment swords, and he and the Scientific Samurai exchange blows. The creature is impressed, not only that Des is blocking his blows, but also that he's coming even closer to hitting him than the Cross Knight had.

The Scientific Samurai uses one of Des's attacks to strike at him, but Des twists so that the strike misses. He then strikes the creature in the back. While the Samurai is stunned, Des grabs him and hurls him to the ground.

Seeing this, Jessica is even more impressed with Des.

When the Scientific Samurai gets to his feet, he says, "Well done, knight. You've proven to be a worthy opponent. Now prepare to die."

Then the Scientific Samurai charges and he and Des exchange thrusts, each blocking the others'.

Then the Scientific Samurai changes tactics and launches an attack at Jessica. Des quickly breaks off his attack and uses his power to raise up a stone to protect her. Then, without warning, the Scientific Samurai strikes Des, knocking him to the ground.

He then grabs Des by the throat and says, "You have fought well, and now you shall die a warrior's death."

In that moment, Jessica attacks, so that the creature drops Des. Even though she fights him with all of her might, he seems to block her attacks with ease. Then, he sees an opening and slaps her, knocking her to the ground.

With this, Des rushes to her side, making sure she is okay. Then he tells Joseph, "I need you all to port out of here, and I'll deal with this poser."

"Don't be stubborn," Joseph says. "This guy can and is looking to kill you."

"I know," Des says, "but right now I'm the only one who can stop him."

With that, they port out.

Once they were gone, Des says to the creature, "Now, let's see how good you really are," and he and the Scientific Samurai begin to exchange blows. These blows come faster and faster, neither of them willing to quit.

The Scientific Samurai finds an opening and knocks Des to the ground. Once again, he grabs Des by the throat, ready to finish him off. Then, suddenly, Des disappears. Furious, the creature begins to shout: "THIS IS NOT OVER, YOU COWARD! I WILL FIND YOU AND DESTROY EVERYTHING YOU CARE ABOUT! DO YOU HEAR ME?"

DES REAPPEARS AT THE BASE. Once there, he falls on his knees. Jessica goes to him to ask if he's okay, and before she can ask, he turns from her, saying, "Leave me alone!"

Jessica asks "What's going on, Des? Why are you being like this?"

Visibly angry, he complains, "Why did you guys pull me out of there? I could have beaten him. I just needed a little more time."

Hearing this, Tasha says, "Des, get a grip. That guy beat all of you, and there is no shame in that. That just means we need to work together and regroup."

Now Des says nothing but heads toward the training area. When others go to stop him, Joseph says, "Let him be for now." They agree.

IN THE TRAINING ROOM, Des puts on the Alpha Dog app and begins to train. As Jessica watches him, she is worried. She wonders why he's being like this.

When Maggie and Britney enter, they see her concern. Maggie says to

Jessica, "Jessica, why are you stressing over this guy? It's so unlike you."

"That's because he's unlike any guy I ever met. I don't know how," she answers, "but I can tell he's hurting. I just wish there was some way I could help him with this?" Her concern was written all over hear face and could be felt in her words.

Tasha says, "Joseph was right for telling us to leave him be. You're right, Jessica, he is hurting, but it's his pride as a warrior and protector that is hurt."

As Des is finishing the training session, the Spirit of Justice appears to him and says, "Are you okay, Des?"

Knowing it's her who is asking, he says, "How can I be? I couldn't beat that guy and he nearly hurt Jessica."

"True," she answers, "but by your own actions right now you are hurting her as well. Des, please understand. When pride comes, then comes disgrace,[2] but with the humble is wisdom.[3] Also, one's pride will bring him low, but he who is lowly in spirit will obtain honor."

As Des struggles to understand this, the Spirit of Justice adds, "Des, you have a lot of knowledge and fighting skill, but in order to defeat this foe, you must abandon your current knowledge, so that wisdom can guide you to victory. Remember: let no one deceive himself. If anyone among you thinks that he is wise in this age, let him become a fool that he may become wise."[4]

With these words, Justice vanishes, and Des falls to his knees and thinks to himself, "How can I abandon knowledge? It's what makes me who I am."

THE OTHERS NOTICE that the Scientific Samurai is still outside waiting for them, so Joseph says, "Let's go deal with this guy."

Eric adds, "Should we tell Des?"

"It's best to leave him behind," Joseph suggests. "The way he is right now to bring him in would only make things worse."

As the knights face the Scientific Samurai, Des is still in the Training Room. Seeing them, the Scientific Samurai says, "Ahhh, so the whole gang is here this time."

Suddenly he realizes that the Earth Knight is not among them, and he says, "Wait! Where is the Earth knight? Where is he?"

Jessica steps up and says, "He's not here. We're your opponents now. You'll have to deal with us."

Smiling, he says, "Suit yourself."

The knights prepare to face him. Then, without warning, the Scientific Samurai moves faster than any of them can see and knocks all of them to the ground at once. "I honestly thought you would be a challenge," he says smirking, "but you're merely a joke. None of you are really able to challenge me."

John gets up and says, "No matter what, we will not quit, and we will stop you."

"I hate to say this," Eric adds, "but he's right. We will not quit. With all that we are, you will not win."

Jessica adds, "You don't understand. We fight to protect our world and the ones we love. With all that we are, you will not win."

Back at the base, Des notices that everyone has gone and he asks Manuel, "Where is everyone?"

"They've gone to fight the Scientific Samurai," Manuel says.

Outraged, Des shouts, "They left without me? That's it! I'm going to help them."

But as he tries to leave, Manuel stops him. He says, "As long as you are like this, you are of no use to them."

"Are you kidding me?" Des protests. "They'll die if I don't go out there."

Manuel answers, "Des, you are part of a team. You are no longer on your own."

With that, Des suddenly realizes this was what Justice had been talking about. For so many years, Des has been alone, was never part of a team. Now , he is part of a team, and the only way this team will work is if they work together. He falls to his knees and cries out, "How could I have been so blind? If I had stopped to think about how we could take this creature down as a team, we would have beaten him the first time around. I know I don't deserve it, but let me go and help them. I know what I need to do now."

Seeing the change, Manuel agrees, and suddenly Des feels a strange energy. He shouts, "Geo Force Armor, engage!" When these words are spoken Des' armor undergoes a transformation that gives him two magnetic maces and secondary armor, and when the transformation is finished, he heads out to help his friends. This time he knows it will be different. This time, he's not fighting alone. He's fighting with his friends, and he's fighting for his home.

CHAPTER 5

STUBBORN AS STONE: A TIME TO ROCK

WHILE ALL THE KNIGHTS ARE DOWN, the Scientific Samurai draws his blades, wanting to finish the job. The first of his targets is the Aqua Knight. Raising his blades in the air, the Scientific Samurai prepares to finish the Aqua Knight, when Des appears and uses his Magnetic Maces to block the Scientific Samurai's attack. The Scientific Samurai is caught completely off guard. Des continues to use his Magnetic Maces to keep the Scientific Samurai off balance, and the other knights are amazed at who it could be. Then they all realize that it's Des.

After recovering from that last attack, the Scientific Samurai asks, "Who are you? I thought there were only twelve knights?"

Des chuckles and says "At least your math is right. There are only twelve of us, and I'm the Knight of Earth. What you see now is an upgrade of my power."

"Well," says the Scientific Samurai, "Let's see how strong your new armor is," and he steps forward in a guarded position, waiting for the Earth Knight's attack. Des turns to his friends and then turns back to the Scientific Samurai. Telepathically he says to his friends, "My friends, please forgive me for my arrogance. I thought I needed to defeat this villain on my own to prove myself to all of you, especially you, Jessica. I realize now that we are stronger together than apart, and I will hold him off while you make your escape."

Des takes a few steps and is almost instantly in front of the Scientific Samurai, who steps to his right, just avoiding the Earth Knight's attack. Des soon realizes that his new armor allows him to use the Earth's magnetic field to move faster than ever before.

While Des keeps the Scientific Samurai's attention on him, the other knights begin to port back to their base. The Scientific Samurai catches wind of this and targets the Aqua Knight in an attempt to capture her. But, before he can reach her, Des is in front of her, blocking his attack. Puzzled by how fast the Earth Knight is moving, the Scientific Samurai then scans his armor and breaks off his attack, saying, "Impressive, Earth Knight! You are indeed the challenge I have been looking for. However, this is far from over. When next we meet, it shall be a duel to the death."

With that, the Scientific Samurai vanishes, and Des returns to the base with the others.

WHEN DES ARRIVES AT THE BASE with the other knights, they gather around him to inspect his new armor. Brad says, "Not bad for a dork!"

John adds, "I wouldn't exactly call you Des the Dork anymore. That creature was more than all of us combined."

"How exactly did you unlock that new armor?" Eric asks.

"After my first battle with the Scientific Samurai," Des answers, "I felt I had to be the one to defeat him. What I didn't realize was that in order to defeat him I needed to remember that I'm part of a team and not alone. Once I acknowledged that, my new armor and powers awakened. I'm sorry for the way I behaved, guys. And, Jessica, I'm really sorry about how I treated you. Will you all forgive me for how I have behaved?"

The knights all nod in agreement, and Joseph says, "So, how are we going to beat this guy? The last time we fought him it didn't go so well."

Des speaks up: "Follow me to the lab. I think I have an idea."

WHILE THE OTHER KNIGHTS HEAD TO THE LAB, Jessica, pulls Des aside and confides in him, "I don't know if I can forgive you just yet. Especially since I just revealed that I care about you. You don't realize how much it took for me to confess to you how I felt. I know you didn't mean to hurt me, but the fact is you did. You hurt all of us because that creature nearly killed you."

At first, Des just stands there silent, wanting to speak, but unable to find the words to say. Jessica continues, "Don't get it twisted. I'm not saying I don't like you, cause I do. What I'm saying is this: you don't need to prove yourself to me because I like you for who you are. When I thought you were all brains and no brawn, I liked you, but after you showed your skills, I was even more impressed. But, what impressed me most was when we were testing the clone, and you noticed that it hurt me when you poked the clone. It was the tenderness you showed when you knew it hurt me. Des, we are all in this together — good or bad — and we need to act as a team."

Their private moment is interrupted by Joseph. "Sorry," he says, "I don't mean to interrupt, but we're all waiting to hear this big plan of yours Des."

"Sorry, Joe," Des says. "We'll be right there, but there's something I have to tell Jessica."

Joseph nods and goes to let the others know what is going on. Des turns to Jessica and pours out his heart. "Jessica, it was never my intention to hurt you or the team. I didn't even realize my pride was that bad. All I can say is that I'm sorry. I know actions speak louder than words, and I will prove by my actions that I have changed. I'm not going to let this guy beat us. I will make sure that I protect you and the others."

With that, the two head to the lab to join the others and tell them of his plan.

MEANWHILE, THE SCIENTIFIC SAMURAI RETURNS TO BRYKAR'S BASE and heads to the ship's workshop, where he begins working on a new weapon and some other special surprises to counteract the Earth Knight's newest armor and the other knight.

As the Scientific Samurai begins working, Brykar walks in. "Why did you retreat?" he asks.

The Scientific Samurai answers, "The reason for my retreat is that the knight's new armor was a surprise I wasn't counting on, and I don't like surprises. Besides, to fight him with those new powers would be unwise and surely would cause me to be defeated. Currently, I'm working on a new weapons that should neutralize the Earth Knight's newest armor. Also, I did a scan of the Earth Knight's new armor, if everything works, I should be able to neutralize his powers quite easily."

"Be sure that it does," Brykar threatens, "or it will be you who feels my wrath."

NOTICING THAT THE THREE HOURS HE GAVE AGENT MARTIN ARE UP, Brykar now enters his chambers and contacts Agent Martin through his cell. When Agent Martin answers, he says, "Time's up, human! Do we have a deal?"

Pausing just a moment, Agent Martin answers, "After careful consideration, we have decided to accept your offer."

"Very good!" Brykar says. "I will be sending you coordinates of where we will meet to finalize this arrangement."

Agent Martin agrees, but he is thinking to himself, "Once we have your tech, we will use it force you off our world."

Agent Martin doesn't know it yet, but Brykar already knows their intentions and is planning to give the earthlings their weakest weapons (which are still stronger than any earthling weapon).

While they are yet speaking, Brykar sends Agent Martin the coordinates. "The coordinates have been sent," he says. "I will meet you there in four hours."

EXAMINING THE COORDINATES THAT HAVE COME IN, Agent Martin realizes it will take him about four hours to reach the meeting site. "Perfect," he says, "we're on our way."

He ends the call, but then he makes another call. "Get the team ready," he says, "we're about to make contact."

The person on the other end of the call asks about the students who escaped. Agent Martin answers, "I'm already on it. Soon they won't have anywhere to hide."

With that, he ends the call and starts to make his way to the hanger.

IN THE LAB, DES HAS HAD BOTH BRAD'S NEW ARMOR and his own scanned in the computer, to see what other secrets their armor might have. While he is reviewing the findings, he notices that the armors aren't just strong; they also enhance their current powers the longer they are used. He also notices something else interesting. "Well, what do we have here?" he says.

Curious, John asks, "What did you find out, Des?"

"Apparently my armor has given me some interesting new powers as well," Des answers, "meaning my armor allows me to adjust the Earth's gravity within a specific range."

"Could you break that down for us, Des?" Eric pleads.

"Simply put," Des replies, turning to them, "I can change the gravity of the Earth itself, and I think I know how I can use that to our advantage." He starts inputting data into the computer and discovers that the gravity change would only affect the area where the knights were at the moment. He then turns to the other knights and says, "I have a plan for how to beat this guy."

"So, what's the plan?" Eric asks eagerly.

"Whenever he fought us, it's been one-on-one, and individually we can't beat him. However, if we were to constantly switch out, we'll be able to keep him off balance enough so that we can finish him."

"That sounds like a plan," John says. "So, how long should each of us fight before we switch?"

Des thinks for a moment and then says, "No more than forty-five seconds. Any longer than that, and he'll be able to gain his balance, and we will lose our advantage."

"Now, all we have to do is find him," Sally adds.

"I hate to be the bearer of bad news," Eric interjects, "but we still have one problem to deal with."

"And that is?" John asks.

"Those guys from ARC," Eric explains. "I doubt anyone has ever escaped them, and I don't think they're going to give up on catching us. And ... going home would definitely put our families in danger."

Now Tasha chimes in, "You're right on that one."

"Guys, guys ... !" It's Max talking this time. "I don't think we have to worry much longer." He has Des pull up a local news station.

The reporter is saying, "Earlier today, three high school buses were destroyed, and the teacher and many students died. But there are twelve students who survived. After being checked out and brought to safety, they were being transported for questioning by authorities, and have escaped custody. If anyone should see them, you are asked to contact the authorities in charge at 1-800-435-7ARC. Please do not approach them as they are considered armed and dangerous."

The knights are amazed to see their pictures flash across the screen. Stunned for a moment, Des soon recovers, and cuts of the newscast.

Eric speaks first, "Well, I guess we don't have to worry about going home now."

BACK ON BRYKAR'S SHIP, the Scientific Samurai begins to review the scan of the Earth Knight's new armor. When he pulls it up on the screen, nothing is there, and as he wonders how this could be. He realizes that the Earth Knight's powers must have shielded him from the scan. He sets it aside and continues to work on his new weapon and other devices to neutralize the knights.

While the Scientific Samurai is in the middle of working on this new weapon, Brykar walks in. He asks, "So, what did your scan of the Earth Knight's armor reveal?"

"Unfortunately my Lord," the Scientific Samurai answers, "the scan didn't reveal anything. The knight's powers have shielded him from my scan. However, I'm working on a new weapon that will allow me to turn the tables on this knight and his new armor."

"So, what do they do?" asks Brykar.

"Well," begins the Scientific Samurai, "my new weapons will allow me to create energy versions of any handheld weapon I desire, and I call them my Energy Emulators. I've also created these." He hands Brykar a disc and explains, "I call these Disc Disruptors. When these are placed on a target, the targets torso will be encased in psychormium, and I've also placed psychic disruptors in each, which should prevent the knights from being able to use their powers to escape."

This causes Brykar to chuckle with delight. "So, do you think these weapons will help you in your next battle against the knights?"

"Oh, yes," the Scientific Samurai assures him. "Between my intelligence and the skills I possess, these knights will fall. My new weapons will give me more of an edge against them. This time there is no retreat. I will make sure that, this time, I finish them all."

Brykar chuckles again, then turns serious. "Well, you had better finish them off this time. Otherwise, I will destroy you myself."

The Scientific Samurai nods his understanding,, and Brykar heads to his chamber.

ONCE INSIDE HIS CHAMBER, Brykar contacts Sadoom. "Lord Sadoom," he says, "I'm ready to give my latest report."

"I'm here, General Sadoom. "Tell me: what do you have to report?"

"I've made contact with the earthling alien hunters," Brykar says, "and I'll be meeting them in the next three hours."

"What about the 'knights' you spoke of? Are they still a problem for you?" Sadoom asks.

"No, my Lord," Brykar replies, "as we speak, my newest warrior is preparing to finish these knights off. They are no match for us."

"Good work!" Sadoom says, "Continue to keep me informed."

BRYKAR HAS THE PSYDRONES LOAD A POD with some weapons and leaves to meet with Agent Martin at the coordinates he sent him.

WHEN AGENT MARTIN AND HIS TEAM ARRIVE at the coordinates, they find they are twenty minutes early. Before they exit the craft, Agent Martin addresses his team: "Okay, team, we are about to make contact with an extraterrestrial being that we have never met before. At this point, this thing is using technology that could revolutionize what we currently know. I need all of you to be alert, just in case this is a trap. Do I make myself clear?"

The team members all nod in agreement."

The ARC team begins to exit the craft. This team consists of seven other people besides Agent Martin. The first member of the team is a former green beret and expert in hand-to-hand combat. His name is Agent Wallace. Next, there is a communications expert. He is Agent Miles. After that, we have Agent Daniels, who is not only one of the team's top female operatives; she is also an expert assassin and hacker. The next member of the team is Agent Rivera. She is a top-ranked robotics expert and weapons developer. This brings us to the fifth team member, Agent Stanton. He's ARC's top martial arts expert and melee weapons master. The sixth member of this team is Agent Saunders. She is an expert strategist and tactician. The final member of the team is Agent Ryan. She is ARC's ranged weapons expert and seductress, able to bend most men to her will.

As the team heads over to the coordinates, where they are to meet Brykar, Agent Saunders notices that they are out in the open. "Not to overstate the obvious," she says, "but doesn't it bother anyone that we're out in the open?"

"I agree," says Staunton, "it does seem weird."

"Will you all calm down?" Agent Rivera interjects. "More than likely this is a hoax. And if that is the case, I'll look forward to testing on whoever thought it was cute to mess with ARC. In fact, if I have the opportunity, I plan to make sure whoever planned this pays dearly ... if it is indeed a hoax."

Agent Ryan adds, "Hey, Rivera, can I use whoever it is for target practice after you're done with him?"

Rivera chuckles and says, "Certainly! In fact, your target practice can be part of my experiments."

Ryan licks her lips and says, "Mmmmmmm, now that sounds delicious." When she says this, the men make sure to focus their attention away from her. They know that if they give her even the slightest bit of attention, they will soon be completely under her hypnotic spell.

Moments after they reach the coordinates Bykar sent, Brykar and his Psydrones suddenly arrive. Their sudden appearance startles agent Martin and his team, causing each of them to take a defensive stance. When they realize who it is, Agent Martin approaches Brykar and says, "I'm here as you asked. By the way, I never did get your name."

Chuckling, Brykar says, "That's because I never gave it to you. Now that you're here, you can call me Brykar." He then points to the pod with psychromium alloy and two Psydrones and says "The pod and the drones are yours to do with as you will."

"Excellent," Agent Martin affirms. "However I know this does not come free. So, what are looking for in exchange?"

This brought another chuckle to Brykar. "All I require in return," he says, "is your help in understanding your world and learning of its beauty."

The members of the ARC team are skeptical of this statement, but, for the time being, Agent Martin agrees to the terms.

Brykar says, "Before you leave, I have a request. May I show you how my people say farewell until we next meet?"

"Certainly," Agent Martin says, "and we look forward to working with you."

Brykar then directs them to line up so that the ARC team is standing before him, and he has them hold hands. He then places his hand on Agent Martin's forehead and begins speaking in an alien dialect. Unknown to the Agent Martin or his team, Byrkar has implanted his psychic link into all of them, allowing him to control them at any given moment.

Moments later, Brykar finishes the farewell, and Agent Martin and his team prepare to depart, unaware of what has truly taken place during this meeting.

Brykar now hands a circular disk to Agent Martin and says, "You can use this to contact me if you have any questions in regard to the tech we gave you."

WHILE THE KNIGHTS ARE IN THEIR LAB, Des's alarm goes off, alerting them of the Scientific Samurai's presence. Des says, "Guess who's back, guys?"

"Let me guess," says Eric sarcastically, "the Scientific Samurai?

"Yep," Des says. "Is everybody ready?"

The other knights nod, but before they can transform, Jessica goes to Des, kisses him on the cheek and says, "I forgive you, Des, and I care about you a lot. But ... if you ever try to take on one of these guys all alone again, I'll beat you myself. Just know that I no longer consider you Des the Dork. You are now Des the Defender."

This brought a chuckle from everyone.

As their laughter ends, Joseph says, "All right, guys, let's get topside and trash this fool."

The knights all raise their hands into the air and transform. Manuel ports them nearby the area where the Scientific Samurai is.

DES PULLS BRAD ASIDE. "Brad, I know you don't like me much," he says, "but after the first attack, we need to engage our new armors so that at least one of us can finish him off."

"You're right," Brad agrees. "I didn't like you much, but I have come to respect you, Des, and I'll follow your lead. Now, let's show him what he's dealing with." The two shake hands and rejoin the other knights.

THE KNIGHTS REACH THE SPOT where the Scientific Samurai is, and Des notices the new weapons in the creature's hands. He telepathically says to the others, "Everyone scatter!"

The knights scatter just in time to miss the attack the Scientific Samurai, has launched upon hearing their approach.

Des says, "Everybody be on your toes. He's got an upgrade since we last saw him."

Joseph says telepathically, "Everybody circle him, and get ready to strike."

The knights circle the Scientific Samurai and begin to approach him. He notices what they have done, but before he can launch another attack Joseph telepathically says to the team, "Knights, let's light the night!"

Brad is the first to attack. As he lunges at the creature, he draws his flame blades and begins his attack. The Scientific Samurai is able to block each attack.

As the forty-five-second mark approaches, Joseph telepathically shouts, "Change!"

Now Brad lunges and uses the Scientific Samurai's block to propel him outward. Before the Scientific Samurai can react, Des draws his swords and launches his attack. With each of Des's attacks, the Scientific Samurai tries to block, but he is finding it increasingly difficult to do. Knowing that the forty-five-second mark is near, Des makes one final lunge and slices the Scientific Samurai.

Now Jessica draws her swords, as Des returns to his position and activates his Geo-Guard Armor. The Scientific Samurai finds it even harder now to block Jessica's attacks.

The Scientific Samurai uses one of his blocks, turning it into an attack, but Jessica is able to dodge it by crouching down. Then, as she springs forward, she knocks him back and is able to wound him even further.

The knights continue this successful pattern, not letting up. However, the Scientific Samurai soon realizes what is going on. He is able to dodge the latest attacks by leaping into the air, then using his Energy Emulators, has them take the shape of double-sided blades. As he comes down, he targets the knights. However, just as his blades are poised to strike, a magnetic field appears over each of the knights to protect them from him.

Surprised by this, the Scientific Samurai shouts, "What happened? Who did this?"

Des steps forward and says, "Guilty, as charged. This time I'm not letting you hurt my friends, you scientific psycho. If you really want to dance, then let's dance."

"No!" Jessica shouts. "Don't do it."

Telepathically Des communicates to them all, "Don't worry, I'm not the same as last time. Last time I fought for myself and my own ego. This time, I'm fighting for you guys. Besides, he's already seen through our first plan, but at least we did some damage. Maybe I can finish him off."

The other knights nod in unison, giving their approval.

As Des faces the Scientific Samurai, the Scientific Samurai speaks: "I've waited for this moment for a long time. Throughout all my travels, I've searched for powerful warriors like yourself. With each victory, I obtained, not just their skills, but also the intellect of the warriors I faced. Once you are destroyed, I will be even more powerful."

Smiling broadly, Des answers, "When we last fought, I fought like you, for my own glory. I realize now that skill and intellect can only take you so far. What carries a true warrior to victory is his heart, and with all my heart I will fight to protect my world and my friends."

The two square off again and the Scientific Samurai attacks. Des, however, uses his magnetic field to dodge this attack. It is almost effortless. Noticing that the Earth Knight is using his magnetic field, the Scientific Samurai flicks a switch on his emulators and throws them so that Des avoids them. As they pass him, the emulators disrupt his magnetic field, causing Des to suddenly stumble.

Watching all of this, the other knights suddenly go to draw their blades as if they were able to attack, but knowing that right now they are prevented from doing so.

When the Scientific Samurai sees Des stumble, he heads straight for him, drawing his original blade. As he prepare to strike the Earth Knight, he smiles and says, "Gotcha!" Suddenly the magnetic fields around the knights disappear, and they are pulled in front of Des and are able to strike the Scientific Samurai all at once, knocking him to the ground, but he remains there for only a moment.

When the Scientific Samurai has recovered, he asks, "What did you do?"

Des answers for them all. "Simple! When I placed the magnetic barriers around the other knights, it had created a polarized field opposite of the one I was projecting. I knew you would see through our first plan, and I knew you would want to disrupt my magnetic field. So, when you did, it allowed my fellow knights to be pulled almost instantaneously to where I was."

Upon hearing this, the Scientific Samurai is furious. He leaps over the knights and grabs his emulators and again takes a fighting stance.

Des prepares to face the Scientific Samurai on his own again, when suddenly a swarm of Psydrones appear. Unknown to the knights, the Psydrones are carrying the Scientific Samurai's Disc Disruptors. The Scientific Samurai says, "These Psydrones will deal with your friends, while I deal with you, Earth Knight."

Eric shouts, "Don't worry, we'll handle these clowns. Take him down."

The other knights then begin to engage the drones, while Des faces the Scientific Samurai by himself. When the Scientific Samurai attacks, Des uses his magnetic field to avoid the Scientific Samurai's attacks, and this frustrates the Scientific Samurai even further. Soon, he realizes that the Earth Knight's plan is to tire him out, so he decides to lunge in for a final attack. Des quickly dodges this attack, but unknown to Des, the Scientific Samurai was counting on that and now blindsides Des, knocking him to the ground.

AS DES HITS THE GROUND, it distracts the other knights enough that the Psydrones are able to place a Disc Disruptor on each of them. The Scientific Samurai has one, this one for the Earth Knight. When the Scientific Samurai approaches Des this time, he says, "In all my travels, I've never met anyone quite like you. I mean, not only did you think you could beat me, but you planned out a strategy that actually would have worked if had you finished me off when you had the chance."

When the Scientific Samurai reaches the Earth Knight, he places the Disc Disruptor on him. As it encases him, Des, shouts, "What's going on?"

"What's going on," the Scientific Samurai answers, "is that you and your friends are trapped by my Disc Disruptors. They are made of pure psychronium and will prevent you from using your powers."

Des struggles to get free, as do the other knights, but none is unable to achieve it. The Scientific Samurai now adds, "Since you are all tied up, I think I shall take care of your friends. I shall start with the Aqua Knight, since you seem to be particularly fond of her."

Des shouts, "Don't you dare harm my, friends!"

"You are in no position to make demands," the Scientific Samurai states. "Still, you can watch as your friends are destroyed before your very eyes. Enjoy the show, Earth Knight."

As the Scientific Samurai approaches the Aqua Knight, Des struggles to break free. He is thinking to himself, "I can't let it end like this. There's gotta be a way to stop him."

Suddenly he hears someone or something say, "Remember the oath."

Des now begins to say, "As days of darkness near, and people run in fear ..."

The Scientific Samurai gets closer to the Aqua Knight, and Des continues to say, "From they who prey on the weak, and silence those who speak..."

Now the Scientific Samurai reaches the Aqua Knight. As he grabs her, Des continues to say, "We will take to the sky with courage and battle cry. TO PROTECT THE WORLD FROM LOSS, I AM A KNIGHT OF THE CROSS." As he finishes the oath, he feels a surge from within his armor, and the Disc Disruptor is absorbed by the armor. Then he uses his magnetic field to hit the Scientific Samurai from behind, causing him to throw the Aqua Knight into the air.

Des leaps up, catching her. As he sets her down, he asks, "Are you okay?" She nods to confirm that she's okay.

Now the Scientific Samurai shouts , "NOOOOOO! THIS ISN'T POSSIBLE! How could you escape?"

The Earth Knight responds, "Your devices blocked our minds and bodies, but they didn't block our hearts." Suddenly, the Scientific Samurai lunges at the him, but he is able to blocks the attack. Then he energizes his magnetic maces, striking the Scientific Samurai, knocking him to ground again.

Now Des has the main spike on his magnetic maces extend, and using his magnetic field, he speeds towards the Scientific Samurai. As the Scientific Samurai turns to face the Earth Knight, he mutters, "What ... have ... you ... done?" He looks down to see that the Earth Knight's mace has pierced his body, revealing that the Scientific Samurai is some kind of bio-robot. As Des removes the mace, the robot falls to the ground.

Breathing a sigh of relief, the Earth Knight walks over to the others and he touches them in turn, activating their armor's ability to absorb any kind of metal. The result is that the knights are all free and able to port back to their base.

UNKNOWN TO THE KNIGHTS, Brykar arrives at where the Scientific Samurai lies. Seeing the end of his experiment, he shakes his head and says, "I should have known better. However you may still be of some use to me." Brykar then ports both he and the Scientific Samurai back to their base. Once there, he places the robot in a revival tube next to Deadly Double.

"These knights are proving to be more difficult to defeat than I thought," Brykar says and he goes to contact Sadoom and give his report.

AS SADOOM RECEIVES THE TRANSMISSION, Brykar says, "Lord Sadoom, everything is going according to plan. I've already made contact with this world's alien hunters and have implanted my psychic connection into them so that I can control them whenever I so choose."

"Good," Sadoom says, "and what is going on with those 'knights' that seem to be giving you problems."

"Lord Sadoom," Brykar says, "the testing of the knights continues. After our this last encounter, I have gained much more intel than I first had. Once I'm done testing their abilities, this world will be ours for the taking. I assure you that I will not fail you, my Lord."

"Very, well," Sadoom says, wondering how much of it is true. "Continue to keep me updated of your progress."

Brykar nods and says "I will, my Lord."

As the communication draws to an end, Brykar goes to his computer and begins to review the footage of this last battle. He is thinking to himself, "Why does this seem so familiar?"

AFTER RETURNING TO THE BASE, the knights gather around Des and ask him how he was able to escape from the Disc Disruptors. Des reports, "To be honest, I'm not fully sure how I was able to escape, but I do know that before I did, I felt something deep inside me saying, 'Remember the oath.' So, I began to recite the oath, and once I had finished it, I felt a surge from within me, and my armor began to absorb the disc disruptors."

The other knights are just as puzzled as Des. He continues, "There's much we still don't know about these armors or the powers they've given us, but one thing is clear: these armors work on a whole different level than simple alien tech."

The other knights agree.

Eric says, "As always, I hate to be the bearer of bad new, but has anyone given thought to what we are going to do now? I mean, as far as the entire world knows, we are wanted fugitives, and I doubt we'll be able to stay down here forever."

Manuel then approaches them and says, "I know this is overwhelming for you, my young friends. However, I do want you to know that, for now, you can consider this place your home."

"No offense, guys," Maggie says, "but where are we gonna sleep and what are we going to wear? I don't know about you, but I'm not wearing this outfit for the rest of my life."

Manuel again interjects something, "Do not worry. There are many rooms here, and each with what you call a bathroom, so you will be able maintain your hygiene, and your armors can transition to be whatever clothes you need."

MANUEL THEN ESCORTS THEM to the hall where their new rooms are located. Before the knights pick out their rooms, Eric says "Manuel, this place is amazing, but I do have a question: What are we going to do for food?"

Manuel answers, "Not to worry, my friend, we also have what you would call a cafeteria, where any food you would like can be made."

The knights are wondering how all of this came about, but they are too tired to care at the moment. They pick their rooms, and each of them lies down for the night, wondering just what the next day might bring.

CHAPTER 6

WINDS OF CHANGE: WHISPERING WINDS

WHILE THE KNIGHTS SLEEP, their families learn of the news of them now being wanted fugitives and have agreed to meet to see if they can figure out what is going on. The plan is to meet at a nearby community center.

The first to arrive is Brad and Joseph's mother, Melanie. Soon afterward, Max's aunt and uncle (who became his guardians when his parents were killed by a drunk driver on their way to pick him up) also arrive. The next to arrive are Maggie's father, Alexander Marks, her mother, and Janet's Aunt Dana. Des's mother and brother arrive shortly after that, followed by Jessica's mother and father. Eric's father, Jason, and his girlfriend wander in moments later. Following behind them are Tasha's grandparents, who have raised Tasha since she was an infant. Not long after that, comes Sally's Aunt Deborah. Coming in behind her is Britney's father, a local District Attorney whose name is David Bolten and her mother, Judge Lara Bolten.

The last to arrive is John's mother. She sits quietly in her chair as the other adults talk among themselves. Melanie goes to the nearby podium, and in a loud, authoritative voice, says, "Everyone, may I have your attention please!"

Not recognizing her, the other adults begin to murmur, "Who's this woman?"

Again, in a loud, authoritative voice, Melanie says, "Everyone, please sit down and let's be quiet. Like the rest of you, I'm worried about my children. I know you are too. I also know that none of our children are so troubled that they should be considered fugitives from the law. I've called you all here so that we could pool our resources, to see if we can find out what's really going on and why there is a manhunt underway for our children." This catches everyone's attention, and the crowd finally ceases its murmuring.

Now Jason speaks up, "So, where do we start?"

Des's brother Graham stands and says, "Hi, everyone. My name is Graham. How about we start with what we know? First, while on their trip, the students' buses were blown up. This leads me to believe something happened that either the government wants to know about or is trying to cover up. I'm not sure which. What we need to do is find out what actually took place out there and what the government is trying to keep secret and why."

"Yes," says Melanie, "That's a very good place to start. Let's all work together to uncover the truth."

"I have some contacts in that area," Alexander says. "They may be able to help me get photos of the wreckage so we can see if there's something that was overlooked."

"Before we begin researching what happened," Graham adds, "I want to point out that going forward it would be best if we are not seen together all that often."

"Why do say that, Graham?" David asks.

"Because whoever is hunting our loved ones may start hunting us, and the last thing we need is to be locked away before learning what is really going on. So, for the time being, it would be best if we use handwritten notes. All other types of communication can be seized or traced. If it's all right with you, I'll work on a code we can use to communicate with each other, something that will be hard to decipher. Until then, only written communications would be best."

"So, what should we use for this communication?" asks Deborah.

"I think the best way," Graham replies, "would be through postcards or greeting cards, considering it's not unusual to see them being delivered."

Max's Uncle Phillip, who works as a postman, now says, "Graham, I work at the post office, and all of you are on my route. So, when you find something, let me know, and I'll deliver it to everyone else."

"That sounds like a plan," Melanie says. "And I'll leave a message with Phillip if we need to meet for any reason."

With that, the group says their farewells, everyone hoping that their children are safe.

THE NEXT DAY, WHEN THE KNIGHTS AWAKEN from their slumber, they all head for the cafeteria. Manuel shows them a machine that will make their food simply by them selecting what type of meal they want. As the knights each select the type of meal they prefer, Joseph says, "While we eat, there's something I've gotta say. If we are going to stand a chance against these things, we need to start training. If not, we just might not make it out alive next time. So, starting from today, we need make sure we give it our all. Are you all with me?"

The knights all nod in agreement. Eric chuckles and says, "Too bad this place doesn't have anything that can simulate a gravity field stronger than Earth's. We could use that to increase our strength."

"That's not a bad idea," Des says, "and I believe the Training Room does have something that can do just that."

Slapping his palm to his forehead, Eric says, "When will I learn to keep my big mouth shut?" The knights finish eating their meal and head to the Training Room.

DES SEARCHES THE COMPUTER FOR A PROGRAM that will allow them to train under higher gravity, and he finds a program called GAS, which stands for Gravity Altering System. He then engages the program and says, "Okay, it's set to 5 GP. Is everybody ready?"

When the other knights nod in agreement, Des presses the button, and they are all ported into the training area. As the knights begin to feel the gravitational pull, they find it increasingly difficult to move. John says, "My muscles feel like dead weights. What's going on?"

Des explains, "What you are feeling right now is a gravitational pull five times that of Earth. The object here is for us to be able to move around freely, just like we did before. Once we do that, I'll up it another 5 GP and continue the process. This should allow us to increase our strength exponentially."

"Des," Maggie interjects, "remind me, when this is, over to hurt you."
"Come on, Maggie," Jessica says. "No pain, no gain!"

"Listen!" Maggie shoots back, "just because he's your boyfriend doesn't mean I have to like going along with this."

"True," Jessica responds, "but we did all agree to do this kind of training. So, there's no real reason to complain."

Des begins to walk toward where some swords are kept in the Training Room. With each step, he notices it is much more difficult than he first thought to move under 5 GP. When he finally reaches the swords, he finds himself struggling to pull one out. When he finally does pull it out, the weight of it under the 5 GP nearly pulls him to the floor.

Des now tries to set his stance and finds each movement extremely difficult. The other knights are experiencing the same thing. Maggie, like the others, struggles with moving under the 5 GP and asks, "How long are we supposed to deal with this?"

Des answers, "Until we can reach the manual shut-off located there." He points to a ledge about twenty feet in the air.

"How are we supposed to get to it?" Maggie asks.

"That part is easy," he says. "We have to be able to jump up there."

"ARE YOU CRAZY!" She is dead serious. "We can barely move down here, and you want us to be able to jump up there to shut this thing down?" She is clearly very annoyed with this idea.

"I've gotta agree. This is a little extreme," John chimes in.

"I also agree," Brad says, "this sucks. But ... the last of these guys we faced tore us apart. If it wasn't for Des, we would all be goners. So, I say we suck it up and get used to this GP, so we can show these alien freaks what the Knights of the Cross are made of."

"Impressive speech, Brad," Tasha says, "and I agree. Complaining won't help us get out of here."

THE KNIGHTS CONTINUE TO MOVE AROUND in the 5 GP environment, each giving it his or her all, so that they can somehow learn to move freely. After several hours in that environment, they begin to find it easier to move around. Now Joseph says, "Everyone start bouncing."

The other knights look at him puzzled, especially the girls. Janet says, "You want us to do what?"

Joseph answers, "If we're going to reach that ledge, we need to strengthen ourselves and increase our abilities, and this just might just be the best way. Now, follow my lead." He begins to bounce on the balls of his feet, and the others follow suit.

Then Joseph begins to bring his knees to his chest and the other knights follow. Although the knights are exhausted from dealing with the strain of moving in the 5 GP environment, they soon start to see that they are able to jump higher than before.

John says, "I have an idea on how to reach that ledge."

"Spit it out," Eric responds, "so we can get done and get out of here."

"Well," John begins, "if I run, and two of you give me a boost, I should be able to reach the ledge."

"Not a bad idea," Max says. "Eric, why don't you and I give him that boost."

"On it!" replies Eric, now excited about the thought of getting done and getting out of there.

John gets to his start point, and then he runs. When he gets to where the other two knights are standing, he jumps. The other two get their hands under him, lifting him higher, and he is able to reach the ledge—barely. He has grasped the ledge, but his lower half is dangling. They can only watch as he struggles to pull himself up.

ONCE HE IS FULLY ON THE LEDGE, John hits the manual shut-off, and the knights are ported back to the Command Area of the Training Room. They immediately feel the difference. Although they are exhausted, they realize that their training exercise was worth it.

"Okay, Des," Maggie says, "I gotta admit I didn't think this would work. But now I've gotta say: this was a very good idea."

"Okay guys," Joseph says, smiling, "let's head to our rooms and relax for a bit." The other knights agree. Joseph, however, heads for the library.

MEANWHILE AT HIS BASE, BRYKAR WALKS down the corridor observing each of the warriors that are with him, trying to decide which will be the next one to face the knights. As he walks back and forth examining them, one particular warrior seems to stand out in his mind. He then approaches the tube where this next warrior is and opens it. He says, "Come forth, Phobia Fighter!"

As he is released, Phobia Fighter falls to his knees and says, "I'm yours to command. What is your desire, my Lord?"

Brykar answers, "I have a little job that requires your special expertise. There are some heroes known as the Knights of the Cross who are becoming a bit of a thorn in my side. I want them removed, and I believe your specific talents will do just that."

Phobia Fighter has the power to make any creatures' fears become a reality to them. Although he doesn't know what their fears are, his power allows him to activate the part of a being's brain that causes them to feel fear. Phobia now answers, "As you command, my Lord."

Before Phobia leaves the ship, he asks Brykar, "How do I find these knights?"

"That's an interesting question," Brykar answers. "However, you won't need to find them; they will find you. Although I have an idea. There is a city nearby. Why don't you go there and test out your powers on the humans and see how they deal with a psychic attack. Just make sure no one sees you."

Rubbing his hands together in delight, Phobia says, "Ohhhhhh, this is gonna be fun!"

Brykar tosses Phobia one of his Vcords and says, "Make sure you turn this on before you begin your attacks, as I need to see how these humans respond to a direct psychic attack."

Phobia puts the Vcord to his chest and then heads to the hangar, grabs a Magnacycle and leaves the base.

AS PHOBIA HEADS TO THE CITY, he presses a button on his belt that allows all he comes into contact with to see him as a native, rather than in his true form. Once he arrives in the city, he is overjoyed at how many targets he has to choose from. He activates the Vcord and looks for his first victim.

In this case, it is victims. He sees a young couple and approaches them. He first touches the girl, then the guy, and before either of them can react, they are literally frozen with fear.

Delighted, Phobia moves on from this couple, looking for more targets. All the while, he is chuckling to himself, "This is going to be so much fun!"

BACK AT THE KNIGHTS' BASE, MAGGIE IS SITTING BY HERSELF. She is thinking about her life before she became a Knight of the Cross and wondering if she made the right choice. Suddenly, but ever so gently, Justice appears in the shape of a human, as a being made up of wind, and asks, "What troubles you, Maggie?"

Maggie sighs deeply and responds, "I'm just wondering if I made the right decision, Justice. I mean, honestly, I can fight and defend myself, but that's not exactly what I pictured myself doing for the rest of my life. In fact, being a soldier was the last thing I ever wanted to be."

"I understand," Justice adds, "however, it is written, 'The wind blows where it wishes, and you hear its sound, but you do not know where it comes from or where it goes. So it is with everyone who is born of the Spirit.'"

"What does that mean, Justice?" she asks, a puzzled look on her face.

Justice turns to Maggie and says, "That, my dear, is for you to find out. I can only point you in the direction of the answer, but you must find it for yourself. What I can say is this: like the wind, you have your times that you can be gentle, and there are time you are like the hurricane. I will be here to guide you. Just know that the choice you made is part of who you are."

Before Justice can say anything else, the alarm goes off, and Maggie rushes to the lab.

AS MAGGIE AND THE OTHER KNIGHTS ARRIVE, they are all wondering what's going on. Des says, "Look at the screen." He shows them the nearby city, and they see the people frozen with fear.

"What happened to them?" Maggie asks.

"I'm not sure," Des responds. "All I know is that their brain activity is spiking like crazy. If we don't do something soon, these people will have a heart attack and die."

Eric asks, "How is that possible?"

"Again, I'm not sure," Des replies. "All I know is that whoever or whatever did this is targeting the part of the brain that produces fear."

Tasha asks, "Does that mean whoever or whatever did this can know our deepest, darkest fears?"

"I don't think so," Des says, "but from these readings, it looks like whatever is causing this is internal, not external."

John says, "Remember, Des, English."

Des shakes his head and explains, "Simply put, it looks like whatever is scaring them is from the inside of them, not the outside."

"Do you have any idea what's causing this?" Eric asks.

"Not at the moment," Des admits, "but all things considering, this sounds like one of Brykar's playmates. Especially given the nature and origin of the attack."

Joseph now says, "All right, I'll take a small team and see what we can do." Eric asks, "Who are you taking this time?"

Joseph answers, "Janet, John, Eric, Tasha and Sally, you are with me. The rest of you should stay with Des, as he tries to pinpoint what's causing this."

Joseph and the knights he has chosen transform. Before they head out, Des says, "Joseph, the armor also has a camouflage mode that should allow you guys to move about easily without being seen." Joseph answers, "How do we activate it?"

Des types something on the keyboard and reads from the monitor, "It's voice activated, and also ... you can only use it for a limited amount of time."

"How much time?" Eric asks.

"According to these readouts," Des responds, "I would say about an hour and a half."

"All right," Joseph says, "let's light the night." He crosses his arms, then extends them to his sides. As he does this, his wings emerge.

Eric says, "Now, that's impressive! But how are the rest of us supposed to get there?"

"According to this schematic," Des says, "you should be able to create wings too, just like Joseph has."

The other knights now begin to focus their minds on creating wings similar to Joseph's, and sure enough, their wings begin to form. Tasha notices that her wings look more like an eagle's. "What's the deal?" she asks.

Des does a scan of her powers and says, "Amazing..."

"Spit it out, Des!" she says, clearly short on patience.

"Okay," he responds, "according to this, your powers allow you to not only shapeshift into different animals; they also allow you to borrow different parts of the animal. In this case, since you wanted to fly, the eagle's wings emerged, so that you can fly."

ONCE THE KNIGHTS ARE READY, MANUEL PORTS THEM outside the base. As they head toward the city, Joseph says, "After we get there, go straight into camo mode, and keep an eye out. I have a feeling this will be one of our deadliest enemies yet."

Tasha says, "It seems like each new enemy is deadlier than the last."

Eric chimes in, "Yeah, but we knew that was part of the job when we signed up."

SOON THE KNIGHTS REACH THE CITY, and as they land, they go into camo mode. Noticing again that the people are literally frozen in fear, Joseph calls Des, "Earth Knight, can you get a read on their vitals?"

Des scans them and responds, "It's not looking good. I would say, at the current rate of progress ... I would say that they have about an hour left before they go into cardiac arrest."

"Let's find whatever is causing this quick," Eric says.

Among the many frozen people, the knights spot one person walking about who doesn't seemed to be in shock. Eric now calls Des, "Could you scan that guy and see if there is anything weird about him."

Des quickly does a bioscan and notices that the person Eric is asking about is not even human. He also notices that the device making the creature look human has also prevented him from being detected by their early warning system. Des says, "Hey, you were right. There is something weird about that guy. In fact, he's not even human."

"That figures," Eric says. "Is there any other info you can give us."

Des quickly does another scan and notices that the same signature causing the attack on the part of the brain that produces fear is being emitted from the guy the knights are currently surveying. "Hey, guys," he says, "I've confirmed whatever is causing the people down there to be frozen is being caused by the guy you are currently watching. I'm going to see if there's anyway I can block the signal and free the people. Just be careful and get him out of there as soon as possible. The last thing we need are the people walking up to a brawl in the middle of the city."

"We're on it," Eric says. Now turning to Joseph, he says, "So, what's the plan?"

Chuckling, Joseph says, "Why do I have to come up with the plan? I mean, all of you have ideas, don't you?"

"Normally," Tasha chimes, "but when it comes to doing things together and working as a team, that proves to be more difficult than expected. You, however, have been able to come up with plans that utilize all our strengths. So, again what's the plan?"

"Touche!" Joseph says, smirking at Tasha. "Okay, and I do have an idea, but first we need to destroy the belt that hides his true form, and we need to do it without him noticing."

"How are we going to do that?" Janet asks.

Joseph looks at Tasha and says, "Tasha, that's where you come in. If you can shapeshift into an animal, you should be able to get close enough to get that belt off of him."

Trying to understand Joseph's plan, Janet interjects, "Even if she does that, how is she going to get away without being seen?"

"This is where John comes in," Joseph answers. "John, you fire a light blast to temporarily blind him so that Tasha can get the belt and get out of there."

WHILE THE OTHER KNIGHTS FINISH formulating their plan, Des uncovers something he hadn't noticed before. Urgently, he says, "Maggie, Brad, Max, Britney and Jessica, the others are walking into a trap."

"What do you mean, Des?" Brad asks.

"What I mean is the second they touch whoever that is, they will be like the rest of the people down there," Des answers worriedly.

"Why not just let them know via their coms?" Max offers.

"That's just it," Des then replies. "After I got done talking to Eric, I tried to reestablish the com link, either via telepathy or their armor comms, and something has been preventing me from reestablishing contact. I need you guys to go down there, while I figure out a way to free the people before they are literally frightened to death."

"We gotcha, Des," Brad says. Then, raising his hand to the sky, he says, "Fire Knight, let's light the night." The other knights also transform, following his lead. Once they have transformed, they get ready to port to the city.

AS THEY'RE TRAVELING TO THE CITY, Joseph and the others begin to execute their plan. Tasha transforms into a doberman and charges the target. John fires a blinding flash to temporarily blind the creature. But when Tasha grabs the belt with her mouth and touches him, she becomes frozen. The other knights are shocked.

Phobia now turns in their direction and says, "Ohhhh goodie! More playmates for me to have fun with! And, since these earthlings are all a bunch of stiffs, you will certainly do. By the way, my name is Phobia Fighter, but you can call me Phobia."

When Phobia drops his disguise, he has the body of a human with what looks like a straw hat on his head. His face has two black holes where his eyes should be, almost as if they were the eyes of a human. His mouth looks like it has been stitched shut. Yet, when he speaks, his mouth is opening and closing. It looks like he's wearing a loose-fitting shirt, revealing his arms, which look like the arms of a human but covered in metal, and shorts, revealing legs that look human but, again, are covered with metal.

As Phobia begins his slow approach to them, Eric says, "What are we gonna do now? We can't touch him—literally."

Joseph draws his sword and says, "I think you're right." He uses his sword to try to strike Phobia, but Phobia blocks the attack. Then he grabs Joseph and throws him into a wall, where he now stands frozen.

"Great!" Eric says. "Now what do we do?"

"I don't know," Janet says, "but we had better think of something fast. Time is running out for these people."

Before the other knights can do anything else, Phobia fixes his gaze on them, and they are also frozen where they stand.

DES DOES ANOTHER SCAN to see what is going on. He gets a visual on the other knights and says, "We're too late! The others have all been frozen."

"Wonderful!" Brad says. "Have you found any way to stop that from happening to *us*?"

"To be honest," Des answers, "I haven't found anything that can even remotely help us." He is so frustrated that he hits the console.

Brad tried to encourage him. "Chill, Brainiac, if there's a way to figure this out, I know you can do it. I mean, you did say this was a psychic attack, right?"

Des' eyes light up. "Brad," he says, "you're a genius."

"What did I say?" Brad asks.

"I've been looking at this whole problem wrong," Des responds. "I've been looking for tech to solve the problem, when I should have been looking for a way to block the psychic connection." He also notices that there are inhibitors all around the city and realizes that this must be what has blocked their communications. He quickly finds a way to hack into them and shut them down.

NOW DES CONTACTS BRAD. "I've disabled the inhibitors that were blocking communication," he says. "I need you guys to lead him out of the city, and I'll port the other knights back here."

"Got it," Brad answers.

Before long, the other knights arrive and see Phobia. Phobia says, "Goodie! More toys for me to play with!"

Brad answers him "You've gotta catch us first." With that, he and the other knights start to run, hoping Phobia will follow.

Phobia now whistles, and his magnabike comes to him. Max sees this and says, "Guys, move it! He's got himself a ride."

"Awesome!" Brad exclaims. "I thought we were gonna have to lead him away on foot."

Jessica adds, "Really, Brad, now is not the time to be stupid."

"Guys," interjects Max, "cool it! Now is not the time to be bickering like children."

The knights lead Phobia out of the city, and Des begins to port the other knights back to their base.

SOON AFTER, THE OTHER KNIGHTS TURN TO FACE PHOBIA. He stops, gets off of his bike, and says "Look what Phobia caught."

Brad says, "You haven't caught anything, you freak. Knights, let's light the night." And he and the other knights prepare to face Phobia.

Phobia says, "How cute! You fools actually think you will be able to fight me? The truth is you can't. Soon you will join your friends and the earthlings. Now, Psydrones, attack!"

Suddenly a swarm of Psydrones appears. As the knights begin to fight the Psydrones, Phobia calmly approaches each knight while they are distracted. First, he sets his sights on Brad. Because he is fighting the Psydrones, he has his back to Phobia. Phobia touches him, and he freezes. Next, Phobia sets his sights on Max, also too busy fighting the Psydrones to notice. After that, he reaches Jessica and touches her, causing her to be frozen as well.

The Psydrones then begin to surround Maggie, who is already feeling overwhelmed by the onslaught and is doing her best to hold them off. When Phobia approaches, the Psydrones back off, and Maggie is left to face him.

"You're the last of them, aren't you?" Phobia says. "Once you are out of the way, we will tear this planet to shreds." He then reaches for Maggie.

Before Phobia can touch her, Maggie uses her powers to lift her away. She shouts, "Not today, you freak!"

Angry that he was so close, Phobia has the Psydrones surround her again.

BRYKAR IS WATCHING what is going on and is pleased with Phobia and his work. He goes to contact Sadoom. When the connection is made, Brykar says, "Lord Sadoom, I'm pleased to report that the defenders of this world will soon be no more. Currently, most of them are frozen with fear, and the final knight is being pursued by Phobia, who, I must say, is enjoying his work."

"Excellent, Brykar!" Sadoom says. "Keep me posted as things develop. I can't wait for us to conquer this world."

"As you command, my Lord," Brykar concludes.

BRYKAR BREAKS OFF THE COMMUNICATION and goes back to watching Phobia, as he pursues the last of the knights. Brykar is saying to himself, "That's it. Once this knight is out of the way, this world will be ours for the taking." He notices, however, that each time Phobia gets close to Maggie, she jumps away, and he says to Phobia telepathically, "Phobia, you are going to have to do better than this. It has become clear that she knows you're trying to keep her distracted. If you want to catch her, I suggest you stop playing around and get serious."

Phobia responds, "As you command, my Lord." He now begins to pursue Maggie with even more determination. But, as he get close to her, she uses her power to carry her away. Seeing it, Phobia waits for her to land, and when she does, he fires a beam from his face. It catches her, and she is frozen in place where she lands.

MAGGIE SHAKES HER HEAD, wondering where she is and what has happened. She suddenly sees her father and mother dead on the floor, their house in ruins, and she wonders what is going on. She begins to look around her and sees that the Psystructs are carrying human bodies. She falls to her knees and hears a voice saying, "You failed. Because you weren't strong enough, the world has fallen to Psystructs."

The next thing Maggie sees is her parents being killed, and she sees it over and over again. As she watches this, she is horrified. She begins to scream, "I'm sorry! I'm sorry I wasn't strong enough!"

BACK AT THE BASE, DES SEES THAT MAGGIE HAS BEEN TOUCHED, and he's the only one left. He begins to wonder how he can stop Phobia without being touched himself. He suddenly has an idea. As he begins working on it, he see's Phobia and the Psydrones getting ready to take his fellow knights back to their base. Suddenly, he is able to port them back to their own base.

CHAPTER 7

WINDS OF CHANGE: WAY OF THE WHIRLWIND

A FRUSTRATED PHOBIA BEGINS TO SHOUT, "WHERE DID THEY GO?" He then turns his rage to the Psydrones and begins to throw them round. After a few minutes of this violence, Phobia calms down and says, "I'll deal with those knights later. Right now there's not much they can do to stop me." He then reactivates his disguise and prepares to head to the next city.

Before Phobia can begin his travel to the next city, Brykar contacts him. "Phobia," he says, "your work with the knights is not done. There is one knight still not under your power."

Puzzled, Phobia asks, "What is the name of this knight?"

Brykar answers, "He is called the Earth Knight, and it was he who defeated your predecessor, the Scientific Samurai. Until he is under your power, we will not be able to take control of the planet."

"I understand, Lord Brykar," Phobia responds, "and I will not rest until he is under my power."

As the communication ends, Phobia thinks to himself, "How am I going to find this Earth Knight? And why hasn't he showed himself? Unless... Of course, if he knows about my abilities, then he must be staying hidden until he can figure out a way to neutralize my power. Unfortunately for him, no one has ever been able to escape my power, and even if he should find the way, it will be too late."

Phobia gets on his magnabike and heads to the city where he froze his first victims. Once he's there, he begins to gather the people together. As he does this, it alerts Des in the knights' base. Des looks at the clock and says, "We only have half an hour left before these people go into cardiac arrest. There's gotta be something I can do."

He remembers the files that showed the vehicles for each of the knights and begins searching the computer for them. When he is able to find the files and open them, he says, "This will definitely work." He has the computer build the vehicles according to the design specs, while he works on a way to free the people.

Suddenly he remembers the device the Scientific Samurai used to block their powers. As he focuses on it, the Disc Disruptor appears in his hand. Quickly, Des opens it and finds the component that was used to block their powers. He then places the chip in the console so that it turns their scanner into a disruptor beam.

Once it's ready, Des fires the beam over the city, and the people start coming out of Phobia's power. Phobia is shocked. Thinking it must be a fluke, he goes to touch someone, and the person turns to him and says, "Do we have a problem?"

"Sorry!" Phobia responds, "I thought you were someone else." He now realizes that the knight has found a way to neutralize his powers, and he says, "When I find that knight, he's going to pay for this."

Des, seeing his plan has worked, now checks on the status of what he has found, which is schematics for vehicles for each of the knights, which he has the computer build, so that they will be ready for the knights when they wake up. However, he realizes that if he has the beam fire on them, it could reveal their location.

MEANWHILE, JOSEPH NOTICES THE OTHER KNIGHTS TRAPPED and Brykar standing before him. Then Joseph hears a voice saying, "Nice job, Boss Man! Not only were your friends captured, but now you're all alone, and there's no one to help you. It's too bad you weren't stronger. Otherwise you could have saved them. Oh, well!"

At first, Joseph wonders if this is a dream or a vision. He slaps himself, only to realize he can feel pain. Clearly, this was no dream.

BRYKAR NOW GOES TO BRAD and says, "I simply adore my collection of knights. However, it does appear that they are beaten up and damaged. Since this is the case, I must get rid of them."

He then turns to Joseph and says, "Cross Knight, you are here just in time to say farewell to your fellow knights."

Drawing his sword, Brykar swings it, cutting through the casing and through Brad. Joseph is forced to watch helplessly as Brykar does the same with the other knights. Enraged, Joseph shouts, "You BUTCHER! THOSE WEREN'T JUST MY KNIGHTS; THEY WERE MY FRIENDS! WITH ALL THAT I HAVE, I'LL MAKE SURE YOU PAY FOR THIS! I'LL MAKE SURE YOU NEVER HURT ANYONE EVER AGAIN!"

Joseph draws his sword and begins to fight Brykar. When the two clash, Brykar begins cutting Joseph's hands. As he gets cut, Joseph suddenly hears the voices of his friends saying, "You could've saved us! It's your fault we're dead!" Overcome with grief and sorrow over the loss of his friends, Joseph falls to the ground. "I'm sorry!" he says, "I'm sorry I failed you all!"

WHILE JOSEPH BATTLES WITH HIS OWN FEARS, Brad looks around and finds himself in a room that, at certain points, seems to be getting smaller and smaller. He notices a creature in front of him and asks, "Who are you?"

The creature chuckles and says, "I'm the Cage Champion." After he says that, he tries to encase Brad in a cage similar to an elevator. With each step, Brad dodges this creature's attacks. When he strikes back at the creature, the creature is able to open a cage below him. He quickly leaps backward to avoid being encased.

Unknown to Brad, the creature has also set a cage behind him, so that as he dodges the one underneath, he gets caught in the one behind him. As Brad enters the cage, it shuts on him. He pounds the cage with everything he has, but he is unable to free himself.

Brad then says to himself, "Okay, I just need to stay calm. It's only a cage." Without warning, Brad begins to sweat, then he notices that the cage is beginning to shrink. He starts screaming, "LET ME OUT! LET ME OUT!" He continues pounding on the walls, trying to destroy the cage, but he is still having no success.

Suddenly Brad thinks that maybe he can fireport out of there. As he attempts to fireport, he is unable to escape and wonders what is going on. Normally, he would be able to beat something like this easily, but for some reason, he can't this time. As the case continues to shrink, his heart begins to race. Then, in a final desperate attempt to escape, he activates his Firebird Battle Armor. As he transforms, the surge in power causes the cage to expand, but just as quickly as it has expanded, it begins to shrink again.

JUST AS BRAD IS DEALING WITH HIS FEARS, Jessica is facing some of her own. Ever since she was a little girl, dogs have always been scary to her, and now she finds herself fighting several man-dog creatures—half man and half dog. She tries to fight them as best she can, but the more of them she strikes, the more of them appear. Soon Jessica notices that she is surrounded, and she shouts, "WHAT DO YOU WANT WITH ME?"

Offering no response, the man-dogs continue to growl. Then, without warning, they transform into real dogs. Now, Jessica uses her powers to try and create a water wall around her to keep the dogs out. However, as the wall goes up, Jessica notices that the dogs have taken on the form of water to get through the wall. As they emerge, they return to being regular dogs. Desperate, she starts screaming, "GET AWAY! GET AWAY FROM ME!"

Jessica creates a blast of water to propel herself away from the dogs, who now begin to chase her. She says to herself, "Calm down! There's gotta be a way to escape these mangy mutts." She then comes to an area where she can land. As she touches the ground, she sees the dogs charging for her. Using her powers, Jessica now covers the floor in water, which she then freezes. The result is that the dogs begin to slide on the ice. However, they undergo a transformation and become creatures of ice, able to charge at her even faster. Again, the dogs surround her, and as they do, Jessica begins to scream and falls to the floor.

AS JOSEPH, BRAD AND JESSICA BATTLE THEIR FEARS, Britney is dealing with hers. It is commonly known as *pediophobia*, the fear of dolls. She looks around and notices that she's in a room that looks much like her own room when she was a child. There are dolls all over her bed, and they suddenly get up and begin to walk toward her. They are saying, "Mama, Mama, Mama!"

Trying to keep a cool head, Britney uses her powers to fry the dolls. They are destroyed, but then the residue from them begins to gel together, and a larger doll is formed. This doll destroys the roof of the house.

Britney begins to run, trying to figure out how to beat this demented doll. The doll continues to say, "Mama, Mama, Mama!" Britney turns, firing a lightning blast, only to have it bounce off the doll. "Oh, great! She says. "Now what am I going to do?"

Without any warning, the demented doll begins firing laser blasts from its eyes. Britney see's a ditch nearby and races toward it. The doll continues firing it blasts, and Britney continues to dodge them. When she gets close enough to the ditch, she slides into it, barely avoiding a laser blast that would've killed her.

The demented doll continues to get closer and closer, then kneels down, trying to grab Britney, but she is able to stay out of its reach. Staying as far from the doll as possible, Britney wonders what is going on. She feels her heart pounding faster than before.

JUST AS THE OTHER KNIGHTS DEAL WITH THEIR FEARS, John finds himself in a house of mirrors and says, "What in the world is this? Where am I?"

Without warning, John is hit from behind. He turns to see a creature who calls himself Mirror Mage. The creature says, "You are in my world, knight, and here I make the rules?"

"You wish, Freak Show!" John answers, and he fires a blast of light, which Mirror Mage easily deflects.

Mirror Mage then uses the mirrors on his body to make himself virtually invisible. John asks, "Where did you go, Freak?"

Now Mirror Mage begins to hit John again and again. As he hits him, he places a mirror in front of him. Then he repeats this process until John is encased in a maze of mirrors. When John can only see himself in the mirrors, he tries to break them, but as quickly as one breaks, a new one takes its place. John says, "What is this?"

"You are in my mirror maze," Mirror Mage says, "and you will never find your way out."

John sees his reflection in so many different mirrors it's difficult to tell which is the right way out. As he becomes more and more frustrated, his heart rate grows faster and faster. John's fear of mirrors starts to overcome him, and he screams and falls to the floor, wondering how he can get free from this living nightmare.

LIKE THE OTHER KNIGHTS, ERIC IS STRUGGLING with his fears. He has a fear of clowns. As he looks around, he notices that he's at a circus. As he begins to walk around, he notices that the biggest act in the circus is the clowns. Angered, he says, "Of all the things it had to be, why did it have to be clowns?"

Making his way through the circus, he notices that he's the only one there. "Where is everyone?" he wonders.

As Eric turns a corner, he sees someone darting into the big top. When he follows them, spotlights are suddenly shining down on him. He looks up to see the ringmaster. "Welcome to the show!" says the ringmaster. "You, my boy, are our star attraction. However, this means it will be your first and last performance. By the way, my name is Clown King, and as you may have guessed, we're all clowns here, and you, my boy, are going to join us as the biggest clown this world has ever seen."

Assuming a fighting stance, Eric responds, "Not on your life, Clown King! And if you think I'm wrong, then the joke's on you."

Clown King smiles and says, "I'll show you how wrong you are." He whistles, a small compact car arrives in the center of the ring, and from it emerges clown after clown, until Eric is surrounded by what seems to be twenty-five to forty clowns. Nervous now, Eric says, "I may have been a bit hasty, but you still have to catch me." With that, he runs toward one group of clowns. As he gets close to them, he slides underneath them. Getting by them, he starts to run with all he is worth.

Noticing a trampoline to his right, Eric races toward it, and the clowns begin throwing explosive pies and shooting acid water toward him. He is able to dodge them, but noticing that these are deadly items, he says, "Looks like you boys aren't clowning around!"

As he nears the trampoline, he jumps onto it, but the clowns hit it with their explosive pies, destroying the trampoline and knocking him to the ground. Dazed, Eric tries to get up, but he is now caught in a net, and is being pulled toward the clowns who have been chasing him. On their faces he can see their sheer glee.

WHILE ERIC TRIES TO ESCAPE THE CRAZY CLOWNS, Tasha looks around and notices that she's in a backyard filled with balloons. At first, she wonders why it had to be balloons. Then she hears a voice that says, "Welcome to the party, Beast Knight."

She turns toward the voice and asks, "What kind of party is this?"

The voice answers, "It's your funeral party, of course."

Before Tasha can say anything else, a balloon is hurled at her. When it pops, it causes a massive explosion, knocking her to the ground. A little dazed, Tasha gets up. As she looks around, she sees a creature that looks to be made from balloons, but it has two cannons on its back. "Well, that was so fun," the creature says, "but destroying you is going to be the best part of the party."

"I'm not dying today," Tasha answers, "and I'm definitely going to bust your bubble." With that, she charges at the creature.

"Not likely," the creature answers, "but before I destroy you, I want to introduce myself. My name is Bubble Blaster, and it's time for me to blast you away."

Bubble Blaster begins firing more balloons. This time, however, as they pop, Tasha notices that the balloons are filled with a gel-like substance that immobilizes anything it touches. She continues to move forward, trying to get closer to Bubble Blaster, but as she is about to reach him, he turns to her. Smiling, he says, "You actually thought you could sneak up on me, Sweetheart? Not a chance! Not today." He then fires a balloon carrying the gel at Tasha. His intent is to immobilize her. As

As the balloon hits Tasha, Balloon Blaster says, "It's been fun, but now it's time to burst your bubble!"

Before the gel can fully immobilize her, Tasha transforms into an eagle and begins to fly away. She is putting some distance between herself and Balloon Blaster, but then the gel begins to work. It is not only immobilizing her; it is also beginning to neutralize her powers. This causes her to crash land and revert to knight form.

Balloon Blaster then makes his way to her side, laughing, and all Tasha can think about is how she can escape from this horrible creature.

JANET, LIKE MOST OF HER FRIENDS, IS NOT SURE WHERE SHE IS. All she knows is that something doesn't feel right. As she looks around, she notices a spooky-looking house and walks toward it ... that is, until she sees a couple of ghosts coming out the door. Now she turns and starts running away from the house, and the ghosts chase her. "Of all things, why did it have to be ghosts?" she is wondering.

Before Janet can get very far, she is surrounded by ghosts. But then the ghosts pull back and make way for a creature who emerges. He says, "Welcome, my dear. Soon you will join our ranks as the new ghoul on the block."

"Seriously?" Janet responds. "You've got to be kidding me. Couldn't you come up with something better than that, you reject from a horror movie." Laughing, the creature replies, "You have a lot of spirit, child. I will enjoy first taking your spirit and then breaking it, so that you will serve me forever.

"By the way," he continues, "my name is Phantom Fighter. Today I will be your judge, executioner and master."

"That's what you think," Janet says. "I'm out of here." With that, she leaps at the ghosts and then turns and runs from them again. "Catch me if you can," she challenges.

"With pleasure," Phantom Fighter responds. He disappears and then reappears in front of Janet, forcing her to slow down, change course and run in another direction. Then Phantom Fighter appears in front of her again and repeats this process until she can no longer run and falls to the ground in exhaustion.

A look of glee on his face, Phantom Fighter now walks over to her and says, "It's over, child! Now you shall join our ranks and be my newest pet."

Using her last remaining bit of energy, Janet gets up and runs again, but she can't run far and falls to the ground. Phantom Fighter calmly walks toward her, knowing that after this last exertion, her spirit will finally be broken.

MAX IS BATTLING WITH HIS FEAR OF SPIDERS, more commonly known as *arachnophobia*. He looks around and notices the cobwebs and the human-sized cocoons and says, "Great! Of all the luck! It would just have to be spiders!"

Before Max can even begin to understand what he is seeing, a webline shoots toward him, grabbing his arm. He draws his sword to cut the line, only to have the hand with his sword webbed up tight. He struggles to escape the web lines, but is unable to do so. Now, from the shadows, emerges a creature that looks like a cross between a spider and a military man. This strange creature says "Welcome! I'm the Spider Soldier, and you will have the honor of being my next meal."

Continuing to struggle, Max says, "Not while I breathe, you bug-eyed freak."

The Spider Soldier replies, "That can be arranged." He then draws his sword to slice Max in two, but Max pulls the webline so that the line holding his arm with the sword is sliced instead. With that hand now free, Max cuts the other webline and begins to run from the Spider Soldier. The creature pulls out what looks like an assault rifle, except that this rifle fires web bullets, which, on impact, begin to encase their victims in cocoons like the ones Max saw earlier.

Spider Soldier begins firing in Max's direction, but notices that he's not hitting his target. Max thinks to himself, "If I wanted to catch my prey, what would I do?" When he realizes the answer, he slides, just missing the webnet the Spider Soldier has set up to catch him.

"Very clever," the Spider Soldier says, "but that is not the only trick in my arsenal. I will find you and feast on your corpse."

Hiding for a moment, Max thinks to himself, "There's gotta be a way to beat this guy."

SALLY AWAKES to find herself in what looks to be a void filled with complete darkness. When she lifts her hands in an attempt to see, she is shocked that the darkness even conceals her hands. Then, suddenly, a voice from the darkness says to her, "Welcome to my world. In this world, darkness rules, and soon it will overtake you, making you my slave."

"I seriously doubt that," Sally responds. "Now, who or what are you?"

She then notices the room going from pitch black to a blue and black combo, allowing her to see the creature, who seems to be the embodiment of darkness. His darkness is so deep that he has no face.

The creature speaks again, "I have no name, yet I have many names. You can call me the Sinister Shadow."

Sally watches as he approaches. She tries to move but is unable to. As the strange creature gets closer and closer, she notices that there are multiple hands holding her. Thinking fast, she suddenly slips downward, dropping to her knees. This move gives her some slack and time to free herself. She is disappointed that she can't move far enough to escape him.

The Sinister Shadow lifts her chin so that she can stare into the darkness that he is. Not intimidated, she says, "Get a life, freak show!" And, with that, she quickly flips backward, breaking the hold they have had on her.

After freeing herself, Sally begins to run, and as she runs, she is thinking to herself, "How can I escape this darkness? There's gotta be a way out of this?"

Sinister Shadow is still nearby. He says, "Run as much as you like. You will never escape the darkness or me. I rule this realm, and you will bow before me."

Despite these threatening words, Sally continues to run, all the while wondering how she can defeat this guy and his realm of darkness. Before she can formulate a plan, the darkness increases, and now she can no longer see anything in front of her. "Oh, great!" she says. "Now what do I do?"

She falls to her knees and begins to crawl, feeling her way, hoping to find someplace to hide while she figures out a way to beat this guy.

BACK AT THE KNIGHTS' BASE, ONLY HALF AN HOUR HAS PASSED. Des watches the vitals of the various knights spike and is wondering how to get them out of this. He then notices that Maggie's vitals are not spiking as high as the others and wonders why. Before he can even begin to analyze this, he notices that the vehicles he had the computer work on are now complete. He looks them over and is impressed. "These things are wild," he says, "but I wonder how they work." He chooses a vehicle for himself, and as he gets inside, he examines the interior, noticing what looks like a scanner. When he places his hand over the scanner, the vehicle's engine suddenly begins to rev, and a voice says, "Hello, Desmond!"

Startled, Des asks, "Who was that?"

The voice again speaks, "Forgive me, Desmond, my name is Rock Racer, but you can call me Rocker."

Still puzzled, Des says, "Okay, Rocker, where are you?"

"If you would step out of the vehicle," Rocker says, "I will show you."

Slowly Des steps out of the vehicle. As he backs away, the vehicle begins to change into a robot. Des shouts, "This is awesome! Can all the other vehicles do this as well?"

Once the change is complete, Rocker says, "Of course, Desmond. In fact, each of the vehicles before you is actually called a Bio Organic Defender Robot or BOD Bot for short."

Excited now, Des says, "Wow! This is an epic moment!"

MAGGIE, CONTINUES TO WATCH HER PARENTS DIE right in front of her eyes, making her feel even more frightened and alone. Then she remembers the choice she made and the oath she took. She made this choice and took this oath so that she could protect her family and friends. She realizes that even if her family is gone, she will not (and cannot) give up the fight. Still on her knees, she says, "I'll never give up. I will fight with everything I have. I don't know if this is real or not, but I'm a Knight of the Cross, and I will not quit."

Maggie then recites her oath, "As days of darkness near, and people run in fear, from they who prey on the weak, and silence those who speak, we will take to the sky with courage and battle cry, to protect the world from loss, I am a Knight of the Cross!"

SUDDENLY, EVERYTHING FADES and Des notices that Maggie is coming out of it. He says, "Hey, Maggie, are you okay?"

She sees him and answers, "Yeah, I'm fine, just a little groggy. What happened?"

"Apparently you frustrated that guy, and he used a fear beam when he realized he wasn't going to be able to touch you. Since then, you and the other knights have been frozen. I found a way to free the people, but it won't last long. So, what exactly happened to you? I mean, you were hit with the fear beam, but your vitals weren't spiking like the rest."

Maggie thinks about it for a moment. She remembers her father always telling her, "Mags, if you run from your fears, they'll always haunt you, but when you face them, your fears will be what runs from you." She says, "That figures. I think I understand how we can beat this guy. His powers are based on bringing our worst fears to life, and my worst fear was that I had made the wrong choice and was going to fail as a knight. When I faced my fear and wouldn't quit, the vision faded."

Suddenly a surge comes from within Maggie, and she shouts, "Whirlwind Armor, engage!" With that, her armor undergoes a transformation, and a new weapon appears in her hand. At first, she thinks it is a sword, until it starts to fall. Upon closer scrutiny, she sees that it looks like a wire. Then she realizes she has been given a whip as her new weapon.

Once the transformation is complete, Des says, "Amazing! You've unlocked a new armor mode as well."

Maggie responds, "What do you expect? You can't have all the fun."

"We need to free the others," Des says, "and we need to distract this guy. Do you think you'll be able to do that while I work to get the others free?"

"Sure," Maggie says, "but how?"

"Just get him to attack you, and, oh, you won't be going alone," added Des as a vehicle is rising next to them.

"What is this thing?" she asks.

"Maggie," Des answers, "this is going to be your backup. It's called a BOD Bot."

Shaking her head, Maggie says, "But, Des, this is a car, not a robot."

"Okay," Des says, "get in and place your hand on the palm scanner."

She does what he has asked and then asks, "Now what?"

Suddenly, a voice says, "Ohhhhhhh man, does it ever feel good to be up and revving!"

"Who or what was that?" Maggie asks. She has an odd look on her face, and is backing away from the BOD Bot. As she watches, the vehicle transforms into a robotic being.`

"My name is Wind Whip," the robot says, "and it is a pleasure to meet you."

Starting to freak out, Maggie says to Des, "Explain and fast!"

After chuckling for a second, Des responds, "Okay, when you placed your palm on the scanner, it scanned your brainwaves to create the AI for the BOD Bot, now known as Wind Whip. BOD stands for Bio Organic Defender."

"You should have started with that first," Maggie says. Recovering her composure now, she says, "Okay, Wind Whip, let's find this freak and show him what the knights are made of."

Des warns, "Hey, Maggie, be careful out there!"

She turns and says, "I will. Just get our friends free of their fears."

"I'll do what I can," says Des, as Wind Whip switches back into his vehicle mode. Maggie gets in, and they leave the base.

JUST THEN DES THINKS TO HIMSELF, "If I can get a message to the other knights telepathically and let them know to face their fears, maybe it will allow them to break Phobia's hold on them." He says, "Hold on, Maggie. I'm going to connect you to the knights, but you need to be the one to free them. He then has Maggie focus all her energy on the other knights, so that the telepathic link can be established.

Once she has the link established, Maggie says, "Everyone listen to me! What you are seeing is not real; it is an illusion meant to keep you prisoner. I know it's not easy, but each of you must face your fears. If you do that, you will be free."

Listening to her words, the other knights are unsure at first. Soon, however, they realize they might as well give it a shot. With that, each of the knights (except for Joseph) stands up and in unison they all say, "I will not be afraid. I will be strong and courageous!" That said, the visions fade, and the other knights (except for Joseph) come out of their frozen trance.

Des notices that Joseph's not waking up and says, "Great! Joseph still hasn't come out of it."

Once the others have had a chance to get their bearings, they ask Des what happened. He replies, "Long story short ... Phobia put all of you under a fear trance. Maggie broke that trance and unlocked a new armor mode as well."

Brad says, "Hmmmm, you look real good, Mags."

She replies, "Brad, how about we fight this guy now, and you can flirt with me later, okay?" He chuckles and nods in agreement.

Des then says, "All right, guys, I've also finished your new vehicles. Take them out and show this freak a thing or two. Also remember to touch the palm scanner first."

Maggie then adds, "Des, shouldn't you tell them ....?"

"Hold on, Maggie, I want to enjoy this," says Des and chuckles.

After each of the knights touch the palm scanners, the vehicles come to life, and the other knights backup and watch as their vehicles change into their robotic form. Brad's vehicle kneels down and says, "Hi, Brad. The name's Blaze Breaker."

Janet's vehicle kneels down and replies, "Dear Janet, my name's Heart Burner."

"Sweet Jessica, my name is Tsunami Slipstream," replies Jessica's vehicle, also kneeling.

John's vehicle kneels and says, "John, my man, my name is Light Stride."

Eric's vehicle kneels and says, "Hey Eric, you can call me Shadow Shifter."

"Britney, you may call me Thunder Trucker," says her vehicle, as it kneels.

Tasha's vehicle says, "Greetings, Tasha, they call me Beast Brawler."

Sally's vehicle kneels and says, "Hi, Sally, you can call me Hope Hunter." Max's vehicle kneels and says, "Max, my friend, you can call me Faithlane Fighter."

After the other knights have witnessed this phenomenon taking place, Brad yells, "How about a little warning next time, Des? You nearly gave me a heart attack."

Des chuckles and replies, "Sorry, Brad! I thought a man of action like yourself was ready for anything?"

Brad starts to get angry, but soon realizes it has been kind of funny and so he let's it slide.

Max then says, "With Joseph still under this guy's spell, we're still down a man, and he's our leader."

Manuel then goes to them and says, "Listen, my friends. You go and deal with Phobia Fighter. Justice and I will work on freeing Joseph."

The knights nod in agreement. Then, as their vehicles shift back into their vehicle forms, the knights climb in and race off to stop Phobia Fighter.

AT THAT VERY MOMENT, Joseph, remembering the words Maggie has spoken, shouts, "I WILL NOT LOOSE! DO YOU HEAR ME?" He then takes his sword and, raising it to the sky, says, "To light the night, Armors unite." Suddenly, the armors from what Joseph believes to be his fallen friends begin to bond with him, and he says, "Apostolic Armor, engage!" Soon Joseph's armor undergoes a transformation unlike anything before.

Manuel and Justice notice something happening, and Manuel tells Justice, "We have to free him now. I know what's going on with him."

Justice says, "I know." The two then touch Joseph and enter the psychic dream where Joseph is now, and they see him in the Apostolic armor.

"Incredible!" Manuel says. "I didn't think it would be possible for that to be unlocked."

"True," Justice agrees, "but we must free him and then make sure he forgets about this armor mode for now." Manuel agrees.

Before they can do anything, Joseph launches a fierce attack at Brykar. Although Brykar tries to block it, the combined power of the knights overwhelms him, and Joseph, Manuel and Justice are returned to the base.

SINCE JOSEPH WAS ABLE TO FINALLY END HIS NIGHTMARE, he feels a little groggy. When he sees Manuel and Justice, he says, "What happened? Where is everybody?"

Manuel replies, "They were able to free themselves and have gone off to fight Phobia Fighter. It appears that the fear he awakened in you was tied to a vision you had, which is why its hold on you was so strong."

Justice then touches him, whispers in his ear and says, "All you will remember is that by the power of your friendship you were able to overcome Brykar. For now, you will forget the new armor mode that was unlocked."

Not realizing what is going on, Joseph feels dazed. He tries to remember everything but finds it very difficult. All he remembers for sure is that a surge empowered him, and he was able to defeat Brykar.

Without a second's thought, Joseph races to go after them, but Justice appears before him and says, "Joseph, while you were trapped, Des finished working on vehicles for all of you." Turning and pointing to the last vehicle, she says, "Place your hand on the palm scanner and then go after your friends."

Joseph enters the vehicle and as he places his hand on the palm scanner, the vehicle roars to life. When it starts to transform, Joseph says, "So, who might you be?"

The BOD Bot kneels down and says, "My dear boy, my name is Cross Cutter, but you can call me Cutter for short. If I may, why are you not shocked to see me in this form? From what I can gather from the security feeds within me, each of your friends was surprised by it."

Joseph then says, "I'm not exactly sure, but considering all the other stuff we've had to handle recently, nothing would surprise me at this point." Cross Cutter then returns to vehicle form, and Joseph gets in. As the engine starts, Cross Cutter says, "Leave the driving to me, my friend." With that, Cross Cutter heads out of the tunnel that takes them to a ramp leading to the surface.

Cross Cutter scans for the others and quickly finds them. Noticing that Joseph is unusually quiet, he says, "Joseph, I know you are worried about the vision you saw and the fact that it was what you feared most. However, you must not let that fear rule you. You are a brave warrior and a good leader, but giving into fear, especially fear of the future, can cause you to ensure that negative future happens. In this case, your fear is that, not only will they be captured, but also killed, and the more you try to fight it, the greater chance this has of becoming reality."

"Cutter," Joseph says, "how do you know about the vision? I haven't told anyone about it."

"Joseph, my friend," Cutter answers, "when my personality was formed, it was made from your brainwaves, and since you've seen that vision, it has been in the forefront of your mind. Which is why I know about it and why I have a calming demeanor and tone. I will not tell the others what you are feeling and seeing. However, I do suggest that you tell them yourself."

"I know I should tell them, but I can't," Joseph answers. "It's bad enough that they followed my lead when I accepted this whole thing."

"Joseph," Cross Cutter says, "stop it! Your friends chose this for themselves, and they knew the risks involved. If something should happen, it's not your fault."

As Cross Cutter says this, Joseph remembers that each of them did have a different reason for accepting. Cross Cutter was right. They were a team, and they needed to trust each other. "Thanks, Cutter," Joseph says. "Now," he adds, "How long until we reach them."

"We should be there in less than two minutes," replies Cutter.

Joseph asks, "Have the knights reached Phobia Fighter yet?"

"According to this," Cutter replies, "they should be reaching him in about a minute."

"How is that possible?" asks a puzzled Joseph.

Cutter answers, "Simple! Although it felt like a while had passed when you were in that psychic trap, it was only about thirty minutes. Although you were under a little longer than the other knights, they had only about a minute's head start before you woke up."

Thinking about the timing of it all, Joseph asks, "Cutter, can we make the ETA thirty seconds instead of two minutes?"

The dashboard on the vehicle lights up and Cutter says, "Hold on, Joseph. We're about to crank this thing up." Suddenly the vehicle speeds up, and the two head toward the other knights.

DES AND THE OTHER KNIGHTS ARE CLOSING IN on Phobia's position when Des notices something coming toward them extremely fast. He says, "Look alive, guys! We've got something coming up on our six."

Puzzled, Brad asks "What are you talking about, Des?"

"He means something is approaching us from behind," interjects Maggie.

Des suggests, "Maggie, you and Brad go and handle Phobia. The rest of us will handle whoever's heading toward us."

"All right," Maggie says. "Come, Brad let's show Phobia what happens when you face fear." With that, the two of them continue to Phobia's current location, while the others stand ready to fight whoever is approaching them.

Des tries to scan the approaching object, but can't get a solid reading on it. He then shouts "Heads up! We should be able to see it any second now." Soon he is able to see who it is, and he shouts, "Stand down, everyone! The object approaching is one of us."

John says, "Seriously? I thought we were the only ones who had gear like this."

"We are," says Eric. "What Des is saying is that's Joseph heading for us. Am I right?"

Des replies, "Correct, Eric."

As Joseph reaches them, he says ,"I hope we're not late for the party."

Des says, "I'm glad your back. I was afraid I was going to have to lead this bunch myself."

"You're not getting rid of me that easily, Des," says Joseph with a grin.

"I'm glad to hear it," Des replies.

Now Joseph notices that Maggie and Brad aren't around and asks where they are. Des replies, "I sent them on ahead cause I thought you were an enemy."

Joseph shakes his head and says, "We need to catch up to them and now."

AS THE OTHER KNIGHTS ARE STILL ON THEIR WAY, Maggie and Brad find Phobia Fighter, and the two vehicles open so that the knights are able to leap from them. As they land, both vehicles leap, transforming into their robotic form. When Phobia Fighter sees this, he is enraged and says, "I don't know how you escaped before or how anyone could escape from the prison I trapped you in, but this time I will destroy you—both of you."

"Listen, you fear-focused freak," says Maggie, "the only thing getting destroyed now is *you*," and she walks toward him, wearing her new armor.

Phobia replies, "Stronger warriors than you have tried to destroy me and failed. Like them, you will fail as well, child." Suddenly Phobia targets the two knights, and his eyes begin to glow. This causes both Maggie and Brad to stumble for a moment.

When the effect wears off, Brad looks and sees Cage Champion coming toward him. He says, "How ... ? Are you real right now?"

Brad raises his hand to the sky and says, "BOD Bot Armor, engage!" Suddenly Blaze Breaker stands at attention, revealing what looks to be a casing for a person. Brad leaps backward into the casing, which now closes. Brad then draws his blade, striking the Cage Champion and knocking him to the ground. As Brad does this, it's actually Maggie who falls to the floor, struck by Brad's attack.

As Maggie gets up, she looks at Phobia Fighter and says, "What have you done to him?"

Surprised that she is not under the same spell as her friend, Phobia Fighter answers, "It's simple! My psychic powers allow me to connect with the part of your brain that causes fear. From there, I'm able to amplify it, and as you've experienced, place you in a trance-like state. There is, however, another delicious part of my abilities. It allows me to create a hypnotic suggestion, so that whenever your friend or any of the knights looks at you, he or she will see the creature of his or her fears that they had to fight in the fear trance."

Before Maggie could respond, Brad's sword came down toward her, but she was able to dodge it. She said, "Mark my words, Phobia Fighter, I'm taking you out!"

Phobia Fighter responds, "You'll have to catch me first." And he gets on his Magnacycle and speeds off.

Maggie shouts, "Wind Whip, cover me while I deal with Phobia Fighter!"

"As you wish, my dear," Wind Whip answers.

Maggie starts to run, and as she leaps into the air, she uses her wind powers to fly after Phobia Fighter.

AT THE SAME TIME, WIND WHIP CHARGES FOR BRAD, who sees everyone as the Cage Champion. Wind Whip changes back into his vehicle form and races toward Brad.

Brad is watching as the Cage Champion is charging toward him. He then points both of his arms forward, revealing missiles that he begins to fire on what he thinks is the Cage Champion. Wind Whip, while in vehicle form, turns around in order to outrun the missiles.

Brad shouts, "Run all you want, Cage Champion! You can't outrun these missiles because once they lock on, they won't stop until they hit their mark."

Wind Whip increase his speed, then makes a hard left and heads straight for Brad. Brad fires another round of missiles toward Wind Whip, who increases his speed again. As the missiles are about to collide with him, Wind Whip makes another sharp turn, so that the two sets of missiles collide with each other, causing an explosion that sends him flying through the air. However, before he crashes to the ground, Wind Whip transforms, allowing him to land safely.

Moments latter, the other knights arrive and exit their vehicles. Des asks, "Wind Whip, what is going on?"

"Well, Des," Wind Whip answers, "apparently Phobia Fighter has another ability that we didn't know about. It makes Brad see me as a creature called Cage Champion."

PHOBIA FIGHTER NOTICES THE ARRIVAL of the other knights and says, "Oh, it looks like your friends have finally arrived. How about we go and greet them." With that, Phobia Fighter makes a sharp turn, heading straight toward the other knights.

Maggie changes direction and follows Phobia Fighter.

As Phobia reaches the knights, Des says, "Everybody get down!" But before he can do anything, Phobia Fighter locks his gaze on the remaining knights (except for Des who is shielded by Rocker).

Phobia Fighter watches as the remaining knights are dazed and says, "Oh, this is going to be fun! Catch me if you can, Wind Knight."

Phobia Fighter then changes direction one more time, this time to lead the Wind Knight away from the others and finish her off for good.

WHILE MAGGIE CHASES PHOBIA FIGHTER, Des notices that the other knights look a bit confused. Suddenly, Joseph shouts, "Brykar, where did you come from?"

Des looks around just in time. Joseph's sword nearly slices him in two. Des shouts, "BOD Bot battle armor, engage," and, like Brad, he and Rocky combine.

Wind Whip then says, "As you can see, they will only see you as an enemy."

Shaking his head in amazement, Des says, "Great! We can't hurt them, but we're gonna have to stop them. Activate BOD Bot override command, Sentient Soldier."

Rocky then says, "What will that do?"

"It's a command program that prevents the knights from combining their BOD Bots. In other words, if they try to merge the way Brad did with his BOD Bot, they won't be able to," Des explains.

The remaining BOD Bots then face the knights, while Des faces off against Brad.

Wind Whip then says "What can I do?"

Des says, "Get out of here and go help the Wind Knight. We'll hold these guys off."

Wind Whip acknowledges the command and says, "With pleasure!" He then transforms and speeds toward Maggie.

DES AND THE REMAINING BOD BOTS SQUARE OFF against the remaining knights, and Des says, "Remember, they don't know what they are doing. So, don't hurt them."

Shadow Shifter says, "That may be true, but they sure do want to hurt us."

Rocky adds, "I may have a way to stop them without actually hurting them."

"What's the idea?" Des asks.

Rocky answers, "Since you've activated the Sentient Soldier override command, why not have the BOD Bots activate the BOD Bot battle armor as a way to trap the knights until they can be freed."

As Des charges towards Brad, he says, "That's not a bad idea, but if I'm not mistaken, won't that allow the knights to control them?"

As he gets close to Brad, Des starts swinging a mace with a chain, and Rocky says, "Since the Sentient Sentinel program has been activated, their commands will not be recognized."

"BOD Bots, did you all hear that?" Des says.

Each of the BOD Bots responds in agreement, and Brad kicks Des. As Des flies into the air, he flings his mace, wrapping it around Brad. When Des lands, he tugs on the chain, pulling Brad forward. Brad sticks out his arm to fire a round of missiles at Des, but he notices that the flaps on Brad's BOD Bot armor are open, so the missiles can be fired. Des quickly wraps the chain around Brad's arm to prevent the missiles from being able to fire.

CROSS CUTTER IS FIGHTING JOSEPH and looking for an opening. Joseph leaps into the air and activates his armors' wings and then dives for Cross Cutter, who barely escapes this attack. Cross Cutter then says, "This is going to be harder than we thought. The only issue with them is they see us as the enemy. Otherwise, they know full well what they are trying to do."

WHILE MAGGIE CONTINUES TO FOLLOW PHOBIA FIGHTER, she starts to notice that she's not able to catch him and wonders why.

"What's the matter?" Phobia Fighter taunts, "Haven't caught your second wind yet?"

Maggie then gets an idea. She begins to focus her powers on her legs and creates a whirlwind effect that propels her forward even faster than before. Phobia Fighter sees this and increases the speed of his Magnacycle. Maggie soon realizes that she's still not fast enough. Then, suddenly, Wind Whip pulls alongside her and says, "Get in, my dear."

As the door opens, Maggie uses her powers to guide her in, and as the door shuts, she says, "Thanks, Wind Whip. By the way, how did you catch up to me?"

"Simple, my dear," came the answer. "While your powers are of the wind, it's this same power that is also slowing you down. You see, when planes fly in the air, there is a bit of wind resistance which creates what is commonly known as *drag*."

"Okay, smart guy," Maggie replies, "then explain how you were able to catch up to me so fast and why I can't catch Phobia Fighter."

Wind Whip scans Phobia Fighter's cycle and says, "Here's why you can't catch him." He then displays the scan on the screen for Maggie to see. "According to this, Phobia Fighter's cycle draws its power from the Earth's magnetic field. By doing this, it actually reduces the amount of drag, allowing it go faster than your current speed."

"Now, as to why I was able to catch up with you so quickly ... ," he continues, "it is because I followed behind you until I was able to pull alongside you."

"Okay," Maggie says. "So, how can we catch him?"

"If you create a vacuum around you while flying," Wind Whip says, "it should reduce the wind resistance to almost nothing and allow you to catch him by surprise."

"Well, let's try it," Maggie says. "Open the sunroof."

With that, Wind Whip opens the sunroof, and Maggie climbs to the top of the speeding vehicle. As they get closer, she leaps forward, but is instantly pushed back past Wind Whip. Before Maggie hits the ground, she straightens her body like a board, with her hands pointed forward like a spear. A spiral of wind begins to form, which creates a vacuum that allows her to fly faster than before, and she speeds past Wind Whip, heading toward Phobia Fighter.

In turn, Phobia Fighter speeds up, trying to avoid her, but Maggie pulls alongside him. Using one arm, she hits Phobia Fighter with a gust of wind, knocking him and his vehicle to the ground.

Phobia Fighter gets back up and says, "Impressive, child! Now that you've caught me, what are you going to do with me?"

Maggie lands and says, "I plan on obliterating you, whacked-out fear factory."

Phobia fighter answers, "I think not, child, for you aren't the only one with a powerful armor." He waves his hand, and his Magnacycle breaks apart and begins attaching itself to him. Once the transformation is complete, he says, "Now, let's see what you've got, child."

Maggie says, "Two can play at this game. BOD Bot battle armor, engage." With that, Wind Whip transforms into a standing position, opens to receive Maggie, who leaps backward into the center of the transformed BOD Bot. As she enters, the entire vehicle becomes her armor.

Once the transformation is complete, Maggie grabs the handles controlling Wind Whip's arms and activates two energy whips. Phobia Fighter says, "Very impressive, child! However, it will be so delicious when I not only break your toy, but also your spirit." Without warning, Phobia Fighter goes from being a distance away to being right in front of Maggie, and he knocks her to the ground.

As Maggie lies there for a moment, Phobia Fighter gets closer and closer. When he reaches her, he turns her over, and she wraps both cables around him in the process of getting to her feet.

Phobia Fighter says, "Again, impressive, child! However, this will not stop me." He then activates blades that were hidden on his arms and shreds the whips holding him. Then he grabs enough of the remaining whip and pulls both, ripping the BOD Bot's arms off. He then draws two blades from his elbows and begins to slash away at the BOD Bot armor, forcing Maggie to eject from it. "Without your armor, you have no chance of beating me," he says.

Maggie stands up and says "That's where you're wrong, Phobia. No matter what happens, I will not give up." She then takes a fighting stance and continues, "I've made a promise to protect the Earth and my friends with my life. Even though you've dismantled my armor, you won't break me. There is only one thing left to say…" She then charges Phobia Fighter, who successfully dodges her attack. Now she turns so that she is able to use her Whirlwind Whip on Phobia Fighter's legs, pulling hard so that he falls to the ground.

Maggie then starts to repeat the oath: "As days of darkness near, and people run in fear …"

Phobia Fighter scrambles to get up, but as he does, Maggie wraps her Whirlwind Whip around him again and says, "…from they who prey on the weak, and silence those who speak…"

With that, she pulls him toward her and punches him in the face.

Although Phobia Fighter is dazed, he manages to get some distance between himself and Maggie, but she looks him directly in the eyes and says, "we will utter our heartfelt battle cry, as we raise our hands to the sky." She then raises her arm up and begins cracking her whip, creating mini-whirlwinds which trap Phobia Fighter. Then Maggie finishes the oath by saying, "To protect the world from loss, I am a Knight of the Cross!"

Maggie now stands at her full height, and the mini-whirlwind presses against Phobia Fighter. She moves her hand to the side and has the whirlwinds move from Phobia Fighter, leaving him somewhat disoriented. Seeing that she is winning the day, she says, "It's over, Phobia Fighter."

Maggie looks to the whirlwinds, which have now become discs of pure wind. She brings her arm forward, points at Phobia Fighter and then, without warning, the wind discs speed toward him, hitting him and cutting him to pieces. As the creature starts to fall apart, Maggie notices the glow in his eyes fading.

BRAD LOOKS AT DES AND NOTICES THE CHAINS ON HIM. Puzzled, he says, "Des, what's the deal, man? I thought we were cool?"

Realizing that the trance must be broken, Des says, "BOD Bots, stand down."

As the other knights begin to come to their senses, Maggie reaches out to Des telepathically and asks him, "Are the other's okay?"

Des replies "Yeah, they're fine, and I take it this means you beat Phobia Fighter."

"Yeah," she says triumphantly, "he's beaten, but Wind Whip is in bad shape." As she says this, she is looking at the scattered pieces of Wind Whip.

Now Des pulls up the schematics for Wind Whip in Rocky's data banks and remotely activates a repair protocol all the BOD Bots have. This causes all of the scattered piece of Wind Whip to reconnect, and within a few minutes Maggie sees that Wind Whip is as good as new.

Wind Whip asks, "What happened to Phobia Fighter?"

"I've beaten him," Maggie says. "Now let's get to the others and head home." As Wind Whip changes to his vehicle form, she gets in and says, "Thanks Des, we're on our way to you now."

MAGGIE ENTERS WIND WHIP, and they head off to meet up with the others. After a while, Wind Whip asks, "Is everything okay, my dear?"

Before she responds, Maggie thinks to herself about what she has learned and then says, "I'm fine, Wind Whip. I was just reflecting on everything that has happened. I don't usually adjust to change well, but I realize now that life is always going to change, and whether the change is big or small, it's how we deal with that change that determines our growth."

"Lay back and rest for now, my dear," Wind Whip says. "I'll get us to the others as quick as I can."

Maggie realizes he is right. She leans back and, for the first time in a long time, her rest is peaceful. Wind Whip has locked onto the coordinates of the other knights, and he is speeding through the land.

UNKNOWN TO THEM, the fallen remains of Phobia Fighter are being teleported back to Brykar's ship and now go to where the revival tubes are and where both Deadly Double and the Scientific Samurai are recovering.

Brykar watches as the remains of Phobia Fighter enter the revival tube, then turns and exits the chamber and goes back to his own chamber, where General Sadoom appears. "What do you have to report, Scout Commander Brykar?" he asks.

Brykar kneels and says, "The testing of the knights and their powers continues as planned. Once we have enough data, this world will fall at our feet."

"Really?" Sadoom questions. A screen appears next to him and it shows the defeat of his last three warriors. They watch it in silence. "So," General Sadoom continues, "let me get this straight. You call three losses a way of testing the knights? Explain yourself now, commander!"

Brykar falters for a moment, then says, "General Sadoom, when I left, I made sure to take the weakest warriors we had because I was confident the Earth had minimal defenses. My discoveries have proven this to be true. The only obstacle we face here is these knights. And, yes, although they have beaten these last three warriors, once I have tested the last of them, there will be nothing to stop us. Why? Because as we speak, the revival tubes are not just healing these warriors; their abilities and powers are also being increased."

"Very interesting, commander." There was a note of scepticism in General Sadoom's voice. "Carry on for now, and keep me updated of your progress."

He turns to go, then thinks better of it and faces Brykar again. "By the way, commander, if you should fail in determining what kind of threat these knights are to us, you know what will happen don't you?"

Brykar feels a brief shudders pass through his body, but he recovers and answers, "Yes, General Sadoom, I know what will happen to me."

"Good, Brykar," Sadoom answers. "I'm glad you understand what is at stake here."

WHEN THE IMAGE OF GENERAL SADOOM HAS FADED, Brykar slams his fists on the ground and declares, "I will make these knight pay if it's the last thing I do! There is much that can be learned from this battle." He then heads back to the chamber where Deadly Double, Scientific Samurai and now Phobia Fighter are recovering. He notices that Phobia Fighters remains are still being teleported into the tube where he will be revived, increased and enhanced. He also notices that Deadly Double and the Scientific Samurai are nowhere near ready.

He then goes back to his chamber to reviews the footage from the last battle. What he now realizes is that the fighting style of the knights is similar to that of several different earthling fighting styles. He says to himself, "So, all this time I've been fighting earthlings. Now, that gives me an idea."

WHEN MAGGIE AND THE REST OF THE KNIGHTS ARRIVE AT THE BASE, Manuel and Justice walk out to greet them. As Maggie gets out of Wind Whip, Manuel says, "You did well, Maggie. In fact, all of you did well."

Joseph adds his praise. "Yes, you did well, Maggie, but this is the first time we've actually seen what their psychic powers are capable of, and we all need to be prepared."

"What are you getting at Joseph?" Maggie asks, walking toward him.

"What I believe Joseph is saying," Des speaks up, "is that if we want to stand a chance at beating the Psystructs, we need to step up our training and expand it to training ourselves mentally, so that their powers will have less of a hold on us. Honestly, if Maggie hadn't broken free, all of us would not be here right now."

As Des is talking, Brad can't take his eyes off of Maggie. Now he walks toward her and returns to his human form. Before he can say a word, she looks at him, returns to her human form as well and pulls him to her, kissing him on the lips."

When the kiss ends, Brad is pleased but shocked. Maggie says, "Mmmmmm, that was good. I've always thought you must be a good kisser, and now I know."

The other knights all laugh. When the laughter has died down, Jessica says, "This is an interesting turn of events, Maggie. I thought you didn't like guys."

"First off, Jessica," Maggie responds, "I never said I don't like guys. Second I've always liked Brad but never had the guts to say anything until now."

Brad is shocked to hear Maggie's confession. Although he has never really looked at Maggie in this way, he does remember thinking to him self on several occasions how cute she was. Now, emboldened, he steps toward her and says, "If you thought *that* kiss was good, try this," and he gently pulls her to him and gives her a passionate, toe-curling kiss. When it ends, there are cheers and laughter all around.

Jessica is not as responsive as the others. She hangs back, a little upset that she and Des are not the only couple anymore. Thinking about it, she decides that now is not the time to make an issue of it.

Joseph asks, "Des, can you go through the computer and see if there is a way to shield us from these psychic attacks?"

"Hmmmmm!" Des replies. "I'm not sure, but I'll get on that immediately. Jessica, would you give me a hand?"

This pulls Jessica back from being lost in thought, and she looks up at him and nods yes, and the two head off to the lab to find a way to shield them all from these psychic attacks.

Joseph says to the rest, "For now, I think it would be good for everyone to go relax, and tomorrow we'll start training again."

The others are a little surprised by the sound of confidence in his voice. It seems that this is the first time he has truly embraced his leadership role.

As the knights disperse, Manuel walks beside Joseph and says, "That was very impressive. It looks like you are starting to walk in the role of leader of this team."

"Thanks, Manuel," Joseph responds. "I'm still not sure why I was chosen to lead this team. Max or Des could easily have handled the job." It dawned on everyone that even though Joseph was still questioning *why* he had been chosen, he was no longer questioning the fact that he had been chosen.

"Always remember, Joseph," Manuel added, "that the important thing is to know why you were chosen, not to question."

What Manual is saying puzzles Joseph at first, but when he turns to ask Manuel something about it, Manuel is nowhere to be found.

Joseph heads to the library. He must find a way to stop the Psystructs' psychic abilities and hopes an answer might it be found in the books in this library.

THE OTHER KNIGHTS ARE STILL TALKING in the Main Hall. Max sees Manuel and asks him, "Manuel, I know Joseph told us to relax, but is there anyplace other than our rooms where we can do that?"

"Have the other knights follow me," Manuel answers, "and I will show you to such a place."

Max shouts, "Hey, guys! Manuel is going to show us where we can relax."

The others are interested and follow Max and Manuel to another chamber of the base. When it opens, they see what can best be described as a recreation center. It has many sections. One area has a pool table and one has a couch with a large movie-sized screen. It also has an olympic-sized swimming pool and what looks like a game room. When the knights see it, they disperse and start having fun.

Watching them go, Manuel says to himself, "Enjoy yourselves now, my friends, for the real battles are about to begin."

CHAPTER 8

AQUATIC ASSAULT: SONG OF THE SIREN

WHILE THE OTHER KNIGHTS RELAX, Joseph is in the library, trying to learn more about the Psystructs. Justice walks in and asks, "Joseph, you may be able to hide it from the others, but I know from the time you came to this area of the base, you have seemed to be troubled about something. If you would like to talk about it, I'm here."

Joseph thinks for a moment and then says, "I'm not sure what's wrong exactly. All I know is: I keep having the same vision over and over again."

Wondering if Joseph is still seeing the battle he had with Brykar in the dream state he was trapped in by Phobia Fighter, she says, "If you don't mind, I could look into your mind and see what you see and help you understand what is going on." Joseph nods in agreement.

As Justice sees Joseph's vision, she realizes that part of it was what Joseph feared most—watching his friends being killed before him. She also sees that when he faced that fear, he was then able to see the rest of the vision, which she had temporarily hidden from his mind." She then asks, "Have you told anyone what you saw?"

"The only other one who knows about the vision," Joseph replies, "is Cross Cutter. Why do you ask?"

"The reason I ask," Justice answers, "is because it's not good for anyone to know too much about the future. For now, it might be best not to tell the other knights." Justice says this because she knows there was much more to this vision, and Joseph is not yet prepared to understand it all.

Justice now says, "I will take my leave for now, but know this, Joseph. The fear from the vision is of your own making. Once you face it, you will see beyond what you could ever know."

Turning to grab a book, Joseph says, "Hey, Justice ... ," but she's nowhere to be found. Shrugging his shoulders, he sits down and begins to look through the book he just picked up. He is hoping it will help him learn something more about the Psystructs.

Before he actually gets started, however, he decides to look through a book Manuel gave him. The title of it is intriguing: *Chronicles of the Cross.*

JUST THEN, JUSTICE APPEARS next to Manuel and says, "We need to talk ... immediately!" Manuel and Justice withdraw to a secret chamber of the base and, once inside, they're hidden from the knights. Manuel asks, "What troubles you, Justice?"

Justice replies, "I've just come from the library and have noticed that Joseph has been seeing visions of the battle between him and Brykar. It was this vision that had him paralyzed longer than the other knights."

"What did you say to him when you discovered this?" asks Manuel.

"I told him to keep it a secret for now," Justice replies. "My concern is that he will continue to have more and more visions, and that he will not be able to handle them."

"I've been aware of his visions since the beginning," Manuel says, "and I will work with him to help him learn to filter and understand what he is seeing."

"If this is the case," Justice says, "then he may be just the one to stop the Psystructs once and for all."

"My dear Justice," Manuel says, "these young ones are the last hope anyone has of the Psystructs being stopped."

"Are you saying that if they don't stop the Psystructs here and now ..." Justice asks with concern, not quite finishing the question.

Manuel understands completely and his answer is: "Yes, if the Psystructs are not stopped here, then there will be no way to stop them." He doesn't want to think of this outcome, but he knows it's a possibility.

"Why is the Earth such a critical piece in the Psystructs' conquest?" Justice asks.

"Because, " Manuel answers, "hidden here on Earth is an element that is stronger than the psychromium the Psystructs are currently using. It is this metal that they seek to increase their power, so that nothing will stand in their way."

IN THE LAB, DES NOTICES THAT SOMETHING IS BOTHERING JESSICA and asks, "Hey, Jess, are you okay?"

Trying to brush it off, Jessica answers, "I'm fine, babe. Why do you ask?"

Des chuckles and says, "I'm asking because you have seemed depressed for the last couple of hours, and I'm wondering if it has anything to do with Brad and Maggie hooking up."

Surprised by this observation, she asks, "Des, were you reading my mind?"

Again chuckling, Des answers, "No, I believe that our thoughts need to be private, and that would be an invasion of privacy. Honestly, though, I do observe things, and I noticed that when they kissed, you started to withdraw. This changes things, especially since we just got together ourselves."

"I'm happy for them," Jessica says, "but I'm starting to wonder where I fit in."

"What do you mean?" Des asks.

"Well," Jessica begins, "when I see everyone, each one brings something different to the table. I mean, honestly I'm not stupid, but I'm nowhere near as smart as you, and I don't want to just be considered a lab rat either."

This makes Des chuckle again. "I see your point, Jess," he says, "but I want you to know I don't see you as a lab rat. I see you as more of an assistant whenever we come to the lab. Also, whether you realize it or not, I tend to spend hours at a time in the lab. To be honest, if it wasn't for you, I don't know if I'd be able to be as social as I have become lately."

Now it's Jessica's turn to chuckle. She kisses Des on the cheek and says, "That's sweet, Des. And it does make me feel a little bit better. Still, this is something I'm gonna have to figure out myself. It does make me feel good to know that you're there if I need to talk about it."

Just then they received a telepathic communication from Joseph, asking all the knights to meet him in the Training Room for one last training session for the night. Des and Jess head over to the Training Room immediately.

WHEN THE OTHER KNIGHTS HEAR THE MESSAGE, they also start making their way toward the Training Room. John, Eric and Max are leaving the Games Room, Tasha and Sally press pause on a movie they had decided to watch, Janet and Britney exit the pool and dry off, and Maggie and Brad are holding hands, waiting for the others by the door.

Janet sees them and says, "Cool it, love birds. We get it. You two are an item now. But if you keep turning up the heat like this, you'll burn this place down."

The others chuckle at Janet's expression, but Maggie says, "Janet, don't be upset just because you couldn't keep Brad."

Hearing this, the other knights don't dare say a word. Janet then answers, "First off, Maggie, I'm happy for you and Brad. Second, I dumped him and don't ever get it twisted. It was never about me keeping *him*, but he couldn't keep *me*. I do think you two will make an awesome couple."

Realizing that she has crossed a line, Maggie says, "I'm sorry, Janet. I never knew what actually happened between the two of you and should never have assumed what I did. Can you forgive me?"

Janet smiles and says, "It's already done. Now, let's see what Joseph has found." The other knights nod in agreement, and they all make their way into the Training Room.

ALONG THE WAY, THEY RUN INTO DES AND JESS. Max asks, "Any luck finding out how to protect us from their psychic powers yet, Des?"

"Nothing yet," Des answers, "but let's see what Joseph wants. He may have found something that will help us."

WHEN THE KNIGHTS REACH THE DOOR OF THE TRAINING ROOM, Joseph is there waiting for them. Brad speaks up first, "What's so important that we needed to meet right now?"

"Calm down, Brad," Max warns. "I'm sure if Joseph called us here, it's for a reason."

"Precisely," Brad answers, "and since we don't know much about the Psystructs right now, any information can and will be useful." He turns to Joseph and asks, "Were you able to find any information on the Psystructs?"

"After spending some time in the library," Joseph answers, "I've found very little about the Psystructs. What I *have* found is that the Psystructs are an ancient race of beings originally known as Psythonians. The Psythonians were apparently a race of psychic beings that had a range of psychic powers. They were peaceful beings ... until one day one of them became too ambitious. I learned that this particular Psythonian led an uprising that nearly destroyed the planet, leaving only three survivors among the Psythonians. Sadly, that's about the extent of the available information."

"Hmmmmm, that's not a lot to go on," Des says. "But ...," he adds, "it's more information than we had before, so there may be something there we can work with."

"The reason I called you all here," Joseph now says, "is so that we could train together for a couple of hours before calling it a night."

Already tired, the other knights all look at each other in surprise. "Are you nuts?"Brad asks.

"I hate to agree with Brad, but I think we should call it a night and start first thing in the morning?" Des says.

"I understand perfectly how you guys feel," Joseph explains, "so, let's do this: I'm going to go train, and anyone who wants to join me is welcome to. Anyone who doesn't will be the target for tomorrow's training exercise." And, with that, he is ported into the Training Room.

When Joseph has gone, Des says, "I don't know about you guys, but I'm getting tired of being used like a human target. I'm going in to train too. I'll see you guys in the morning."

He looks at Jess, kisses her on the lips, and asks her, "Would you care to join me, Jess?"

Jess thinks about it for a second and then says, "I might as well. There's not much I can do standing here, now can I?"

The two of them are then ported to the Training Room. Janet says to the rest of the knights, "I know we are all tired, but Joseph does have a point. If we're going to beat these guys, then we need to train with everything we've got." She steps forward and is ported into the Training Room.

She is followed by Tasha, who shouts, "I'm not letting those two pampered princesses leave me in the dust." Turning to the others as they depart, she says, "Make your decision quickly!"

John then says, "No one ever said saving the world would be easy," and he steps forward to be ported into the Training Room. He looks at Eric and says "Are you coming?"

Eric shakes his head and says, "I think I'm going to regret this," but he, too, ports into the Training Room.

"I guess that answers my question," John says, and he enters the Training Room door.

Sally then looks at the others and says, "I hate work, but the world is counting on us. How else am I gonna find a cute guy like you, Max?"

"Seriously?" says Britney, shaking her head. "Do you ever stop flirting?" Then Britney grabs Sally and says, "Let's go, you little flirt." And the two girls port into the Training Room together.

Maggie then looks at Brad and says, "If you don't want to train, that's cool. That just means I'll have to beat you down tomorrow 'cause I'm going to join them." She kisses him on the cheek and goes into the Training Room.

Max then looks at Brad and says, "If we don't go now, we are going to get slaughtered tomorrow."

Brad replies, "I know. I guess if we can't beat them, let's join them." And, with that, the two remaining knights port into the Training Room.

ONCE INSIDE THE TRAINING ROOM, the knights are surprised to find that they can move normally. Joseph sees the looks on their faces and says, "For this training session, I've turned the AG system off, so that we can focus on learning how to use our powers. Also, this is more of a free training session. You train how you want to train. There is, however, a time requirement of two hours. We each have to workout that long before the system will allow us to leave. Does everyone understand?" All the other knights, including Brad and Max, nod in agreement and each of the knights find a spot to begin training.

MEANWHILE, BRYKAR IS PONDERING how he can find a weakness in these knights. As he is walking through the chamber where his remaining warriors are kept, he comes to the chamber holding the Seductive Siren, a creature able to change her appearance just by using her voice. "Hmmm," thinks Brykar, "I know these knights are human. Perhaps the powers of this seductress will be enough to tear them apart."

Brykar releases her, and she stretches toward him and attempts to use her powers on him. Brykar grabs her by the throat, slams her to the wall, and says, "Don't even think your powers will work on *me*. If you ever try it on me again, I will cut your throat myself."

He releases her but says, "Now, Siren, I have need of your unique skill-set."

She moves closer to him and asks, "So, what do you need me to do?"

"I've been sent here," Brykar answers, "to see what kind of defenses this world has, but I've encountered a group of heroes who call themselves the Knights of the Cross. I've just learned that these particular knights are humans and, since most humans are driven by pride and lust, this is where your powers come into play."

The Seductive Siren licks her lips in anticipation and says, "This sounds interesting! So, what is it exactly that you want me to do?"

"What I would like for you to do," Brykar responds, " is to use your powers to enslave the men and divide the women of a nearby city so that it will draw the knights out. When they emerge to stop you, I want you to use your powers on *them*, so that *they* will be divided and no longer be able to interfere with my plans."

The Seductive Siren is delighted with the idea. She says, "Mmmmmm, sounds like fun, Brykar. Maybe not as much fun as you and I could have, but fun nonetheless."

He turns on her and shouts, "I have no time for your tricks, Siren. You will find your weapons in the lab. Now be gone from my sight."

The Seductive Siren swaggers out of the room and heads to the lab.

AFTER THE SEDUCTIVE SIREN LEAVES, Sadoom appears before Brykar and says, "So, you have released the Siren?"

Brykar turns and kneels, saying, "Yes, I have, Lord Sadoom. I thought her powers would be a good way to test the people of Earth, especially these knights."

Sadoom chuckles and says, "That was a wise choice, Brykar. Keep me updated on your progress."

"Yes, Lord Sadoom," replies Brykar.

IN THE LAB, THE SEDUCTIVE SIREN GRABS HER SONIC SONG SPEAR, an instrument used to amplify her powers, as well as allowing her to use sound itself as a weapon and modifying any vehicle she desires. She then grabs her Siren Soul Shield, which allows her to be seen as what males of any race would consider "beautiful." After securing her gear, she sees a Psystruct psycycle and uses her staff to modify the vehicle to become one that will amplify her powers even more. A few minutes later, her vehicle is assembled, and she walks around it and says, "Now, this is more like it! I think I'll call this the Siren Street Screamer." She then enters her new vehicle.

As the Seductive Siren leaves, Brykar's ship heads toward the town that Phobia Fighter went to when he faced the knights. She thinks to herself, "This will be so much fun!"

THE KNIGHTS ARE IN THEIR TRAINING ROOM. As Jessica trains to use her powers, she's having a hard time focusing. The others notice, but each of them is having their own challenges. Justice then appears to Jessica in a liquid form and says, "I notice you are having some trouble focusing. Would you like to talk about what is bothering you?"

Jessica says, "I'm not even sure how to talk about what I'm feeling, Justice."

Suddenly the alarm goes off, releasing the lock on the training room, and the knights head to Des's lab to see what the disturbance is. Jess starts to follow them, but Justice says to her, "Hold on! Let them see what the problem is. Let's talk about what is bothering you."

"I guess what's bothering me," Jess says, "is the fact that I don't know where I fit in within the group. I mean, Joseph is the leader. Des is the brains. Brad is the hothead. Sally is the flirt. Maggie is the courageous one. John is Mr. Positive. Eric is Mr. Depression. Tasha is a natural fighter. Brittany is the socialite. Janet is more vocal than any of them. And Max is like the voice of reason in most cases."

As she says all this, Justice gives her a quizzical look. Jessica explains, "I was referring to Max when it come to the dynamics of the group, not when it comes to the wisdom you provide, Justice. I just wish I knew where I fit in in all this."

Justice then says, "That is quite the dilemma, but I do believe you bring more to this team than you realize. I could tell you what I think you bring, but the problem with that is if you don't see what you bring, you will never truly know. Although it is said, 'The simple believe everything, but the prudent give thought to their steps.' "[5]

Jessica asks, "Are you calling me a prude?"

Justice chuckles and says, "Well, yes, in a manner of speaking. You see, the term prudent in your language originally meant "cautious," but it has been twisted to mean something else now. Right now, you are being what is called "sober minded," as you look at yourself and where you fit in. This is a very rare quality that few people possess, and you should consider yourself lucky to have such a trait."

Jess shakes her head and says, "When you put it like that, I guess I am a prude. Thanks for the talk, Justice. It helped a lot. Now, if you'll excuse me, I'm gonna join the others and see what the alarm was about."

WHEN JESSICA ARRIVES AT THE LAB, Des had just pinpointed where the disturbance is and says, "According to the readings, it looks like the city Phobia Fighter attacked is where a new disturbance is coming from."

Brad asks, "How can we know if it's one of Brykar's warriors?"

"Simple," Des says. "I've altered the scanner within the base to scan for non-earthling biosignatures. Also, when a drone was sent to that particular city I saw this…" He pulls up a screen where a woman is standing with hundreds of men at her feet. And the women of the city are fighting each other like it is an all-out war.

"Between my scanner and this," Des says, "it's safe to say Brykar is definitely behind this."

Joseph then says, "Do we know if it's her that is causing this or if it's a device planted somewhere in the city?"

Des does a quick scan of the city and answers, "At the moment, it's hard to say, but it looks like it coming from her."

Joseph then says "All right, let's Light the Night. Everyone to your vehicles."

AS THE KNIGHTS HEAD TO THEIR VEHICLES, Jessica asks, "Joseph, is it okay if I sit this mission out?"

He looks at her with a puzzled expression for a moment and then replies, "May I ask why, Jess?"

"I've got some stuff I've got to deal with," she answers. "Until I figure it out, I'm not going to be any good to you guys out there."

"All right, Jess," Joseph says, "just stay in touch in case this goes south and we need you out there."

She nods in agreement. Then, as the other knights head for the city, Jessica says, "I need to figure this out. Time to do some training."

WHILE THE OTHER KNIGHTS HEAD FOR THE CITY, Des notices that Jess isn't around and privately asks Joseph why. "She asked to sit this one out," Joseph informs Des. "I told her to be on standby just in case."

Joseph then asks Des, "Is there more that you aren't telling me, Des?"

Des replies "No, I just wish there was more I could do for her."

"So do I," Joseph agrees, "but right now we have to keep focused on the task at hand."

AS THE KNIGHTS ENTER THE CITY, they are hit with a sonic wave. It doesn't affect them or their vehicles physically. However, Des notices the disturbance and tries to pinpoint it. Then he hears a voice that starts to say, "Come to me, my darling"

Without a second's thought or hesitation, Des heads toward the voice, which is the same direction as the disturbance. Soon, the other guys also start hearing a voice that calls to them, and they head in the same direction. The girls start to notice this, and Maggie says, "Where do they think they're going?"

"What's the matter, Maggie?" Janet taunts, "Afraid Brad is tired of you already?"

Maggie shouts at her, "What did you say, you cheap whore?"

Britney chimes in, "From where I'm standing, both of you are whores."

Tasha adds, "This coming from the number one trick of our school!"

Britney then responds, "Slow your roll, Tasha. The number one spot is reserved for Sally."

"That's not what the football and track teams would say, Britney," replies Sally.

The girls then switch their vehicles into their fighting form and begin to square off against each other. It is Maggie against Janet and Tasha, Sally and Britney against each other. As Maggie and Janet square off, Maggie says, "All right! You wanna go at it. Let's go. I'm tired of you acting all high and mighty like you are better than the rest of us."

Janet chuckles and says, "Who says I'm acting trailer trash."

Without hesitation, Maggie charges at Janet. Janet is able to dodge her and then throw her to the floor. She says, "If that's all you got, then this will be quick."

JOSEPH AND THE OTHER MALE KNIGHTS ARRIVE to where the mysterious voice has led them. As they exit their vehicles, they kneel down. Seeing them, the Seductive Siren says, "Well! Well! Well! What do we have here?" Walking toward them, she says, "Could it be that you are under my power?" She then looks at Des but says to them all, "Who do you serve?"

In unison they all say, "We serve you, oh beautiful Siren."

Hearing that, she is pleased. She turns from them, smiles and says, "This is perfect! I must tell Brykar this at once. If I remember correctly, he said there were twelve knights, but only six of them are here."

Now turning to Joseph she asks, "Where are the remaining knights?"

Although under her power, Joseph replies, "The remaining knights were behind us, beautiful Siren."

The Seductive Siren then gets in her Siren Street Screamer and heads off to find the other knights. When she finds them, she chuckles, for they are fighting among themselves. "Oh, my!" she says, "This is just too delicious!"

BACK AT THE BASE, JESSICA CONTINUES TO TRY TO TRAIN, to try to get past the block she is having, but with no luck. Manuel and Justice see this and Justice says to Manuel, "The block she's having is because she questions her own worth and is comparing herself with the others."

Manuel replies, "That is definitely a hard thing to deal with. No matter what we say, she must realize her own self-worth. But I do have an idea to help her."

Manuel then goes to Jessica in the Training Room and says, "Still having trouble training with your powers?"

Jessica says, "Of course. Can't you see that?"

Manuel says, "I can, and that is why I wish to help you. Jessica, remember: your power is the power of water, which can be both gentle and strong. I know you question your place on the team, but know that your powers are a reflection of who you are."

Before Jessica can say anything, Manuel disappears, and she starts to think about what he has said. She comes to the conclusion, "Manuel is right! My power is the power of water. Now that I think about it, that is how I am. No matter what situation I've ever been in, I've always been able to adapt and adjust quickly."

With that being said, she tries to use her powers again and finds that she has a much different result this time. She is able to control the flow of water, causing it to be as bendable as a rope or as hard as steel.

Before she can celebrate, the alarm in the lab goes off, and as she races to see what's going on. She sees that this issue is with the girls and their vehicles. As she pulls up the screen, she sees them fighting. She tries to communicate with them, but their coms are not responding. When she tries to communicate with them telepathically, she also gets no response. She then says, "Great! What am I supposed to do now? If I go out to help, I may fall into the same trap."

JESSICA THEN NOTICES THAT THE GUYS AREN'T THERE and searches for them. She opens their comm and hears the guys saying, "We love you, beautiful Siren."

When Jessica hears that, she then has the computer scan for sound waves and, in doing so, is able to find that the source of the disturbance is the one the guys were calling "Siren." She says to herself, "Now it makes sense why Des couldn't pinpoint it before. She's been using sound, and that's probably why everyone has gone nuts."

When she turns to go, she sees Manuel. He asks her, "Where are you going, Jessica?"

She smiles at Manuel and says, "To help the others."

"Does that mean you've found the answer to what has been bothering you?" Manuel asks.

Again Jessica smiles and answers, "Yes, I have, and I realize now that I'm not the lab rat I thought I was. I realize that I do have value and that, like water, I flow, and I adapt."

Manuel smiles and says, "Very well, then! Go and help the others, Jessica."

BEFORE JESSICA CAN LEAVE THE BASE, she starts to feel a surge of energy inside herself and then she shouts, "Aqua Armor, engage!" Suddenly, she is engulfed in a column of water, and her armor begins to transform. As it does, a trident appears in her hand and a shield in a large oval shape.

Moments later, when the transformation is complete, Jessica says, "This is unreal. I can't believe how strong I feel."

Manuel chuckles and says, "Well, it looks like you've unlocked your new armor. Still, how are you going to be able to break the hold the Siren has on the men without being put under the same trance?"

Jessica answers, "I've thought about that. If she's using sound as her weapon, then I should be able to use my powers to neutralize her sound."

"That's an interesting theory," Manuel concludes. "Just be careful, Jessica. There is still much we do not know about this new enemy."

"I will, Manuel," she replies, "because my team needs me, and I know now where I fit in."

JESSICA HEADS TO WHERE TSUNAMI SLIPSTREAM IS, and she gets in. He immediately says, "My dear Jessica, is everything all right?"

As she shuts the door, she says, "No! The team is in trouble, and we've gotta save them. Are you ready?"

Tsunami Slipstream revs his engine and says, "Ready to roar like the raging sea, my dear!"

She chuckles and says, "Let's ride this wave, Tsunami."

With that, the bay door opens, and she and Tsunami Slipstream race to help the other knights.

AGENT MARTIN HAS NOTICED the disturbance the Seductive Siren has caused. He slips away from the cameras and, using the circular disc that Brykar has given him, he contacts Brykar. Pressing the button, he sees a holographic image of Brykar appearing before him. Brykar replies, "Hello, Agent Martin. Is there something I can do for you?"

Unknown to Agent Martin, Brykar has already scanned his mind and knows that he's calling regarding the Seductive Siren. Agent Martin says, "I thought you came here with a peaceful intent. What I'm seeing from my end is anything but peaceful."

Brykar then telepathically communicates to the Seductive Siren, "Have the knights act as if they've captured you. Then have them drag you away."

She, in turn, responds, "As you command, Brykar."

As she does what Brykar has commanded, Agent Martin sees it on his screen. Brykar is seeing it too and he now says, "They are not with me. In fact, these warriors have hunted me and my people for generations. We thought we had lost them when we had come to Earth, but it looks like they even followed us here."

Brykar then uses his psychic powers to enhance the illusion that the knights are the evil ones. Brykar adds, "We may be able to defeat them with your help."

"On one condition, Brykar," Agent Martin says.

Intrigued as to what Agent Martin would want in return, Brykar asks, "What is that, Agent Martin?"

"I want the bodies of these warriors that have chased you for so long," Agent Martin demands. "Do we have a deal?"

Brykar chuckles and says, "Very well, Agent Martin. Once they are beaten, you can have their remains. They call themselves the Knights of the Cross."

AGENT MARTIN ENDS THE COMMUNICATION suddenly before entering ARC's central command. He then makes a call and informs the person on the other end about his discovery of the knights and their goal of world domination.

MOMENTS LATER, JESSICA IS NEARING THE CITY. She says, "Tsunami, stop here."

As he stops, he says, "My dear, why have we stopped here. Your friends are in the city?"

"True," Jessica says, "but whatever has the knights is able to disable you guys as well. Otherwise they would have stopped them by now."

"That's a very interesting observation," says Tsunami.

"Thanks," Jessica replies, "but if you were impressed with that, this will blow you away." She then raises her shield to the sky and shouts, "Sonic Tsunami Shield, engage."

Once she says that, a column of water appears around her and Tsunami, then begins to shrink rapidly until it's gone. Tsunami asks, "What was that all about?"

"Before we left the base," Jessica answers, "I found that whoever this is is using sonic waves to control everyone's minds. What I just did was use the elemental power of water to shield us from her sonic vibrations, which apparently are able to disable the Bod Bots as well."

"Very impressive, dear Jessica!" Tsunami says.

Jessica now enters Tsunami again and, as the two head into the city, she says, "Hopefully we won't be too late."

CHAPTER 9

AQUATIC ASSAULT:
SERENADE OF THE TSUNAMI

JESSICA AND TSUNAMI HAVE ENTERED THE CITY. Jessica says, "Tsunami, scan for the knights and see where they are."

Tsunami scans the city, notices that the knights are split into two groups and tells her what he has discovered: "Apparently the girls are fighting, and the guys appear to be in a trance-like state."

"Let's get the girls first," Jessica says, "before they destroy each other."

She has Tsunami lock in the coordinates, and they race to stop the girls from destroying themselves.

WITHIN A FEW MINUTES, THEY REACH THE GIRLS and see them fighting in their BOD Bots. Janet is dodging Maggie's punches, but now Maggie finds an opening and throws Janet to the ground.

Tasha, Britney and Sally are also locked in combat in their BOD Bot Armors. Tasha, for the most part, has been dodging the attacks of the others and using them to attack each other. When Jessica and Tsunami see this, Jessica says, "I think I have an idea about how to get them to stop fighting, but it will involve them chasing us. Are you up for it?"

"My dear, I will always follow your lead," says Tsunami. "Let's do it!"

Jessica then exits the vehicle. Raising her trident to the sky, she shouts, "Tsunami, strike!" He then hits each of the female knights with a blast of water, knocking them to the ground.

Jessica then gets back in Tsunami and says, "Time to go, Tsunami." And, with that, the two speed away.

WHEN THE FEMALE KNIGHTS ARE ABLE TO STAND, they see that it was Jessica who hit them and knocked them down. Janet says, "I can't believe she did that. Oh, is she gonna pay! I'm going to ..."

"Not if I get to her first," replies Maggie, suddenly in a rage.

Tasha then shouts, "Neither one of you will beat me to her."

Britney then shoves Tasha, knocking her to the floor and says, "How are you gonna beat anyone from the floor? I'll see you all after I get her."

Sally starts to walk behind Britney. As she passes Tasha, Tasha stands to her feet, picks Sally up and throws her at Britney. She falls into Britney, and the two of them fall onto Janet and Maggie. Tasha runs past them saying, "Awww, poor babies! Did that hurt? Maybe this will make it better." She then lifts a giant slab of concrete, throws it on them and races off after Jessica.

AT FIRST, JESSICA NOTICES THAT ONLY TASHA IS BEHIND THEM, but very soon the others are gaining ground as well.

Tsunami asks, "So, what's the next part of the plan?"

Jessica says, "That's the tricky part. We need to have them all within range. We will spray them with my Tsunami shield, and hopefully that will free them from the Siren's power."

About the same time Jessica notices a spot for her shield on the console and says, "Let's see what this does."

Tsunami says, "It allows me to use your shield' lower in vehicle form."

Jessica notices that the girls are closing in fast, and she says, "Tsunami, I need you to speed up and then do a hard u-turn."

Just as Jessica has asked, Tsunami speeds up, giving them about a five miles of distance between them and the other female knights. As they turn back to face the others, Jessica says, "All right, Tsunami. As soon as they are in range, hit em."

AS SALLY AND THE OTHERS GET CLOSER, they stop, preparing to strike, Just then Jessica shouts, "Now, Tsunami! Let em have it," and Tsunami hits them all with a water blast that circles each of them, like it did Jessica.

As the force of the blast fades, the female knights start to shake their heads, trying to figure out what's going on. "What happened to us?" Janet asks.

Jessica answers, "You were placed under a trance by one of Brykar's warriors, a Siren apparently. Her powers seem to have lured the guys and caused females to fight each other."

"If that's the case," Maggie asks, "how come you weren't affected?"

Jessica smiles and then answers, "I was back at the base when I learned that you girls were fighting, and I noticed the men of the city calling her Siren. Thankfully I remembered that a Siren uses sound to lure men to their doom. Once I realized that, I was able to use my armor's new ability to create a shield from her sonic powers that were causing you all to fight each other."

"That was pretty clever, Jess," Tasha says. "So, what do we do now?"

"To be honest," Jessica answers, "I'm not sure. But I think if *we* can defeat her, the hold she has over the guys will be broken as well."

Britney then asks, "Couldn't you use what you used on us on them?"

"That's possible," Jessica responds, "but if I did, the blast would harm the normal guys under her control. And that's not a risk I want to take right now."

"So, what's the plan, Jess?" Britney asks.

Jessica answers, "First, we need to separate her from the guys, get them away from her. Otherwise we won't stand a chance of defeating her ... if she has them protecting her. Do you girls think you would be able to cause a big enough distraction to lure her or the guys away?"

Now Thunder Trucker says, "Pardon the intrusion, ladies, but from what I can tell, the Siren and the guys have moved away from the humans."

Smiling, Britney says, "Perfect! Looks like we won't have to create a distraction after all."

"True!" Jessica adds. "But, still, we can't just go charging in there. Especially if she's already seen you girls fighting."

Janet watches as Jessica tries to devise a plan and notices that she's different than before. Janet says, "Jessica, I have an idea. Why don't the rest of us approach her, showing that we've broken her control, to lure the guys away while you take her out."

"That just might work," Jessica replies.

The girls then get in their vehicles, with the exception of Janet and Jessica. Janet says, "Hey, Jessica, listen. Can I talk to you for a second?"

"Normally I would be fine with that Janet," Jessica says, "but I think we should save the boys first." Knowing that Jessica is right, Janet nods in agreement.

AGENT MARTIN IS GATHERING HIS TEAM for an attempt to capture the knights. He goes into the facility where the ARC team is located and enters the lab where Rivera is. He notices that she's been working with the Psystructs' tech. With her back to him, she asks, "What can I do for you today, Agent Martin?"

Agent Martin chuckles and says, "Observant as always, aren't you, Agent Rivera?"

"Yes," she answers, "but that's not why you're here. So, tell me what can I do for you today?" It is apparent that she is annoyed with Agent Martin's pleasantries.

He then says, "I need you to alert the team, because we have a mission."

"What kind of mission?" she asks.

Agent Martin explains, "There's a disturbance in the city where we met Brykar, and apparently they're being chased by another alien race and causing quite the problem."

"Interesting!" Agent Rivera says. "I shall alert the team, but I want them to meet us here. I have a surprise as well." She then presses a button on the console and says, "Attention! Attention! Will the following ARC members report to the lab: Agent Wallace, Agent Miles, Agent Daniels, Agent Stanton and Agent Ryan."

She releases the button and turns to Agent Martin. He asks, "What about Agent Saunders? We'll need her too."

Chuckling, she says, "Why should I call her when she is right behind you."

"Surprise, Agent Martin. What's going on, Agent Rivera?" says Saunders, causing Agent Martin to jump slightly in surprise.

Regaining his composure, he says, "Let's wait for the others to arrive, shall we? I'm only going to say this once."

Before Saunders can say anything, the other agents arrive. Agent Martin does a head count to make sure they are all present and accounted for. Then, when he is sure they are all there, he says, "Welcome, everyone. I had Agent Rivera call you here because we have a situation that we need to look into immediately."

Agent Wallace stands with his arms behind his back and asks, "What kind of situation is it?"

"As you know," Agent Martin explains, "we have met with an alien race that said their intentions were peaceful. However, today we noticed that not only are they out among the populace, but apparently they are being hunted by an alien group, and now their fight has been brought to our world. So now, I need you to investigate just who and what these things are so we can stop them."

"I really hate to say this," Agent Miles speaks up, "but how do we even know that these new aliens are evil? I mean, technically we don't know much about Brykar and his people."

"Very true," Agent Martin answers. "This is why I want you to research both groups and see what you can find?"

Agent Rivera motions for a chance to speak. "Quick question!" she says. "How are we supposed to research and investigate these things when this is the first time they've made contact with us?"

Agent Daniels answers, "While dismantling the ship they gave us, I found what we would consider a black box, which might be able to give us some useful data on both groups. I have connected it to the lab's computer, so whenever you are ready, we can begin."

Agent Rivera claps her hands together and says, "Perfect! Well, it looks like you've got some work to do."

Agent Wallace asks, "What about the rest of us?"

"That is for you to determine, Agent Wallace," Agent Martin says. "As for me, I will be back to check on your progress. If you find something substantial, notify me immediately."

With that, Agent Martin leaves.

AS THE AGENTS TALK AMONG THEMSELVES, trying to figure out what to do, unknown to them, Brykar is hearing every word of their conversation through the psychic link he planted in Agent Martin and his team. He chuckles now and says, "Interesting! These humans aren't as easily fooled as I thought." He then goes to his console and transmits a false history, one that shows that the Knights of the Cross are evil and have been hunting the Psystructs for years.

Brykar then heads to his chamber and contacts General Sadoom. As the link is established, Brykar kneels and says, "Greeting, General Sadoom!" Sadoom replies to Brykar, "What do you have to report, Brykar?"

"Everything is going according to plan," Brykar reports. "I have sent the Seductive Siren out to test the humans and the knights, and she currently has the male knights under her power."

"Very good, Brykar!" General Sadoom says. "Keep me informed of your progress. Is there anything else you wish to tell me?"

Brykar adds, "Also, I'm convincing the humans that the knights are aliens that have been hunting us for years."

"Excellent, Brykar!" General Sadoom says. "Again, keep me informed on what you learn of these humans and their protectors."

Brykar looks up at General Sadoom and says, "As you command, General."

AS THE COMMUNICATION ENDS, Brykar stands and walks toward the computer console in his chamber. He turns it on and watches as the Seductive Siren has the knights lead her away. Just then he notices something approaching her from behind. To his surprise, it is the remaining knights (with the exception of the Aqua Knight). He then sends a telepathic message to the Seductive Siren: "Siren, I don't know how, but the female knight broke your control, and they are quickly approaching you."

"Even if they found a way to break my hold on them," she responds, "they will find that breaking the hold I have on their men will be a much different story. Still, I will be ready for them, Brykar."

He ends the communication. Thinking over the fact that there were only five knights, he says to himself, "So, that's what happened. The Aqua Knight must have been the one to free them. Still, this confirms what I thought, which is that these knights are mere earthlings. Now that I know that, dealing with them will be simple."

NOW BRYKAR RECEIVES A TELEPATHIC SPIKE, a sort of early warning system to let the Psystructs know when anyone is close to discovering their true intentions. He then notices that the ARC team is doing a scan for the knights and the Seductive Siren. As the ARC team locates them with their satellite, Brykar uses his powers to have the ARC team see what he wants them to see.

WHEN THE FEMALE KNIGHTS REACH THE SEDUCTIVE SIREN and the guys, Maggie leaps from Wind Whip and says, "So, this is the whore you left me for?"

Janet chuckles and says, "It's over, Siren! Now, let them go!"

The Seductive Siren laughs and says, "Ohhhhh, you girls really are some-thing! Do you really think that because you broke free of my hold, I'll just let these guys go. Sorry, I don't think so! Besides, I thought every girl wants a knight in shining armor, and look! I've got six!"

"Seriously?" Britney says. "Not all of us are that desperate for a guy's at-tention that we need to enslave their minds."

"True," Siren says, "but these knights are more than my slaves; they are now my own personal guards." Turning to the guys, she says, "Knights, will you take care of your former teammates for me, please."

The male knights under her power nod in agreement and signal for their vehicles. Within seconds, their vehicles arrive, and the guys enter them, switching them from Vehicle to Armor mode. Sally says, "Okay! We've got their attention. Now what do we do?"

Tasha answers, "How about we take them out, Beast Brawler? You take Shadow Knight, and I'll take the Light Knight."

"Sounds good to me," says Beast Brawler, as he transforms. Tasha exits and charges at John.

Sally shakes her head and then says, "Then I'll take Faith Knight."

Britney charges toward Des, and as she does, she declares, "I've got the Earth Knight."

"Maggie turns to Janet and says, "I guess that means I've got the Fire Knight. What about you?"

"The Knight of the Cross is mine," Janet says.

The two remaining female knights move toward their targets.

"This is going to be quite entertaining!" says the Seductive Siren. "Let's see what you girls have got." She is taking delight in watching the knights fight each other.

Beast Brawler charges at the Shadow Knight, and as he does, he says, "Let's see what you've got." The Shadow Knight is able to dodge him and throw the BOD Bot to the ground. "So, ya got some moves after all," Beast Brawler replies, rising from the ground. "This is gonna be great fun!"

On his feet now, Beast Brawler circles the Shadow Knight, who suddenly activates his Shadow Sickles. They extend from the wrists of his BOD Bot. Beast Brawler finds this to be very funny. In response, he then activates his Beast

Blades—five blades that extend from his wrists. While these two circle each other, Beast Brawler looks for an opening but finds none. He thinks to himself, "If I can't find an opening, I'll have to make one."

Beast Brawler lunges in with one arm for an attack, forcing the Shadow Knight to block, using both of his Shadow Sickles. With the other arm, Beast Brawler comes around, catching both Shadow Sickles. Then, with a quick turn, he's able to disarm the Shadow Knight.

As the Shadow Knight recovers, he says nothing. Beast Brawler says, "Still giving me the silent treatment are ya?" He then throws the Shadow Sickles behind him and says, "If you wanna get to them, you have to go through me."

The Shadow Knight takes his stance and the two of them continue to lock horns in combat.

WHILE BEAST BRAWLER IS FIGHTING SHADOW KNIGHT, Tasha has been fighting the Light Knight and having a harder time than she thought she would. Each time she steps forward, the Light Knight uses a blinding light to stop her and change his position. Tasha then says, "If only there was a way to move without being seen. Wait a minute! That's it!"

Now that Tasha has a plan, she is suddenly excited. The Light Knight uses his ability once more, but Tasha uses the ability of the chameleon to blend in with her surroundings. In this way, she becomes virtually invisible to him.

At first, the Light Knight is puzzled, wondering where she has gone. As he looks around, he wonders why he can't see her. Tasha uses this to her advantage and jumps on the back of his BOD Bot, trying to disable the power core. Before she can do this, however, the Light Knight grabs and throws her.

As she is thrown, Tasha twists, allowing herself to recover and land safely. She then says, "This is going to be harder than I thought."

Suddenly the Light Knight begins to fire on Tasha, who manages to dodge his attacks and says telepathically, "Jessica, you'd better hurry up cause we won't last long like this."

While Sally fights Faith Knight in her BOD Bot, she dodges his attack and says, "Aww, come one! These guys aren't that tough. Cute maybe. Tough? Not so much."

Suddenly the Faith Knight grabs Sally in a choke hold and says, "Okay, they may be a bit tougher than we thought."

As Sally struggles to get free, she remembers a self-defense move she learned, and she bends her knees while leaning forward, causing Faith Knight to flip over her, breaking his hold. Then she uses her BOD Bot's specialized weapons, known as the Hatchets of Hope, which are spears that have an axe and a spike at their tip. These weapons come from the wrists of Sally's BOD Bot. "All right, Hunter," she says, "let's show him what we've got."

Faith Knight stands and engages his BOD Bot's specialized weapons, known as the Flails of Faith. They are spiked spears with a chain attached to a pole coming from his forearm. Hope Hunter then says, "This is definitely going to be interesting!"

Faith Knight then attacks, using his Flails of Faith, throwing them so that the chains extend to wrap around Sally. Amazingly, Sally is able to use the Hatchets of Hope to block this attack. Faith Knight then begins spinning both Flails and uses both of them to bind Sally.

Struggling to get free, Sally says, "This is just perfect! Now, what are we going to do?"

"I have an idea, Sally," says Hope Hunter. "I just need you to give me control for a moment."

"Go for it, Hunter," she responds. Hope Hunter then rotates his forearms, grabbing the chain of Faith Knight's Flails. Then he turns, pulling the Faith Knight toward them. The result is that the chains release, and Sally and Hope Hunter are free.

She says, "Okay, I was wrong. These guys are definitely tougher than we thought. If we're going to do something, we need to do it quick."

Britney then says, "No kidding! You would think it would be easier since we train with them. Still, this is definitely harder than we first thought."

As Britney says this, she is dodging the Earth Knight's attacks. He then activate his BOD Bot's signature weapon, the Dirt Drills. Like the other BOD Bot weapons, these come from his wrists.

Britney then activates her BOD Bot's weapons, the Bolt Blades. As they extend from the wrists of her BOD Bot, she notices that they are pure electricity, and this gives her an idea. She charges the Earth Knight, who uses the Dirt Drills on the ground to knock her off balance. As she falls to the ground, Britney says, "Great! Now, what do we do? How can we fight him if we can't even get close to him?"

Thunder Trucker then says, "Britney, if I may interrupt you. I believe I have an idea about how we can get to him." He then shows her his plan via a display that only she can see.

Britney says, "It might just work. Let's try it."

As before, Britney charges at the Earth Knight, and as he uses his Dirt Drills to knock her off balance, she leaps and, using her Bolt Blades, she is able to create a charge that allows her to hover over the ground. As she charges at the Earth Knight, she knocks him to the ground.

Britney chuckles and says, "Not so smart now, are you?"

The Earth Knight gets up, grabs a huge stone and places it in front of him. Using his Dirt Drills, he begins drilling through the stone so that it begins to shatter, causing the fragments to act as daggers that start to hit Britney and dig into her BOD Bot.

Britney says, "Great! I just had to gloat, didn't I?"

Thunder Trucker then says, "That would be a yes."

Maggie then says, "We all knew this wouldn't be easy, but we've got to get past them if we are going to have any chance of stopping this witch. I know we don't have the strength the guys have, but we have our wits, and last time I checked brains always win out over brawn."

The Fire Knight engages his signature weapon, the Blaze Bat, which extends from the wrist of his BOD Bot like the others. When Maggie sees this, she says, "What do you think a bat is going to do against me?"

Fire Knight points at her, and flames begin to engulf the bat without burning it to a crisp.

"Why did I have to open my big mouth?" Wind Whip says. "I believe I have an idea about how to deal with this situation."

"Great!" Maggie says. "Spill it!"

"Remember," says Wind Whip, "fire needs oxygen to survive, right? So, let's take his breath away, shall we, my dear?"

"True," says Maggie, "but our goal is to distract them, not kill them. Wait a minute! I have an idea." She is remembering how Joseph beat Brad when they fought.

The Fire Knight begins using his Blaze Bat to create fireballs that he hits toward Maggie. She dodges them and charges Fire Knight. Once she gets close, she kicks him and then has Wind Whip transform, and they speed off, the Fire Knight following close behind them.

Wind Whip asks, "So, what is your plan, Maggie?"

She says, "When Joseph beat Brad, he knew a head-on fight would be pointless and would only end up with both of them hurt. So, he basically got him to overexert and exhaust himself, which is what we are going to do now."

"Good plan!" replies Wind Whip. "But how exactly are we supposed to do that?"

Maggie smiles and says, "By doing this…" She now uses her wind powers to create a wind spear in front of her and a tunnel behind her so that she and the Fire Knight have no resistance.

As the Fire Knight chases them, Maggie is able to drive faster than ever. The Fire Knight is unaware of the fact that his BOD Bot system is starting to overload. When he notices what's going on, he transforms and starts to use his Blaze Bat to hit fireballs all around Maggie. This uses up the air around her, canceling out the tunnel she has created.

Maggie notices what's going on, and Wind Whip says, "So, what do we do now?"

Maggie chuckles and says, "Good question! I wish I had an answer right now."

LIKE THE OTHERS, JANET IS NOT HAVING AN EASY TIME fighting the Cross Knight. She dodges his attacks, but he also uses his BOD Bot weapons, the Cross Claws. These are claws that have three prongs on each.

Janet now begins speaking to the girls telepathically. She says, "Listen, girls! We know the boys are not responsible for their actions right now, and although we don't want to hurt them, they have no problem hurting us. So we need to fight them like they are the enemy. Not because we don't believe they will be free, but so that, no matter what, we will know how strong each of us has become. Each of us has our own doubts about different things, but each of us has a place here."

Even as Janet is speaking to the other girls telepathically, she continues to dodge the attacks of the Cross Knight. After dodging his most recent attack, one of Cross Knight's Cross claws pins Janet to the ground. She struggles to get free and says to the girls, "Look at me!"

Each of the girls look in her direction, while remaining locked in combat. Janet continues, "Even though I'm pinned to the ground and Cross Knight is stronger than me, I'm not beaten. We are Knights of the Cross, the same as the guys, and each of us has our own strength. We just need to remember that true strength comes from the heart. Let me show you why. Heart Burner, engage the BOD Bot weapons called Love Lances."

Suddenly, two lances with a heart-shaped tip emerge from Heart Burner's wrists. As Cross Knight prepares to finish her off, Janet uses her lances to break the grip of his Cross Claw then springs to her feet and lunges toward the Cross Knight, with one lance toward him and the other across her chest.

The Cross Knight grabs the first lance, unaware that Janet was counting on this. She now strikes with the second lance, knocking the Cross Knight to the ground. The other girls are inspired and begin to launch their counterattacks, knocking the rest of the guys to the ground. The guys just lie there for a moment.

NOW THE SEDUCTIVE SIREN STEPS FORWARD and begins to laugh. "Very impressive, ladies!" she says. "However, your attempts to stop me or the army of men I have under my control are pointless."

Britney says, "What are you talking about? We've beaten the male knights."

"Oh, is that so?" the Seductive Siren says with a swagger. She then turns to the knights and says, "Come on, boys! Show these girls how real men fight." With that, the male knights begin to get up and attack the girls again, pinning them all to the ground.

"You see, girls," the Seductive Siren says, "the only way to stop the men is to kill them. Women were always meant to rule, for males cannot help themselves when it comes to us. And why not? We females are smart, cunning and beautiful—at least in most cases."

Jessica then emerges and says, "Enough Siren! This ends! Now!"

The Seductive Siren turns to the Aqua Knight and says, "I was wondering when you would show up. I take it that you are the one who figured out how to break my hold on the females, which is rather impressive. Still, you are no match for me."

Jessica puts her left leg forward and says, "We'll see about that."

NOW THE SEDUCTIVE SIREN HAS HER SILENT STREET SCREAMER drive toward her. As she get into it, she says, "You aren't the only one with powerful armor." Then the Silent Street Screamer begins to become like a liquid metal, enveloping the Seductive Siren.

As the armor begins to form, it takes the shape of the Seductive Siren. When the process is complete, she says, "Now, let's see what you've got, little girl."

"I'm no little girl," Jessica says, "as you are about to find out."

"Very well," the Seductive Siren says. "Let's see how you deal with this."

Suddenly, the circuits of Janet's BOD Bot begin to go haywire, and she asks, "Tsunami, what's going on?"

Before he can say anything, his voice circuit is damaged, and he can no longer speak. "Great!" Jessica says. "I guess I'm on my own!" She then leaps from her BOD Bot and has it transform back into vehicle form.

"Aww, did I take away your trump card?" the Seductive Siren taunts. "How are you going to beat me now? Oh, that's right! You aren't going to beat me."

Jessica responds, "You are wrong. I will beat you, for I am a Knight of the Cross."

The Seductive Siren is now almost double the height of the Aqua Knight, who stands with her shield and trident in hand. The Siren attacks Jessica, who dodges but is clearly puzzled as to how she can win this fight. Getting an idea, she says, "You no-talent whore, is using your armor the only way you can beat me? How pathetic!"

Siren then says, "Oh, you think you are clever, don't you? Do you really think that by taunting me I'll fight you in a fair fight? I've got news for you, honey. I don't ever play fair."

The Seductive Siren then uses her Shockwave Scream to try to knock Jessica down. Jessica uses her Tsunami Shield to absorb the Shockwave Scream, then says, "Gotcha!"

"What did you just do?" asks the Seductive Siren.

Jessica says, "I figured you wouldn't ditch that armor, but I knew absorbing your attack would allow me to do this." She then stands and touches her Tsunami Trident to the shield, points to the Seductive Siren and says, "You are done!"

Jessica then charges the Siren, who also charges. As the two come closer, the Siren strikes downward. Jessica leaps out of the way and says, "Tsunami Storm, strike!" With that, she stabs her trident into the chest of the Seductive Siren's armor.

AS JESSICA LANDS, the Seductive Siren is stumbling, and with the trident still in her armor, begins to break apart. Suddenly, there is an explosion, and the trident is thrown into the air. Jessica leaps to catch it, and the Siren says, "You will pay for that." She then takes her Siren Soul Shield and her Sonic Song Spear and combines the two to form a new weapon. It looks like an oversized spear tip, which then splits. Half goes on one arm and the other half on the other arm. She then says, "This is my Siren Spear Shield. Let me show you how it works." The Seductive Siren then points at Jessica and sends a shockwave, knocking her to the ground. She then speeds toward Jessica and begins pounding her. As Jessica falls to the ground, she starts to question if she is strong enough to endure, then remembers what she has learned. In her heart, she begins to repeat their oath: "As days of darkness near, and people run in fear..."

The Seductive Siren reaches her, ready to deliver the finishing blow. As she is about strike with her shield spear, Jessica remembers that water is balanced, meaning both hard and soft. She turns to face the Seductive Siren, blocking her final strike.

Shocked by this, the Seductive Siren doesn't see that Jessica is standing to strike her. In her heart, the Aqua Knight continues to say, "from they who prey on the weak, and silence those who speak..."

The Seductive Siren, although stunned, leaps backward and brings both her hands together to fire a deadly sonic blast at the Aqua Knight. For her part, the Aqua Knight continues moving toward the Seductive Siren and, in her heart, says, "We will take to the sky with courage and battle cry."

As the Seductive Siren fires the blast, the Aqua Knight sticks her hand forward, neutralizing it effortlessly, and she finishes by saying, "To protect the world from loss, I am a Knight of the Cross!" The Aqua Knight now reaches the Seductive Siren, who leaps even further back and again puts her hands together so that her arms form an arrowhead, and she hurls herself toward the Aqua Knight. As she speeds toward the Aqua Knight, she creates a sonic charge that she believes will destroy the knight. The Aqua Knight sees this, and this time she puts her left hand forward, stopping the Seductive Siren dead in her tracks. With her right hand, she grabs her trident and strikes her, sending the Seductive Siren flying.

The Aqua Knight grips her trident as the Seductive Siren lunges for her, to attack one last time. The Aqua Knight blocks the attack and strikes the Seductive Siren with the trident, impaling her on it. Suddenly, it's all over. The Seductive Siren lies on the ground, her spell broken.

AS THE KNIGHTS AWAKE FROM HER SPELL, they gradually become aware of going on. "We'll explain it all later," the Aqua Knight says, "but right now we need to get out of here." All the knights agree and they head toward the base.

AFTER THE SEDUCTIVE SIREN HAS BEEN THERE A WHILE, Brykar has her brought back and placed in a chamber similar to those his other fallen warriors now occupy. Angry, he shouts, "This time those knights will pay. I will destroy them ... if it's the last thing I do."

AGENT DANIELS, WHO HAS BEEN LOOKING THROUGH THE ALIEN BLACK BOX, suddenly slams her fist on the console, causing Agent Rivera to ask, "Having trouble, are we?"

Agent Daniels turns to Rivera and says, "Shut it, Rivera! This is already hard enough! I don't need your sarcasm!"

"Very well," Agent Rivera says, "although I was just asking a question. By the way, I came across what appears to be a translator, and I thought it might help." Agent Rivera then places a small box down and says, "If you wish to use it, let me know, and I'll install it immediately."

Agent Daniels then turns to Rivera and says, "You already know the answer to the question. Install the translator so we can learn the truth of what's going on."

Agent Daniels tosses the translator to Rivera, who catches it and says, "It'll be my pleasure, Agent Daniels."

AGENT RIVERA TAKES THE BOX TO THE MAINFRAME and opens it, revealing a drive that can be easily inserted into the mainframe. As she plugs it in, Agent Daniels watches and says, "I so hate you right now."

Agent Rivera turns and says, "Like you said before, I already knew the answer. I just figured it would be best to suggest instead of assume. Don't you agree?" Agent Daniels.

Shaking her head, Daniels says, "I hate to agree with you, but that does make sense."

Agent Daniels now turns her attention to the computer and begins to have the translator work on the alien black box. She receives a notification saying that the translation will take a few hours, so she stands and says, "I'm gonna go work out for a bit. Let me know if the translator finishes earlier than expected."

Agent Rivera replies, "Very well, go have fun."

Agent Daniels shoots her a nasty look. Before she says anything, she realizes Agent Rivera may already have a response for it. So, she says nothing as she leaves the lab.

Agent Rivera waits for her to be out of earshot and then says, "I do believe Agent Daniels is learning."

AGENT DANIELS MAKES HER WAY TO THE TRAINING ROOM. When Agent Wallace sees her, he asks, "How's the project going?"

She walks to a table, grabs five throwing blades, and with her back to her targets, throws the blades over her left shoulder, hitting the dead center of four out of the five targets. The one that is off is off by merely a millimeter from dead center.

When Agent Daniels turns around, she screams, "Are you kidding me?"

Agent Wallace then says, "What's wrong? They all hit the center?"

She then scowls at him saying, "Yes they hit the center, but they all didn't hit *dead* center. You see, by it being off by even the fraction of an inch, it gives my target a chance to live, and my targets need to have zero chance to live."

Agent Wallace chuckles and says, "Okay, so what's got you so distracted?"

"I guess Rivera got under my skin more than I realized," Agent Daniels answers.

Wallace starts laughing. "Oh, now I get it," he says. "Well, if it helps, she has a way of getting under everyone's skin—especially mine. Why do you think I rarely go to the lab? Don't get me wrong, her seduction skills pale in comparison to Agent Ryan's, but she still knows how to distract and frustrate men easily. I honestly believe that's why she is attracted to Agent Martin, because he's the only one I know who can frustrate her."

She sighs and says, "I hate to admit this, but you're right. I guess I'm still bothered by what happened between us."

She remembers an incident she had with Rivera years earlier. Then she grabs five more blades and throws them the same way as before. This time, all five hit their targets dead center, splitting the previous blades."

Wallace is impressed. "Impressive!" he says. "By the way, what did happen between the two of you that makes you so angry with her?"

Agent Daniels turns and replies, "Agent Rivera and I had been the best of friends when we got recruited here. At least, that was until after we took the seduction course taught by Agent Ryan. After that, she started realizing that her beauty and brains could get her whatever she wanted, and she decided to test her skills by going after my now late husband."

Wallace interrupts. "Wait a minute! You were married?"

She scowls at him and says, "I was ... until I caught her and him together, in *our* house and in *our* bed. Without a thought, I killed him and made it look ike an accident. I was about to kill her too, but Agent Martin stopped me and told me that she was off limits. Since then, I don't deal with her unless I absolutely have to."

Agent Wallace says, "Wow! No wonder you two are so distant. Hey, Daniels, I know we don't usually hang out together, but would you like to get a bite to eat some time?"

Before Daniels can respond, Agent Saunders comes in and says, "Hey, Wallace, I have an idea about what can be done while we wait for intel on the Psystructs and the knights."

"Oh, I'm sorry," Agent Saunders adds. "Did I interrupt something?"

Agent Daniels, with a hint of sarcasm, replies, "No, you are right on time, Saunders. I gotta get going anyway. And, Wallace, since you asked what I like to eat, I like Italian."

AFTER AGENT DANIELS HAS WALKED OUT, Wallace, with a slightly annoyed tone, asks, "What have you got, Saunders?"

"Well, I was thinking. While Daniels focuses on finding out about the knights and the Psystructs, I thought maybe it would be best to focus our attention on those teens who escaped from Agent Martin. Granted, it's not a top priority, but it might provide some clue as to what is going on, since the destruction of the bus happened around the same time."

"That's not a bad idea," Agent Wallace agrees, "but how do you suppose we find them, since they've gone off grid?"

Agent Saunders replies, "That's what I was wondering ... until I did some digging in their backgrounds and thought, 'What if we do some surveillance on their families?' If they decide to contact them, we will be there waiting for them."

Agent Wallace says, "Gather whatever information you can on them, so we can get the team together (except for Daniels) and get Rivera working on surveillance tech. At least, this way, we won't just be here twiddling our thumbs."

"I'm on it!" Agent Saunders responds. As she leaves, to go gather the others, she thinks to herself, "Agent Wallace is mine, and I won't let anyone else have him."

GRAHAM HAS FINISHED DEVELOPING THE CODE AND TWO CIPHERS. The first cipher is actually a decoy meant to be given if anyone should find their coded messages, throwing them off the trail. The second cipher is the actual code, and it is small enough to fit into their wallet or purse, so that it's always with them. Graham then creates copies of both ciphers, puts them in a manila envelope, then checks the time and notices that Phillip should be passing by on his daily rounds. He also grabs a package that needs to be mailed and places the envelope under it.

As he goes out the door, he sees Phillip stopping in front of his house. Phillip notices him and waits. As Graham reaches him, he says, "Where's the fire, Graham?"

He chuckles and says, "Sorry! I have this package I have to get out today, or it will be late. And you know I can't have that."

Graham slides forward the manila folder so that Phillip notices it, and Graham nods slightly so that it doesn't draw any undue attention. Phillip says, "Don't worry, I'll make sure it gets mailed out asap." He puts it in his truck and continues to make his rounds.

A FEW HOURS LATER, WHEN PHILLIP GETS OFF, he heads home. In the bedroom, his wife looks at him and asks, "Has there been any word on the kids?"

"Not yet," Phillip answers her, "but I do have something to show you." He then opens the envelope, and they see the note from Graham.

The note reads, "Hi, Phillip, in this envelope are documents known as ciphers, which are meant to help everyone understand the code I will be sending out. The cipher on the larger paper is meant to be a decoy, while the smaller ciphers are the real way to understand the code. I need you to deliver a copy of these to all of us, including myself, so no one suspects anything. Now that we have the code to communicate, I will begin the search for my brother and the others. I'm sorry it's taken so long just for this part, but we need to be careful because the people we are dealing with are dangerous—if they can get the media to look at our family members as wanted fugitives. Be safe, until the next communication." It was signed "Graham."

Phillip looks at his wife and says, "I don't know what's going on, but I believe Graham will be able to find the answers no one else can."

His wife begins to sob. He holds her and comforts her, and he says to himself, "Max, wherever you are, stay safe! We *will* find you."

CHAPTER 10

LIGHTING STORM SHOCK: SHOCKING SITUATIONS

AFTER RECEIVING THE PACKAGE FROM GRAHAM, Phillip begins working on the mail to deliver to the others.

DAVID AND LAURA BOLTEN ARE MEETING FOR COFFEE WITH MELANIE Sabre-Masters, Joseph and Brad's mother, concerning a different matter altogether. As David sips his coffee, he says, "How long has it been since Darren went missing?"

Melanie bows her head and thinks. Then says, "Longer than I care to admit, but I would have to say it's been about five years since he vanished."

"Were there any signs that he was unhappy?" Laura asks.

Melanie looks at her and says, "I know it sounds crazy, but my husband didn't run away. He wouldn't and couldn't do that, not to Joseph, after all *he'd* been through. All I remember was coming home before the boys and I heard the door open, and it sounded like Darren, saying, 'Hi sweetheart.' But, when I turned to greet him, he was gone. The only thing left was a watch that his previous wife had given him before she died."

Melanie sips her coffee again and adds, "I'm sorry if I came off rude, but Darren was the best man I had ever met, and I loved him, just as he loved me."

David jumps back into the conversation. "Melanie," he says, "I've known Darren a long time, and we hate having to ask these questions, but this is necessary if we're going to find out what has happened to him."

Laura adds, "Yes, I know these questions are hard and I hate seeing you in pain, but David is right. If we're going to have this be a missing persons case, we need to rule out all other possibilities."

She pauses a moment, then resumes, "Which brings me to my next question. Did Darren have any enemies that you are aware of?"

Melanie thinks to herself for a moment and then says, "None that I can think of. Why do you ask?"

"Based on what you've told us," Laura replies, "it sounds like it's possible that maybe Darren could have been abducted before he got inside. I know that's a very slim possibility."

When there seems to be no answer, David interjects, "If you know anything hat could help us, please tell us. We want to help."

He, too, pauses a moment, then continues, "We noticed you were hesitant. Why was that?"

Melanie sighs and says, "Darren told me that his wife died, but he never did tell me *how* she died. And, what's worse, he would always have nightmares about it and wake up screaming. Before he disappeared, I did a search on him and found nothing. Then I remembered that he had told me his wife's name years ago. When I searched for it, I found an article about a woman who was brutally murdered by her husband's co-worker. When I first saw that article, I thought it must be a coincidence, until I saw the date of the article and noticed that the name of both the husband and the child were left out."

"Why was the date significant?" David asks.

"Because that was the date my brother was arrested and went to jail for murder," Melanie answered. "When I realized this, I broke down and cried. That night I talked to Darren and told him what I had found, and he told me the whole story."

"Darren had told me that when he came home that night, the door was partially open, and he found my brother leaning over his wife's body in the living room. Joseph was in the playpen nearby when it happened. He also said that before he could confront my brother, the police arrived and found my brother in that position. He was immediately taken into custody.

"Darren said that after the trial he changed his and Joseph's names, so as to protect them. The reason I paused is because I thought maybe it was my brother, but he's still in jail."

Stunned to learn this news, David and Laura sit there and silently wonder what to do next.

AS THE KNIGHTS RETURN FROM THEIR BATTLE with the Seductive Siren, they all look at Jessica's armor. Everyone is amazed at how it looks. Des walks up to her and says, "I thought you were beautiful before. Now there are no words to describe you."

Janet chimes in and jokingly says, "It took you long enough to stop the Seductive Siren. Please try not to cut it so close the next time."

Jessica says, "Sorry, Janet. I'll make sure not to cut it so close next time."

Tasha interjects, "Just exactly how did you stop her? I mean, I didn't see all of it, but it looked like she had you beat. Then, in the end, you seemed to beat her effortlessly."

Looking curiously at Tasha, Joseph asks, "What are you implying, Tasha?"

"Nothing," she replies, chuckling, "other than the fact that this is the fourth time this has happened?"

"Explain what you mean!" Des asks, curious.

"Des," Tasha says, "I'm not anywhere near as smart as you, but since we got these powers I've noticed the Psystructs are getting stronger and stronger. We have grown stronger as well. Still, it happened with Brad, you, Maggie and now Jessica, which makes me wonder why."

"It's a fair question," Joseph says. "Does anybody have an idea as to why?"

Des pauses for a moment and then says, "I believe I do. Although each of us was given powers, those powers are limited to our imagination, and each time we unlocked a new level of power, it has been because of personal issues that each of us has had to face. For Brad, it was his anger and jealousy. For me, it was my pride. For Maggie, it was fear. Jessica questioned her worth."

Eric steps forward now and asks, "So, what are you saying?"

Des then explains, "If I'm correct, as we grow as people, so do our powers. And, apparently, the increase is exponential, resulting in a new armor being created."

"Hey, Des, could you repeat that in English?" pleaded John.

"Simply put," Des says, "each increase in power is so great that a new armor is created because of it."

Now Britney asks, "Do you think we can unlock those powers before we face them in battle?"

"It's possible," Des says, "but it would be a lot more difficult than any of us realize."

Max is puzzled. "What do you mean, Des?" he asks.

"What I mean is that not all of our issues are surface issues or issues easily identified. In order to unlock these new levels of power, we must get at the root of a problem, which is, in most cases, on a subconscious level."

The others look at Des, who now bows his head and adds, "Simply put, the issues that cause the growth are not obvious and are on a deeper level than we realize."

WHILE THE KNIGHTS DISCUSS THIS, Manuel steps forward and says, "Des is correct in what he has said. There is a reason for this, one that I may be able to explain. As you all know, when you received the armor, it bonded with you, not just to your body, but in every aspect, which is why you can communicate with each other telepathically."

"If this is the case," Joseph asks, "then training alone won't give us the power to beat these things. How can we grow so that we will have the power to defeat them?"

They all look to Manuel for his answer. "Joseph," he begins, "I believe you already know the answer?"

Joseph stares at Manuel with a puzzled look and asks, "What do you mean?"

Manuel says, "How did you learn about the history of the Psystructs, what they really were?"

Joseph's eyes widen, and he says, "Of course! But I thought there was only one copy of the book?"

Smiling, Manuel answers, "Bring me the book, and I will take care of the rest." Joseph immediately heads to the library.

IN THE LIBRARY, JOSEPH GRABS *THE CHRONICLES OF THE CROSS* and returns to the others. He hands the book to Manuel, who then gives a copy to Brad, Des, Maggie, Jessica, Britney, Eric, John, Tasha, Sally, Max, Janet and, finally, Joseph."

Joseph is amazed. There was one book. Now they all have a copy of the same book. "How is this possible?" he asks.

Smiling, Manuel says, "As Joseph has learned, this book is called *The Chronicles of the Cross*. It contains the history of how the Psystructs began, as well as the history of the very first heroes to wear the armor that has bonded with you. I believe having a personal copy of it will help you to discover things about yourself and help you grow, allowing you to unlock even greater power."

MANUEL NOW BACKS AWAY. The knights look down at their individual copies of the book, and when they look up again, Manuel is gone.

"This is crazy!" Max says. How are we going to grow by reading a book?"

Joseph replies, "You're absolutely right, but at this point in time, what do we have to lose? I mean, do you have a better idea of how to unlock these powers and defeat the Psystructs?"

Frustrated, Max says, "No, but are you telling me you want us to read a book that is in a language we don't understand, about people we don't even know, and somehow that's going to help us?"

"How do you know that you can't read it?" Joseph asks. "You just got the book and haven't even opened it yet?"

Max sighs. "You're right, Bro," he says. "I'll give reading this a shot."

The other knights nod in agreement. Soon they each go to their quarters in order to examine the books they have been given.

AS BRITNEY ENTERS HER QUARTERS, she tosses the book on the bed and lies down, thinking to herself about what has been said. "I've never been the best student," she thinks, "so, how am I supposed to use this book to figure out what's holding me back?"

Suddenly Justice appears in a lightning form to her and asks, "Are you okay, Britney?"

Britney sits up and says, "Not really. I was just thinking about what was said, and when it comes to problems, I have to admit I have a lot of problems, not to mention that I haven't really been the best of students. So, using a book to figure out what's holding me back as a person doesn't seem like the easiest thing."

Justice looks at her compassionately and says, "It may not seem like it, Britney, and I understand that this is not easy for you. I know this whole thing hasn't been easy for any of you. What I can tell you is this: you are stronger than you realize."

Britney smiles and says, "Thanks, Justice."

As Justice leaves the room, Britney lies down on her bed and begins thinking of her parents and how much she misses them. She then begins to think about how often her mother and father would give her advice on how to do things, and she would just shrug it off by thinking, "I've got beauty and money, what else could a girl ask for?" She now says to herself, "Yeah, money and beauty really help me out a lot here."

BRYKAR RETURNS TO HIS CHAMBERS after placing the Seductive Siren in the regeneration chamber, when he is alerted to a transmission from General Sadoom. He activates the communication devices.

As General Sadoom appears, he notices that Brykar is not pleased, He says, "I take it from the look on your face that the Seductive Siren was beaten."

Brykar angrily nods. General Sadoom looks at him and says, "Brykar, remember: your mission is to observe and report intel on the humans and their defenses. This includes these knights. Once we know more about them, we will be able to move in and destroy them. So, continue with your mission, or what has happened to your warriors will look like a walk in the park compared to what will be done to you."

Brykar nods and says, "As you command, General Sadoom."

THE COMMUNICATION ENDS, and Brykar makes his way toward where his remaining warriors are located. As he enters the chamber, he thinks to himself, "Who should I send against the knights next?" He goes to a computer and inputs the known data he has accumulated and in seconds, the computer finds a match. Seeing it, Brykar chuckles and says, "Yes, this should be perfect!"

Now Brykar goes to the tube holding the Elemental Enforcer, a being that has the ability to tap into the elements of whatever planet he touches. Once released, the Elemental Enforcer falls to his knees. As he begins to wake up and sees Brykar, he says, "How may I serve you?"

Brykar answers, "We have traveled to a planet called Earth, and I've been tasked with gathering intel on its defenses. One of its particular defenses has become a rather large pain to me. This is the problem I need you to take care of."

"It will be my pleasure to take care of it for you," the Elemental Enforcer replies.

Brykar chuckles and says, "I was hoping you would say that."

BRYKAR POINTS ELEMENTAL ENFORCER in the direction of the weapons chamber. As he enters the chamber, he looks for a particular weapon, known as the Elemental Eye. It is a jewel-like orb that can amplify his powers exponentially. In the process of finding it, he notices another item that he was going to look for next. It is called the Elemental Extractors. It consists of two gloves that have the ability to drain elemental power from any source, including the planet itself. Delighted, he says "This will be perfect!"

He then looks to see what vehicles are there and notices a vehicle that looks like a giant eagle. As he approaches it, he chuckles at the name, for it reads, "The Elemental Eagle" He then says "I don't know who or what these knights are, but it's time to show them the true power of the elements."

The Elemental Enforcer grabs the chain on the back of the Elemental Eagle and hooks his feet into what look like stirrups. After securing himself, he activates the Elemental Eagle and opens a bay door, and the Elemental Eagle takes flight from Brykar's base.

BACK AT THE ARC FACILITY, Agent Daniels has been looking through the translated data from the alien black box, and she notices that it does verify that the knights have been hunting the Psystructs. Daniels also finds that, according to the black box, the knights are a race of immortal beings that do not age, and that they take on whatever life form they first encounter.

Agent Daniels now contacts Agent Wallace over the com system and says, "Agent Wallace, we need you in the lab immediately."

A few minutes later, Agent Wallace arrives in the lab and says, "What did you find, Agent Daniels?"

She then begins pulling up the translated documents, showing that the knights have been indeed hunting the Psystructs. Then she shows him a document which reveals that the knights are immortals that take on the shape of whatever life form they come into contact with. As Agent Wallace reads this, he says, "Good work, Daniels! But we need to find out more about them and what exactly they can do. I'll take this info to Agent Martin and then have Rivera use the tech we have to create weapons that might allow us to put these things down."

Before Agent Wallace can leave, both Agent Martin and Rivera walk in. Agent Wallace says, "Agent Martin, I was just coming to inform you of what Agent Daniels has discovered."

Agent Martin chuckles and says, "Is that so?" He then walks over to Agent Daniels and says, "So, tell me what you've found?"

When Agent Daniels pulls up documents confirming that the knights have been hunting the Psystructs, Agent Martin says, "Perfect! Now, just keep digging. We need to make sure we know the kind of enemy we are dealing with."

As Agent Martin walks toward the doorway, with Agent Rivera following, he says, "Agent Daniels, please be aware that when you find anything in regard to the knights or the Psystructs, please report it to me immediately."

Agent Daniels replies, "Yes, sir! I will remember that going forward."

AFTER AGENT MARTIN LEAVES, Agent Wallace slams his fist on a table and says, "Sometimes I really can't stand Agent Martin."

She turns to him and says, "True, but last time I checked, he is the head of the organization. So, right now, we have to endure it. By the way, what was Saunders planning for the rest of you guys to do while I sift through this garbage?"

He turns to her and says, "Do you remember the students that escaped from Agent Martin's custody?"

"Yeah, what about them?" replies Agent Daniels.

"Agent Saunders thinks they may have some knowledge about the Psystructs and wants us to investigate them and their families."

Agent Daniels chuckles and says, "That's actually not a bad idea. Although it's still surprising that they escaped."

THE KNIGHTS ARE SCATTERED THROUGHOUT THEIR BASE. Des, in the lab studying the info he got from Jessica, notices that the tech the Seductive

Siren used is similar to the tech used to design their BOD Bots. Just as he notices this, the alarm goes off, and each of the knights heads for the lab.

Joseph waits for them all to arrive and then asks, "What's going on, Des?"

Des, lost for a moment in thought, realizes that Joseph is talking about what set off the alarm. He points to the screen, and says, "Look at this?"

As an image comes into view, Brad says, "It looks like a giant turkey." The others chuckle. Des says, "I wish it was just a turkey. From all appearances, it seems to be a giant eagle."

Joseph asks, "Is there anything in the computer about this guy?"

"No!" Des replies, "and I've checked everything I know to try and find out more about it."

"So what do we do," Eric asks, "just go charging in?"

"No," Joseph says, "we need a plan, and I think I have one. First, we need to see just what this new warrior of Brykar's can do."

Eric says, "Okay, but how do we do that? The last couple of times we did that, we either got captured or put under some kind of spell."

Joseph then says, "Simple, we send in a clone squad to find out just what this new creature can do. Des can monitor the fight from here, so we can know what we are up against." The others seem to like this idea.

Max says, "I thought we were supposed to only use the clones during battle or an emergency?"

"Okay, Max," Joseph says, "do you have a better idea about how we can find out what this thing is and what it can do? We need to do something that won't put us at risk of being caught or captured?"

"No," Max admits, "but there's gotta be a better way. Des, you were the one working on understanding how the clones work. Are you sure this is a wise idea?"

Des stays silent for a minute, trying to analyze the situation. Then he says, "I've only learned a small part of what the clones can do, and although it might be risky to use them in this situation, it might just be the best idea we have. Although ..."

"Although what?" Max says, "What is it Des?"

Des chuckles and says, "Joseph, how about this idea? Rather than each of us creating a clone, how about I create a clone that goes out with you guys, while I monitor what's going on from here? By doing this, it limits the clones to one rather than half a dozen."

Joseph nods in agreement. "What's the status on the BOD Bots?" he asks.

Des checks on them, using the computer, and finds that they're all ready except for Thunder Trucker, who apparently had more damage than realized.

"All right, since Des is staying here, the rest of us will go, except Britney, to see what this new warrior of Brykars can do. Britney, when your BOD Bot is ready, you can join us."

Britney nods in agreement, and Des activates a drone that will record the fight. Then he transforms and creates a clone of himself that will join the knights.

AS THE KNIGHTS LEAVE, Britney can't help but feel alone. Des notices that something is wrong, but he knows he has to focus on the task at hand, so he leaves it alone for the moment.

MOMENTS LATER, THE KNIGHTS ARRIVE near where the Elemental Enforcer is located and exit their BOD Bots. When he sees them, he leaps from the Elemental Eagle and lands in front of them and threatens them by saying, "So, you are the knights that have been giving Brykar so much trouble? I wish I could say that I was impressed, but I'm not. By the way, you may call me the Elemental Enforcer, and I will have the pleasure of destroying you."

Joseph steps forward and says, "I highly doubt that."

The Elemental Enforcer chuckles and adds, "How about I show you then?" With that, the Elemental Enforcer crosses his hands and begins throwing ice daggers from one hand and lighting daggers from the other.

The knights scatter and Joseph telepathically asks Des, "What is going on? Did he do what I think he just did?"

Des says, "He did. Apparently this guy is able to use the elemental energy of a planet to his advantage."

"Oh, lovely!" Joseph replies. "I guess we really angered Brykar if he's pulling out guys like this one."

Des telepathically says, "In this kind of a situation, I would suggest we keep him off balance, since he can use the elements to his advantage."

The knights signal their agreement, but before they can do anything, the Elemental Enforcer begins to speed toward Jessica. When he reaches her, Des' clone moves to block him. When the Elemental Enforcer grab his arm, he uses the Elemental Extractor to drain his elemental power.

The clone falls to the ground, and Des screams as he feels the elemental power being drained from him at the same time. Hearing this, Joseph tries to contact Des. Jessica rushes to the clone's side and asks, "Are you okay?"

He says, "Yeah, but my powers are gone."

Joseph turns to the Elemental Enforcer and asks, "What did you do to him?"

"What I did is simple," the Elemental Enforcer answers. "I've drained him of his elemental power, just like I will the rest of you."

Joseph then says, to Jessica, "Get him out here. The rest of you guys scatter."

As the knights disperse, the Elemental Enforcer says, "Don't you get it? You can't run from me." He then creates an electrical dome to keep the knights close. Then he has it start to shrink.

As the knights see this, Eric says, "Talk about being trapped? What do we do now?"

Joseph says, "Everyone get behind me…"

BACK IN THEIR BASE, DES KNOWS what Joseph is planning, and he looks for a way to short-circuit the force field. For the moment, he is unable to find it.

The Elemental Enforcer also knows what Joseph is planning and it makes him laugh. "If you think you can stop me, Cross Knight," he says, "you are sadly mistaken. And I will show you why."

As the Elemental Enforcer charges at them, Jessica, Brad and Maggie leap in front of Joseph to defend him. The Elemental Enforcer grabs Brad and uses the Elemental Extractors to absorb his powers. Maggie and Jessica hold their ground and try to think of a way to keep him from touching them. As he moves toward Maggie, she uses her powers to move the other knights away and prepares to fight him. Jessica stands next to her, ready to fight as well.

Jessica and Maggie then activate their armors. As they transform, the Elemental Enforcer says, "Am I supposed to be scared by your costume change?"

"This is more than a costume change," Maggie says, "as you are about to see."

Jessica adds, "By the way, you don't have to be scared of us for us to beat you down."

Joseph shouts, "What are you two doing?"

The Elemental Enforcer replies, "I'm starting to grow tired of this. Let me show you how to truly use your powers." He has his body become complete water. Then he creates a body double that appears behind Jessica and Maggie, grabbing them and stealing their powers.

John and Eric rush toward them, but suddenly the Elemental Eagle takes the form of wind and sends the two knights toward the Elemental Enforcer. He then touches both of them and takes their powers as well.

Seeing it, Max says, "This is crazy! Are we just going to stand here and let him pick us off one by one?"

Joseph says, "Stand down, now. If we are going to fight him, we need to come up with a plan."

Max says, "Fine, you plan. I'm going to do something."

As Max charges at the Elemental Enforcer, he then takes the form of wind. Then Max draws his sword and tries to attack, but he has no effect. The Elemental Enforcer then grabs Max and drains his powers.

Seeing what has happened to the others, Des realizes that the best course of action is to port them all out of there. He prepares to have the BOD Bots fire missiles to create a smoke screen so that he can get them out.

Before the BOD Bots can fire their missiles, the Elemental Enforcers uses an electrical charge similar to an electromagnetic pulse, shutting down the BOD Bots.

Even though his smokescreen idea has failed, Des activates the port system. He soon notices that it isn't working and, as he tries to figure out why, he notices the electrical field and soon realizes that it is preventing them from being able to port out.

BRYKAR WATCHES, VERY PLEASED, as the Elemental Enforcer drains the knights of their powers. He has the scene sent to General Sadoom, who is also watching. General Sadoom says, "Your newest warrior is doing well, Brykar. However, it looks like you are missing one of the knights."

Brykar looks and notices the same. Then he connects to the Elemental Enforcer and says, "Continue to drain their powers, but there is a knight missing. She is the one they call Bolt Knight."

The Elemental Enforcer replies, "As you command, Brykar." He then uses his lightning ability to trap the drained knights in cages, and he and his Elemental Clones continue to drain the powers of the other knights till only Joseph remains.

Now, as he looks at Joseph, the Elemental Enforcer uses his powers to bind him and begins speaking, "I know you can hear me, Bolt Knight. I do not know why you are hiding, but if you wish to save your friends and your leader, come and face me."

The Elemental Enforcer continues to taunt the knights, knowing that they can't get free. He notices that the Earth Knight is starting to dissolve and the other knights watch. He chuckles and says, "Clever ploy, sending in a clone to stand in for one of you. However, as you may have noticed, Earth Knight, your powers created the clone, and without your powers, you will not survive, Earth Knight. Soon neither will any of you."

BACK IN THEIR BASE, Britney sees Des fall to the floor. Manuel goes to him and says, "If we don't restore their powers soon, Des will die."

Britney says, "Manuel, I would really love to, but there's one problem. I don't know how. I'm not Des or any of the others. I have no idea where to begin to see what's holding my powers back. All I know is how to use my family's money to get out of problems, and there's no amount of money that can stop these creatures."

Manuel looks at her and says, "You're right in what you're saying when it comes to 'no amount of money will stop them.' But you are wrong when you say that is all you know. If you were not worthy, the armor would not have chosen you. Take a breath and look deep inside, and you will find the answers you seek."

As Britney takes a breath, she thinks of when she was young and how her father had taught her archery. She had said to him, "Daddy, if we have money, why do I have to learn this?"

He chuckled and said, "Sweetheart, money is a form of power, but it isn't *all* power. Archery will help you develop skills that will come to your rescue when money cannot. People constantly come to me with money, thinking it will solve their problem and, as tempting as it is, the truth is this: even if I took the money, it wouldn't change what happened. This is why I have you learning this, so you can look at the heart of a matter and understand that true power comes not from a person's wealth but from their heart."

From that time on, Britney developed a love for archery and became a skilled archer. But, because she had also become a socialite of the school, she had hidden this talent. Suddenly a phrase came to her mind: *"And he sent out his arrows and scattered them; he flashed forth lightnings and routed them."*[6] Without thinking, Britney raises her head and shouts, "Thunderbolt Burst Armor!" With that, lightning begins to surround her, and her armor begins to take on a new form. In her hand, appears a bow.

Manuel says, "Britney, is that you?"

She nods and says, "Thanks, Manuel. I know what I have to do now."

THAT SAID, BRITNEY DISAPPEARS in a flash. Now Justice approaches Manuel. "They are growing stronger and stronger," she says, "which means the threats will increase even further."

Manuel looks at her and says, "I know, but I believe they will all be up to the task."

CHAPTER 11

LIGHTNING STORM SHOCK: ELECTRICAL ENHANCEMENT

WHILE THE ELEMENTAL ENFORCER HAS THE KNIGHTS TRAPPED, he approaches the Cross Knight and says, "Well, the time has come to take your powers. I'm going to enjoy this." Before he can do anything, a huge surge of electricity hits the electrical dome surrounding them, and it shatters. "So," the Elemental Enforcer says, "you must be the Bolt Knight I've heard about. I wish I could say I was impressed, but you will fall, just like your friends."

Britney speaks up, "I doubt that, but if you would like to try it, then go ahead."

He then creates water, fire, wind and earth clones, while he himself takes on a lightning form. As the clones approach her, she leaps into the air and does a back flip while pulling the energy string at her back. As she does this, a bolt of lightning forms, to become an arrow that she fires at the Elemental Clones. They dodge it.

When Britney lands, she looks at him, and the Elemental Enforcer says, "That was actually impressive. Too bad it's still not good enough. Let me show you why." Now he starts throwing bolts of lightning that take the form of thin beams.

Britney pulls the energy string back, but this time several lightning arrows appear. As she fires them, each arrow deflects the lightning beams the Elemental Enforcer has fired at her. She taunts him, "I thought you were going to show me why I'm not impressive enough, you egocentric enforcer?"

This causes him to chuckle, and he says, "You may have stopped that attack, but let's see how you fare against the other elements."

The Elemental Enforcer now has his Earth Elemental clone attack her by throwing boulders at her.

Britney leaps toward the boulders with her sword in hand. She has charged her sword with sound, so that as she hits the first boulder, it shatters into pieces. She destroys all but one of the boulders. This makes the Earth Elemental clone so furious that he decides to charge at her himself. As Britney destroys the last boulder, the Earth Elemental clone hits her, causing her to be slammed to the ground. When she starts to get up, he pins her to the ground and says, "Last time I checked, lightning has no effect on stone?"

Britney looks at him and smiles, "That may be true, but aren't you just a bit curious as to how I smashed your oversized golf balls?"

Thinking that she won't be able to escape, he says, "I'll bite. How did you smash through those boulders?"

She answers, "Come closer, and I'll tell you?"

He leans in, but as she speaks, he is thrust from her and to the ground. He is able to get up, but he is in shock. He shouts "What was that?"

Britney replies, "That was the other end of my power. Lightning is not my only power. My power is the power of thunder and lightning. What you just witnessed is the power of thunder throwing you, and it happened by me just using my voice."

The Earth Elemental clone charges her once more, and this time she uses her Bolt Bow. As she pulls back on the energy string, nothing appears. As she lets the string go, no one sees that a thunder arrow has formed. When it hits the Earth Elemental clone, he is stopped for a moment and then begins to disintegrate.

The Elemental Enforcer says, "Impressive! No one has ever taken down one of my clones before. Still, your luck ends here." He signals to the Elemental Eagle and has it attack her in its wind form. As it charges her, she notices something shiny within it. She pulls back on the energy string and aims for that spot. When the bolt of lightning flies and hit its target, the Elemental Eagle stops and begins switching between different elements. Then it crashes to the ground and explodes into pieces.

Looking up, Britney says, "I thought you said my luck was going to run out?"

Now the Elemental Enforcer has his Wind Elemental clone attack her, and as she's thrown to the ground. He says, "Don't taunt me, child, for you do not know who you are dealing with."

Getting up, Britney now wonders how she will be able to beat the Wind Elemental clone. She notices that dust is being created as he comes in for another attack, and she gets an idea.

BRITNEY NOW STARTS TO HEAD TOWARD a sandy area nearby, and the Wind Elemental starts to chase her. When she reaches the right spot, she turns to see the Wind Elemental getting closer. She then pulls out her sword and stabs it into the ground, causing sand particles to be thrown toward the Wind Elemental. While he is distracted by the sand, Britney pulls the energy string back and fires several bolts at him.

When the Elemental Enforcer arrives where she is, he laughs: "Your lightning bolts will not have any effect against my Wind Elemental."

"Don't be so sure about that," Britney says. "Check it out!"

The Elemental Enforcer notices that his wind elemental has now been encased in glass, and he shouts, "What have you done?"

"Here's a fun fact about lightning," she says. "A bolt of lightning can reach about 53,000 degrees, and it takes about 3,200 degrees of heat to make glass. So, when your wind elemental got caught in that sand cloud, I targeted the sand encasing your wind elemental in glass. So, what do you have next?"

Enraged, the Elemental Enforcer then shouts, "Do not lecture me about the power of the elements, child!"

Britney sees that his body is starting to solidify the angrier he gets, and this gives her an idea.

AGENT WALLACE IS TRAINING when Agent Saunders comes in and says, "Here is the information on those students and their families." She hands the list to Agent Wallace.

Agent Wallace looks at it and says, "Good! I'm going to check on the devices we'll need to do proper surveillance. While I do that, go gather the team."

"Yes, Agent Wallace," Saunders replies, "but if I may speak freely: I think it would be better if *you* gathered the team and I check on the devices, since the team would respond better to you than to me."

Agent Wallace thinks about this for a moment and agrees that the logic is sound. "Very well," he says, "go check on the devices while I gather the team."

While she makes her way to the lab where Agents Daniels and Rivera are, Agent Saunders is smiling more than normal. Her plan to keep Agents Wallace and Daniels apart is working.

MOMENTS LATER, WHEN AGENT WALLACE REACHES AND ENTERS the lab, he notices that Agent Daniels is still looking through the translated documents. Suddenly the alarm goes off, and they see the battle occurring between the Bolt Knight and the Elemental Enforcer.

Agent Daniels uses the communication system to contact Agent Martin. "Agent Martin," he says, "we have a disturbance involving one of the knights and an alien. How do you want us to proceed?"

"At the current time," Agent Martin replies, "do not engage, but watch for any weakness that we may exploit and see what you can learn."

"Very well, sir," Agent Daniels says. She then sets the satellite to record the battle, as she continues to look through the documents.

Now Agent Saunders asks, "Hey, Daniels, have you seen Rivera around?"

Turning, Agent Daniels sees Saunders and replies, "I don't know and don't care, but if I had to guess, I'd say she might be in her workshop, which is to the left of me."

"Thanks," Agent Saunders responds, then asks, "By the way, how is the research going?"

"At the moment, nothing new," Daniels answers, "but the more I look at these documents the more I feel that something is off. I just can't put my finger on it yet."

Before she can expound any further on this matter, Agent Saunders walks in to the main part of the lab. When Agent Rivera sees her, she says, "Why, hello, Agent Saunders. What brings you to my lab today?"

Smiling Saunders says "Agent Wallace is gathering the team and sent me to come check on the surveillance devices that we recently requested."

Rivera pauses a moment and then says, "What surveillance devices are you talking about? I don't remember getting any request for surveillance devices?"

"Cut your garbage, Rivera!" Agent Saunders says. "I came to you specifically with the written request. Now, where are the devices?"

Smiling, Rivera answers, "The devices are right here."

Suddenly eleven more Agent Rivera come walking into the main part of the lab. They all say in unison, "How may we help you, Agent Saunders?"

Startled, Saunders asks, "What are these things?"

The twelve Agent Rivera then revert to robots, and the real Agent Rivera says, "So, what do you think of my SUDs?"

Shaking her head, Agent Saunders answers, "Rivera, we asked for surveillance devices, not these things?"

"True," Rivera answers, wiping her glasses. "Originally, I was working on the wireless handheld devices, but I realized there was a major problem."

Now looking at her with a scowl, Agent Saunders says, "What problem?"

"Simply put," Agent Rivera responds, "there are twelve students that have escaped from Agent Martin, which means there are twelve targets, and we only have seven, including Daniels and myself on the team. So, what I've done is create these SUDs, which stands for Special Undercover drones. Their purpose is to observe, track and report any and all activity coming from the families of the twelve students."

Clenching her fists, Agent Saunders shouts, "This is not what we requested!"

JUST THEN AGENT WALLACE COMES IN WITH THE TEAM. Seeing this confrontation, he asks, "What's going on here?"

"Nothing," says Rivera. "I was just explaining to Agent Saunders that there was a problem in regard to the surveillance gear requested, and I fixed that problem by creating what I call SUDs, which stands for Special Undercover drones. These drones can assume any human likeness and blend in, using cloaking technology that we were able to adapt from Brykar and his people."

Agent Wallace begins to examine the SUDs, and as he does so, one of them transforms to look just like him. It even starts moving like him. He grabs for the drone and is surprised to find that it feels human. "How is this possible?" he asks.

"Apparently," Rivera answers, "some of the tech Brykar gave us has the ability to look and feel like human tissue. So, using that tech, I created these."

Wallace is now smiling broadly. "These are fantastic, Rivera," he says, "what is their main purpose?"

She smiles in return and answers, "Their mission is to observe, track and report any and all activities among the families of the twelve students."

"So, let me get this straight," Wallace says. "With these SUDs, as you call them, we will be able to view and assess the data that they collect?"

"Precisely," Rivera answers, feeling very proud of herself. "Follow me," she adds, "and I'll show you where you can monitor the data they collect."

WHILE THE ARC TEAM GOES to the area where they can view the data sent by the SUDs, Britney continues to hold her own against the Elemental Enforcer. She reaches out to Manuel telepathically and asks, "How is Des doing?"

"He won't last much longer," Manuel answers, holding Des, who is twitching in pain. "We need to restore their powers immediately."

"I have an idea that I'm working on," Britney says. "Stand by."

Manuel replies, "Hopefully, it'll work. I'll keep you posted on Des' condition."

"No need, Manuel," she says. "Besides, I don't want Jessica coming after me, thinking I'm going for her guy. Although, if we're going to beat this guy, Des will probably be the best one to come up with an answer."

Even as she says this, the Elemental Enforcer sends his Fire Elemental after her. As he walks toward her, the sand under him starts to turn to glass. He says, "You aren't the only one who can make glass, little girl."

"True," she says, looking at him, "but you are the one I'm least worried about."

Chuckling at that, he asks, "Why's that?"

"Simple," she replies. "Fire safety was the very first thing I learned about. So, bring it on, hot stuff!"

Now laughing, the Fire Elemental says, "Very well! Take this!" And he sends a blast of fire at her. Britney is able to leap away from it and fire three lightning bolt arrows. "What are those supposed to do to me?" he asks.

"To you, nothing," Britney says, landing safely on her feet, "but they weren't meant for you ..."

Before she can finish her sentence, the lightning arrows hit the Elemental Enforcer's hands, causing the elemental extractors he is wearing to short out. When he sees this, he shouts, "What have you done?"

Smiling, she answers, "Hopefully, I've gotten my friends their powers back."

Now the Elemental Enforcer's hands begin to shake and his gloves self-destruct, freeing the powers absorbed by them.

AS THE POWERS OF THE KNIGHTS BEGIN RETURN TO THEM, Manuel watches as Des returns to normal. He immediately contacts Britney and informs her: "Whatever you did ... it worked! Their powers have returned and Des is okay."

Now Britney's smile broadens to fill her whole face. "Perfect!" she says. Then she turns to the Elemental Enforcer and says, "I hate to leave a party early, but this is simply boring. See ya around, hun." And, with that, she ports to where the BOD BOTS are, and the other knights port back to their base.

BRITTANY NOW GOES TO THE EACH KNIGHT'S BOD BOTS, and touches it. As she does this, she is able to undo the negative effects of the electromagnetic pulse they were hit with earlier. Once they are all fully online again, she says, "Let's get back to the base before the Elemental Enforcer gets here. Besides, I think I have an idea about how we can beat him."

BRYKAR AND GENERAL SADOOM BOTH WATCH as the knights escape. Brykar observes, "These humans are like bugs, and they're becoming a nuisance."

"Yes," General Sadoom agrees, "but you never mentioned to me you suspected they were human."

"Forgive me, General Sadoom," Brykar answers. "I wanted to be sure before I let you know. Now I'm almost positive they *are* human."

"You should have informed me," Sadoom says. "What is evident is that these knights are very clever and resourceful. Be careful when dealing with them, Brykar, or they might destroy you and your crew."

The communication fades.

WHEN THE ELEMENTAL ENFORCER RETURNS TO BRYKAR'S SHIP, Brykar is anxiously waiting for him. "What happened?" he asks. "I watched you. You nearly had the knights. And this girl ... this human girl bested you."

Kneeling, the Elemental Enforcer says, "Commander Brykar, she has not bested me yet, for it was my elemental forms she faced. She still has to face *me* and my full power. I know you do not tolerate failure, and I assure you I will not fail. This time, when I face her, she and her fellow knights will fall."

Looking at him with contempt, Brykar says, "Lucky for you, I feel like giving you one last chance to defeat her and the knights. However, you will not be given additional equipment, seeing as how you squandered the previous equipment that I gave you. So, whatever you have left is at your disposal. Now, get out of my sight before I vaporize you myself."

"As you wish, Commander Brykar," the Elemental Enforcer replies.

AS BRYKAR LEAVES, the Elemental Enforcer goes to the lab and uses the equipment there to salvage pieces of the Elemental Eagle. Once he has all the pieces he can find, he begins to combine those pieces with the tech for the Elemental Extractors, so that his new creation will steal the powers of the knights, while he handles the Bolt Knight.

As he is making the last adjustments to his new creation, Brykar comes in. Seeing what the Elemental Enforcer is doing, he says, "I thought I told you that you were not allowed any new equipment. Now, give me one good reason..."

Before Brykar can finish this statement, the Elemental Enforcer says, "Commander Brykar, forgive me for interrupting you, but what I've done is combine the tech from the Elemental Extractors and the Elemental Eagle, to create the Elemental Eagle Extractor, which will steal the powers of the knights while I deal with this girl. You told me before that I could use what I had, and that is what I have done."

For a moment, Brykar thinks to himself, then says, "Very well, you may use it." Then, without warning, he slaps the Elemental Enforcer, knocking him into the wall. "You are not forgiven," Brykar adds. "Always remember: never interrupt me."

Getting the point, the Elemental Enforcer replies, "Yes, Commander Brykar." As the Elemental Enforcer leaves the ship, he sends the Elemental Eagle out to find the knights.

MEANWHILE, AS THE KNIGHTS SPEND TIME RECOVERING in their base, everyone is in the lab trying to figure out how to beat the Elemental Enforcer. Britney says, "I think I know of a way to beat him, but I'm not sure if it will work or not."

"What's your idea?" Joseph asks.

Before she can answer, Des interjects, "I agree. It's not like we were able to do anything ourselves."

Britney takes a breath and then says, "I noticed that the Elemental Enforcer can only hold his Elemental forms when he's calm and focused. So, I was thinking: if we can keep messing with his temper enough, we'll have a shot at beating him."

Thinking about what she has said, Des goes to the computer to look at the data. After going over it, he says, "Britney's right. Apparently, from these readings, it takes an enormous amount of energy and focus to maintain those clones and forms. In fact, if we can get him to recreate all four elemental clones, he might not have enough energy to use his lightning form, as that apparently uses the most energy."

Concerned, Eric says, "I have a question. What if he tries to steal our powers again. If he does, that will mean Britney will have to fight him on her own again."

Looking over the recording of the fight, Des notices that their powers were restored when the gloves of the Elemental Enforcer were destroyed. He begins typing on the console and then says, "Hey, everyone, come check this out."

As the knights gather around the screen, which shows two gloves, Eric asks, "What are we looking at, Des?"

"The gloves you see on the screen," Des answers, "are called Elemental Extractors, and from the data of the fight, plus looking through the archives, I see that these are his particular weapons of choice."

"Okay," Eric says. "Now that we know what he used to put us down, how do we stop him from using it again? I mean, even though Britney damaged them, more than likely he'll want to repair them and use them again."

Des again scans through the footage of the fight and notices that there was a gem that glowed on each glove, just as it began to drain their powers. "Look at this!" he says, and he freezes the screen. "Those gems on the gloves, I believe, are the power source and also where our powers were stored. If we can destroy the gems, we should be able to prevent him from being able to absorb our powers again. Any questions?"

Shaking his head, Eric answers, "Yeah! How exactly are we supposed to do this?"

Just then the alarm in the lab goes off. Des uses the scanners to find out what is going on, and notices the Elemental Eagle. When Britney sees it, she is astonished. "What the heck?" she says. "I destroyed that thing."

"Apparently he has rebuilt it," Des says.

Just then Des notices a shine coming from the wings. As he zooms in, he says, "We might have just caught a break. Look at this." What he is showing the other knights is that the gems from the Elemental Extractors have been placed on the wings of the Elemental Eagle. "Britney," he says, "do you think you would be able to hit those gems with your Bolt Bow?"

She smiles at the thought of it and replies, "Easily!"

"Good," Des continues, "cause I have plan. I'll need you to create a clone in your new armor and have it lure out the Elemental Enforcer with the rest of us. As this new creation of his starts to drain our powers, you use your lightning arrows and destroy those gems. Once they are destroyed, we should be able to get him to generate those Elemental clones again, causing him to exhaust his powers." It sounds good to everyone, and they all nod in agreement with this plan.

WHILE BRITNEY CREATES HER CLONE, Eric is still feeling a bit uneasy about the plan. Still, even he can admit that the logic of the plan is sound. When Britney is finished, she sends the clone out, then goes to Des and asks, "Where do you want me to be, so we can take out this flying freak?"

Des uses the scanners to look for a good position and notices a cliff above the cave where they had the emergency team find them. Pointing to the screen, he says, "This looks like the best vantage point because it's far enough away, while providing the right amount of cover."

"Good," she replies. "Hopefully, this will work."

Concerned now, Des asks, "Hey, Britney, are you okay?"

"I'm okay," she responds. I've just never had a plan rely on me before, so I'm kind of nervous."

"I understand your concern," Des says, "but to be honest, if it wasn't for you and your quick thinking, we might not have even have gotten this much information."

"What do you mean by that?" she asks.

He chuckles and replies, "What I mean is that *you* shouldn't feel nervous because you showed a lot of skill, taking out two of those elemental clones and the Elemental Eagle. On top of that, you were able to destroy the devices that stole our powers and so those powers were restored to us."

Realizing that Des is right, Britney is now all smiles.

AS BRITTANY LEAVES, SHE PASSES BY ERIC, who seems to have been watching her intently. She notices this and asks, "Hey, Eric, what's your deal?"

"What do you mean?" he asks in return.

"I mean, I know you always look at what can go wrong with a plan, but this time you seem overly concerned about me, and I would like to know why?"

Shaking his head, Eric says, "Sorry if I have weirded you out. I was just concerned about putting you in harms way, especially since this guy came so close to ending us all. Just be safe out there, okay?"

Smiling again, Britney says, "Wow! So, there actually is a heart underneath that brooding exterior. Even if you won't admit it, it's nice to know you care." She then blows him a kiss and ports out of the base to where she needs to be.

Eric now joins the other knights. Noticing what has just taken place, John makes a mental note to talk to his friend about it later.

ONCE BRITNEY'S CLONE REACHES THE AREA where the Elemental Eagle Extractor is located, she shouts, "I see that you fixed that, flying freak, but I'll make sure this time that it is destroyed for good."

The Elemental Enforcer appears and says, "Yes, I did, you foolish girl, but this time it has some modifications, as you will soon see. By the way, where are the rest of your fellow knights? Don't tell me they are afraid of facing me again?"

Before Britney responds, the other knights arrive, and Joseph says, "We're not afraid of you or your ego. We just had something more important to take care of."

Laughing, the Elemental Enforcer says, "Oh, so there *is* something more important than me? I sincerely doubt it."

Britney's clone replies, "What's the matter? Can't handle the fact of being second place?"

"I'm second to no one, child, as you and your friends shall soon see," responds the Elemental Enforcer, and he recreates the four elemental clones. Then the rest of the knights suddenly appear.

AS THE ELEMENTAL EAGLE EXTRACTOR FINDS AND FLIES toward the knights, preparing to steal their powers again, the gems in its wings begin to glow. The real Britney pulls the energy string of her bolt bow back and fires three lighting arrows, shattering both gems. The third arrow strikes the Elemental Eagle Extractor, causing it to explode.

When the Elemental Enforcer sees this, he is horrified and shouts, "My Eagle! But how? All of you are here."

He then remembers that one of the knights had used a clone before and says, "Clever!" He points to Britney and says, "So, this time *you* are the clone. You have humiliated me for the last time, child." And he has the four elemental clones attack her.

Now a huge stone wall appears and Des says, "Did you forget about us so quickly?" He and the other knights surround Brittany, and the real Britney appears, recalling her clone. She steps in front of her friends and says, "It's time to end this. And you," she adds, addressing the Elemental Enforcer.

The Elemental Enforcer smiles at this and says, "Let's see what you've got, child?"

Joseph looks at Brittany and says, "Now we've got them! Go take this guy out."

Hearing this, the Elemental Enforcer shouts, "Do you really think she is capable of defeating me when you knights stood by and did nothing? Let me show you my power!" He surprises the knights by switching to his lightning form.

Seeing this, Des tells Britney telepathically, "Don't let him rattle you. If I'm right, he's doing this to show his strength. But without our powers fueling him, I don't think he'll be able to keep it up long."

"Let's see what you've got, Enforcer," she now shouts, and she charges the Elemental Enforcer.

WHILE BRITNEY IS FACING THE ELEMENTAL ENFORCER, the other knights face the elemental clones. Maggie, Tasha and Sally take on the Fire Elemental. Brad, Joseph and Max make their stand against the Earth Elemental. Jessica and Janet get ready to deal with the Wind Elemental. And, finally, Des, Eric and John take their stand against the Water Elemental.

The Fire Elemental grins and says, "Let's see what you girls got?" He starts throwing fireballs at them, and the girls scatter.

Maggie shouts, "Is that the best you've got, hot stuff?"

"Do you really have to antagonize this hothead?" asks Tasha, looking askance at Maggie.

"Why not?" Maggie replies. "It's not like he can actually touch us."

The Fire Elemental points his hand and starts firing fireballs from that hand. As the girls run for cover, the Elemental Enforcer pauses for a moment in his approach to Britney. She then tells the others telepathically, "That's it! Keep it up! The more energy you cause his clones to use, the harder it will be for him to maintain his lightning form."

Tasha shakes her head and says, "Hey, fire fool, who taught you how to shoot the three blind mice?"

Sally chimes in, "Naw! this fire freak is as blind as a bat."

The Fire Elemental begins shouting at the girls, "You will *not* mock me!" He aims at them with both arms and fires blades from his hands. The blades begin to extend, and he tries to slice the girls, who, nevertheless, continue to taunt him.

BRAD, JOSEPH AND MAX BEGIN TO ATTACK the Earth Elemental, who says, "Don't think I will be as easily angered as the Fire Elemental. It won't happen."

Brad shouts, "We wouldn't dream of insulting the all-powerful Earth Elemental."

Seeing what Brad is doing, Joseph chuckles and joins in, "I agree.

It would be futile for us to try to anger the great and powerful Earth Elemental."

Max follows suit, "Oh, great Earth Elemental, don't destroy us with your *great* power."

The Earth Elemental says, "I will *not* be patronized by you children. If you want to see my power, I will show it to you." With this, he takes a stone boulder from in front of him, breaks it into thin sharp spikes and hurls them at the three boys. Joseph puts one hand forward and creates a shield, blocking the spikes.

Actually impressed by this, the Earth Elemental says, "Very impressive! Let's see how you handle *this*." Now he has the earth beneath them open up, and as the three knights begin to fall, he starts to cause the ground above them to seal back over.

WHEN THE THREE BOYS START TO FALL, Joseph looks at Brad and Max, and the three of them in unison engage their knight wings. Joseph tells Brad. "Drill a hole for us, will ya, Bro?"

Brad answers, "On it!" He takes the lead. He has two beams of fire come from his hands, to act as a drill, and they soon fly back to the surface.

The Earth Elemental, thinking that he got rid of the knight, says, "Just as I thought! They were all talk!"

Suddenly, the earth shakes beneath him, and the three knights emerge. Brad says, "We're back! Did you miss us?"

Max shouts, "You showed us your power. Now we'll show you *ours*." He then creates two clones, and the three of them begin to attack the Earth Elemental.

The Earth Elemental now puts two of them in stone cases. He then has spikes emerge from within the cases, to pierce the two knight clones. Max has the clones return to him. Max falls to one knee as he begins to feel the pain his clones are feeling. The Earth Elemental now begins to get angry, and the Elemental Enforcer pauses once more. Britney notices that he's having a harder and harder time maintaining his elemental form and knows that their plan is working.

JESSICA AND JANET ARE FACING THE WIND ELEMENTAL. Janet says,

"Quick question! How do we hit something that's not there?"

The Wind Elemental smiles and says, "The answer is simple. You don't! Now, let me show you why you will not beat me, little girls."

Undaunted, Jessica smiles and says, "Get real! No one is invincible. Whatever your weakness is, we will find it."

"Okay," he answers, "let's see what you girls have then."

"Tell me how we got stuck with this overgrown wind bag,"Janet says.

"I don't know. I guess we were just the lucky ones," Jessica replies.

As the two female knights try to come up with a plan to defeat the Wind Elemental, Jessica looks to Janet and says, "I have an idea. Follow my lead."

The two knights then charge at the Wind Elemental, and Jessica uses her water powers and begins firing ice beams at him. When the beam hits the arm of the Wind Elemental, that part of his arm is encased in ice, and he is unable to move it.

Before Jessica can fire another shot, he severs the arm encased in ice. Since the Wind Elemental is made of wind, a new arm forms immediately. He then says, "Big mistake, girls! Now I'm about to blow you all away."

WHILE JESSICA AND JANET DEAL WITH THIS, Des, Eric and John are busy with the Water Elemental. Eric looks at Des and says, "Have any idea about how we are going to beat this thing?"

"To be honest," Des says, "I have no clue."

The Water Elemental then says, "I will not be beaten by you knights, and I will show you why."

Des looks at the Elemental Enforcer and says to the knights telepathically, "It looks like the plan is working. The Elemental Enforcer is flickering more and more in his lightning form."

As Des and the other continue to dodge the elemental clones' attacks, he has an idea. He now faces the Water Elemental and says, "You don't have any power, you wet blanket."

Laughing at this, the Water Elemental says, "Unlike the other elemental clones, my personality is not so easily provoked. However, if you wish to see my power, then I will show you."

Before Des the others know what's happening, they are hit with a powerful blast that knocks them off their feet. Eric looks at Des and says, "It looks like you got his attention."

BRITNEY WATCHES as the other knights fight against the elemental clones. The Elemental Enforcer just looks at her. She says, "You know, if you take a picture, it will last longer, right?"

He answers, "You and I both know what is happening. Although you and your friends were clever to figure it out, I will not be beaten so easily. Now, let me show you my true power."

Using the power of lightning, the Elemental Enforcer charges himself and begins to attack Britney, who tries her best to dodge his attacks. He shouts, "What's the matter, child? Are you afraid of me now?"

Britney knows that if she's hit by one of these attacks, she will be toast.

The Elemental Enforcer says, "If you won't fight me, I'll make sure your friends pay with their lives."

AS THE OTHER KNIGHTS WONDER WHAT HE'S TALKING ABOUT, the elemental clones unleash an unbelievable assault against them, pinning them to the ground. "Now, fight me or your friends are finished!" shouts the Elemental Enforcer.

"Fine!" Britney replies. "I'll fight you, but if I win, you have to let my friends go."

He chuckles at that and says "That's a very big *if*. But, yes, if you win, I'll let your friends go."

Britney steps forward, her eyes locked on the Elemental Enforcer. Just then, he charges for her. With her sword in hand, she dodges and strikes his side, knocking him to the ground.

The Elemental Enforcer quickly recovers, but he is wondering how he was able to be hit him in his lightning form. Britney wonders the same. Then she remembers that lightning can have both positive and negative charges. She says to him, "Looks like you're not as smart as you thought you were. I was able to channel my power through my sword to produce a charge opposite of the one you generate."

"Foolish girl!" he shouts in answer. "I'm the power of all the elements combined, as you will now see." He now has his elemental clones return to him.

The other knights now watch as Britney faces the Elemental Enforcer with all five elements. He shouts, "I will not be beaten by the likes of you, little girl." He charges and hits her, sending her flying to the floor, while the other knights remain pinned. The only thing they can do is watch as Britney faces the Elemental Enforcer alone.

When Britney gets up, he begins to pummel her. With each strike, she is wondering how she might beat him. Then she remembers what her father once said, "… look at the heart of the matter and understand that true power comes not from a person's wealth, but from their heart." She realizes that even the Elemental Enforcer has a heart, just as she does. As his next strike is about to hit her, she ports away and starts to say, "As the days of darkness surround, where no hero can be found…"

The Elemental Enforcer is shocked at how she has escaped and says, "You will not escape me."

She turns to face him and continues to say, "While those who descend and prey on the weak, who do not rise or dare to speak…"

He starts to throw fire, water and wind blasts. He even throws boulders at Britney, but she is somehow able to dodge them all effortlessly. She continues to say, "We will utter our heartfelt cry, as we raise our hands to the sky…."

Angry and shocked at what she's doing, he charges at her, but she is able to finish what she was saying, "To protect the world from loss, I am a Knight of the Cross!" When she finishes saying this, she ports away from him. Then, drawing her bow, she pulls back on the energy string, and a combination thunder and lightning arrow appears. Just before letting the arrow fly, she ports to a position in front of the Elemental Enforcer and says to him, "Gotcha!" With that, she lets the arrow fly so that it pierces his lightning form and strikes his very heart, causing him to crash to the ground.

As he gets up, he grabs his chest. His powers are beginning to go haywire. He tries to speak, "What … have … you … done?"

Britney can't help herself. She chuckles and says, "Simple! Everything has a heart, including you. All I did was make sure to hit my target."

The Elemental Enforcer falls to the ground and where his legs should have been are now stones and a smoldering fire. Where his arms should have been is lightning and a puddle of water. Where his chest should have been is a small tornado and a microscopic cube that looks to be nearly destroyed. Suddenly the prison holding the knights fades.

AS THE KNIGHTS BEGIN TO GET UP, they all rush to Britney's side. "Are you okay?" Eric asks

She starts to chuckle and then answers, "Awww, I never knew you cared!"

"I just wanted to make sure you were okay," he responds, "cause it looked like you really took a beating is all." He walks away, and they all port back to the base.

ONCE THEY ARE ALL BACK AT THE BASE, Des says to Britney, "I have to admit, the way you beat the Elemental Enforcer was genius. It gave me a deeper insight into how our powers work, but I'll need time to test my theory."
Joseph agrees with Des, "How you beat the Elemental Enforcer was genius, and going forward I don't think any one of us should be doubting ourselves."

MEANWHILE, THE ARC TEAM IS IN THE SUD REVIEW ROOM WAITING. Agent Rivera is about to activate her newest creation, so that they can learn just what happened to the teens who escaped from Agent Martin. Impatient, Agent Wallace asks, "How much longer do we have to wait, Rivera?"

"My! My! Why such a hurry, Agent Wallace?" Agent Rivera asks. "This procedure is very delicate. Are you in such a hurry with everything?" She has asked it in a slightly seductive tone, all the while looking toward Agent Daniels.

Agent Saunders says, "Honestly, Rivera, can you stop and stay on target for once? None of us has time for your garbage."

"My! My! Aren't we the touchy one, Saunders!" Rivera says. "I was only having a little fun. And, besides, the SUDs need to be activated at the same time in order not to arouse suspicion. If they know they are being watched, our efforts will be for nothing."

Just then Agent Rivera receives the notification that all the SUDs are in place, and she presses a button on the console. A voice says, "SUD activation code required."

Agent Rivera says, "Activation code, SNOOPER."

The voice then responds, "SUDs are now fully active."

Once they are activated, Rivera then has them begin to scan for people who can blend in and watch the houses of the teens, still not realizing they are the knights.

As the SUDs begin to blend in with their surroundings, by taking on human faces, Agent Wallace says, "This is fantastic! With these things watching their homes, we'll be able to find out just where these teens are and finally get some answers."

"All right, Miles and Stanton," he continues, "you two take the first shift. Agents Rivera and Ryan, you two take the second shift. Agent Saunders and I will take the third shift. Is that understood?" The agents agree.

As Agents Miles and Stanton sit down, Agent Wallace walks over to Agent Daniels and asks, "Have you found anything else that may be of use to us?"

She turns and looks at him. Then, shaking her head, she says, "Not really, although I recorded the last fight the knights had and noticed something that may be of use to us. But I will need more time to analyze it. More than likely, before I can do it, I'll have to call Agent Martin to see if I may review the data."

"Good," Agent Wallace replies, "because we definitely need to know what exactly we are dealing with here."

Now Agent Daniels asks, "Why is it so important for you to know what's going on?"

"Let's just say," he answers, "that I don't trust anyone who is willing to just share specialized tech, like we've received." Without fully explaining what he means by this, he adds, "I gotta run. I'll check in later." And he quickly exits the lab.

WHILE THE ARC TEAM MONITORS THE SUDS, Graham has just finished the very first cipher message to the families and is beginning to put addresses on the envelopes. He gets up to stretch and notices a weird-looking figure outside his window. He thinks to himself, "I need to keep an eye on *that* guy." Then he goes back and finishes addressing the envelopes, for he knows that Phillip will soon be by to pick up the mail.

When he finishes, he puts the letters in a big envelope and puts that envelope in the mailbox. Within minutes, Phillip comes by, making his afternoon rounds.

He takes the envelope out of the box and walks back to his postal vehicle. He is excited and anxious to open the envelope, hoping that Graham has discovered something that will be useful to them all in locating their loved ones.

Phillip makes the drive back to the postal center and then takes all of the outgoing mail he has collected with him into the post office, minus the large envelope, which he takes home with him.

He opens the envelope only when he is safe in the privacy of his study. There he finds a paper with some very weird wording on it. He needs the cipher that Graham sent to read it. With the aid of the cipher, he is able to translate it. It says: "Wait three days before delivering these to avoid suspicion."

Also inside the large envelope are twelve smaller envelopes. One of them is addressed to him and his wife. Just as he opens it, his wife comes downstairs. "Are you okay?" she asks.

He smiles and answers, "Yeah! Just going through the mail."

"Did we get anything from Graham," she asks, "that may help us to know what's going on?" Although he wants to tell her the truth, Phillip decides to tell her no, at least not until he's gotten used to using the cipher and to understand the messages Graham will be sending. "Well, okay," she says. "If we haven't gotten anything, then come and have dinner."

"I will, sweetheart," he says, smiling, "I just want to sort through this mail. Can you give me about twenty minutes?"

"Of course, my love," she responds, kissing him on the cheek. And then heads to the kitchen.

Phillip looks at the mail in front of him and has second thoughts. He puts the coded message underneath his nightly crossword puzzle for safe keeping and heads to the kitchen to have dinner with his family.

CHAPTER 12

SHADOWS AND SECRETS: SHADOWS OF THE PAST

WHILE PHILLIP AND HIS WIFE, LINDA, EAT DINNER, his mind is elsewhere. She can tell that something is wrong with him, so she asks again, "Is everything okay, sweetheart?"

Hearing her voice, he snaps out of his thoughts and replies, "Yeah, I'm just worried about the kids and wish there was more we could do for them."

She smiles at him and says, "I know. This has been hard on both of us, especially since he's the last piece of my sister I have. But he's more than our nephew; he's become our son, and I don't know what to do without him."

Looking at his distraught wife, Phillip thinks, "She's right." He had become their son, and he was going to do everything he could to find out what really happened. Then, nervously, he says, "Darling, I have something to tell you. Please don't be too upset with me."

"What's is it, dear?" she asks, suddenly alarmed.

He continues, "You came into the study earlier as I was going through the mail, and when you asked me if I had heard from Graham in regard to the kids, I lied. I had just gotten a package, and the note inside stated that I should wait to deliver the test page of the communications Graham will be sending and the way to decode it until three days from now. I haven't had a chance to use the cipher Graham sent to decode the test message to us, but I was concerned about telling you, because I knew how much you were hurting."

She bows her head for just a moment and then asks, "Then how about we decode that test message after dinner and find out what news Graham has for us?"

He likes the idea, and it brings him a moment of joy. "That sound like a plan," he says. Then he continues, "Although ... I do have a question to ask."

"What is it, sweetheart?" she asks with a coy smile.

"I honestly thought you would be more upset with me for not telling you about this," he explains. She gets up, walks over to him and, kissing him on the cheek, says, "Darling, it does bother me that you didn't want to tell me about the package, but I also know that it was because you were concerned for my feelings, which is really sweet and thoughtful. Now, let's finish up here so we can get that message decoded."

Smiling broadly at his wife, Phillip replies, "Okay, my love." He returns her kiss, and then carries the dirty dishes to the kitchen, placing them in the sink.

When he returns to the dining room, he finds his wife looking expectantly at him. "Are you ready, sweetheart?" she asks. He nods and they go together to the study.

IN THE STUDY, PHILLIP PULLS OUT THE MESSAGE addressed to him and his wife. They open it, and Phillip gets out the cipher they will use to decode it. Together, the two begin the arduous process. It takes time, but when they have finished, they are able to read: "I've just begun my research into what happened with the bus incident, and am not finding a lot of information. I've sent this message as a test to let you all know and so that everyone can be informed. Updates will be made weekly."

The couple looks at each other. This is a disappointment. They were both hoping for more. They can only hope that Graham will be able to find more information about what has happened and where their children are.

THE SUD STANDING OUTSIDE PHILLIP'S HOME has been monitoring the house, as directed, while Agents Miles and Stanton watch the monitors, trying to find out if the families know anything about the escaped teens. Agent Stanton asks Miles, "Hey, do you have any idea what we're supposed to be looking for?"

"To be honest, no," Miles responds. "Although my specialty is communications, that's more with hidden communications and with communication tech. If I had to guess what we need to do first, it is to look for any weird or abnormal patterns, so we will know where to go from there."

Agent Miles has an idea. He begins to use the SUDs audio sensors to listen in and see what the range is, and he notices that he's only able to hear anything within a seventy-five-foot radius. While he wonders why the range is so short, Agent Rivers comes in and asks "How's it going, boys?"

"It's going as well as can be expected," Agent Miles answers. "I have a question. Why is the range of the SUDs so short?"

"The reason for that," Agent Rivers answers, "is that most of our long-range listening devices would interfere with the SUDs' other functions, so I had to shorten the range so that they would be fully functional while in the field."

Agents Stanton and Miles look at each other, thinking the answer is a little odd. But, given the fact that Agent Rivera is the robotics expert, they don't question it further. Instead, they go back to watching the monitors.

After a while, a slightly annoyed Agent Stanton asks, "How many more hours do we have to do this?"

Agent Miles shakes his head and says "We still have six hours to go. Like you, I can't wait for this detail to be over. But it *would* be good if we can at least find some information that would give us a clue as to what is going on. For now, all we can do is monitor what's happening and report anything suspicious."

"You mean like that?" Stanton asks, pointing to the screen, where they see April, the girlfriend of Eric's father, sneaking out, getting in her car and driving off.

"Yes," replies Agent Miles, "like that." He has the SUD follow her. "Let's see where this girl is headed?" he adds.

FURIOUS WITH THE KNIGHTS and his own inability to finish them off quickly, the next day Brykar goes to where the Elemental Enforcer was defeated and makes sure to collect the microscopic box that was the heart of the creature. Upon his return, he places the cube in the restoration chamber. Then, as he enters his quarters, General Sadoom appears. Brykar falls to his knees and says, "Greetings, General Sadoom! What can I do for you?"

"Brykar," Sadoom says, "we are not pleased with your performance right now. Out of all the scouting commanders, you are and have been the one to always get the most results. However, since you've encountered these 'knights,' you have had one failure after another. So, here's what I suggest you do: stop focusing on the knights and begin understanding the earthlings' normal defenses. Once that has been discovered, we will deal with the knights, and they will be no more. Also," he continues, "I suggest that if you must send a warrior to fight them, let it be to distract the knights from our purpose."

Brykar can only nod in agreement. He asks General Sadoom, "What did you mean by *we?*"

Sadoom chuckles and replies, "Why, me and the other nine generals. Trust me, if this were to go any further, you would already be pulled off that planet and tortured beyond your wildest nightmares. Brykar, you yourself know that failure is not tolerated. It is only because of your past achievements that we have granted you amnesty for your most recent setbacks."

"There will be no more setbacks, General Sadoom," Brykar replies. "I promise you that."

"There had better not be," Sadoom warns, "but just so that you understand: whether the knights defeat your warriors or not is of little concern. What we need to know is if the earthlings have other tech that could be used against us once the invasion begins. Now, do not disappoint me further, Brykar. If you do, this will be the last time." And the transmission abruptly ends.

BRYKAR WALKS TO THE CHAMBER where his remaining warriors are stored. He slowly passes by them, stopping to consider each. When he comes to Brillander, a crystal warrior who can both disperse and focus energy, he makes his decision. "Yes," he says, "he will do nicely!"

Brykar releases Brillander, who says, "Now, that's what I call a nap! How may I serve you, Brykar?"

"I need to handle some business outside the ship," Brykar explains, "and I need *you* to keep some pests out of my hair. Can you do that?"

"No problem, Brykar," Brillander replies. "This will be my time to shine like the star I am. So, who are these pests I'm fighting?"

Brykar points to a monitor that shows clips from previous battles with the knights and says, "They call themselves the Knights of the Cross, and they have become a bit of a nuisance that needs to be dealt with. Is that clear?"

Chuckling with delight, Brillander responds, "We're clear. Crystal clear."

Pointing to the hanger where Brillander can get his weapons and vehicle, Brykar says, "In this hanger, you will find your weapons and vehicles. Choose a vehicle and keep those knights busy."

Brillander immediately heads into the hanger. He grabs his Gemstone Gloves and sees a Magnacycle he likes. With one touch, he converts it into a Crystalcycle and races off to find the knights.

DES HAS BEEN GOING OVER THE DATA OF THE LAST BATTLE and notices that the Elemental Enforcer was able to absorb powers that, as far as he knew, were not elemental powers. While he continues to look over the data, Joseph and the other knights all enter the lab and wonder the same thing. Joseph asks, "Any idea on how the Elemental Enforcer was able to absorb the others' power the way he did?"

"To be honest," Des answers, "I'm not exactly sure. I'm just as puzzled about it as you are."

Suddenly Manuel appears behind them and steps into the conversation. "I believe I can answer that question for you, my young friends."

"Okay, Manuel." Eric says, "if you know how he was able to absorb our powers, spill it."

"Eric," Joseph warns, "step back." Then he continues, "Manuel, if you know something, please tell us, so we can understand what's going on."

Manuel says, "Follow me, and I will explain." As they follow Manuel to the library, Eric says to Joseph, "I hope we get some answers cause I hate being left in the dark."

"I know how you feel," Joseph replies, "but all things considered, I understand why nothing has been said up until now." Before either of them can say anything else, they reach the library.

AS THEY ENTER THE LIBRARY, Manuel says, "When the Psystructs first started attacking other planets, the armors you are wearing were created, but in order to power them, we needed elemental energy from the core of a planet."

Des interrupts, "Are you saying that our powers are elemental powers from another planet?"

"No," Manuel answers patiently, "each of your powers comes from a planet."

"Let me get this straight," Eric buts in, trying to understand what Manuel is saying. "Each of our powers came from a different planet?"

"Yes," Manuel continues, "each of your powers comes from the elemental energy of a planet. And, just as there are twelve of you, there were twelve planets that gave their elemental energy so that your armors could be complete."

The knights stand awestruck by this explanation. Then Manuel continues, "As you know, the Psystructs began conquering whatever planets they could, and while there was a chance to stop them, the armors you're wearing were forged, one from each of the twelve planets. But, just as the armors were completed, the Psystructs attacked each of the twelve planets at the same time, forcing each of the planets to send their armor as far away as possible. Then, shortly after the armors were launched into space, each of the planets exploded, as the armors traveled here to Earth, where Justice and I were able to track them down."

"Okay," Des says, "that explains how the Elemental Enforcer was able to absorb our powers, but what about the Seductive Siren with that BOD Bot of hers?"

Manuel shakes his head and replies, "Even I'm not fully sure how she did that, but in time we shall see. I'm sorry I didn't tell you all of this sooner, but I didn't want to overwhelm you with the origins of your armor."

Obviously agitated, Eric now jumps up and says, "Good point! Don't tell us something that might help us know not to engage a crazed Psystruct warrior capable of absorbing our powers!" And, with that, he storms off. John goes after him.

BEFORE ANYTHING ELSE CAN BE SAID, Des's alarm goes off, and he checks on what the disturbance is, using the computers in the library. After a few moments, he says "What a surprise! It looks like we have another of Brykar's warriors looking for a fight."

Joseph responds, "If they want a fight, then let's give them one."

Britney adds, "What about Eric and John?"

"I'll tell John and Eric," Manuel replies, "and have them join you."

The other knights quickly transform, race to their BOD Bots, and once they're activated, head out to deal with Brykar's newest warrior.

WHILE THE KNIGHTS PREPARE FOR THEIR UPCOMING BATTLE, Eric is already in a battle of his own. When he stops to catch his breath, John catches up with him and asks, "What's going on?"

Shocked to see his friend behind him, Eric asks, "Where did you come from?"

"Let's see?" John says, "I followed you after you took off. So, what's the deal?"

With his back to his friend, Eric answers, "Listen, I know you mean well, but I don't want to talk about it. Just leave me alone, bud."

Now Manuel arrives and says, "John, there's a disturbance, and the other knights need you to help them. Let me talk with Eric, and you go and help the others."

"I'm on it, Manuel," John answers. Then, to Eric he says, "See you out there, Bro."

ONCE JOHN IS OUT OF EARSHOT, Manuel asks Eric, "What is bothering you?"

Lifting his head, Eric replies, "The problem is: I'm the Shadow Knight, and I hate secrets."

Manuel chuckles at this. "So, you hate secrets," he says, "and yet you keep your own secrets, holding them in."

Eric looks at him puzzled and asks, "What do you mean by that?"

"Look behind you," Manuel replies.

As Eric looks behind him, he sees Justice in her shadow form. She says, "What Manuel means is this: there are secrets about your past that you don't want anyone to know, not even yourself. So, rather than accept them, you have hidden them away, and in doing so, you are doing exactly what you hate. For it is written, *"For I do not understand my own actions. For I do not do what I want, but I do the very thing I hate."*[7]

"Eric," Justice continues, "I can see that there is a lot of pain within you, but I also see that you are a protector. That is why you were chosen to be the Shadow Knight. Manuel told you of the origins of your armor. Now let me tell you the cost of making the armors you and the others now wear.

"When it was known that the Psystructs had started to conquer the Cosmos, the last three remaining Psythonians created the armors you wear and searched for a power source. When they came to the twelve planets, they met together with the leaders of each planet. Then, as they prepared to infuse the armor with elemental power, they were left with one major question: how were they going to delay the Psystructs if they were to show up? And that is where the source of your armor comes into play."

Shocked and confused by this revelation, Eric asks, "How does an armor of evil play a part in stopping evil?"

"That's just it," replies Justice. "The armor of shadow is not evil. The armor of shadow is the armor of protection."

AS ERIC LEARNS THIS NEWS, THE OTHER KNIGHTS ARE SEARCHING for Brillander. Using the BOD Bot's communication system, Joseph says, "Hey, Des, have you got a lock on whatever this thing is?"

"Not really," Des, responds. "It seems like every time I get a lock on him, he reappears somewhere else. It's getting really annoying."

Rock Racer then says, "Des, didn't you say this guy was made out of crystal?"

"Yes," Des answers with a chuckle. "You're right, and that gives me an idea?"

"What's that?" Joseph asks.

"I was using light waves to scan for him," Des replies, "and when Rocky reminded me that he was made of crystal, I remembered this: crystals can disperse light, and that's why I haven't been able to figure out where he is. Maybe we can use sound waves."

Jessica asks, "Do you even have that kind of tech in your ride?"

Laughing, Des says, "No, I don't, but you and Tsunami do. To activate it, just say, 'Tsunami Sonic Search, activate!' Once you do that, we should be able to find him.

"All right," Jessica laughs. "Let's do this." Then she repeats, "Tsunami Sonic Search, activate." That said, Jessica's BOD Bot begins to use a sonar-like device to locate Brillander. After only a few moments, she notices a result on her screen. "Tsunami," she says, "show this to the others." As the other knights see the new coordinates, they all change course and head for Brillander.

EN ROUTE, BRITNEY ASKS, "What's the plan once we find this guy? I mean, it's not like fighting these guys is getting any easier."

"Good point!" Janet says. "What are we going to do?"

Joseph says, "To be honest, I haven't thought that far ahead yet?"

"Are you insane?" Janet interjects. "Each time we go after these guys, they nearly kill us, and you're telling me you don't have any kind of plan yet?"

Joseph knows it isn't funny, but he still can't help but laugh. "Easy, Janet," he says, "I just thought I would see how you would respond if I said no. The only thing I can say right now is this: we need to assess his powers. So, I need to ask everyone not to use full power. If we do this, it might just give us the advantage we need."

To the other knights, this plan, as far as it goes, seems sound, and they all signal their agreement. No sooner do they come to agreement when they reach Brillander.

UNKNOWN TO THE KNIGHTS AT THAT VERY MOMENT, Brykar uses his psychic link with Alexander Marks and has him meet with him several miles away from his office. As Alexander approaches, Brykar uses his psychic powers. "My name is Bryan K. Arsen," he says, "and you will escort me to your office building. Once there, you will go to your office like normal and inform the others that I'm a visiting supervisor and that this is a surprise inspection."

Even as Brykar says this, he scans Alexander's mind so that he knows the chain of command and so that humans are unaware of his secret. The two of them get into Alexander's car and head for his office. About twenty minutes later, they are getting near, so Brykar scans for Alexander's supervisor. Once he finds him, he plants a psychic suggestion in his mind, letting him know of a surprise inspection.

Moments later, as they enter the local office of Homeland Security, Alexander shows his ID to the guard. When he asks for Brykar's ID, Brykar uses his psychic powers to make the guard believe he's handed him the proper credentials. Alexander then heads to his office. Brykar, using his powers to mask his identity, so that he appears human, says, "My name is Bryan K. Arsen, and I've been sent here to inspect this facility." Alexander's supervisor, Marcus D. Wild, nods and says, "Of course, we've been expecting you. Follow me." And Marcus takes Brykar throughout the facility.

They come to a room with four or five people seated at computers, and Marcus says, "This is our WMD (Weapons of Mass Destruction) room. From here, we scan the globe in an attempt to stop new weapons from being developed and/or deployed."

Brykar replies, "Mmmmm, may I have a closer look?"

Marcus nods, and Brykar enters the room. He uses his psychic powers to blind the employees to himself. He actually moves one of the researchers and sits down in his place. He notices that the computer the man was using has a USB port and chuckles to himself. "These humans are truly archaic, to be using such ancient tech," he says to himself.

Bykar then pulls on a small rectangular box, and as he touches the center of it, a USB port emerges. He plugs in an apparatus he has brought with him and begins to copy all the information the officials of Homeland Security have gathered.

After Brykar has finished copying the files he wants, Marcus resumes the inspection. Once it is all over, Brykar leaves.

BRYKAR PORTS BACK TO HIS SHIP. Then, as he goes over the data he has acquired, he laughs. He is assured that the only ones preventing the conquest of this planet are the knights.

THE KNIGHTS ARE MOVING FORWARD with their plan for testing Brillander and his abilities. Des telepathically says, "Well, it looks like your plan is working so far. This isn't going to last long."

Brad responds, "No kidding! It's like we're not even hitting him."

"That's it," Des says. "I know now why we haven't been able to beat him. Each time we attack, the crystals on his body flash and, like crystals, deflect the damage done."

Joseph signals for the knights to regroup. As they do, Brillander says, "Is this the best you knights could do? I was hoping for more of a challenge, considering the warriors you've beaten. Still, I know you are all more capable than what you are showing me. So, either show me what you pathetic knights have, or I will make sure you all suffer a slow and painful death." With that, Brillander charges at the knights, and they scatter. Then he begins firing crystal blades from his hands, as he adjusts them for scattering. As the knights dodge the crystal blades, they try to figure out what to do next.

Brillander then says, "Do not continue to insult me with these weak attacks. I've seen you all fight better than this." When the knights fail to respond to him, he says, "Very well, if you wish to see my power, then I will show it to you gladly." He then begins to absorb the light from the sun and to fire energy blasts at the knights.

The knights dodge these blasts, but they can't help but notice that the blasts disintegrate everything they touch. Des says telepathically to Joseph "We can't keep this up much longer. We need to attack."

Joseph replies, "Fine! Des, Brad, Maggie, Britney and Jessica, activate your armors and attack at the same time. After that, the rest of us will launch a second wave of attacks."

When the knights all nod their agreement, Brad steps forward and says, "Firebird Battle Armor, engage," and his armor begins to transform.

Des then rises and shouts, "Geo Guard Armor, engage," and his armor begins to transform as well.

Maggie leaps backward and shouts, "Whirlwind Armor, engage," and her armor begins to transform.

Jessica flips forward and says, "Aqua Armor, engage," and her armor begins to transform.

Britney leaps forward and says, "Thunderbolt Burst Armor, engage," and her armor begins to transform.

In little more than an instant, the knights' armors are activated.

Seeing this, Brillander chuckles and says, "Looks like you have been holding out on me. Now, let's see what you knights have really got."

BACK AT THEIR BASE, Eric is in shock at Justice's words and asks, "Are you serious?"

"Yes, we are," Justice and Manuel answer in unison.

Eric shakes his head and walks off, but he does not go far. He stops and ponders, thinking to himself about how all of his life he has longed for a protector. As a child, he'd had to protect and guard himself. When he was bullied, he expected his dad to help him, but his father had just said, "You just have to stand up to them." Even though Eric did, and things changed, even if only slightly, there were times when he wanted someone to protect him from the abusive nature of his father because he was verbally abusive at times.

Eric clutches his fists as he continues to remember and reflect on all of this. Then he falls to his knees, as both Manuel and Justice watch. Manuel knows that what's about to happen is necessary. Without even realizing it, Eric becomes lost. In his mind, he tries to understand this entire concept. He remains there kneeling for sometime ... until finally he hears Justice's voice saying, "Eric, I know this is a lot for you to take in. And I see all the hardships you've had to endure. But I want you to know that you are not alone. The power of shadow is to protect, not destroy. Do not let the hardships of the past define you. Instead, let them refine and reforge you for the task ahead."

Suddenly, everything around Eric fades, and he sees a bright light. He sees Justice, but not in her normal form, for now as he see her, she's almost a silhouette. He wonders why he sees her like this and remembers that when she speaks to the knights individually, she appears to them in accordance with their powers. She then says, "Eric, look around you." As he does this, he sees the light around him, and Justice continues to say, "Light doesn't destroy shadow. It strengthens it. Light and shadow work together, just as you and John have for years now."

Now Justice kneels before him and, looking him in the eyes, says, "It's time for you to rise and be the protector you were born to be."

The moment Justice says that, Eric raises his head and then begins to reflect on his life, knowing that all he has experienced was meant to lead to this.

MANUEL AND JUSTICE WATCH AS ERIC STANDS and then they hear him say, "Shadow Star Armor, engage." Suddenly, Eric's armor begins to transform, and it looks as if he is now wearing a black leather jacket. The top of his helmet becomes like that of a top hat, and the colors of his armor start to change to a combination of black, gray and purple. Then, on Eric's back, appears a triangular shield and two swords with a twelve-sided star as the hilt.

After the transformation is complete, Eric's eyes open, and he marvels at what has happened. "How did this happen?" he asks. "The last thing I remember, I was in a room of bright light, and Justice was speaking to me."

Manuel answers, "Because of the human rules of right and wrong, it was difficult for your mind to understand what we were trying to explain. So, your powers, along with your mind, created a place where your mind would be protected until you could accept this truth."

Then Justice says, "Now do you accept and understand this: you have unlocked a new armor. Now, get going. Your friends need your help."

Chuckling, Eric says, "You got it, Justice. I'm on my way now." With that, he races to the hanger. Using his gauntlet, he signals his BOD Bot, Shadow Shifter, who drives behind Eric while he races through the hanger.

As Shadow Shifter gets closer, Eric flips backward, Shadow Shifter opens the top, and Eric lands inside. "Need a lift, Bro?" Shadow Shifter asks.

"Yea," Eric answers, "and we've gotta get to the others fast."

The hanger doors open, and the two speed off.

"ANY IDEA WHAT WE'RE DEALING WITH?" Shadow Shifter asks.

"Not a clue," Eric answers. "All I know is that we are a team, and our team needs us. So, let's pick up the pace."

As Shadow Shifter increases speed, and they race to the others, Eric says, "Shadow Shifter, can you get a lock on their position?"

"Activating scanners now," Shadow Shifter answers. A few seconds pass. Then Shadow Shifter says, "I've got them ... and we're heading to them now. We should be there in three minutes."

"Hopefully, we are not too late," Eric says.

THE OTHER KNIGHTS ARE CONTINUING TO FIGHT Brillander. Brad now shoots a beam of fire toward him. It hits Brillander, but he seems unfazed and continues walking steadily toward the knights. Brad says, "What is it going to take to beat this guy?"

Des does his part by shattering stones to make spear-like darts and then throw them at Brillander. This receives the same reaction—none. Brillander keeps on coming. Brad says, "You've got to be kidding! So far, everything we've thrown at this guy barely makes a dent."

Now Jessica fires a water blast at Brillander, but, like the other attacks, this doesn't seem to have any negative affect on him. Frustrated, she says, "There's no way this guy is unbeatable. There's gotta be something that we are missing here."

Hopeful, Maggie uses a wind tunnel to lift Brillander up and send him backward. It helps a little, but doesn't seem to be a real solution. It only delays the inevitable. Disappointed, Maggie says, "We can't keep delaying him forever."

Agreeing with this observation, Joseph asks everyone, "Do any of you have an idea how his powers work?"

"Working on it," Des says.

As Des goes over the data, he notices that just before each attack the crystal on Brillander's chest lights up. This inspires him to take a closer look. What he sees is that their attacks are having no effect because of that crystal. Not only does the crystal increase Brillander's powers; it also allows him to deflect *their* powers and render their attacks useless. "In order to stop him," Des concludes, "we need to destroy the crystal on his chest."

"I'm on it," Britney says, and she prepares to fire a thunderbolt arrow at the crystal.

Seeing this, Brillander chuckles in amusement and says, "Take your best shot." Brittany fires the thunderbolt arrow, but Brillander uses the crystal to deflect her attack.

Unknown to Brillander, Britney has a second arrow ready. When Brillander deflects the first one, she ports close enough to him so that when she fires the next arrow, it should shatter the crystal. She ports at just the right moment and fires her arrow. As she does this, Brillander has an odd smile on his face. He calmly holds his other hand forward, crystallizing the arrow before it ever reaches him. "Nice try!" he says. Now let me show you what I can really do."

Brillander now moves closer to Britney and reaches for her in an attempt to crystallize her. Suddenly, however, she is wrapped in a shadow and dragged back toward the others. In that moment, Eric leaps from Shadow Shifter and says, "If you want them, you're gonna have to go through me. You got me?"

"How interesting!" Brillander says. "You're a little late to the party, aren't you?"

Eric is unintimidated. He chuckles to himself and says, "True, but better late than never! Now, show me what you've got."

The other knights watch as Eric unlocks his new armor.

Joseph asks Des, "What do you think his chances are?"

"It's hard to say," Des replies, "considering we don't know much about his armor."

Brillander now begins firing crystal darts that transform anything they hit into crystal. Eric reaches for the shield behind him. As he brings it in front him, it transforms from a triangle into a twelve-sided star that fires a blast, destroying each and every crystal Brillander fires.

As the other knights watch this in fascination, Des says, "He might actually have a fighting chance."

"Don't be so sure!" Brillander says. "That was impressive, Shadow Knight, but that was just the beginning. I have many more tricks in store for you."

"Then bring it on," Eric replies.

Before the two can resume their fight, Brillander notices that the sun is about to set. He realizes that this will leave him vulnerable. Before anything else can be said, he uses his crystal to create a blinding light that allows him to disappear.

The knights are left wondering what has happened and why. Eventually, since it appears that the fight is over for the moment, Eric says, "Let's get back to the base and regroup." The others agree, and they get into their BOD Bots and head back.

CHAPTER 13

SHADOWS AND SECRETS:
SECRET OF THE SHADOW STAR SWORDS

AFTER ARRIVING BACK AT THEIR BASE, THE KNIGHTS CHECK OUT Eric's new armor—especially Britney. She says, "You didn't have to save me, but thanks," and she gives him a quick kiss on the cheek. When the others see this, the guys start to chuckle, and the girls "ohhh and ahh," like girls do.

This, however, is short lived as Joseph says to Des, "We need to analyze this data. Everyone to the lab so we know what we're dealing with and exactly why our foe pulled that disappearing act."

As Des uploads the data from his gauntlet, the knights talk among themselves. After going over the data, Des looks puzzled. He says, "It doesn't make any sense."

Jessica goes to his side and asks, "What doesn't make sense?"

His eyes locked on the screen, he answers, "According to this, he still had enough power to continue the fight for several more hours. But he didn't."

Jessica asks, "Do we have a video of what happened just before he disappeared?"

"Yes," Des answers, "after our last few battles, I found a way to have the BOD Bots record the fights. Let me upload the videos."

Once the videos are uploaded and they have a chance to start reviewing them, Jessica notices Brillander's head turning slightly, as the sun started to set. "There!" she says. "That's it!"

Des is also watching, and he responds, "Now it makes sense. How could I be so dumb?"

Brad says, "Do you really want me to answer that?"

Maggie slaps him playfully and laughs. "Shut up, Brad," she says.

Chucking, he says, "Easy! I was just kidding."

Concerned, Joseph now asks Des, "What exactly did you learn?"

"When Brillander did his disappearing act," Des explains, "it wasn't because he didn't have the power to continue. It was because he knew that he would be at a disadvantage at night, when he wouldn't have the sun to feed off of. So, rather than take the chance and battle us at night..."

"He chose to fight another day when he would have a nearly limitless supply of sunlight," Jessica finishes his sentence for him.

Des smiles at Jessica, and Joseph says, "So, at least he does have some sort of weakness."

Des chuckles and says, "That and his dependency on sunlight also weakens his abilities."

Now Des pulls up the video footage of the moment when Eric arrived, and they begin to review it too. "Look at this," Des says, pointing to Eric using his shadow powers against Brillander's crystal attack. "When Brillander used this attack earlier," he explains, "it turned whatever was touched to crystal, but when Eric used his powers, the crystals not only didn't turn things to crystal; they fell to the floor and shattered. So, if my theory is correct, Eric's power just might be the key to stopping this new warrior of Brykar's."

WHILE DES BEGINS TO FORMULATE A PLAN, using the computer in the lab, the other knights decide to go relax for a bit. Eric, in his usual fashion, goes off by himself, only to be followed by Britney. She thinks he hasn't noticed her, and when he turns to see if someone is there, she ducks out of sight. When he reaches where he wants to be, he starts chuckling and says, "You can come out now, Britney. I know you've been following me."

Britney remains hidden, wondering how he knew she was following him. Before she can speak, he appears right in front of her and says, "Now that you see that I've seen you, can you tell me exactly why you are following me?"

She looks at him and replies with a bit of disappointment, "Honestly, you intrigue me. I mean, when it came down to me fighting the Elemental Enforcer, you were more concerned about *me* than some of the other girls. Then, there was the timing ... with you saving me."

Before she can say anything else, he interrupts her. "Britney," he says, "if you want to know if I like you, the answer is, Yes, I do!"

"Then why are you always so guarded and distant with everyone," she asks him. "Why are you always by yourself?"

Eric turns to her now. "Do you remember how I ran off after we were told about the origins of the twelve armors?" he asks.

Still puzzled, she answers, "Yes." It was more of a question than an answer.

Eric goes on, "When we first received our powers, I thought my powers were of darkness and that all the bad things that had happened to me were the result of something I did, as if I attract evil to myself. It is because of this that I have kept to myself most of the time. Now I realize that whether I like it or not, bad things are bound to happen. I can either choose to let the bad things in my life define me or refine me. So, from now on, I'm going to let them refine me."

That being said, he pulls Britney to himself and kisses her deeply. As they kiss, she wraps her arms around him, and the two young knights enjoy their special moment in time.

THESE MOMENTS OF BLISS ARE QUICKLY INTERRUPTED by Des. Using the base's communication system, he is calling everyone to the lab. As their kiss ends, Eric looks at Britney and says, "I knew you must be a good kisser, but that was *amazing!*"

This brings a full smile to her face, and she responds, "You're not too bad yourself. In fact, I don't think I've ever kissed anyone like that before."

Eric is laughing now. "That's very interesting," he says. "We'll definitely have to explore that some more later. Right now, we need to get to the lab before they come looking for us."

Playfully, Britney says, "Okay, if we *have* to."

The two knights then walk to the lab hand in hand. As they get closer to the lab, they let go of each other's hands, but not before Jessica notices. She doesn't say anything but decides she'll ask Britney about it later.

ONCE ALL OF THE KNIGHTS HAVE ARRIVED AT THE LAB, Joseph says, "Okay Des, what have you come up with?"

"While I was working on a plan to defeat Brillander," Des explains, "I noticed that as soon as the sunlight was blocked, not only did the crystals he fired lose their powers, but it also caused anything that was turned to crystal before to revert back to it original form."

"How is that possible?" Joseph asks.

"That's the same thing I was wondering," Des continues. "That's when it dawned on me that he needs solar energy, not just to keep him charged, but also for his powers to work at all."

Now Eric chimes in. "If I understand this correctly, you're saying that if I can cut him off from the sun, he'll be powerless?"

"In theory, yes," Des replies.

Eric shakes his head and says, "Fine! I'll do it. Just come up with a backup plan in case he finds a way to deal with that little issue."

John then speaks, "Normally I hate to agree with Eric, but he does have a point here. I mean, granted this time none of us got captured, but we need to be ready because Brykar's soldiers seem to be stronger than the last."

Des agrees and offers, "I'll work on a couple of contingency plans."

Joseph says, "Good! We don't need to be taking unnecessary risks right now. I think we should all take a breather for the next few hours."

All the knights gratefully agree.

AS ERIC GOES OFF ON HIS OWN AGAIN, Jessica asks Britney, "Could you stay behind a moment? I have question for you?"

Britney goes closer to her and asks, "What's your question?"

Jessica chuckles and says, "It's nothing major. Just wanted to ask you when you and Eric decided to hook up?"

For a brief second Britney blushes. Then she says, "I don't know what you're talking about?"

Jessica looks at her curiously and says, "I'm not trying to upset you, but I think it's really cool if you two are together."

Knowing she can't hide her feelings for Eric, Britney pulls Jessica to the side and says in a lowered voice, "I still can't believe it happened and all ... just before Des called us. I had followed Eric while he went to go brooding, like he usually does, and I had kept out of sight. At least I thought that ... until it became obvious that he saw me. It was then that he told me he did actually like me, and he explained his reason for always being by himself. After that, we kissed. It was amazing! But I think the most amazing part of the kiss was that I could feel how much he really cared for me. See, most guys, when they've kissed me, it was because of what I could *do* for them. But with Eric, he kissed me because I was me. That's what made it so special."

MEANWHILE BRILLANDER HAS BEEN IN BRYKAR'S WORKSHOP, working on a way to neutralize the effect the Shadow Knight's power has over him. While he does this, Brykar walks in and says, "I take it the reason you are here is because the knights found some way to defeat you."

Brillander chuckles and says, "I take it you've seen this before, Brykar."

Chuckling, Brykar replies, "I've seen it far too often, but this time I realize that the more I focus on *them*, the more I'm kept from my main objective. This is why I have warriors like you, so they can handle these issues for me, while I keep my focus on my true objective. Besides, as long as you keep them occupied, that allows me to move around without being noticed."

Brykar leaves and Brillander continues to work on the crystal that gives him his powers. He is able to enhance it so that it will work in both darkness and light. He knows that if he should fail this time, he will not get another chance.

Once he's finished, he uses his powers to create two swords that he calls the Crystal Cutlasses. Anything they touch will turn to crystal. He is pleased with them, for his test of them seems to be successful. "Now," he says to himself, "let's see how the Shadow Knight's shield stands up to these."

ERIC AND THE OTHER KNIGHTS ARE RESTING, knowing that their next battle with Brillander will be their most dangerous yet. Eric joins the other knights. Noticing his arrival, Brad says, "Are my eyes deceiving me, or has Eric just joined the land of the living?"

This causes Eric to chuckle. He says, "That was a good one, Brad, but let's not forget: I'm the one who avoids people, unlike you, where people avoid you on purpose."

At this, everyone begins to chuckle. They know it is all too true. If it was not for the fact that Brad is a knight, most of them *would* avoid him.

Brad is momentarily upset by this comment, but he soon recovers and laughs along with everyone else. "I guess I deserved that," he says, "but seriously, it's good to see you hanging around, Eric."

Maggie chimes in, "I agree with Brad. If we are going to do this, we have to work together."

"Yeah, I'm sorry about that," Eric offers. "I just had a lot that I had to sort through."

Joseph interjects, "Either way, Maggie's right. We need to work together, and that means your problems are our problems. If we are going to save the world, we have to grow as a team and as friends."

Just then Britney and Jessica come walking in. Jessica says, "Hey, everyone, Des has finished the battle plan for tomorrow with Brillander and wants everyone in the lab at once."

Brad notices the glance between Britney and Eric, and he slaps Eric on the shoulder and says, "All right, Eric!"

As the other knights look at Brad, Eric says, "What are you talking about Brad?"

He chuckles and says, "Ohhhh, so you didn't want them to know, did you?"

John says, "Really, Brad, what are you talking about?"

Brad says, "What I'm talking about is Eric and Britney becoming a couple."

Joseph then says, "Ohhhh, that! I thought you were talking about something else."

Eric, to his surprise, asks Joseph, "Was it that obvious?"

Joseph chuckles and says, "Not really! But if we pretend it was known about, Brad will feel like a moron because he was the last to know rather than being the first."

The other knights begin to join Joseph in admitting that they saw this coming, and Brad starts to feel silly for pointing out something everyone already knew.

ONCE THEY REACH THE LAB, Des says, "Eric, do me a favor. Activate your shadow armor."

Eric then transforms into the Shadow Knight and says, "Shadow Star Armor, engage" Once that is said, his new shadow armor begins to engage.

Once this is done, Des says, "Eric, let me see your shield and swords."

Eric takes his shield and swords and hands them to Des, who begins to scan them.

Joseph says, "Jessica said you were done with the contingency plans, so why do you need his weapons?"

Des says, "I have, but in order to make sure everything is correct, I needed to check out his new weapons and armor."

While Des scans the weapons from his new armor, he notices something very interesting. He murmurs to himself, and this causes Eric to be worried. "What is it, Des?" he asks.

Des chuckles as he's snapped out of his thoughts and says, "Sorry, Eric. While examining your weapons, I noticed that depending on how the star on the hilt of each your swords is pointed, they can gain power from either the day or the night, and I found that fascinating."

Eric shakes his head and says, "Please don't scare me like that, Des."

"Sorry, Eric," Des answers, "but your powers are truly remarkable. They function on levels I never even thought possible. Take your shield, for instance. It's design allows it to be thrown, and with each throw, it can actually move like a buzz saw. But it also has the ability to fire a focused blast or allow you to capture objects and projectiles, opening wormholes that would allow an attack to be sent to somewhere deep in space. These weapons are truly remarkable." He then passes the weapons back to Eric.

As Eric puts the weapons back in place on his armor, he asks, "So, what are the contingency plans you came up with, Des?"

Des clears his throat and says, "If my calculations are correct, and he does modify the crystal on the center of his chest to allow him to use his powers in the light as well as the darkness of night, then, Eric, your swords might just be the key."

"How's that?" Eric asks

Des replies, "Well, according to this scan I did, there seems to be a third setting for the two swords that would allow them to use both the power of light and shadow at the same time. However, I'm not sure how to trigger it. I *am* sure that the key to unlocking it is somewhere in the hilts of both swords."

Britney then asks Des, "If you can't help him to unlock it, then how can it help?"

Des wipes his forehead and says, "Britney, I'm sure Eric will find a way to unlock this new mode for his Shadow Star Swords."

Britney gets annoyed and repeats herself, "Not to be a downer, but what if he can't unlock it in time, and something happens to him, genius?"

Des looks down and shakes his head and says, "Listen, I know everyone thinks I like sending you all on these what seem to be suicide stunts, but I don't. I don't like being asked what the plan is or to rely on anyone else when I could do it myself. The problem is I can't do it all by myself. We have to trust each other and trust each other's skills. If we don't, then there's no way we'll survive as a team.

"Turning to Eric, he says, "All I can ask, Eric, is that you try to unlock the secret mode of these swords. Once you do, all you need to do is strike the crystal. And once it is destroyed, defeating Brillander should be easy."

Before anyone can say anything else, Joseph says, "With that being said, everyone to your chambers. Rest up for the fight ahead."

WHEN THE KNIGHTS MAKE THEIR WAY TO THEIR RESPECTIVE CHAMBERS, Eric sits on his bed, wondering how he will be able to unlock the secret of his Shadow Star Swords. Before he can think much about it, he sees Britney standing in his doorway. She says, "Sorry if I went a bit crazed back there!"

Eric chuckles and replies, "You did, but it was nice to have someone care about me like that. Still, Des has a point. None of us can do this on our own, and he's putting a lot of trust in me. To be honest, I never thought anyone would put as much trust in me as they have already."

Britney comes in and sits with Eric on his bed. "It's not just you, Eric," she says. "We all have to start trusting each other more. Like Des said, if we don't, then there's no way we'll survive as a team.'"

Eric chuckles and says, "I never thought I'd hear you agree with Des like that, but I've got to admit this whole thing has caused us all to adapt and grow."

Britney looks at him and says "True, just do me a favor. Don't die on me tomorrow! Okay?"

Eric chuckles and says, "I promise I won't. Now, you should get to your chambers and get some rest."

She looks at him and says, "What if I want to stay here for the night?"

Eric chuckles again and says, "I don't think she would let you." He points to the doorway where Britney had stood a little earlier, and there stands Justice, with her arms crossed.

Justice says, "While I think it's awesome that you two have gotten close, if you don't get back to your chambers, Britney, you are not going to like what happens."

Now Britney chuckles, kisses Eric on the lips and says, "Till next time, baby."

Eric watches her go. While she is still within earshot, he says, "Till next time, my angel."

Britney turns and smiles at him, but Justice makes her go to her chambers.

ONCE JUSTICE IS SURE that Britney is in her chambers, her form changes to that of a shadow, as Eric had seen her before, and she asks, "Is something bothering you, Eric?"

He shakes his head and says "It's hard to explain. I mean, there's a part of me that's relieved that I'm not a dark force for this group. But, at the same time, there is a lot of pressure on me to defeat this newest warrior of Brykar's."

"True," Justice agrees, "but remember: you are not alone. I and your friends are all here for you." With that, she leaves, and Eric lies down on his bed and eventually drifts off into a restless sleep.

AFTER SEVERAL HOURS, THE KNIGHTS ARE AWAKENED by an alarm Des has set up so they would know when Brykar's forces show up. The knights make their way to the lab and find that Des is already there. He says, "Brillander's back, and it definitely looks like he got an upgrade."

Eric asks, "So, do we have a plan or has just charging in without thinking become the new plan?"

Des shakes his head and says, "Funny, Eric! But, no. Stage one of the plan is for you to create a dome, blocking him off from the sun's light. Stage two: we need to keep him off balance and give Eric time to unlock the secret of his Shadow Star Swords. Stage three: smash that crystal and send Brillander packing."

Joseph then asks, "How exactly do you plan for us to keep him off balance?"

Des turns to his computer, has it pull up an image on the screen and says, "Like this…" The image Des has pulled up shows the knights and their BOD Bots surrounding Brillander.

Des says, "The pattern is similar to what we used on the Scientific Samurai."

Eric chuckles, says "Okay, do we know how long before Brillander figures out what we are up to?"

Des runs through his calculations and says, "If my calculations are correct, about eleven and a half minutes. And that's providing each exchange doesn't last longer than thirty seconds … And providing we don't give Brillander a breather, which would allow him to see what's happening."

Eric says, "So, if everyone is keeping him busy, what exactly should I be doing?"

"While we fight him," Des replies, "I want you to watch his movements to see if you can find a pattern. At the same time, I need you to figure out how to unlock that new mode of your swords."

Eric says, "All right, Des. I think this plan is crazy, but we have no other options right now. So, let's do it, and I'll do what I can. I just hope I don't let you down."

Joseph now steps toward Eric and, placing a hand on his shoulder, says, "Eric, I know this is a lot on you. But the only way you would let us down is if you refused to try at all. Each of us believes in you, and we need to believe in and trust each other. Otherwise, we will fail."

Eric chuckles at this and nods in agreement. Then he warns, "Let's not get too sentimental, boss. We still have a job to do."

Joseph chuckles too and says, "All right, knights, let's light the night."

With that being said, the knights transform and head to their BOD Bots, board them and head out of the hangar to face Brillander.

AS SOON AS THE OTHER KNIGHTS ARE OUT of the hangar, Des begins to track Brillander's exact location. When he finds it, he relays it telepathically to the others. "Okay, guys," he says, "I found Brillander's coordinates and am transmitting them to you now. Everybody remember the plan. Once Eric casts the dome, we need to keep Brillander distracted as much as possible."

When Eric hears this, he shakes his head and says, "Well, it's now or never."

Des replies, "Don't worry, Eric, we'll distract him as much as we can. Just focus on how he fights."

Joseph interrupts them and says, "Look alive, guys. We're almost there."

THE KNIGHTS ALL STOP WITHIN A FEW FEET of Brillander and leap from their BOD Bots. As they do this, Brad, Des, Maggie, Jessica, Britney and Eric transform into their secondary armors, while the others remain in their base armor. Turning to see them, Brillander smiles. "I was wondering," he says, "when you knights would show up. Especially you, Shadow Knight. I've got a particular punishment planned for you."

Eric leaps backward and claps his hands together, so that as they part they create a shadow dome, as planned. Eric says, "Bring it on, Brillander. This ends ... today."

This causes Brillander to laugh. "Interesting!" he says. "Very interesting! You seem much bolder today. I'm going to enjoy crushing you and your friends."

Brillander then switches the crystal on his chest to night mode and charges at the knights, going straight for Des.

Joseph shouts, "Knights, scatter!"

As the knights scatter, Brillander looks for his next target. Des decides to be the first to attack, but when he does, Brillander blocks each of his attacks. "Is that really the best you've got?" he asks.

Des chuckles and says, "You'll see."

Des breaks off his attack and Jessica leaps in and begins attacking Brillander.

ERIC WATCHES as Brillander continues to block their attacks. He notices that he's reflecting their attacks back at them. Brillander then notices the Shadow Knight has yet to attack. As he faces the Aqua Knight, he says, "Enough of this…" He then grabs her, and she becomes paralyzed.

Before the other knights realize what's going on, he begins to touch each of them until they are all paralyzed, except for the Shadow Knight. When Eric sees this, he says "What have you done to them?"

Brillander answers, "They're simply in a temporary state of paralysis while they're bodies crystallize. That is ... if you can defeat me, which I doubt. But they will watch as I crush you like a bug."

Now Eric chuckles. "I seriously doubt that, Brillander," he says. "Now, let's see what you've got."

Before Eric engages him, Joseph reaches out to him telepathically and says "Eric, we may not be able to move or talk, but we are still with you."

When Eric laughs to himself, Brillander asks, "What's so funny?"

Eric then lifts his head and says, "You wouldn't believe me if I told you."

Suddenly Eric draws both of his swords and charges at Brillander, who begins to fire crystals from his palms at Eric. Firing a shadow blast at them, Eric watches as his shadow blast becomes pure crystal. Then he halts his charge, and Brillander says, "As you can see, I've neutralized your advantage and have made myself functional both in the night as well as daylight."

While Brillander speaks, Eric's removes the shadow dome and for a brief second Brillander is hurt by the sun ... until he switches the crystal on his chest from night to daylight. To Eric's surprise, the crystal growing around the knights has spread even faster now, covering their calves and feet in crystals.

Brillander laughs and says, "You fool! By removing the dome, it speeds up the paralyzing effect of my touch."

Remembering that Brillander's fighting styles relied on reflecting their attacks back on them, Eric says, "I still have more than enough time to defeat you, you crystallized creep."

With that, Brillander charges at Eric, who dodges the attack. Eric continues this, causing Brillander to become slightly winded and says, "Fight me, or your friends will become my crystal trophies."

Although only a few moments have passed, the knights are now crystallized from the waist down. Eric sees a slight opening and forms the shadow dome once again, in order to slow down the effect Brillander's ability is having on his friends.

As Brillander comes toward him, Eric switches his Shadow Star Swords from their sun mode to their shadow mode. When Brillander strikes, Eric uses his blade to block the attack, damaging Brillander's gem gauntlet in the process. This causes Brillander to say, "I see I'm not the only one with new tricks at their disposal. Still, your powers are not enough to beat me, Shadow Knight."

Using his undamaged gauntlet, Brillander fires a blast, destroying the shadow dome and, in doing so causes a shockwave, knocking Eric to the floor. Slightly dazed, Eric watches as Brillander walks toward him. Looking at the stars on the hilt of his blades, he notices that there are two small triangles that have both the sun and shadow mode on them.

Brillander keeps getting closer, but Eric gets an idea. As he gets up, Brillander says, "It's been fun, Shadow Knight, but this game ends now."

Still slightly dazed, Eric says, "It's not over yet." He ports himself away from Brillander, who uses the crystal on his chest to redirect the port, actually bringing the Shadow Knight closer to him.

As Eric emerges from the port and sees Brillander closer than before, he falls to his knees with both swords in his hands and begins to recite their oath, "As days of darkness near, and people run in fear…"

With each step, Brillander gets closer. Thinking he has won, he begins to gloat. "Really, Shadow Knight," he says, "you're making this too easy for me."

Eric continues to recite the oath, "From they who prey on the weak, and silence those who speak…"

Continuing his gloat, Brillander says, "Are you really going to just cower there on your knees like that? At least make this interesting."

Still not moving, Eric continues speaking his oath. "We will take to the sky with courage and battle cry."

As Brillander makes his way to the Shadow Knight, he notices him saying something. Before Brillander can react, the Shadow Knight lifts his head to finish the oath, now shouting with all his strength: "To protect the world from loss I'm a knight of the Cross!"

This surprises Brillander, who replies, "Oh, so there is still some fight left in you! Good! I'm going to enjoy this."

Quickly Eric stands and turns the stars on the hilt of his swords so that both the triangles from the sun and shadow mode are connected to the blade. Then he says, "Shadow Star Swords Twilight mode, engage." That being said, both swords begin to glow with an almost purple-like color. Now Eric charges for Brillander, who is saying, "Show me what you've got, Shadow Knight!"

Like before, with the other knights, Brillander blocks many of Eric's attacks, but with a major difference. Each of Eric's strikes are slowly breaking down Brillander's defenses. As Eric sees this, he attacks from above in order to bring Brillander's guard up. Then he attacks with his second sword from below, hitting the crystal on Brillander's chest and slicing it in two. This causes Brillander to fall to his knees.

Before Eric can strike the final blow, Brillander claps his hands together to create a flash of light and charges at the Shadow Knight. Eric, without even thinking, blocks the attack with one sword and immediately strikes with the other sword. As he does this, Brillander shatters into crystallized dust, leaving only the split crystal that Eric has destroyed.

The Shadow Knight breathes a sigh of relief and looks at each of the other knights as the effect of Brillander's touch is undone and crystals shatter around the knights. Each of the knights then walks toward Eric. Joseph says, "We're done here. Let's head back to the base."

The knights agree and as they get in their BOD Bots, Shadow Shifter notices something is bothering Eric. He says "Is everything okay?"

Eric says, "I'm not sure. Usually there's more of a plan to these attacks, but this one seemed like he didn't do as much planning as the other warriors in the past had. Still, that's something I can let the others know about that when we get back to the base."

ONCE THE KNIGHTS HAVE RETURNED to their base, they return to their human forms, and the knights congratulate Eric on defeating Brillander. Still he can't shake the feeling that there was something weird about this attack. As the knights disperse to relax, Eric goes to Joseph and Des and says, "May I have a word with you two?"

Both Joseph and Des are puzzled. The three go to the lab and as they enter, Joseph asks Eric, "What's on your mind?"

Des adds, "If something is bothering you, please tell us?"

Eric then says, "That's just it. I beat Brillander, but I feel like something was off. Usually, when we fight these guys, there's more of a plan or a depth to their attack, but with Brillander, it just felt ... weird."

The other two knights listen to Eric, and then Joseph asks, "What do you think about it, Des?"

Des rubs his chin for a moment and replies, "I've been wondering the same thing." He then goes to the computer and pulls up the data on each battle they've fought since becoming knights. He continues, "According to this, it looks like each of the warriors we've fought have been meant to test us as a whole. But, apparently, due to our powers, it has allowed Brykar to gather data on each of us."

"Does that mean," Joseph asks, "that he knows who we are?"

"At this point in time," Des replies, "I doubt it. We don't communicate with each other by our names, not to mention it took three of us to take down one of their Psydrones. But I do believe he's found out that we are human. Also, I do agree that the other warriors we've dealt with planned a lot better than Brillander."

"Do you have any idea why?" Eric asks.

Des shakes his head and answers, "Not really. The only thing we can do right now is wait and see what Brykar will throw at us next. Although I have an idea that might help us to get a leg up if you are up for it, Eric?"

This causes Eric to chuckles, and he asks, "What have you got up your sleeve, Des?"

"Well," Des says, "as you know, usually I'm the one looking for patterns in these fights. But from what I've noticed, you have the same habit as well. So what I propose is that going forward, when we go into battle, I want you to hang back and study each of the warriors Brykar sends against us. This will allow us to have some kind of strategy rather than getting blindsided by their powers each time."

"Not a problem!" Eric answers. "That I can handle."

Joseph then asks, "If that's it, are we done here?"

"I'm good," Eric says. "I just wanted to let you two know."

"Same here," Des replies.

With that being said, Joseph heads to the library, Des stays in the lab, and Eric goes off to join the others for once.

THE SUD FOLLOWING APRIL, the girlfriend of Eric's father, has been tracking her since she left the house several hours ago. It has now tracked her to a gentlemen's club called Songbird. After being there for about four to five hours, she goes to a restaurant with another man. Agent Stanton says, "Awwww, come on! I thought we had something."

"If you would shut up," Agent Miles replies, "we might."

He then has the SUD go into the restaurant and sit about fifty feet away from April and the other man and place an order, all the while listening in to and recording their conversation.

However, before Miles can listen to it, their shift-change occurs. Agents Rivera and Ryan arrive. Agent Miles fills her in on what he has found. Agents Rivera and Ryan then take their seats and begin to monitor as they have been directed. Agent Rivera informs Agent Miles, "When monitoring, don't get too focused on one person, or you might find yourself down the wrong rabbit hole."

As the rotation continues, both Agents Rivera and Ryan fail to see anything new. Agent Rivera sets up a notification on the screen so they will be alerted when possible suspicious activity occurs.

After that, Agent Wallace and Saunders arrive for their shift, and Agent Rivera informs Agent Wallace of what she has been told by Agent Miles and what she and Agent Ryan have discovered on their shift.

Agent Saunders and Wallace are watching the screens when Saunders notices Graham put a large envelope in the mailbox, when the postal worker, Phillip Max's uncle, was within a few feet. As Graham leaves the mailbox, the postal service worker picks up the package and continues his route. Agent Saunders says to Wallace, "Didn't that seem a bit odd to you?"

Chuckling, Agent Wallace and says, "Not really! Still, I wouldn't rule anything out, but Agent Rivera did make a point when she told me what she told Agent Miles, which was: When monitoring, don't get too focused on one person, or you might find yourself down the wrong rabbit hole."

"What's that supposed to mean?" Agent Saunders asks.

"It means," Wallace explains, "you have twelve different targets. If you become too focused on any one of them, you might find yourself looking at the wrong clue or even the wrong target. Besides, right now we need to focus on establishing patterns with each of these people, not just one random one, or we might not even come close to finding out if they know anything."

"I hate to admit it," Saunders replies, "but you're right. Still something, bothers me about what we just saw."

"So," Agent Wallace says, "mark it and when the time comes. Maybe we'll find out if there is more to it."

After Phillip picks up the package from Graham, he keeps it with him until he gets home. When he walks through the door, he's surprised to see Melanie and his wife there talking. He says, "What brings you here?" "Honestly," Melanie answers, "I'm still worried about the kids and thought maybe I'd stop by to see if you've heard anything?"

Phillip remembers what Graham said the last time they met, thinks it's a little odd and says, "We haven't heard anything, but if we do, we'll let you know."

Then he adds, "I'm gonna grab something to drink. Excuse me, ladies."

Phillip then goes into the kitchen to get something to drink and Linda soon comes in after him. He pours a glass of water, then writes down on a piece of paper so that she can see, "Don't tell her anything. I don't think that is Melanie."

Linda takes the pen and writes, "I haven't told her anything, and I don't think it's her either."

When the two return to where Melanie is, Phillip says, "I'm gonna go to the bedroom and relax for a bit. Melanie, it was good to see you. If we hear anything, we will let you know."

Linda gives him a kiss and he disappears into his bedroom. She sits down next to Melanie and gets ready to continue their conversation, when suddenly her cell phone rings. Looking at her phone, she sees that the person calling her is "Melanie." She says "Melanie, I'm sorry but this an important personal call. Can we finish this later?"

The fake Melanie says "Sure, I'd like that."

Linda walks the false Melanie to the door and then answers the call. She says, "Hello?"

Melanie then asks, "Is everything okay?"

Linda responds, "It is now. Just out of curiosity, where are you?" Surprised by the question, Melanie answers, "I'm home. Why do you ask?"

Linda looks to make sure the door is locked then heads to their room and puts Melanie on speaker phone. "We have a major problem," she says. "We need to meet ASAP."

Melanie suggests a place and time, and the two agree. Seeing that his wife is alarmed, Phillip cuts the phone call off and asks "What happened?"

She takes a deep breathe and says, "I was getting ready to continue talking to my visitor when Melanie called me. It happened while the false Melanie was right there in front of me. I thought it was weird when she came by, because Melanie has always called before coming over. When she just showed up earlier, it made me cautious. So, when I saw Melanie was calling me, I knew the one in front of me had to be fake. The question is: why is this happening? And what have the kids done that someone is willing to impersonate us?"

"I don't know," he answers, "but I know who might."

He then pulls out the envelope he has received earlier that day from Graham. When his wife sees it, she says, "I thought Graham was paranoid before, but now I see how right he was to use this system."

CHAPTER 14

DARKEST BEFORE THE DAWN:
DESCENT INTO DARKNESS

AFTER CALLING LINDA, Melanie is shocked to hear that there is a problem and wonders what that problem could possibly be, especially since they dared not talk about it over the phone. She has known that, since their children are now wanted fugitives, there would be people wanting to know if they had any information. She also knows that all she can do, at this point in time, is wait until she can speak with Phillip and Linda to find out what exactly what's going on.

She goes to her room, changes from her work attire into a pajama shirt and pants, then goes to the kitchen to make herself some tea. She grabs the teapot, fills it with water, places it on the stove and turns it on. Then she grabs a tea bag and some honey and lemon. As she waits for the tea to boil, she thinks to herself, "Darren, I really wish you were here."

A few minutes later her thoughts are interrupted by the teapot whistle. She turns off the stove, fixes her tea and sits in the armchair where Darren used to sit. While sipping her tea, Melanie remembers her times with him and remembers the look on Joseph's face when they were told that he had gone missing. It was the look of every hurtful emotion a child could possibly experience, and the only thing she knew to do was to be there for him, just as his mother and father would have had these tragedies not happened.

She remembers that it was hard for Joseph at first, and Brad didn't make it any easier. The memory that now warms her heart is of the day where she and Joseph had a breakthrough. As usual, she had picked him and Brad up from school. Back at home, Joseph went to his room. She waited a bit and then passed by his room on her way to her own bedroom. That was when she heard him crying. Joseph had not shed a tear when he heard the news of his father's disappearance, and now she knew why. She opened the door, went in and held the young man who was so lost because all that he had known was gone.

When Joseph had stopped crying, she looked at him and said, "I know I'm not your mom, but I loved your father very much, and if you would allow me to, I will take care of you, just as he or your own mom would have done."

Up until that point, she had allowed him to call her Melanie, but in that moment, he said, "Thanks, Mom." He hugged her, and although she knew the road ahead would be long, she was confident that she and "her boys" would make it through.

Soon, she finished her tea and her memories. As she headed to bed, she thought to herself, "Brad, wherever you two are, look out for Joseph. He needs you."

BACK AT THE VIEWING ROOM FOR THE SUDS, Agents Miles and Stanton are back on their shift. Suddenly, Agent Rivera storms in and says, "Who is the genius that decided to do this?" She is pointing to a tablet showing an image of one of the SUDs posing as Melanie.

"How did you get that?" Agent Miles asks.

"I have my ways," Agent Rivera answers. "More importantly, explain to me why you would think it was a good idea to have a SUD act as one of the targets."

"Actually, it was my idea," Agent Stanton explains. "I thought, since we can't hear them from outside, maybe by going inside we would have a better shot."

"That may be true," Agent Rivera admits reluctantly, "but a tactic like this needs to be planned and orchestrated properly. Right now, we need to pull the SUDs back before the wrong people start asking the wrong questions." She then presses a blue button on the upper right of the SUD viewing console, and this sends a signal to each of the SUDs in the field, informing them to return to the ARC base. She then proceeds to contact Agent Wallace and inform him of the situation.

He shakes his head and says "This is just great! Stanton, Miles, all you had to do was watch and listen. Do you understand what kind of position this puts us in?" Before either can say a word, Agent Wallace says, "Shut it! I really don't want to hear what either of you has to say. You're lucky all I'm doing is letting Agent Ryan use you for target practice. Now, get out of my sight!"

"So what do we do now?" Agent Wallace asks.

"Simple!" Agent Rivera answers. Before I had the SUDs return, I had each of them leave hidden minicameras by each of their homes. This allows us to still watch them, but from a stationary point rather than being able to follow them."

Agent Wallace replies, "That idea was pretty good."

"Look," Agent Rivera says, rubbing her forehead, "I agree. The idea was a good one, but in order for us to do that we need to capture the people we are having the SUD replace, or it could cause major problems. I was going over their backgrounds, and some of these people have a great deal of influence. So, we need to be careful when doing something like this."

Agent Wallace nods in agreement and asks, "So, where does this leave us?"

"I'm pulling the SUDs for about two weeks," Rivera answers. "Then we'll send them out again. In the meantime, I suggest you and your team keep training. Now, if you'll excuse me," she adds, "I need to see what damage they did."

With that, Agent Wallace leaves, slamming his hand against the wall in frustration. Agent Daniels joins him. "She does that to everybody, doesn't she?" she suggests.

"I haven't seen you around much," he says.

She answers, "Yeah, well, that's what happens when you get chosen to rummage through an alien black box and have to sift through what's good, bad and pointless." Before she can say anything else, she gets a notification, informing her that something of interest has been found. "Listen, she says, "I gotta go, but can we catch up later?"

Agent Wallace nods and says, "Yeah, that would be cool."

Agent Daniels heads back to the computer, and Agent Wallace heads to the training area to deal with his frustrations.

AFTER WATCHING THE KNIGHTS defeat Brillander, Brykar contacts General Sadoom. "General Sadoom, as you ordered," he begins, "I have begun gathering intel on the earthling defenses and am sending what I've learned to you as we speak."

General Sadoom immediately reviews the data, then says, "Well done, Brykar! Now, stick to your mission and continue to learn about the earthlings' defenses. Once you are sure these knights are their only defense, you have my permission to destroy them."

With that being said, the transmission ends.

BRYKAR GOES TO THE CHAMBER WHERE HIS RECOVERING WARRIORS ARE and uses his technology to recover the broken crystal of Brillander, as well as the core crystals that formed his consciousness. He then places the broken crystal and Brillander's core crystals into the restoration chamber and moves on to the chamber holding the remaining warriors he has brought with him.

For the first time, he notices that there are only five chambers remaining. He then begins to think about which of the remaining five warriors would be best to test the knights. He comes to the conclusion that a creature of darkness will be more than capable of handling them.

He goes to one of the tubes holding it and opens it, and a creature emerges from the tube. It has a humanoid body and the wings of a bat and is wearing psychromium armor. The creature looks at Brykar, then kneels and asks, "How may I serve you, Brykar?"

Chuckling, Brykar says, "Direct as always, aren't you, Nosvorat? Still, I have need of your abilities. Currently we are on a planet called Earth, and there is a team of defenders who call themselves 'knights.' The problem is that they keep getting in the way of my plans. I need you to take care of them for me. If you go into the next room, you will find weapons and a vehicle of your choosing."

Nosvorat stretches and says, "It shall be my pleasure, Brykar! Besides, it has been a while since I've last been able to feed."

Brykar chuckles again and says, "I believe you will find the darkness in these humans to be a rare delight." Brykar now returns to his chamber, and Nosvorat heads to the hanger where the vehicles and weapons are stored.

NOSVORAT, THE CREATURE OF DARKNESS, LOOKS AROUND and then chooses for weapons what look like a top hat and a white-tipped cane. When it comes to vehicles, he sees no need for one. When he puts on the top hat, it covers his body in a shroud of darkness that will protect him from light. Once the shroud is completely in place, he exits the base and flies toward the city. He needs to gain strength to take on the knights.

THE KNIGHTS HAVE STARTED JOGGING IN THEIR TRAINING ROOM, using their GP system. For the past hour, they have been jogging with the level set at 10 GP. No sooner do they finish their current lap than their alarm goes off. As it does, the GP system deactivates. It's a new feature that Des created so that when they are training they will be able to respond faster. The knights all head for the lab.

AS THEY ARRIVE AT THE LAB, Des scans for any alien life and finds Brykar's newest warrior heading toward the city. Joseph then says, "Des, can you tell us anything about this new creature?"

Des quickly scans the creature and replies, "From what I can tell, this thing is a humanoid bat. Aside from that, I don't have much data on it."

"Then we'll have to be extra careful," Joseph concludes. Then he addresses the group. "All right, team, everyone transform, and let's see exactly what we're dealing with here."

THE KNIGHTS TRANSFORM and then head to the hanger where their BOD Bots are located. Each of the knights gets into his or her BOD Bot and exits the hangar. When all the knights have exited the hangar, they speed together to the spot where Brykar's newest warrior has been spotted. On the way, Des says over their com system, "Here's the plan, people. Eric and I will hang back to analyze and observe, to see if we can find out any of its abilities before it can use them on us."

"Why do you two get to hang back," Brad asks, "while the rest of us put our lives on the line?"

"Okay, Brad," Eric says, "how about you and I switch places. I will be on the front lines with the rest of the team, while you come up with a plan for how to defeat Brykar's newest warrior before the rest of us are captured. How does that sound?"

"Point made!" Brad says, chuckling, "Still, does anybody have an idea about how to keep him busy before he can use his powers on us?"

Des responds, "Well, since this warrior can fly, I would suggest that you and Maggie attack him from the air (should he not yet go airborne). The rest of us will surround him, so that it will make it harder for him to target us."

Now John chimes in, "Not bad, Des! Let's light this dude up!"

Shaking his head, Eric cautions, "Calm down, bud. We still don't know what this guys is capable of."

"True," John replies, "but we're a team, and I'm confident that we'll be able to win as a team."

"I can't argue with that logic," Des says. Still, everyone be careful!"

AS THE KNIGHTS REACH THE NEWEST OF BRYKAR'S WARRIORS, they leap from their BOD Bots. Brad and Maggie hang behind, and the other knights surround Nosvorat. For his part, Nosvorat places both of his hands on his cane and says, "Well! Well! I see you've found me ... and sooner than I expected. Allow me to introduce myself. My name is Nosvorat, and it will be my pleasure to destroy you all."

Noticing that the knights have surrounded him, Nosvorat says, "Do you really think surrounding me will work?"

Stepping forward, John says, "Pretty much!"

Nosvorat grabs his cane with one hand and lunges at John, but John is able to draw his sword, block the strike, and move to the right, to keep Nosvorat in front of him. Then, using the telepathic connection he has with the other knights, John says, "Listen, I'll keep him busy. You guys rush him when his guard is down."

Nosvorat now twists the tip of his cane, so that it creates a sonic blast. When he points it at John, it sends the knight to the floor. "You are a fool," Nosvorat says, "to think you could ever handle me, and allow me to show you why!"

Before any of the knights can react, he leaps into the air and begins to fly into the sky. Joseph signals to Brad and Maggie to follow him. As the two knights follow Nosvorat, he doubles back and uses a hypnotic stare to bring out their darkest emotions. In doing so, he paralyzes them, making them unable to continue the battle.

Noticing both of these knights falling to the ground, Des says to the others, "We have a problem! Both the Wind and Fire Knights are falling fast! We need to catch them quick!"

With no hesitation, Eric and Britney leap into the sky. Eric catches Maggie, and Britney catches Brad. However, just at that moment, Nosvorat comes close to both of them and is about to use his stare on them. Just then, John speeds past the two knights and says to Nosvorat, "Surprise, fly boy!" He hits Nosvorat with both of his fists.

Although slightly stunned, Nosvorat says mockingly, "Not bad, boy! But you have little chance of defeating me." He then opens his mouth and begins to drain energy from both Maggie and Brad, causing their bodies to become limp.

As Britney and Eric land and regroup with the others, Joseph asks, "What happened to *them*?"

Eric replies, "Apparently, when they went up, he used a stare on them that paralyzed them, and he was about to do the same on us ... until Light Knight showed up, knocking him back a bit. Then it looked like he was able to drain their energy."

John rejoins the group and confirms what Eric has said. This causes Joseph to say, "We need to get them out of here ... NOW?"

"What about the rest of us?" Max asks.

Joseph replies, "We hold the line and fight this thing?"

"Are you crazy?" Max says. "If we stay, we could end up like them."

Now, without any warning, Nosvorat appears behind Max and says, "Mmmmm, such delicious negativity. You shall do nicely." He then opens his mouth and drains Max's energy, causing him to fall nearly lifeless to the ground.

Drawing his sword, Joseph points it at Nosvorat and says, "What have you done to him?"

Delighted, Nosvorat answers, "All you need to know is that he's fine for now. However, I cannot say the same for you." He then uses the same stare on the Knight of the Cross. Like the other two knights, Joseph is placed under a hypnotic trance that brings out his darkest emotions.

However, just as Nosvorat opens his mouth to feed on Joseph's negative emotions, Des uses his power to have a stone slab rise up from the ground, creating a barrier between them. "Everyone," he urges, "we need to get them back to the base ... and now."

John grabs Joseph, and Des grabs Max, but then Nosvorat uses his cane to destroy the stone slab with one of his sonic blasts. Then he uses his stare on Jessica, then Janet, Tasha and Sally. He open his mouth again and drains away their energy. "Do you still think you can defeat me?" he taunts.

Undaunted, John steps up and says, "I know we can!"

Nosvorat chuckles again. "Oh, yeah. Just look at your friends."

First Brad's body and then Maggie's begin to stir. They suddenly hit Eric and Brittany with the same kind of stare, causing them to go into a paralyzed trance, just as Nosvorat had done. Then, together, they say in unison, "We are yours to command, master?"

Without wasting another second, Des and John port back with the remaining knights, including Brad and Maggie, who apparently are now under the control of Nosvorat.

ONCE THE KNIGHTS ARE BACK IN THEIR BASE, Des activates his Geo Guard armor and creates an electromagnetic cage to keep these two at bay. John asks, "What's happened to them?"

"I'm not sure," Des responds, "but from what I can tell, he's put them under a trance. After draining their energy, they become like ..." He doesn't finish that thought. Instead, he now suggests, "John, get all the other knights into the cage—now!"

As John turns, the remaining knights who were paralyzed start to stir and begin to move as Brad and Maggie have been. John is then put under the same trance. Startled, Des says, "Great! This is the last thing we need!" He then uses his power to extend the cage so that all of the knights are held in one place.

In that moment, Manuel and Justice walk toward Des and ask, "What's happened to them?"

Des explains, "Brykar's newest warrior is a creature who calls himself Nosvorat. From what we know, he has powers similar to a vampire." Using the computer to scan the other knights, he notices something. "This is interesting!" he says.

"What is it?" Manuel and Justice ask simultaneously.

"According to these scans," Des replies, "the trance they're in is one that brings out the negative emotions that are inside them." He remembers that

Nosvorat didn't put Max under a trance. He just fed off of him. Realizing that this is another issue that will have to be dealt with, he says, "I'm not sure how to help them get out of this."

"All we can do for now," Manuel offers, "is hope that the knights find a way to break it on their own."

"Still," Des says, "we need to keep Nosvorat from getting anyone else. If he does, there will be no stopping him." At this point, he remembers the BOD Bots and activates their sentient mode, saying to them, "Right now, the knights are out of commission, and we need you all to keep Nosvorat busy until we find a way to free them." Each of the BOD Bots acknowledges the command and speeds off after Nosvorat. Now Des looks for a way to free the knights from Nosvorat's power.

FINDING HIMSELF LYING ON THE GROUND IN A DARK WORLD, John sits up. Wondering what's going on, he stands and starts walking, hoping to find some way out of this place. At first, he feels positive about finding that way out, but before long a voice is whispering in his ear, "You'll never get out of here, so why try?"

Then another voice is heard. "Even if you find your way out," it says, "you're still not strong enough to beat Nosvorat."

Unfortunately, these voices continue to whisper such negative things in John's ear. Soon, he has stopped walking and is standing still. He suddenly remembers the day his father died. He was about ten years old at the time, and he was having the worst day he thought he could ever have ... until he discovered that no one had come to take him home from school. Usually his parents were prompt. The school authorities had called his mother, and she, too, thought it was terribly odd. John's father had left more than an hour before to go get him. As she hung up the call from the school and opened the door to leave, two police officers were standing there. She looked at them, curious and, at the same time, disturbed, and offered, "May I help you?"

The lead officer said, "Ma'am, please forgive the intrusion, but we have some news about your husband. May we come in and speak with you?"

She looked at the officers and said, "I'm sorry, gentlemen, but I need to get my son from school. Could you tell me whatever it is when I get back?"

The officer shook his head and said, "Ma'am, unfortunately what I have to tell you is very important. If you would like, my partner and I could take you to get your son, and we can explain the situation on the way."

Not having time to argue with them, she said, "All right, we need to get there quickly! He's already been waiting at the school for more than an hour because his father didn't pick him up."

As they got in the car, the officer began to explain to her that there had been a bad accident involving her husband. A driver running a red light had t-boned her husband's car, causing it to flip. By the time the ambulance got there, it was too late. Her husband had been found dead in the damaged vehicle.

AFTER IDENTIFYING THE DRIVER OF THE VEHICLE, the two officers felt they needed to inform her, his wife. As she hears this, she begins to break down and cry. Soon the officers reach John's school, and she wipes her eyes and goes in to get him.

She finds him by the main entrance, and as she goes to him, she takes his hand and walks him to the police car. Once inside the car, John asks her, "Mom, is everything okay? What happened to Dad?"

Again fighting back tears, John's mother answers, "I'll explain later. Just sit back and enjoy the ride." The lead officer tries to make small talk, knowing this is a lot to take in at the moment.

WHEN THEY GET BACK TO HER PLACE, John's mother walks him inside. The lead officer follows them to the door. "Ma'am," he says, "I'm sorry to have been the bearer of this bad news, but I want you to know we have in custody the person responsible for the death of your husband. I know that doesn't mean much now, but we'll do everything we can to make this as easy as possible for you. Also, the DA will be getting in contact with you. He will make sure that the person responsible for this tragedy doesn't get away with it."

The officer leaves, and John's mother goes inside. Little John can sense that something is very wrong. "Mom," he asks, "what's wrong? Where's Dad?"

She now rushes to her son and explains to him what happened. As he hears what she is saying, he slams his hands against the floor and starts pounding them out of sheer rage. She wraps her arms around him and says, "I know this hurts. I wish I could make the pain go away, but I can't. This is a part of life. I know your father wouldn't want us to be unhappy."

John looks at her and says, "Are you *happy* Dad's gone?"

"No!" she says, shaking her head. "I am *not* happy he's gone." She pauses for a moment, then continues, "but, your father taught me that no matter what life throws at you, you've got to stay positive. And, right now, doing that makes me feel connected to him. So, I want you to promise me that no matter how bad things get, you will always find a way to stay positive, just like your dad would." Reluctantly John promises, doing as his mom has asked.

Soon she is contacted by the DA, but it isn't for the reason she expects. He tells her that the person responsible for her husband's death was connected to some official, so, in order to keep the whole matter quiet, the case has been settled out of court. She and John have been given the offer of a very large cash settlement. The DA explains that he wants to hold this person accountable, but to do so would cost him his job and ensure that the case got buried. At least, this way she and her son will be taken care of. Reluctantly, she agrees.

AS TIME GOES, ON JOHN LEARNS how to remain positive, as his mom has made him promise to be. This makes him into the person his friends have come to know. Now, as he stands there, voices continue to bombard him with questions. Still, he hears another voice. It is saying, *"The light shines in the darkness, the darkness has not overcome it."*[8] Although the voice sounds familiar, John doesn't know where it is coming from. But, as he hears it, he remembers the promise he made, and a renewed determination rises in him. He says, "I didn't quit then, and I won't quit now! There are too many people depending on me ... on us."

BACK IN DES'S LAB, HE NOTICES a light coming from John and says, "This is interesting!" Before he can say anything else, John starts to stand, begins walking toward the electrocage Des created and walks out. In shock, Des replies "This is impossible! There's no way he should have been able to do that."

Once out of the cage, John begins to shake his head. When he sees Des, he asks, "What happened? I feel like I got hit by a truck."

"Well, Des answers, "for starters, the other knights hit you with the same stare that Nosvorat did, and it put you in a trance-like state. How you came out of that I don't know."

"To be honest," John responds, "I'm not sure how I got out of it either. All I remember is being bombarded by different voices telling to quit and give up, and when I refused, I suddenly found myself back here."

"That makes sense," Des says. "If Nosvorat feeds off of the negative feeling of others, then it's possible that positive feelings may weaken him as well. I'll see what I can do to free the other knights. Right now, I need you to go and assist the BOD Bots in stopping Nosvorat."

Starting to loosen himself up, John asks, "Do we have any idea how I can stop him?"

"No," Des says, "I don't have any idea how we can stop him. All I know is that we need to stop him ... if we are going to save the others. I've already sent a return signal to Light Stride, and he's on his way back here now. I'm sorry. I wish I knew how we can beat him."

John puts a hand on Des's shoulder and says, "It's okay, Des. What matters is that we stay positive, even when the days become their darkest."

"It's weird," Des says, "how positive you are sometimes, but right now I'm glad you are."

This causes John to chuckle. He says, "You're not the first person to tell me that. By the way, there's something I do remember before I woke up here. I heard a voice that was different from the others. It said, *'The light shines in the darkness, the darkness has not overcome it.'*[9] Do you have any idea what that means?"

"I don't have a clue as to what that means," Des replies. "I see that Light Stride has just entered the base. Get going now and take out Nosvorat."

"I'm on it!" John says, and he heads toward the hanger.

ON HIS WAY TO THE HANGER, John begins to hear those voices again. He says to himself, "Even if I have no chance at beating Nosvorat, I have to try. My friends wouldn't give up on me, and I'm not giving up on them."

Suddenly, John stops, for he hears the words, "Light speed Armor, engage," and, in a flash of light, his armor begins to change. Where his helmet has been, he now gets a crown. Then comes a golden chestplate with a cape, and he then receives golden gauntlets and leg plates. Then, in his hands, form both a jousting lance and a shield.

Once the transformation is complete, John takes a quick look at himself and says, "I guess I may have a shot at beating him after all."

As Light Stride finds John, he says, "John, is that you?"

John chuckles and says, "Yeah, but we can talk about this on the way. Right now, we've got to stop Nosvorat."

John gets in, and they head off to stop Nosvorat before he can do any more damage.

MEANWHILE BRYKAR IS IN HIS BASE researching the weapons and defenses the earthlings have. He decides to check in on Nosvorat. When Nosvorat receives a signal from Brykar, he stops, holding his forearm in front of him. A video screen appears, and Nosvorat says to Brykar, "I'm here, Commander Brykar. What can I do for you?"

Brykar then replies, "What's your status?"

Nosvorat chuckles and says, "All but two of the knights have had their energy drained by me, and now that they're connected to me. The only way to break the connection is to destroy me."

Brykar shakes his head and says, "Excellent! But don't let your guard down! We've been here before, and somehow, some way they always find a way of defeating each of the warriors I've sent."

"Understood, Commander Brykar," Nosvorat says. "I will stay on my guard."

Suddenly hearing the BOD Bots coming toward him, Nosvorat says, "Forgive me, Commander Brykar. It appears that I have company coming."

Brykar chuckles and says, "This is exactly what I mean. Just when I think they are beaten, they still find a way to remain a thorn in my side."

As the communication ends, Brykar watches as Nosvorat turns to face the knights' BOD Bots. As they reach Nosvorat, they begin to transform into their warrior modes.

Nosvorat chuckles as he sees that it's just the vehicles and not the knights themselves. He says, "I see that since your masters are unavailable, they are reduced to sending in their pet tin cans after me. Oh, well, I guess it's time to play Kick The Can."

The knights' BOD Bots say nothing to Nosvorat, but they surround him. Nosvorat then says, "This little trick didn't work before, and it won't work, now." He then flies into the sky, and as he does, he twists the tip of his cane to its second mode, revealing a psychronium blade. Then, as he speeds toward the BOD Bots, they scatter. "Ahhh!" he says, "so you tin cans actually can think. Too bad the knights weren't as smart as you! If they were, I wouldn't have defeated them so easily."

Before any of the BOD Bots can respond, John and Light Stride arrive, and John leaps into the air to face Nosvorat. He says, "Back off, you horror movie reject. I'm your next opponent."

Nosvorat notices that there's something familiar about the warrior in front of him and says, "You look familiar, but who are you exactly?"

"I'm the Light Knight," John replies, "and I'm here to end you."

Nosvorat chuckles and says, "Just because you've had a costume change doesn't mean you have the power to defeat me. Still, let's see what you can do."

CHAPTER 15

DARKEST BEFORE THE DAWN: LIGHT OF THE KNIGHT

BACK AT THEIR BASE, DES MONITORS JOHN, while, at the same time, looking for a way to break the connection Nosvorat has over the other knights. As he scans Nosvorat, he's unable to find any way to sever the connection. In frustration, he slams his hand on the console.

Just then, Manuel and Justice come in. "What's wrong?" Manuel asks.

Des turns to Manuel and says, "I've tried everything I can think of, and I still haven't found a way to break the connection Nosvorat has over the other knights."

"Okay," Manuel says, "I can see that it's frustrating. Mind if I have a look?"

Des shrugs his shoulders and says, "Go ahead! I'm all out of ideas."

As Des steps back, Manuel goes to the console and begins going through different screens ... until he brings up one showing the connection between the knights and Nosvorat. He asks, "Is this what you're looking for?"

Des rushes back to the console and says, "Manuel, how did you do that?" Manuel chuckles. "Simple," he says, "I stopped looking for a physical connection and started looking for a soul-like connection. That was when I found this."

Des looks more closely at the scan now. It shows that the darkness within the knights is what's growing. This causes him to realize what the connection is. "Of course," he says, "now it all makes sense."

"What is it, Des?" Manuel inquires.

Des explains, "At first, I was scanning Nosvorat for his connection to the knights, and I found nothing. But, then, as I scanned the knights, I noticed that for a moment the darkness drains from them. Then, it grows larger each time. It is the darkness that is keeping them under his control."

Now Justice asks, "Is there anything that can be done to free them from this?"

Looking at the console, Des says, "It looks like the only way to free them would be to destroy the force feeding on them — which is Nosvorat."

Using their telepathic powers, Des contacts John. "John," he says, "I've got good news and bad news. Which do you want first?"

John chuckles and replies, "What's the bad news?"

"The knights won't be able to help you this time," Des responds.

Shaking his head, John asks, "So, what's the good news?"

"I've found a way to free the knights?" Des says.

"Awesome! says John. "So ... what do we need to do?"

Des hesitates a moment and then finally says, "The only way to free them is to destroy Nosvorat."

"Ohhhhh, lovely!" John responds. "And just how am I supposed to do that exactly?" He can't help the sarcastic tone.

"I'm not sure," Des has to admit. "If I get any ideas, I'll let you know."

NOSVORAT WATCHES AS THE LIGHT KNIGHT HOLDS HIS STANCE. He says "What's the matter, young knight? Are you scared that you can't defeat me?"

John looks straight at him and says, "Get real! Why would I be scared of a reject from a horror film like you."

John pulls the arm holding the shield behind him, while the hand holding his lance crosses his chest. As he pulls his arm down, he moves with blinding speed and charges for Nosvorat. Surprised by this maneuver, Nosvorat uses his mouth to create a sonic wave that allows him to dodge, John's attack. He says, "Impressive, young knight! I see that you have gained some power. Still, it will not be enough to defeat me. But ... if you think you can, let's see what you've got."

John chuckles. He is just as surprised at how fast he is able to move as Nosvorat is. He turns and says, "Nosvorat, you haven't seen anything yet." Then he charges in for an attack.

Just as before, he moves at blinding speed. When Nosvorat uses his sonic blast, John is able to avoid it. At the same time, he hits Nosvorat with his shield, sending him flying into the air. As Nosvorat flies through the air, he uses his wings to change his direction and heads straight for John, who is able to dodge him easily.

Frustrated,, Nosvorat continues to attack the Light Knight, and yet he is unable to land a single blow. Still he boasts, "If you think you can beat me like that, you are sadly mistaken!"

Before John can respond, Nosvorat opens his mouth, letting out a sonic blast that disorients the Light Knight, causing him to fall to the ground. Then Nosvorat charges at him with his arm across his chest. He is holding his cane, having the exposed blade, and, as he gets closer, he swings his arm away from his chest in hopes of striking the knight.

As he does this, Light Stride gets in the way, and Nosvorat's blade slices Light Stride's armor. "Don't forget," he says, "we're here too!"

"Oh, I haven't forgotten about you," Nosvorat says with a chuckle. "The thing is I don't concern myself with inferior opponents."

With that, Nosvorat flicks his pinky, which hits Light Stride, sending him flying to the ground several hundred feet past the Light Knight. When John sees this, this he grips his lance tight and says, "Big mistake, Nosvorat! No one hurts my friends!"

Nosvorat chuckles again and says, "You call that ... that thing your friend? It's not even human. How can it be your friend?"

"You're right," John answers, "he's not human, but that doesn't mean he's not my friend, and you're going to pay for hurting him and for what you've done to my other friends."

Upon hearing the Light Knight's words, Nosvorat gets an idea. He says, "You know what? I do believe you're right. And now let me introduce you to *my* new friends."

Suddenly, Nosvorat's eye begins to glow, and he says, "Come to me, my servants! Aid your master in this hour."

Before John can says a word, the knights under Nosvorat's trance appear before him. He says, "Meet my new friends. Oh, that's right. I do believe you may have met them before."

When John sees who it is, he says, "What have you done to them?"

Nosvorat laughs and says, "That is my secret. They are my servants, and with them on my side, you cannot win."

Looking at Nosvorat, the Light Knight replies, "Really? How did you come up with that?"

Nosvorat says, "Simply put, I know that you, being a hero, would not dare to harm your friends. And, with them under my trance, I have access to their powers as well — as you shall see." He touches the Bolt Knight's shoulder with one hand, then, with his free hand, he fires a lightning blast at the Light Knight. John is able to use the tip of his lance to redirect the blast back at Nosvorat.

Nosvorat has the Aqua Knight jump in front of the blast, to protect him. It hits her, and she is thrown to the ground. When John sees this, he shouts, "You coward! How dare you do that to my friends!"

Waving a finger in the air, Nosvorat says, "I'm not the one who did that. You did it when you attacked me, and my new servants will protect me with their lives, as you can see. Although there is one more surprise I should show you, knight. Or should I say, 'show him, Earth Knight.'"

The Light Knight watches as the Earth Knight emerges from among the knights under Nosvorat's trance. "You'll pay for this, Nosvorat!" says the Light Knight as he tries to think of a way to defeat him.

Nosvorat says, "Now, Earth Knight, why don't you and your friends join with vehicles and get rid of this knight."

The Earth Knight steps forward and says, "BOD Bot Sentient mode, disengage, and BOD Bot armor mode, engage." Suddenly the BOD Bots return to their vehicle form and join the knights. They each get in their respective BOD Bots. Transformed into their warrior mode, the knights control them.

This causes Nosvorat to laugh heartily. "Get him, my knights!" he says. "Destroy your former friend!"

The knights under Nosvorat's control step forward. The Light Knight says, "If you think using my friends as a shield will keep me from stopping you, then you have another thing coming. Let me show you why."

The Light Knight charges at his friends, going for the Earth Knight first. As he reaches him, the Light Knight hits him and says, "Even my friends won't be able to hit what they can't see."

Using his speed, John attacks and dodges, so that he can lure the Earth Knight away. Once they're far enough away, John, says, "I don't know how you got caught, but I will put you down if I have to."

The Earth Knight attacks. John, using his speed, dodges this attack easily, and as he charges at the Earth Knight, the sun reflects off his shield, shining in the Earth Knight's face, causing him to stagger for a moment.

Noticing this, John decides to use it to his advantage. Leaping into the air, he uses his shield to reflect the sunlight into the face of the Earth Knight, causing him to stop. As John lands, he slowly approaches the Earth Knight and says, "Hey, buddy, are you in there?"

Shaking his head, the Earth Knight says, "Yeah, what happened?"

John responds, "You tell me! Last time I saw you, you were in the base, and the next thing I know, you're under Nosvarat's trance."

The Earth Knight starts to remember what has happened. He says, "Now I remember. I went to check on the knights, when one of them used that stare Nosvorat uses on me. The next thing I knew I was here with you."

Before anything else can be said, the Earth Knight starts to double over in pain. John moves back, noticing that the Earth Knight is once again under Nosvorat's trance. Looking up, John notices Nosvorat and the other knights coming closer. He takes a moment to think and says to himself, "Okay, so going by what we know, his powers are weak against sunlight. So, I might be able to use that against him."

Once Nosvorat and the knights are in front of the Light Knight, Nosvorat laughs again and says, "If you think you can beat me, you are sadly mistaken, for my power comes from the negative emotions of any and all life, and your friends are so full of negative emotions that it will make me unstoppable—as you shall see."

Nosvorat opens his mouth, and the knights come to standstill. Then, with nearly the same speed as the Light Knight, Nosvorat charges at the knight with a barrage of strikes. At first, John blocks and dodges the attacks, but then he finds it difficult to block them all. Nosvorat uses a sonic blast, knocking the Light Knight to the ground. He is dazed for a moment.

Using this, Nosvorat begins to launch another barrage of attacks, preventing the Light Knight from being able to block this newest onslaught. With one last strike, Nosvorat hits the knight in his stomach, causing him to fall to his knees. Nosvorat then lifts the knight's head and using his powers, puts the Light Knight under a paralyzing trance, so that the knight is only able to speak.

Haughtily looking at the knight, Nosvorat says, "As you can see, Light Knight, there is no way you can defeat me, for where there is light, there is also darkness, and the power I possess is the very power of darkness itself and the darkness within each living being. As you have seen, your friends are under my power and have not been able to resist me."

The Light Knight replies "True, but I did and I have."

Chuckling again, Nosvorat says, "True, but once your light is extinguished, there will be no being in the universe that can resist my powers."

Nosvorat then draws his cane. Twisting the top, he activates its third and final mode, revealing the blade from his cane's second mode, but with a dark energy around it now. The Light Knight groans as he struggles to break free of Nosvorat's trance. He is able to reply, "That's where you're wrong, Nosvorat! No matter how dark things become, darkness will never overcome light. The power of light will shine even in the deepest darkness. You may have my friends under your power, but you won't win, for I am the Light Knight, and I will extinguish you."

Suddenly the Light Knight stands to his feet. As Nosvorat watches him stand, he says, "Very Impressive! I've never met anyone quite like you, but it will make my victory over you that much more enjoyable."

John moves to the side, to take his stand against Nosvorat. "We'll see about that!" he says. "Give me your best shot."

Locking eyes with Nosvorat, the Light Knight breaks the trance, and the two warriors draw their weapons. As they charge at each other and begin to exchange blows, neither warrior is willing to back down. Nosvorat hits the Light Knight, sending him to the ground. He shouts, "It's time for me to end this dance!"

Stunned and dazed from the last exchange, John shakes his head and starts to recite the oath, "As the days of darkness surround, and heroes can be found." Nosvorat leaps into the air and speeds toward the Light Knight, his cane in front of him. His plan is to impale the knight on it. But even as Nosvorat speeds toward him, John continues the oath: "While those who descend and prey on the weak, who do not rise or dare to speak…"

Suddenly Nosvorat's attack is deflected by John, as he stands and finishes the oath, saying, "We will utter our heartfelt battle cry, as we raise our hands to the sky. To protect the world from loss, I am a Knight of the Cross!" Surprised by this, Nosvorat charges at the Light Knight, who also charges. As John grips his lance, he has it become a beam of solid light. The two clash, but he knocks Nosvorat's blade away and then stabs him in the heart with his beam of light. It pierces Nosvorat, and he falls to ground shouting, "NOOOOOOOOOO!"

Before Nosvorat can utter another sound, he turns to dust. John, for his part, breathes a deep sigh of relief and rushes to his friends. He notices that, with Nosvorat's defeat, they have been freed from his power.

AS THE KNIGHTS AWAKEN FROM THEIR TRANCE, John makes his way to Light Stride, and while his self-repair is underway, John asks, "Are you okay?"

"I'll be fine," Light Stride replies. "Just give me a few minutes to put myself back together."

Moments later, as Light Stride finishes repairing himself, the other knights join John. "I see that congratulations are in order," Joseph says. "By the way, I see that you unlocked a new armor as well."

"Pretty much!" John answers. "Still, I'm glad you guys are okay."

Tasha asks, "Can anyone explain what just happened to us?"

Des steps forward and responds, "Let's head back to the base, and I'll explain."

AS THE KNIGHTS HEAD BACK TO THEIR BASE John is relieved to have his friends back. Light Stride says, "I'm sorry I wasn't able to help you more back there."

John chuckles and replies "It's fine! Just don't let it happen again."

Light Stride, says, "Excuse me?"

John says, "Easy, Bro! It was just a joke. Although the new armor is awesome, I have to admit: even I wasn't sure if I would be able to beat him at first."

"So, what changed?" asks Light Stride.

For a moment John is silent and then says, "I guess what changed was when he started talking about how powerful darkness is. It was as if something inside of me confirmed that as a lie. No matter how dark things may get, even the smallest gleam of light can drown out the darkness. Once I realized that, I felt a surge of power I had never felt before, and that's when I focused my power into my lance and used it like a giant stake, piercing Nosvorat through the heart and freeing the others from his trance."

BEFORE JOHN CAN SAY ANYTHING ELSE, they all arrive back at their base and make their way to Des's lab. There he powers on the computer. Tasha says "Now that we're back, can you tell us what exactly happened to us?"

"Well," Des replies, "when Nosvorat put you all under his trance, it caused all your negative emotions to surface. And, as they did, he began to feed off of them to increase his own power."

"Is there a way to prevent this from happening again?" Joseph asks.

"Yes," Des replies, "but it's not an overnight fix."

Tasha asks, "What do you mean by that?"

Des puts his hand to his chin, then responds, "What I mean is this: we all come from different backgrounds and have different experiences, which means different events bring out different emotions. The only way we'll be able to defeat a creature that uses this kind of power will be to do as John did and not give in to the negative emotions that Nosvorat was using. Since John's powers were based on the power of light, he was able to resist the darkness better than we were, but if we each learn to overcome our negative emotions in that kind of situation, we should be able to break the power of darkness, just like John did."

"Wait!" Tasha says. "So you're telling me that they are able to use our own emotions against us?"

Des nods and says, "Exactly! Although I have noticed something interesting about these last few battles!"

"What's that?" Joseph asks.

"What I've noticed," Des explains, "is that, although the Psystructs do have psychic abilities, the warriors Brykar has been using don't seem to have any psychic powers." He looks at the computer screen.

Now Brad asks, "Hey, Des, if these guys don't have any psychic powers, then how are they able to either gain control over us or put us under these 'trances' as you call them?"

Chucking, Des responds, "I was just about to explain that. Although these warriors Brykar has been using don't have psychic powers, the powers they *do* have are more hypnotic powers, which is why they've been able to gain control over us. Also, when we first got our powers, I noticed that the armors we've been given protect us from the Psystruct's psychic abilities, but not abilities or powers that are hypnotically based."

"What's the difference," Tasha asks, "between hypnotic powers and psychic ones?"

"The difference." Des explains, "is that psychic powers don't just control; they manipulate your mind and your psyche, whereas hypnotic powers simply allow control."

Coughing, Joseph says, "Hey, would you mind repeating that in English?"

After thinking about how he has said it, even Des realizes he wasn't very clear, so he says, "Basically, the Psystructs' psychic powers would be able to access our memories, along with our emotions, fears and desires, but the hypnotic powers of his warriors don't have access to our memories or thoughts."

While the knights listen to Des' explanation of what has been going on, some of them start to question if this was a good idea or not. Joseph, noticing the looks on their faces, says, "Hey, everyone, listen up! I know this news is not the best we've heard, and I know some of you are thinking, 'Did we make the right choice?' I believe we did. I mean, think about it: if we hadn't done this, Brykar and his crew would have all of us and our families by now. I know it's been hard, but we have to keep fighting. If we don't, everyone and everything we know will be destroyed. I don't know about the rest of you, but I won't let that happen."

As the other knights listen to Joseph, they realize that he's right, and they all nod in agreement. Joseph then adds, "All right! For now, I want everyone to go and relax for a few hours, and then we'll link up to start training again. Agreed?" The knights agree, and they each start to go their separate ways.

JOHN HEADS TO THE REC ROOM, and Tasha decides to follow him. Getting close, she calls, "Hey, John, can I talk to you?"

He turns to Tasha and says, "Sure, what's up?"

"Well," she continues, "I wanted to know how you were able to escape

Nosvorat's trance?" She seems nervous for the first time since they have all became knights.

Noticing this, John says, "To be honest, I'm not fully sure. All I remember was that I was reliving the day my dad died, and I heard voices telling me to give up. I was just about to do that when I remembered a promise I had made to my mom. Remembering that, I felt a surge and awoke back in the base with Des and the rest of you under Nosvorat's control."

Puzzled by this statement, Tasha says, "Do you mind if I ask: What was the promise you made to your mom the day your dad died?"

Now it's John's turn to chuckle. "She made me promise to always stay positive," he says, "no matter how hard or dark things got. Because I've been doing that for the last several years, it's become almost second nature to me."

"Wow!" Tasha replies. "I don't know if I could do that."

"To be honest, at that time I wasn't sure if I would be able to do it either," John admits. "All we can do is take things one step at a time."

WHEN THEY REACH THE REC ROOM, and as they enter, John says, "Are you up for a game of pool?"

Now Tasha chuckles and says "You're on! Just watch your hands?"

John shakes his head and says, "I wouldn't dream of touching you ... unless you want me to." He pauses for a moment, then decides to continue, "And I don't think there's a man alive who wouldn't want to hold or touch you."

This causes Tasha to smile. She says, "When did you become the sweet talker?"

"I'm not trying to be a sweet talker, just stating what's true," John says, as they make their way to the pool table.

MEANWHILE BACK IN THE ARC TEAM'S BASE, Agent Wallace and the others continue their surveillance of the knights' families. Agent Daniels has been reviewing the alien black box. After she received the notification, she has returned to the computer. As she sits down and clicks on the item of interest, it is a video that shows the knights attacking the Psystructs, but on an alien planet. After verifying that the video is authentic, she contacts Agent Martin via a video link and informs him of her discovery. He says, "Gather the team! I need to speak with them ... now!"

USING THE COMMUNICATION SYSTEM WHERE SHE IS, Agent Daniels makes the announcement: "All ARC team members, assemble in the lab at once!"

Moments later, Agent Wallace and the rest of his team arrive in the lab, Agent Wallace asks, "What's going on?"

Agent Martin says, "Agent Daniels has verified that what the Psystructs told us is correct. The knights have been hunting them and have brought that fight to our planet. Now, I need all of you to focus your attention on these knights and how we can exterminate them."

Agent Rivera says, "That's easier said than done. If we are going to have any chance of defeating them, we'll need more advanced tech from Brykar."

"You make a good point," Agent Martin replies. I'll contact Brykar to see what other tech he can give us that will help us to destroy these so-called knights."

Suddenly the video link ends, and Agent Wallace says, "Daniels, what info do we have on these knights?"

She then starts going through the video logs and says, "Not much really. The only thing we know for sure is that there are twelve of them."

When Agent Wallace hears this something strikes a cord. "Is it possible," he asks, "that the kids we're looking for are these knights?"

Agent Daniels shakes her head and says, "I seriously doubt it. The date of the video taken on that alien planet is several thousand years before these teens were even born."

"Still," Agent Wallace replies, not yet satisfied that he is wrong, "it's kind of weird that the twelve teens we are looking for are the same number of the knights we are now hunting."

"Well," Agent Daniels says, "I'll go through the videos more to see, but if these teens were somehow connected to the knights, they would be waging war, not just against the Earth, but also against their families. From the profiles we were given, they don't seem to match the sadistic nature that would be needed for someone to side with the destruction of their own world."

"I can't argue with you on that point," Agent Wallace concedes, "but, still, we need to know more about these knights."

"Okay," Agent Rivera interjects, "while you all do that, I'll be working on gear to give you a fighting chance."

BRYKAR IS RETRIEVING THE DUST that is the remains of Nosvorat, when he notices Agent Martin is trying to contact him. He opens the link between them and says, "Greetings, Agent Martin! What can I do for you?"

Agent Martin says, "Brykar, after a thorough search of the alien black box you gave us, we have seen that these knights do intend to harm you and your kind, with no just cause. My team is ready to join you in your fight against these knights, but we will require more advanced tech in order to fashion weapons that will be able to destroy them."

Brykar smiles to himself. Then he scans Agent Martin's mind and notices that the ARC team has seen the fake video of the knights fighting the Psystructs. He says, "I see, Agent Martin. Give me a few hours, and I will gather the tech I have available and contact you with the pick-up location."

"Very well," Agent Martin replies. "My team and I will be ready, and together we will destroy these pesky knights."

AS THE COMMUNICATION ENDS, BRYKAR NOTICES that General Sadoom is also trying to contact him, and he opens the corresponding communication channel. "Brykar," General Sadoom says, "give me a status report on your mission."

"Well," Brykar replies, "the knights have just defeated my newest warrior, and while I was collecting his remains so that he can be revived and improved, I was contacted by the Earth's alien hunters. They have agreed to help us against the knights ... provided we give them the tech to fight the knights."

Skeptical, General Sadoom asks, "How would a bunch of Earthlings help to defeat the knights?"

"They *would* help," Brykar replies, "because I believe these knights are humans. Also, the alien hunters found the fake video of the knights attacking us thousands of years ago. By them seeing this, it will increase their drive to defeat the knights."

"Very well," General Sadoom says. "Give the alien hunters the tech they are asking for. Just make sure it's nothing that would be a threat to *us*."

Brykar bows and says, "Of course, General Sadoom."

With that, the communication ends, and Brykar has the Psydrones get the tech ready for the ARC team.

WHILE THIS OCCURS, MELANIE IS MEETING WITH PHILLIP and Linda at a nearby cafe, when they see Graham across the street. Melanie walks over to him and asks, "Graham, would you join us for a moment?"

Knowing that this is a bit odd, Graham also knows that Melanie wouldn't ask him to join them if it weren't something serious. So, he says "Sure, lead the way."

As they rejoin Phillip and Linda, Melanie has them tell Graham about what happened. When they are done, he says, "Well, there's good news and bad news. What do you want first?"

The three look at each other and say, "What's the bad news?"

Graham takes a breath and says, "I honestly haven't found anything about why Des and the others are being hunted."

"And what's the good news?" Phillip then asks.

"Although I haven't found out *why* they are being hunted," Graham replies, "I did find out *who* is hunting them. It's a secret government agency that goes by the name of ARC. It is associated with hunting aliens."

Melanie shakes her head in disbelief and says, "Graham, if this organization is as secret as you claim it to be, how do you know so much about it?"

This causes him to chuckle. "Well," he says, "that's because my dad happened to be one of their agents until he died, and while there are no hard documents about this organization, he left a journal which I recently found. It talks about this organization a lot. I will study it more as I have time."

He pauses for just a moment and then continues, "I also found that, according to the fire department, whatever caused the bus to explode was not normal, and if these alien hunters think aliens did this, that may be why they want Des and the others so badly and why they would try to use a duplicate of Melanie to get information out of us."

Melanie is again shocked. "Graham," she says, "you can't be serious!"

He turns to her and says, "Unfortunately, I am *very* serious, and these people are *very* dangerous, which means we have to make sure that we maintain a low profile ... at least until we can find out more about why Des and the others are on their radar."

Phillip, his wife and Melanie all nod in agreement and soon head their separate ways.

AS GRAHAM WALKS AWAY, he pulls a journal from his pocket. Looking hard at it, he says, "What other secrets are you hiding, Dad?"

CHAPTER 16

BATTLE OF THE BEASTS: CORNERS AND CAGES

WHILE GRAHAM IS ON HIS WAY HOME, Tasha's grandparents, James and Claudia Velios, are home doing what they normally do. Claudia is cooking, while her husband has his nose in a book. He puts it down, goes to his wife, and says, "I really hate this!"

"You really hate what, dear?" she asks.

Realizing that he wasn't as clear as he should have been, he says, "I hate feeling useless. I wish there was more we could do to find out what happened to Tasha and the others."

Chuckling, she says, "Is it really that or that no one asked what you could do to help find out what happened?"

Now it's her husband's turn to chuckle. He can never hide his feelings from her. In his prime, James Velios was an ace reporter, known for doing a number of exposés on military and government corruption. He had done so well, in fact, that his family never had any real financial worries.

As James looks at his wife Claudia now, he says, "As always, you have me pegged. I am upset that no one asked me what I could do."

"Well," she answers, "why wait for them to ask? You never did that before. Whenever you needed answers, you went and found them."

Now chuckling to himself, he realizes that she's right. He pulls out his phone and makes a call to an associate. When they answer, he says, "Hey, do you have a minute?"

The person on the other end let's him know he can't talk long. James says, "Listen, I need a small piece of the wreckage from the bus my granddaughter was on, so we can figure out what's going on." When the person on the other end starts to get difficult, James says, "I know that's going to be difficult, but I need to know what happened to my granddaughter and her friends. Please help me."

Reluctantly, the person on the other end voices their agreement, and James says, "Awesome! I'll give you the address of where I want it dropped off."

Claudia has been listening to the conversation and notices that her husband has given an address other than theirs. When he gets off the phone, she asks, "Whose address did you just give him?"

Laughing, James says, "I gave him Graham's address. If there's anyone who can find out anything from that wreckage, it's him."

Claudia walks over to her husband and kisses him. "See!" she says, "I knew you could do it. You just had to be reminded of what you can do."

Pleased, James says, "Thanks for reminding me who I am and what I can do."

BACK AT BRYKAR'S BASE, he places the remain of Nosvorat in the reconstruction tube. As it begins to rebuild his body, Brykar makes his way to the chamber containing his remaining warriors. Once there, he realizes that if he's going to stop the knights, he will need a hunter. Then he remembers a creature that will do nicely. As the chamber opens, a creature with the face of a lion but the body of a human being emerges. He is dressed in a leather vest, leather-like pants and boots. Around his waist are discs known as terra traps. These can alter the terrain of any past planet to meet his needs. On one wrist he has a scrambler that will "mess" with any and all scanning devices (with the exception of his own). On the other wrist he has a scanner that lets him know when something is coming near or enters his terra trap.

Looking at Brykar, he asks, "What do you require of me, Brykar?"

Chuckling, Brykar answers, "Leo Untaros, I have need of your unique abilities."

Leo Untaros responds, "Who do you need me to eradicate for you this time?"

"They are a group known as the Knights of the Cross, they have become a nuisance, and I need them gone. Are you up for the challenge?" Brykar asks.

Stretching, Leo Untaros says, "I'm always ready for a challenge, Brykar."

Brykar then points to the hanger and says, "In there, you will find weapons and vehicles that will help you against the knights. I must leave now as I have other matters that need my attention."

Kneeling, Leo Untaros says "Very well! But do you have a specific way you want me to deal with these knights?"

This causes Brykar to chuckle again. "No," he says, "do with them as you will.

AS BRYKAR LEAVES TO CHECK ON THE STATUS of the equipment being gathered for the ARC team, Leo Untaros goes to the hanger. As he enters, he notices the chain blade, a sword made of chains that can extend like a whip at the will of the user. When he picks it up, he notices single links of chains called link cuffs. Picking one up, he throws it at a nearby Psydrone, it hits him, and the Psydrone is paralyzed and unable to move. This causes Leo Untaros to chuckle, and he says, "This is going to be fun. Still, I need something more before I take them on."

Looking around, he notices one of the Magnacycles. He walks over to it and, using the chain blade, has it wrap around the Magnacycle, converting it into a Magnachaincycle. This is like the Magnacycles, except that it is made out of chain links, much like the chain blade. Once the process is complete he says, "Now this is much better!" Then he gets on his vehicle and heads out of the hanger, eager for the hunt ahead.

AFTER RIDING SEVERAL MILES FROM THE BASE, Leo Untaros notices that the land is dusty and barren, pulls a terra trap and sets it on the ground. When he activates it, it expands, creating a jungle-like terrain about an acre in width. When the process is complete, he says to himself, "Perfect! When the knights come to investigate this, I'll have them."

MEANWHILE, AS THE KNIGHTS ENJOY THEIR DOWN TIME, Maggie, Jessica, Britney and Janet notice that something is going on between Tasha and John, who are playing pool. Britney walks over to them and says, "Sorry to bother you guys, but could I borrow Tasha for a moment, John?"

Not knowing what this is all about, he answers, "That's up to her. If Tasha's fine with it, I have no problem with it either."

Tasha turns to Britney and says, "You've got five minutes."

"Okay," Britney says, "follow me."

As she leads Tasha to where the other girls are, Tasha says, "What's this all about?"

Maggie chuckles and says, "Why don't you tell us? I mean, you and John seem to be getting pretty close, don't you think?"

Snapping at Maggie, Tasha says, "What are you talking about?"

Jessica shakes her head, says, "Tasha, listen! We all just noticed that there's something going on between you and John, and we'd like to know about it. It's not a bad thing, just surprising."

Now Tasha sighs. "Is it that obvious?" she asks.

Janet chuckles. "To us it is," she says, "to the boys, not so much. So what happened?"

"Honestly," Tasha answers, "I wanted to talk to John about how he broke Nosvorat's control. Then, after he told me, he asked me to play pool, and I accepted. Although now that I think of it, guys don't really approach me that often, and John was the first guy to actually approach me."

"That makes sense," says Britney, "so do you like him?"

Tasha shakes her head and says, "I'm not sure. I know I like hanging out with him, but I don't know if it goes any further than that."

"Really?" Maggie says. "Why don't we ask John how he feels about you?"

"Don't you dare," Tasha replies. "If you do I'll make sure you pay."

Maggie chuckles again and says, "Relax! I'm not going to say anything, but your response shows you really like him a lot."

Janet then adds, "Tasha, listen! We're not trying to upset you. We just want you to be happy. But, most of all, we want you to be honest with yourself. If you like John, then tell him. I mean, it's obvious he's into you ... although he may be unsure about how *you* feel."

Just then Sally walks over and says, "What are you all talking about?"

Britney pulls her close and whispers, "We're talking with Tasha about her love life."

Tasha then interjects, "It's more like the lack of a love life, from what I'm starting to notice."

"Well if you ask me," Sally says, "you and John would make an awesome couple. And, there's something you might want to know."

Tasha looks at her in surprise and then asks, "What are you talking about, Sally?"

Sally smiles and says, "Well, do you remember the freshman dance?"

"Yeah, what about it?" replies Tasha, puzzled by what Sally is saying.

Again Sally smiles and then continues, "Well, I remember too, and what I remember is that you were by yourself for most of the dance ... that is, until the last slow song. Then I watched as someone asked you to dance. Do you remember who it was that asked you to dance, Tasha?"

Suddenly Tasha remembers. It was John, and she loved the way he held her. "Yes," she says, "it was John."

"Bingo!" Sally says. "You may not know it, but I've watched him reject girl after girl, waiting for the right time to ask *you* out."

Surprised by all of this, Tasha asks, "How do you know that?"

Sally now giggles and says, "Because I have watched him do this and was curious about it, I asked him. When he described the girl he's waiting for, I knew it was you."

Before anything else could be said, the alarm goes off. Sally shakes her head and says, "I guess this means we'll have to finish this conversation later."

WHILE THE ALARM STILL SOUNDS, the knights all head to the lab. Once there, they find Des looking to see what has caused it to go off. Joseph says, "What have we got, Des?"

Shaking his head, Des answers, "That's just it. I'm not exactly sure what is going on. As far as I can tell, the only thing out of the normal is that there looks to be a jungle growing about seventy miles from here. The weirdest part is that it's growing in the middle of nowhere."

"What do you mean," Joseph asks, "in the middle of nowhere?"

"Simply put," Des replies, "there's nothing out there but barren wasteland. In fact, I don't even know how it's possible for anything to grow out there in the first place."

Brad then says, "Does this mean what I think it means?"

"If you're thinking this is a trap," Eric says, "then most definitely it is. Still, we can't just ignore it and hope it goes way. So, what's the plan?"

Joseph asks, "Des, didn't you set the scanners to find alien life signs that might give us more info on what's going on?"

"That's the problem," Des replies. "From what I found, there are too many alien life signs that are throwing the sensors off. So, I'm not able to pinpoint who or what is causing this."

Eric says, "Des, rather than scanning for life signs, how about scanning for any alien tech in that area?"

"Well," Des says, "at this point, I'm willing to try anything."

As Des scans for the alien tech, he notices that there are two different signals. The first is at the center of where the anomaly is taking place, and the second is moving throughout the anomaly. After he finds the moving anomaly, he adjusts the scanners to lock on it and get an image of it. This accomplished, the knights see Leo Untaros for the first time.

John asks, "Who's that?"

"I'm not sure," Des says, "but the best I can tell, he's half lion and half man, most likely one of Brykar's warriors who's trying to lure us out."

"So," Eric says, "not only is this a trap, but we don't have much info on who's setting the trap."

"That's pretty much it," Des replies.

Just then Manuel walks in and says, "What seems to be the problem, my young friends?"

Des answers, "Well, we've got a jungle growing in the middle of nowhere and an alien we know nothing about. We know it's a trap, but we are flying blind as to who is setting this trap."

Looking at the screen, Manuel says, "That is a bit a of a predicament. Des, may I see the computer a moment?"

Stepping back, Des answers, "Sure, go ahead!"

Manuel moves to the computer, and as he does, he looks intently at the screen. With a few keystrokes, a profile of the alien is on the screen, and Des is impressed. He says, "Manuel, how did you do that?"

Manuel chuckles and says, "All I did was unlock the DNA scanner, which will allow you to know what kind of alien you are dealing with, as well as the types of powers associated with their race."

Manuel steps away from the computer, scans the data and says, "According to this, he's from the planet Leorano, a planet of hunters. It also says that they are trained to hunt from birth, and the more challenging the hunt, the more deadly they are."

Eric shakes his head and says, "Perfect! This is the last thing we need, a crazed hunter after us! Although this might work to our advantage if we play it right."

Des now chuckles and says, "What's your plan, Eric?"

Eric answers, "I'm glad you asked. If this guy is a hunter and he's hunting us, then odds are he's planning on trapping us or has a way to trap us."

"What exactly are getting at, Bro?" John asks.

"What I'm saying," Eric suggests, "is we let him capture us, and while he thinks he has us, we escape and trap him instead."

Chuckling, Des says, "That might just work, but that would mean we would have to know exactly how he plans on trapping us. Although I might be able to short-circuit them, using the BOD Bots, still it's risky."

Joseph says, "True, but still, it's the best plan we have right now. So, let's meet this new warrior of Brykar's and show him why we're the Knights of the Cross."

The other knights nod in agreement and all head for the hanger. When they reach the BOD Bots, the hanger doors open, and they race off to where the anomaly has been identified.

MEANWHILE. LEO UNTAROS HAS BEEN SETTING TRAPS all throughout the area. As he finishes setting the final trap, he says to himself, "Now, all I need is for those knights to show up."

Suddenly the scanner on his arm starts to beep. As he looks at it, he notices something approaching and says, "Perfect! Once I trap these knights, I will have the pleasure of hunting them down one by one."

NOW LEO UNTAROS GETS ON HIS MAGNACHAINCYCLE and takes off into the jungle. As he does, he looks for a vantage point where he can watch the knights as they enter. Coming to the edge of the terra trap, where the jungle and barren land meet, he notices a tall tree and heads toward it. He stashes his Magnachaincycle in the bushes and climbs to the top of a tree to wait for the knights to enter.

When Leo Untaros reaches the top of the tree, he can see the knights as they approach. He says to himself, "That's right, young knights, enter the jungle! Become my prey!"

He watches as the knights stop at the edge of the terra trap. Activating his scrambler on his left arm, he waits for them to enter. Soon he will begin his hunt.

As he waits for the knights to enter, Leo Untaros notices that they are staying just outside the terra trap. Chuckling to himself, he says, "If you think hiding just outside the terra trap will help you, you had better think again."

Using, the scanner on his right arm, he presses a button, causing the terra disc to expand even further. As it does, the knights speed away from it in hopes of outrunning it. Now Leo Untaros begins leaping from tree to tree, as the terra trap expands. Then the knights have their BOD Bots continue, while they leap from them and come to a stop. Leo Untaros watches as the trees of the jungle grow around the knights, and they are caught in his terra trap.

He leaps down and says, "Welcome, knights! My name is Leo Untaros, the Beast King Hunter, and you are my prey."

The Light Knight steps forward and says, "You wish! We're nobody's prey."

"You have spirit," Leo Untaros says with a chuckle. "I will give you that, young knight. But you will need more than that if you are going to best me. Still, I'm a good sport and will give you a chance. If I capture all of you by sundown tomorrow, then you will give up your fight against the Psystructs, but if even one of you escapes or manages to defeat me, then I will surrender to you. How's that for fair?"

The Shadow Knight answers, "How do we know you will keep your word?"

Leo Untaros looks intently at the Shadow Knight and replies, "You will just have to trust me, Shadow Knight." The rest of the knights are also wondering if he can be trusted.

The Cross Knight steps forward and says, "If that's how you want to play it, we accept your challenge. When does the clock start?"

"The game starts now!" Leo Untaros replies. "Let the hunt begin!"

That being said, Leo Untaros draws his chain blade from his hip and begins to attack the knights, and they scatter.

Brad is the first to launch an attack, using his flame blades. Leo Untaros counters by leaping over and past the Fire Knight, so that as he passes him, he's able to kick him in the back, sending him flying to the ground.

Landing, Leo Untaros taunts, "Really? Is that the best you knights have got? If, so you will be no challenge at all."

As the Fire Knight gets up, he says, "I'm not done by a long shot."

Again the Fire Knight charges. Leo Untaros says, "Are you really trying the same attack twice? You are pathetic, Fire Knight."

Leo Untaros leaps as he did before. As he gets ready to pass the Fire Knight, the Fire Knight turns and strikes him in midair, wounding him, causing him to miss his opportunity for attack.

While Leo Untaros gets to his feet, the Fire Knight says, "How's that for pathetic, you crazed kitten?"

Looking intently at the Fire Knight, Leo Untaros says, "Impressive, Fire Knight! But make no mistake, I am no kitten, and here's why?"

Suddenly he charges at the Fire Knight. Before he can react, Leo Untaros grabs the Fire Knight and throws him into a tree, snapping the tree in two. As the Fire Knight gets to his feet, Leo Untaros charges at him again. Now in front of the Fire Knight, he throws him again, so that he slams violently into the ground. Leo Untaros now walks menacingly toward him with his chain blade drawn. He says, "Get up! I know I didn't throw you hard enough to knock you unconscious."

The other knights watch as Leo Untaros walks toward the Fire Knight. Then the Wind, Aqua and Earth Knights move to stand in front of the Fire Knight. Seeing this, Leo Untaros says, "Do you really think you will stand a chance against me?"

The Earth Knight says, "There's only one way to find out."

As Leo Untaros continues to walk toward them, the Knight of the Cross telepathically says to the other knights, "Grab him and let's get out of here! There's no way we're going to win like this."

The Shadow knight responds, "I'll provide the cover! Just be ready!"

Using the same telepathic link, the Beast Knight says, "Why are we running? He's not using any special powers to trap us."

"That's the problem," the Cross Knight responds. "Besides, we need to stick to the plan. If we are going to let him capture us, then we need to move now and come up with a plan." The other knights nod in agreement.

Shadow Knight points both of his hands at Leo Untaros, creating a shadow dome, to blind him so that they can make their escape. As the dome closes, the Earth Knight touches the Fire Knight on the shoulder. When he doesn't move, they roll him over and notice that there is chain link-like cuff on his hands. The Cross Knight says telepathically, "Grab him and let's move!"

Just as they get ready to move, Leo Untaros walks out of the dome. He says, "If you think your tricks will work on me, you are sadly mistaken."

Cross Knight shakes his head and says, "I'll hold him off. Everyone else run!"

The other knights watch as he walks toward Leo Untaros. Drawing his swords, as he stand in front of the Earth, Wind, Water and Fire Knights. Then he turns and says, "I gave you all an order! Now move!" With that, the other knights disappear into the surrounding jungle.

The Cross Knight says to Leo Untaros, "If you want a fight, I'll give you one."

Leo Untaros looks at him smugly and says, "Bring it on, little boy!"

RACING THROUGH THE JUNGLE, the other knights come to a spot where they can regroup. The Earth Knight slams his fist on the ground and says, "How could I could I have been so stupid?"

"It's okay," the Water Knight says. "There's no way you could have known."

He turns to her now and says, "I wish I could believe that, but Cross Knight saw it and told us to move. And, whether we admit it or not, we all questioned it."

"You're right," she agrees, "we all did question it, but what's done is done. And, like the Cross Knight said, 'We need a plan.' So let's come up with one."

The Earth Knight tries to scan the cuffs that now bind the Fire Knight, but he gets nothing but static. "This is just great!" he says.

The Wind Knight asks, "What's wrong?"

He replies, "Apparently something is jamming my scanners, and all I'm getting is static. So I have no idea how to undo these cuffs."

As he pauses a moment, the Earth Knight realizes something. "That's it!" he says. "That's why he wanted us here."

A bit puzzled about the outburst, the Shadow Knight says, "I think I'm understanding as well."

"Hey, guys," the Light Knight says, "do you plan on filling us in on what's going on?"

The Earth Knight says, "Forgive me! I just realized: the whole point in bringing us here was not just to trap us, but also to make our scanners useless. So, there's no way I can undo these cuffs."

"True," the Shadow Knight interjects, "but maybe there's another way to undo them."

The Earth Knight notices two small pin holes, but before he can say anything else, Leo Untaros's chain blade extends and wraps around him, dragging him into the bushes.

The Shadow Knight says, "We need to move and now."

The Water Knight says, "What about the Earth Knight? We have to go help him."

He turns to her and says, "We can do more to help right now by figuring out how to unlock these cuffs, not by getting captured. So, now, come on!"

With that, the knights race off through the jungle. The Shadow Knight says telepathically, "We need to split up, to buy us more time to figure this out. So let's split into teams of two."

The Shadow Knight then has the Aqua and Wind Knights go in one direction, the Hope and Love Knights go in another direction. As the rest of the knights are getting ready to split up, the Faith Knight prepares to hold off Leo Untaros. He says, "I'll stay and hold him off. The rest of you get out of here!"

The Light Knight says, "Are you crazy? He's already got Cross and Earth Knights, and he's immobilized the Fire Knight."

"That's true," he replies, "but honestly I haven't done much for the team up until now, and I think it's at least time I tried."

The Light Knight is about to plead with him when the Shadow Knight says, "Very well, Light Knight. You and Beast Knight take the Fire Knight and go. The rest of us will make our stand here and face Leo Untaros."

Looking at his friends, the Light Knight says, "This is suicide!"

The Shadow Knight says "True, but it's part of the plan. Now Go!"

With that, the Light Knight and Beast Knight disappear into the jungle.

AFTER DISAPPEARING INTO THE JUNGLE, the Light Knight and Beast Knight spot a nearby cave. As they head for it the Light Knight says, "This is just wonderful! He's picking us off one by one, and who knows when or how he will find us."

The Beast Knight looks at him and says, "I thought you were Mr. Positive?"

Shaking his head, the Light Knight says, "You're right! I have to remain positive, even in this situation. Thanks." He then continues, "So, let's look at what we know. It looks like these cuff paralyze you, and somehow Leo Untaros can find us, no matter where we go."

As the two try to figure this out, the Beast Knight realizes the answer and says, "Our scent! That's got to be it and also why the Shadow dome didn't work. He wasn't relying on his sight to get him through."

The Light Knight answers, "Okay, so if he's tracking us by our scent, is there a way to throw him off of it?"

"Yes," the Beast Knight says, "but you aren't going to like it."

"At this point," replies the Light Knight, "I don't care what it is ... as long as it helps us stay clear of him."

The Beast Knight says, "Okay! First, we may have to leave the Fire Knight here, cause he may also be how he's tracking us. Second, we need to find some mud and cover ourselves in it to cover our scent."

As the two knights look for mud to change their scents, they hear some rustling in the bushes. The Light Knight pushes the Beast Knight into the bushes just as Leo Untaros appears. He says, "Well, well, well! Looks like I found you. Now, tell me where your friend is, and maybe I'll you go."

"Not a chance, you feline freak!" the Light Knight says, looking squarely at Leo Untaros. If you want her, you'll have to go through me first."

"Considering I've already caught the rest of your friends, that shouldn't be too difficult," replies Leo Untaros, "but if you think you can beat me, bring it on."

Taking a step forward, the Light Knight says, "Light Speed Armor, engage," but, to his surprise, nothing happens.

Leo Untaros says, "I'm fully aware of your secondary armor, but my scrambler prevents those of you who have unlocked this armor from being able to use it. If you still think you can fight me, bring it on!"

Taking a deep breath, the Light Knight says, "I may not be the strongest of the knights, but I know this: even if you beat me, you won't win."

Leo Untaros chuckles at this and says, "If you think your girlfriend will beat me, you *are* a fool."

Chuckling in turn at this statement, the Light Knight answers, "She's not my girlfriend, no matter how much I want her to be. But I made a promise long ago that no matter what, I would look out for her—whether she knew it or not—and I'm not about to let some crazed kitty cat hurt her or our friends or this planet."

"That was so touching," Leo Untaros says sarcastically, "but it was also foolish. Come on! Let's see what you've got." He draws his blade and charges at the Light Knight.

Telepathically the Light Knight tells the Beast Knight, "Sorry about pushing you in the bushes, but if I'm caught, you are the only one who can beat him. Watch for a weakness, something we can exploit. And I meant what I said: I want you to be my girlfriend. Sorry I didn't say it before now."

With Leo Untaros now in striking range, the Light Knight blocks the strike, and the Beast Knight watches the two clash. As the Light Knight continues to block his attacks, Leo Untaros says, "Of all the hunts I've been on, this has been the most fun. Too bad this will all end soon. You see, I was raised as a hunter, and to me you knights are a simple prey."

Knowing that he has to help the Beast Knight find some kind of weakness, the Light Knight channels his power into his blade. He says, "If I go down, I'm going down fighting," and he prepares his attack.

Leo Untaros dodges this attack, and then slips the link cuffs on the Light Knight. As the Beast Knight watches, she sees what look like a two-pin key. She shapeshifts into a chameleon, and, using its ability to blend in with its surroundings, she moves quietly, grabs the key and escapes into the jungle.

Before heading back to his camp with the Light Knight, Leo Untaros shouts, "I know you can hear me, Beast Knight. If you are brave enough, find me, and if you beat me, I will free your friends. You have until the sun is high in the sky. Otherwise I will hunt you and end you." With both the Light Knight and the Fire Knight, Leo Untaros disappears into the Jungle.

THE BEAST KNIGHT NOW HOLDS THE KEY that could free her friends. She wonders, "How can I beat him if he has beat all the others?"

Suddenly Justice appears to her, in the form of a mutant lioness, and she asks the Beast Knight, "What's the matter, dear Beast Knight?"

The Beast Knight shakes her head and says, "Leo Untaros has captured the others. I think I've got the key to free them, but even without hypnotic powers, like Des said, he still beat the others, and I don't know if I will be able to beat him."

Justice looks lovingly at her and says, "Dear Beast Knight, you have all the power to defeat him. All you have to remember is to be *as shrewd as a snake but as innocent as a dove.*"[10] If you do this, there will be no stopping you."

When the Beast Knight turns to ask her what she means by this, Justice is gone, and the Beast Knight decides to take a breath. Then she says, "Let's look at everything we know so far. First, his cuffs can paralyze us, but I have the key to unlock them. Leo Untaros is a strong hunter ..." Before she can continue, she remembers a similar situation that happened when she was just a child. Her grandfather was teaching her how to fight, and he said, "When facing a stronger opponent, always use their strength against them. You see, no matter how strong someone is, it's not the strongest move that wins the day, but wisdom and grace to overcome even the greatest obstacle."

In that moment she realizes what Justice and her grandfather are both saying, and she says, "Beastial Beauty Armor, engage."

Once the Beast Knight says this, her armor begins to change. Wings appear on her back. They are as white as a dove. Her helmet forms to the shape of a dove's head. Her armor transforms into a kimono-like dress with slits on both sides, allowing her ample movement. Then, on the back of each of her hands, are four blades made of pure energy. When the transformation is complete, she looks at herself and says, "It's time for the hunter to become the hunted."

CHAPTER 17

BATTLE OF THE BEASTS: BEAUTY OF BEASTS

AFTER UNLOCKING THE POWER of her Beastial Beauty armor, the Beast Knight works on a plan, not only to defeat Leo Untaros, but also to free her friends in the process. Just then, a sparrow lands on her shoulder. It says "What kind of bird are you?"

Beast Knight turns and says, "That's just it. I'm not bird; I'm a human." Just then she realizes what happened, and she says to the sparrow, "Did you just speak to me, little sparrow?"

The little sparrow says, "Yes, and I'm talking now. Also, I've never seen a human quite like you before."

The Beast knight then asks, "Are there more of you around, little sparrow?"

The little sparrow answers, "Ohhh yes, there are a bunch of us."

"Little sparrow would you call your friends for me?" asks the Beast Knight, as she formulates her plan to defeat Leo Untaros.

As the little sparrow calls to his friends, the Beast Knight is surprised at how many of them there are. She says, "I need your help. My friends have been captured by a creature called Leo Untaros."

Looking at her friends, then looking back at the Beast Knight, the little sparrow says, "How can we help. We're all so small. If this creature is big like you, what could we do?"

"It's simple," the Beast Knight answers. "All I need you and your friends to do is rush toward him, while one of you takes this key and uses it to free one of my friends. They will take it from there." Thinking about it for a moment, the little sparrow and his friends agree.

The Beast Knight has the sparrows fly around to find the knights When one of them signals that they have found something, the Beast Knight is able to see what they are seeing, confirms they have indeed found her friends the knights and informs them of it.

Only a few hours remain until the deadline is up, and as the Beast Knight arrives to distract Leo Untaros, she has the sparrows speed toward him. As he walks, not intimidated by them, the Beast Knight steps forward. He sees her and says, "Now this is something I was not expecting. I don't know how you were able to access that armor, but it still won't matter because I will destroy you before you can ever use it."

She looks at Leo Untaros and says, "Let's see what you've got, you crazed kitty cat."

With that, Leo Untaros charges at her. With a single step, she dodges his attack and says, "Awww, did you miss me?"

Leo Untaros chuckles and says, "Clever move, little girl, but it will take more than a clever move to defeat me."

Using his felone, he charges toward her again. As she dodges his advance, Leo Untaros uses the momentum to spring back toward her, but she is again able to dodge his attack.

Unknown to him, however, the little sparrow flies to where the Light Knight is held, and, using the key, unlocks the cuffs.

As the paralysis wears off, he sees the Beast Knight fighting in her new armor and also sees the key for the cuffs that had held him. Grabbing the key, he quickly begins to unlock the cuffs of the other knights.

Still unable to land a single blow, Leo Untaros is getting rather annoyed. He says, "If you think you can dodge me forever, you are sadly mistaken."

The Beast Knight chuckles as she notices that the other knights are free and says, "I don't need to dodge you forever, but I have dodged you long enough. Don't you agree, guys?"

The Fire Knight says, "I don't know! It is kind of fun seeing him swing and miss each time."

The Shadow Knight says, "I feel the same way."

Leo Untaros looks around, sees that all the knights are free, and says, "How is this possible?"

"Simple," Beast Knight answers. While you were gloating over beating the Light Knight, I stole your key, and a little birdy helped me do the rest. All I had to do was distract you long enough."

Before anything else could be said, Leo Untaros draws his blade, begins to have it spin and attacks the Beast Knight. Using the blades on the back of her hands, she catches the blade. And, with a shift of her hips, she throws Leo Untaros into a tree.

As he get to his feet, she says, "Hmmmm! That's interesting! I always thought cats landed on their feet!"

Shaking his head as he stands to his feet, he says, "I'm going to have fun ripping you to shreds, little girl."

"You've got to catch me first?" she responds, as she flies into the sky.

Leo Untaros uses his chain blade, having it extend and wrap around her legs. But, instead of him being able to pull her down, she soars higher into the sky, dragging him with her.

THE BEAST KNIGHT THEN TURNS and begins to fly through the jungle. Leo Untaros is doing everything in his power to avoid hitting or being hit by the trees, as she speed past and in between them. Just then, she sees two trees close together and speeds toward them. As Leo Untaros sees this, he gets ready to place his feet on the trees. Just then, however, she flies straight up so that he is hit by the trees and their branches, causing him to lose his grip on the chain blade. It falls to the ground.

As the Beast Knight lands, she faces Leo Untaros and says sarcasstically, "You know, I think it's really sweet how you've fallen for me."

Again he gets to his feet. Extending the claws on his hands, he says, "Little girl, I'm a hunter—born and raised. I will not be beaten by some child."

The Beast Knight looks intently at Leo Untaros and says, "It's true, you are a hunter born and raised, but I'm no child. Now, you can either choose to stand down, or we can end this right here and now."

This brings a chuckle to Leo Untaros. He says, "We shall end this here and now, but first I' think I'll pay your boyfriend a visit and carve my name into his corpse."

Grabbing his chain blade, Leo Untaros leaps past her, he uses the trees to propel himself back toward the knights. When he reaches them, he goes straight for the Light Knight. As the other knights try to rush him, he throws them off, shouting, "You all are pathetic! With all the power you possess, not one of you has been able to defeat me!"

Then, looking at the Light Knight, he says, "Still, I will enjoy carving my name in your corpse, Light Knight."

Suddenly the Beast Knight flies from the jungle, kicks Leo Untaros into a nearby tree, and says, "Don't you dare touch any of my friends!"

Shaking his head, he says "I will do whatever I please because even you cannot stop me."

With his claws drawn, he begins to slash at her. She uses her own claws to block his attacks. He then sees an opening and, with a quick stab, pierces her armor with his claws.

As the Beast Knight stumbles back, Leo Untaros watches in amazement as her wound starts to heal almost instantly. As she notices this, she says, "Looks like my armor is full of surprises."

Desperate to defeat her, he now leaps past her, and charging toward the Light Knight, begins to pummel him into the ground. The other knights try to stop him, but each of them in turn is thrown off as if they were rag dolls.

As Leo Untaros prepares to land the final strike, the Beast Knight speeds toward him, and flips, kicking him in the back and sending him flying deep into deep the jungle. She then turns toward the Light Knight and asks, "Are you okay?"

He chuckles and says, "As long as I get to see you, I'll be fine."

The Earth Knight looks at him and asks, "Can you walk?"

Barely able to stand, the Light Knight says, "I think so." But when he tries to walk, he falls.

"This isn't good!" the Earth Knight says. He then notices that blood is dripping from the Light Knight's arm. "Lay down," he tells him, and let us take a look at you."

Walking over to the Cross Knight, the Earth Knight says, "Without being able to scan him, it doesn't look good. And, to be honest, he's bleeding through his armor."

Hearing this, the Beast Knight says, "There's gotta be something we can do. We just can't let him die."

Looking at her, the Earth Knight says, "Trust me, I don't want him to die either, but I have no way of knowing how hurt he is or even the slightest idea of how to heal him." She rushes to his side, and the knights are surround them.

"It's gonna be okay," he says to her. "I'll be fine. You need to go stop Leo Untaros so we can get out of here."

She shakes her head and asks, "How can I leave you, after realizing how much you mean to me and knowing how much you care about me."

He reaches for her helmet, and assures her, "You can do it, and once you do, we'll be able to talk about where to go from here."

She nods in agreement and says, "I'll take him down! I promise!"

Putting a hand on her shoulder, the Earth Knight says, "We'll take care of him and figure out a way out of this trap. Once we do, we can port back to the base, and I'll check him out."

She looks at him uncertainly and says, "You'd better, or it'll be me gutting you like a fish rather than Leo Untaros. Do you understand?"

The knights head toward Leo Untaro's camp, to see if they can find anything that will set them free.

MEANWHILE, DEEP IN THE JUNGLE, Leo Untaros is licking his wounds. Shocked that he's been defeated in battle, he now finds himself hiding, waiting to catch the Beast Knight as she searches for him.

He signals for his chain Magnachaincycle, and at the same moment, Brykar attempts to contact him for a status report. As he opens the line, Brykar says, "What's your status? Have you captured the knights yet?"

Leo Untaros answers carefully, "I captured the knights ... except for the Beast Knight."

Brykar says, "We need all of them captured. Do you understand me?"

"Yes, Commander Brykar," Leo Untaros answers. "I will make sure to capture them all."

Brykar, then goes to his viewscreen, looks at Leo Untaro's camp, and notices the knights reentering the camp. He says, "Leo Untaros, if you've captured the knights, why are they walking around in your base?" Shaking his head, Leo Untaros says, "Commander, I *had* captured the knights, just as I told you, but the Beast Knight stole the key and then distracted me while she had the other knights freed."

"If she was fighting you," Brykar asks, "how were the knights set free?"

Leo Untaros bows his head in embarrassment as he slowly admits, "A little bird did it."

"Are you telling me that one of the best bounty hunters in the galaxy was outwitted by a girl and a little bird. Are you serious?" Brykar demands.

Pausing for a moment, Leo Untaros says, "That is correct, Commander Brykar. However I have a plan to recapture all the knights, and one of them will soon be dead."

Not sure if he should ask, Brykar feels that he must. "What do you mean 'one of them will soon be dead?'"

Leo Untaros then responds, "I attacked the Light Knight and pummeled him while the other knights were helpless to interfere. I would have finished him had the Beast Knight not interfered."

Brykar then checks his viewscreen, confirms what Leo Untaros is saying, and says "Good! Just make sure you capture the rest of them. If not, I will destroy you myself. Are we clear?"

Leo Untaros nods, then says, "Yes, Commander Brykar."

As the communication ends, Leo Untaro's Magnachaincycle arrives behind him, and as he gets on it, he's suddenly thrown from it. Shaking his head, he gets up saying, "What just hit me?"

Standing before him is the Beast Knight, and she says, "Awwww, did the kitty cat fall down and go boom?"

Leo Untaros leaps back and says, "What's the matter, Beast Knight? Did I hurt your boyfriend?"

She shakes her head and answers, "First off, he's not my boyfriend, and I'll never know if he would have been. But, with everything I have, I will end you if it's the last thing I do."

He chuckles and says, "If this is my last battle, I at least have the joy of knowing I'm taking one of you knights with me."

He then lunges at her. As he slashes at her, she turns so that rather than dodge the attack, she's able to grab his wrist and slam him into the ground. When he gets up and attacks again, she repeats the same movement. This time, however, as she slams him into the ground, she doesn't let go. She slams him left and right into the ground several times.

Before she can slam Leo Untaros into the ground one more time, he manages to catch himself and break free of her grip. As he gets to his feet, he says, "I have to admit it: you're stronger than I anticipated. But I will not quit or be defeated by the likes of you."

Just then, Leo Untaros sets his stance, roars with all his might and as he does this, he takes his chain blade and has it wrap itself around him. Puzzled by this, the Beast Knight wonders what's happening. Then, suddenly, the chain blade releases, and Leo Untaros has been transformed into a being made of chains.

The Beast Knight looks at him and says, "Am I supposed to be impressed by this or what?"

Leo Untaros chuckles and says, "I don't care if you are impressed or not. In this form, I am superior, and I will destroy you."

"We'll see about that," says the Beast Knight, as she prepares to take on Leo Untaros in his new form.

Now, raising his arm, he points his open hand at the Beast Knight, and suddenly all five of his claws extend to form individual chains, and they try to wrap up the Beast Knight. She is barely able to find a way to dodge them.

Looking at her, he says, "Don't you realize how hopeless it is to try to defeat me. It's true that you had the advantage before, but now I have even more power, and I will make sure that this is your last battle, child."

She then responds, "I made a promise to stop you, and with everything I have, I'm going to keep that promise."

Just then, the chains Leo Untaros has fired wrap around the Beast Knight's arms, legs and body. He says, "Silly girl, did really think that first attack was supposed to land? Even I knew it wouldn't. I just waited for your guard to be down so I could do this. Even though you have the ability to heal, let's see if you can heal from having your head chopped off."

Leo Untaros then has a new chain blade form in his hand, and he walks toward her. As she struggles, the Beast knight begins to recite the oath: "*As days of darkness near, and people run in fear …*"

At this point, Leo Untaros is enjoying the fact that the Beast Knight seems to be helpless. He walks slowly and menacingly toward her. Struggling to break free, she continues to recite the oath: *"From they who prey on the weak, and silence those who speak, we will take to the sky with courage and battle cry ... "*

Now Leo Untaros is chuckling as he watches her struggle. "This is the end for you, child," he says, "although I must admit: no one has ever challenged me like you. Nor has anyone ever come as close to beating me as you have."

Raising his sword, he prepares to strike. Then she shouts, *"To protect the world from loss, I am a Knight of the Cross!"* As Leo Untaros swings his chain blade, the Beast Knight shapeshifts into a snake and slips away through the chains, causing him to stumble. Once she is free, the Beast Knight returns to her armored form. She leaps toward Leo Untaros, and before he can react, she cuts off his head, and he falls to the ground.

As the Beast Knight takes a moment to catch her breath, the jungle they are all in starts to dissolve. She contacts the Earth Knight and asks, "How's he doing?"

The Earth Knight scans the Light Knight and replies, "We need to go now!"

With that, all the knights, including the Beast Knight, port back to their base.

UNKNOWN TO THE KNIGHTS, even as the jungle continues to dissolve, Brykar arrives where Leo Untaros' head and body lie. As he gathers them, he shakes his head. He takes them back to his ship. As he enters it, he goes to the revival chamber where the rest of his fallen warriors are. He places Leo Untaro's body in the chamber, then goes to check on the gear he said he was going to give the ARC team. He needs to make sure it will help them in defeating the knights, and also that the necessary failsafes are in place that will prevent them from using the tech against the Psystructs. He then heads to his chamber, where General Sadoom is trying to contact him.

Once the communication link is activated, General Sadoom says, "Brykar, what is your status?"

Brykar goes down on one knee and says, "I regret to inform you that Leo Untaros has been defeated, But, before he was defeated, he informed me that he was able to kill one of the knights."

"Brykar," General Sadoom replies, "I want you to understand that these constant defeats will not be tolerated. If Leo Untaros has indeed killed one of the knights, then we might be able to overlook your failures. Still, the remaining knights are a problem that must be dealt with."

Brykar replies, "General Sadoom, even if my remaining warriors are defeated, I do have a plan for defeating these knights. If you would just give me the opportunity to explain."

Intrigued by this, General Sadoom says, "Then tell me, Brykar, what is it that you have planned for the knights?"

Brykar begins to tell General Sadoom of his plan and how he is reviving and enhancing each of the fallen warriors, so that when they next face the knights, he can capture and destroy them. General Sadoom listens to Brykar's plan and then says, "Very well! Continue as you have planned, but if this plan of yours fails, you know the punishment that awaits you."

"Yes General Sadoom," Brykar replies, "I understand." With that, the communication ends.

BRYKAR SITS DOWN IN HIS CHAIR located in his chamber and contacts Agent Martin. As Agent Martin opens the link, Brykar says, "Greetings, Agent Martin. As you requested, I have gathered the gear that will help you in defeating the knights. I will send you the coordinates of where you can receive it. It will be there one hour from now, so I would suggest you mobilize your team so that you can get the gear without any interference from the knights."

Agent Martin replies, "They'll be there, Brykar."

As the communication ends, Brykar leans forward and says, "I will destroy these knights ... if it's the last thing I do."

THE KNIGHTS ARE AT THEIR BASE. They have gathered in the lab, and Des is doing a scan of John to determine the extent of his injuries. Once he has finished, he has Joseph port John to his room. Tasha then asks Des, "How bad is it?"

Des shakes his head and says, "It's worse than I even imagined. In fact, the only reason he's alive right now is because of his armor."

"How much time does he have?" she asks.

Pausing a moment, Des replies, "I'm not quite sure. The only thing we can do right now is make him comfortable."

Now Eric walks over to Des and asks, "Isn't there anything we can do?"

Looking at Eric and the other knights Des says, "I wish there was something that could be done, but right now I don't know what we can do."

Brad says, "There's gotta be something we can do. We can't just let him die."

"I don't want him or anyone else to die," Des replies, "but I'm not a doctor, and that's really what he needs right now."

"Des," Jessica asks, "what exactly are his injuries?"

Des pulls up the screen and says, "According to the scans, his injuries include three fractured ribs, multiple bruises on his torso, and to top it off, he's bleeding internally."

Max shakes his head and says, "Just listening to his injuries hurts."

Maggie adds, "Do you think Manuel might know of something that would be able to heal him?"

"That's another problem," Des explains, "Manuel and Justice are nowhere to be found. So, right now, we're on our own."

Overwhelmed from hearing all of this, Tasha storms out, heading toward John.

SALLY AND JANET BOTH FOLLOW her. As she walks down the hallway, Sally calls, "Tasha, wait up!"

Angry and frustrated, Tasha turns to Sally and says, "Leave me alone, Sally."

Knowing that Tasha is hurting, Sally wraps her arms around her and says, "Tasha, I know you are hurting, but you can't give up hope. We'll find a way to save John. I promise."

Unconvinced, Tasha pulls away and says, "Don't make promises you can't keep. Des promised me he would find a way to heal John, and right now he's saying there might not be any way to do so."

Janet catches up to them and says, "That may be true, but remember what Des said, 'He's no doctor.' He can only go by what he knows, and that doesn't mean that there's no way to heal him. It just means that we all have to think about and look for a solution. I know it's hard, but Sally's right. You can't give up hope. We'll find a way to heal John."

As Tasha turns from them and heads to John's room, she says, "I really wish I could believe that, Janet."

The two female knights watch as Tasha walks alone toward John's room. As she does, she sees Joseph and asks him, "How is he?"

Joseph pauses and then says, "Right now, he's stable, and he's asking for you."

Without saying another word, she heads toward John's room. As Joseph joins Sally and Janet, he says, "I really wish there was more we could do right now." Both Janet and Sally nod in agreement.

WHILE WALKING DOWN THE HALLWAY to John's room, Tasha is clenching her fists, angry with herself for not stopping Leo Untaros sooner. As she enters John's room, he sits up and says, "Hey! I was hoping you would come by. Are you okay?"

Tasha wipes tears from her eyes and says, "I don't know."

John smiles at her and says, "Come, sit next to me. We need to talk."

As Tasha walks closer to him, she notices him wincing in pain. Still, he holds her close to him and says, "Listen, I know I don't have much time left, but there's something I want you to know."

Looking up at him, Tasha asks, "What is it you want me to know?"

Smiling at her, John says, "As you know, I care about you a lot, and I have waited for a long time to tell you how I feel. But what I want you to know is what I see when I look at you. Like most people, I see how strong and fierce you are, but I've also seen what an amazing beauty you are. I know we've gotten closer in a short time, and no matter what, I'll treasure whatever time we have together. I just want you to know I have no regrets. If I had to endure another beating from Leo Untaros to protect you, I would do it gladly."

Tasha is chuckling now. "You're an idiot," she says. "You know that, right?"

John chuckles as well and replies, "Yeah, but I would still do it because I love you, Tasha, I know it sounds silly, but I do and will always love you."

As the two knights look into each others' eyes, Tasha says, "This is isn't fair. I mean, I just realized there's this amazing guy that cares about me, and now he's being taken away from me." She wraps her arms around him and starts to sob. "I'm sorry it took me so long to realize you were always there," she says.

While Tasha sobs, John rubs her head. "It's okay," he says. "What matters is that you know how I feel, and I know how you feel." He then gently lifts her head and kisses her on the lips. His kiss is slow and tender.

When the kiss ends, John says, "Wow! That was amazing and well worth the wait!"

Tasha looks at him and says, "You're not too bad yourself!" She then slips from John's side. Looking back lovingly at him, she says, "Rest now, my love," and she helps him lie back down. As she does this, she is saying to no one in particular, "I wish there was a way for him to be healed."

Suddenly her hands start to glow, and as she places them on John, she is inspired to recite their oath:

As days of darkness near, and people run in fear,
From they who prey on the weak, and silence those who speak,
We will take to the sky with courage and battle cry.
To protect the world from loss, I am a Knight of the Cross!

Now the glow on her hands becomes brighter, and without a second thought, she says, "Be healed, Light Knight."

Then, just as suddenly, John's body starts to glow and becomes enveloped in a blinding white light that seems to last several minutes. When it ends, Tasha falls to her knees from exhaustion. She begins to cry, and as she does, John says, "Hey, beautiful, are you okay?"

Thinking that she's hallucinating, Tasha says, "I'm not okay. You just died, and I miss you already."

But John sits up, looking like he was never wounded. He reaches down, lifts her to her feet and kisses her again. As they kiss, she feels his arms wrapping around her. When the kiss ends, she says, "Is this real? Are you really okay?"

He looks at her and says. "Looks that way. How about we go show the others?"

BACK IN DES'S LAB the other knights are unaware that John has been healed and as the two walk in they see the knights, with saddened faces and John says, "Why do you all look like someone died?"

Thrilled to hear his voice, the other knights all all rush toward him. Des says "Amazing! how did this happen?"

"I'm not exactly sure," John answers. "All I remember is Tasha reciting the oath, then saying, 'Be healed.' The next thing I knew I was sitting up and feeling fine."

Des then scans him, using the computers in the lab. After the results appear on the screen, Des says, "This is amazing! According to these scans, John is completely healed."

Eric says, "Not that I'm complaining, but how is it possible ... if he was just on death's doorstep?"

Des admits, "I'm not fully sure, but if I'm correct, there's another aspect to Tasha's power which is the ability, not only to heal herself, but also to heal others from serious injuries."

"So, wait," Tasha says, "you're telling me that if any of you are seriously wounded in battle, I can heal you?"

"Exactly!" Des says.

Obviously surprised by this, Tasha asks, "How is this possible?"

Scratching his head, Des says, "I'm not sure, but with each new armor that we unlock, it seems like new powers and abilities emerge."

Brad turns to John and says, "No matter how it happened, we're all glad you're okay, John."

Joseph chuckles and says, "I agree! What matters most is that you're okay. Although ... learning that Tasha has healing abilities is an added bonus. Now, everyone go and relax for the next five hours, and we'll meet in the training area to continue our training. If I'm right, Brykar is working on a new plan to destroy us even as we speak." Each of the knights nods in agreement.

AS THE KNIGHTS GO THEIR SEPARATE WAYS to relax, Tasha and John walk towards the recreation area. Tasha pulls John to herself, and this time she kisses him. "So, John," she boldly asks, "do you want to be my man?"

Chuckling, he says, "I thought you would never ask."

The two knights hug and share another quick kiss and then continue toward the recreation area.

"Wanna play a game of pool?" John asks.

Tasha laughs with delight. "Sure," she says, "just don't expect me to go easy on you."

MEANWHILE AGENT MARTIN VISITS AGENT WALLACE and the others. As he enters their training area, he is greeted by Agent Rivera. "Welcome, Agent Martin," she says, "it's been awhile."

Adjusting his tie, Agent Martin says, "It has, Agent Rivera. Tell me, how are your plans to defeat the knight coming along?"

Wiping her glasses, she says, "So far I've ... I've come up with the armor designs, but that's about it. Without the proper tech, that's all they are ... designs."

Agent Martin chuckles as he says, "Well, it looks like I arrived just in time." Handing her a paper with the coordinates, he adds, "Mobilize the team, and go to the coordinates on this paper. You have forty-five minutes to get there and the equipment you need."

As Agent Rivera takes the paper, she uses her wireless mic and says, "ARC Team, meet me in the hanger bay immediately. This is a priority one alert. I repeat: this is a priority one alert."

With that, each of the ARC team members heads for the hanger. Agent Rivera heads there herself and on the way runs into Agent Saunders. She asks, "What's up with the priority-one alert?"

Agent Rivera replies, "I'll explain once everyone is together. Still, we need to move."

Soon the two agents are joined by Agent Wallace. He says, "I heard the alert, and I'm having a transport prepped, ready for cause. I take it this means we know where to get the tech we need."

"Good guess, Agent Wallace," she answers, "and that's exactly the case. Now, let's get to the hanger, and I will explain everything."

WITHIN TEN MINUTES, all of the ARC team is assembled, and Agent Rivera has them board the transport. As it prepares for takeoff, Agent Daniels says, "Okay, Rivera, what's this priority-one alert about?"

Agent Rivera answers, "Agent Martin, just gave me the coordinates of where to meet the aliens and get the tech we need so we'll be able to face these so-called knights."

Agent Stanton says, "Awesome! But why is it a priority one?"

Rivera shakes her head and says, "Simply because, Agent Stanton, we have less than an hour to get to the coordinates and get the gear before we are noticed. So, we need to move fast."

ABOUT THIRTY MINUTES LATER, the ARC team arrives. As they exit the transport, the Psystructs arrive with the gear. Agent Wallace has the gear loaded onto the transport. Once all the Psystruct gear is loaded onto the ARC team transport, Agent Wallace goes to Agent Rivera and says, "All the gear has been loaded onto the transport. Is there anything else we need?"

She pulls her glasses down and wipes them as she replies, "No, there's nothing else. Let's head back to the base."

With that, the ARC team heads back to their base with the new gear.

BACK AT THEIR BASE, Agent Wallace goes to Agent Rivera and asks, "Do you think this is enough gear to help us defeat the knights?"

She turns to him and says "To be honest, I'm not sure. I'll need time to examine it and see what it can actually do."

AT THAT VERY MOMENT, GRAHAM IS SEARCHING the web for any clues to help him understand what happened to his brother and his friends. He is startled by a knock at the door. Getting up from his desk, Graham goes to the door. As he opens it, he sees no one. He looks down, and there is a package with his name and address on it. As he brings it inside, his cell phone starts to buzz.

Pulling his phone out of his pocket, Graham notices that the text message is from Tasha's grandfather, James. It reads, "I need to talk to you. May I come over?"

Graham replies, "Yes, when do you want to meet."

Almost immediately he gets another text saying, "Could we meet now?"

Puzzled by this, Graham responds, "Sure, where do you want to meet?"

The next text reads, "Your house. Is that ok?"

Graham texts back, "Okay."

Just then Graham's doorbell rings again. When he goes to the door, he sees Tasha's grandfather standing there. "Graham," he asks, "did you just receive a mysterious package a few minutes ago?"

Graham looks at James and says, "Yeah, but how did you know?"

"Simple," James replies, "because I sent it."

Graham now opens the package and notices that it's a piece of wreckage from the school bus that was destroyed. He looks at James and asks, "How did you get this?"

James chuckles and says, "I was an ace reporter, and I still have resources at my disposal. I was able to get this. Let's leave it at that. I figured you would be able to learn more from this than I could."

As Graham examines the damaged piece of the bus, he says, "This is amazing, but why are you doing this?"

James shakes his head and replies, "I'm going to level with you. The reason I did this is that I want to feel useful, and I was kind of feeling left out."

"I'm sorry, Graham replies. "I never meant to leave you out. I just wasn't sure what role everyone should play. Let's check out this piece of wreckage and see what we can learn from it."

CHAPTER 18

BEYOND ALL HOPE:
DARKNESS OF DESPAIR

While Graham and James examine the wreckage, Sally's Aunt Deborah is working as a waitress at a restaurant called Mariano's. She is finishing with her latest customer when Melanie Sabre-Masters, who is also Brad and Joseph's mother, walks in. When Deborah sees her, she walks over to the hostess area and says, "Hey, Melanie, It's been a while?"

When Melanie sees her, she smiles and says, "Yes it has. How've you been?"

Deborah says, "A bit stressed, but not more than usual. Do you need a table for one?"

Melanie then says, "Actually it's going to be for three. I'm meeting with David and Laura Bolten. They should be arriving here soon."

Smiling at her, as is her normal when working and taking care of her guests, Deborah walks Melanie to an area of the restaurant that is used for private meetings and says, "You guys can use this room as it's been a bit slow today. By the way, could I get you something to drink?"

As Melanie sits she says, "I'll take a water for now."

Deborah places three menus on the table. "Okay," she says, "I'll grab that for you and be right back." And she heads to the kitchen to get the water.

A few moments later, when Deborah comes back, she place the glass of water on the table, along with a note and she goes to check the door.

Melanie looks at the note. It reads, "Melanie, I'm sorry for lying, but I'm really worried about Sally and the other kids. While I'm at work, I have to smile and put on a brave face, and it's not easy. Please tell me that there is some news about what is going on."

Melanie then pulls a small pad from her bag and writes a note for Deborah, letting her know about everything she has learned recently. Although it isn't much, Melanie hopes this will help ease Deborah's mind.

When Deborah comes back, she is followed by David and Laura Bolten. As the two sit down, Deborah asks, "What can I get for you all to drink?"

David and Laura both order a lemonade, and Deborah goes to get their drinks.

Melanie informs them of what happened when she met with Phillip and Linda, and as she recalls what happened, both David and Laura are furious, wondering who would go to such lengths to do this. Before Melanie can say anything else, Deborah comes back. "Here are your drinks," she says, and she places the two lemonades in front of David and Laura. Then she asks, "What can I get for you this afternoon?"

David looks briefly at the menu and says, "I'll have a center-cut steak with mashed potatoes and gravy."

Laura looks at Deborah and says, "I'll get the spicy chicken wrap with broccoli for my side."

Then it's Melanie's turn. She says, "I'm going to just order some mozzarella sticks for now."

As Deborah heads back to the kitchen to have the cooks start working on their order, David says, "Why does this waitress look familiar?"

Melanie chuckles and says, "She should. Her niece, Sally, is one of the students missing, along with our children."

Then David realizes who she is and says, "I never knew she worked here."

AT THAT VERY MOMENT, unknown to them, Agent Rivera is examining the tech they have been given by Brykar. As she goes through it, she is amazed by one piece of equipment that can increase a normal person's strength a hundredfold.

Agent Martin asks, "What do we know so far about the equipment we just received?"

Agent Rivera shakes her head and replies, "Not much, but the amount of tech given is amazing." She then shows Agent Martin the piece she's looking at. "For example, look at this piece. It may not look like anything special, but it actually has the ability to increase the strength of whoever is using it a hundredfold."

"Good," Agent Martin says, "how long do you think it would take for the equipment you are working on to be online?"

Agent Rivera pulls down her glasses and wipes as she replies, "That's what I'm not sure about."

Agent Martin asks, "Why is that?"

"Simple," Agent Rivera answers, "there's too much tech here for me to just throw something together. And, before we can send anyone out in the armors I'm working on, the gear needs to be tested to make sure that it won't malfunction in the field."

Frustrated by this, Agent Martin says, "I want this new equipment up and running as soon as possible. Do you understand me?"

Smiling at him, Agent Rivera replies, "Of course! I'll have it ready as soon as possible. But just remember, Agent Martin," she warns, "whoever these knights are, they are skilled warriors, and the last thing we need is to go in unprepared."

Knowing that what she has said is true, Agent Martin adjusts his tie and responds, "You're right, Agent Rivera, but we need to deal with them as soon as possible."

Chuckling at this, she says, "We will, but while we're waiting for everything to be just right, I've developed new recording equipment, so that now whenever the knights attack Brykar and his forces, we'll be able to watch how the knights fight. And we'll have more intel so that when we do face them, our team will be better prepared."

"That's good," Agent Martin says. "Keep me posted on your progress with the tech. Also, how many armors are you working on developing?"

Looking at him, she says, "I've plans for seven armors so far. Why do you ask?"

He answers, "According to what we know, we have only seven operatives on this team, and there are twelve knights. So, I'm going to be going through a list of operatives that would even up the playing field, but, at the same time, give us an advantage over these so-called knights."

"Well," Agent Rivera says, "I'll get started on it right away. But I would recommend that you inform Agent Wallace, as he might have an opinion about who would be best suited for this team."

As Agent Martin turns to leave, he says, "That's perfect! I'll inform him immediately and have him make the selection."

BRYKAR IS WALKING TO THE CHAMBER that hold his three remaining warriors. As he enters, he wonders who should be next to face the knights. He looks at the empty chambers that held the previous warriors who faced the knights and then at the three remaining chambers. They hold the last three warriors. Considering them all, he notices one that he thinks would be absolutely perfect to face the knights. He opens the chamber, and the warrior falls to his knees. "Rise, Dispotier," Brykar says, "I have need of your unique skills."

On his knees, Dispotier is a fearsome sight. His body and face are as black as the night, and he wears only a cloak with a hood. Rising now from his knees, he puts the hood over his face and replies, "I am at your service, Brykar. What is it you need of me?"

Brykar says, "We are on a planet known as Earth, and I have been charged with testing its defenses. So far, the only opposition we have seen is from a group of warriors who call themselves the Knights of the Cross. What I need from you is to find a way to either capture or eliminate these knights?"

Dispotier replies, "As you command, Brykar."

Brykar chuckles and says, "Go to the hanger, and you will find weapons and vehicles that you can use to deal with the knights. I have other matters that I must attend to." That being said, Brykar departs and Dispotier makes his way to the hanger.

IN THE HANGER Dispotier sees an armor that has two scythe blades on it and a shield made of scythe blades that spin. Walking toward the armor, he says, "This will be perfect!" He puts the armor on, takes the blades, and says, "Now, all I need is a ride."

Looking around the hanger, he notices a magnacycle. As he examines it, he touches it with his scythe blades, and the magnacycle transforms and becomes a scythecycle with blades on the front of it similar to the scythe blades he has. Its colors become a mix of silver and black.

Once the transformation is complete, he says, "This shall do nicely. Now, all I need to do is find these knights and bring them to their knees." Dispotier then gets on his scythecycle, and, as the hanger doors open, he rides off, looking for the knights.

WHILE THE KNIGHTS ARE ENJOYING their recreation time, Sally starts to wonder about her role and also about why she doesn't have a boyfriend yet. She is sitting by herself, and Janet notices this. She walks over to Sally and asks, "Something on your mind, Sally?"

Sally chuckles and says, "Is it that obvious?"

Janet says, "Well, you've never really been the quiet, thinker type, so I thought I would check and see if you're okay."

Shrugging her shoulders, Sally says, "I'm honestly not sure. I think it's awesome that Des is with Jessica, Brad and Maggie make a cute couple, Eric and Britney are amazing, and now John and Tasha are like the sweetest couple. I guess what I'm saying is: I'm happy for them…"

Janet finishes her sentence for her, "But you want the same for yourself, right?"

Sally chuckles and says, "Pretty much. Normally this wouldn't be a problem for me, but right now my choices of guys is kind of limited."

Now it's Janet's turn to chuckle. She says, "True, but you still have a choice between Joseph and Max, don't you?"

Shaking her head, Sally replies, "That's just it. Joseph is cool and all, but he's kind of taken. Which leaves Max, who is really cool and all, but I'm not sure if he's into me."

Puzzled by this, Janet says, "What do you mean, Joseph is 'kind of taken?'"

Giggling at the question, Sally says, "Well, if you need me to spell it out, I know you really like Joseph and have liked him from the beginning … even before all this happened."

Shocked, Janet responds, "How can you be so sure?"

"I may not be the smartest on the team, Janet," says Sally, "but I can tell when you have eyes for somebody. And, even though Joseph is an amazing guy and I would love to have someone like him as my boyfriend, it just wouldn't feel right for me to go after him, knowing you like him as well."

Taken aback by what Sally has said, Janet asks, "Is it that obvious that I like him?"

Sally shrugs her shoulders and says, "I'm not sure if the others know you like him, but I'm pretty sure the only one who would have a suspicion about you two is Brad. Especially since you broke up with Brad, after seeing how he treated Joseph. Not that I blame you. The only thing that concerns me with Max is that I don't want to be his last or second choice. I want to be his first choice."

Before anything else can be said, the alarms go off. Janet chuckles and says, "It looks like we'll have to finish this conversation later." And the two female knights race to the lab.

THE OTHER KNIGHTS JOIN THEM. As they enter the lab, Joseph says, "It looks like Brykar isn't wasting anytime. Des, what kind of info do we have on this guy?"

Des replies, "As usual, not too much at all. The only thing I can determine is that this guy has a thing for scythe blades."

As Des scans the warrior, Manuel walks in and says, "His name is Dispotier, and he's one of the most dangerous warriors Brykar could unleash."

The knights tun to Manuel. Des replies, "How do you know who he is, Manuel?"

Manuel answers, "Just as the armors were completed, the Psystructs sent him to attack each of the twelve planets where the armors had been forged, in order to prevent them from ever being used. However, as the armors were completed, they were combined into a single armor, sent here to Earth along with Justice and myself."

Joseph asks, "Is there anything you can tell us about his powers?"

Manuel says, "Unfortunately, no. All I know about him is his name and that he was a feared warrior that would drive people from their worlds or to the grave."

Eric then asks, "So, what's the plan guys?"

The other knights look to Joseph. He says, "To be honest, I'm not sure, but what I do know is that we need to face this guy and whatever he throws at us." Pausing a moment, Joseph gets up and adds, "Although, now that I think about it, I think I do have an idea."

Brad, chuckles. "Well, bro," he says, "don't keep us in the dark. What is it?"

LOOKING AROUND AT THE VARIOUS KNIGHTS, Joseph says, "Des, can you scan his vehicle and see if there are any weaknesses we can exploit?"

Knowing where Joseph is going with this, Des says, "I'm on it." While Des scans Dispotier's vehicle, Joseph says, "While Des is looking into that, Britney, I want you in the distance so that the second he tries to attack, you can let us know, and we can evade the attack."

Des then says, "Hey, Joseph! Your hunch was right. I scanned the vehicle Dispotier is using. For the most part, there's no real weak part ... except for where the power core is."

Pulling up the scan on the screen, Des continues, "As you can see, the power core is surrounded on all sides, except from the right side, which is usually protected while he's on it. But, once we get him off, it becomes vulnerable to attack. Here's the best part," he adds, "once its hit, the blast should be strong enough to weaken Dispotier so that we can finish him off."

Turning to Britney, Joseph, says, "Hey, Britney, do you think you can hit that power core?"

She chuckles and says, "Of course."

"Good!" Joseph replies. "Now, the rest of us are going to keep him busy so Britney has her shot."

With that, the knights agree and run for the hanger. They enter and get into their BOD Bots, and when the hanger doors open, they head out.

AS THE REST OF THE KNIGHTS GO AFTER DISPOTIER, Britney breaks off and heads off to take up her position. While the other knights race toward Dispotier, he comes to a mountain range that he believes will give him an advantage. As he comes to a stop, he can sense the knights behind him. He grabs his scythe blades and says, "Soon the knights will arrive, and when they do, I will show them what horrors awaits."

Moments later the knights arrive. When they see Dispotier, he's standing there by his scythecycle. Even before turning around, Dispotier says, "Well, if it isn't the knights. I was wondering when you fools would show up."

As the knights surround him, he chuckles and says, "If you think surrounding me is going to work, then think again."

Unknown to him at that moment, the Bolt Knight takes up her position and activates her armor. Using her Bolot Bow, she fires a bolt at the scythecycle. It speeds through the air, and Dispotier uses his scythe to split the bolt, causing it to hit each of the knights, knocking them to the ground. "I knew you would all fall by my hand," he says, "but you make it too easy."

The Shadow Knight says, "How did you do that?"

Dispotier chuckles and says, "Unlike the previous warriors you've faced, my powers won't simply affect your mind, as you will now see."

Each of the knights begin to rise. As they do, Dispotier walks toward the Fire Knight, who activates his secondary armor, the Firebird Battle Armor, and as he transforms.

Dispotier chuckles again and says, "If you think that is going to stop me, you are sadly mistaken."

Once the transformation is complete, the Fire Knight charges toward Dispotier, and Dispotier uses the dull end of his scythe to trip the Fire Knight. As Dispotier turns to face the Fire Knight, he chuckles yet again and says, "If you wish to defeat me, you will have to do better than that."

Dispotier goes to grab the Fire Knight, but, without warning, he is hit with a blast of wind that sends him flying. Dispotier uses his cloak to change his direction, moving back to where the knights are. As he lands, he looks at the Wind Knight, only to see her in her secondary armor. He says, "Nice try, Wind Knight! However, as you can see, I will not easily be defeated. Let me show you why."

Then, without warning, Dispotier suddenly appears behind her. As he touches her shoulder, she falls to her knees. The Fire Knight sees this and charges Dispotier, shouting, "Get away from her, you cowled creep!"

Dispotier chuckles as the Fire Knight charges at him. When the Fire Knight gets close to him, Dispotier is hit with a blast of water that causes him to stumble. When this happens, the Fire Knight gets ready to strike. But somehow Dispotier is able to strike first. He plunges the handle portion of his scythe blades into the gut of Fire Knight, causing him to fall to the ground. He then whispers, "Don't worry about your friend. You will be joining her soon, but first ... ."

Again Dispotier vanishes, then appears behind the Aqua Knight and, before she can react, he touches her and she falls to her knees.

The Earth Knight rushes to her side. Seeing Dispotier walk away, he says, "What have you done to her?"

Chuckling, Dispotier says, "That's for me to know and you to find out, Earth Knight."

The Earth Knight lays the Aqua Knight down, activates his secondary armor, and launches his own attack against Dispotier. As he attacks Dispotier, so does the Fire Knight. Even with two knights attacking, Dispotier seems to dodge them effortlessly. The two knights continue their attacks, but Dispotier taunts them, "This has been fun, but now I'm growing tired of it."

Now Dispotier uses his scythe blades to strike both knights, stunning them. As they are still stunned, he walks in between them. Touching both of their shoulders, he says, "Relax, young knights. Your friends will be joining you soon."

After watching their fellow knights be brought to their knees with no explanation, the Cross Knight says to the remaining knights, "Get the Earth, Fire, Wind and Water knights out of here while I hold him off."

Standing next to him, the Light Knight says, "You mean, we'll hold him off."

The Shadow Knight says, "We're on it."

"You knights won't be going anywhere," Dispotier says.

As the Shadow Knight moves toward the Earth and Fire Knights, Dispotier appears behind him, like before, with the other knights. He touches the shoulders of the Shadow Knight, causing him to fall to his knees as well.

The Cross Knight and Light Knight then charge at Dispotier, who, like before, with the other knights, dodges effortlessly. The Light Knight activates his lightspeed armor, and using his super speed as he attacks Dispotier, he is surprised to find that Dispotier is able to match his speed. He says, "There's no way."

Looking directly at him, Dispotier chuckles and says, "Surprise!" Dispotier swings his scythe blades, hitting the Light Knight with the handle part of it, knocking the Light Knight to the ground. As Dispotier walks by, he touches the Light Knight, and before the Cross Knight understands what has happened, Dispotier says, "If you think you and your friends are going to beat me like this, you are sadly mistaken."

Suddenly the knights who have been touched by Dispotier begin to disappear. As he notices it, he says, "If you think saving them will stop me, you truly are a fool."

Cross Knight then attacks with both of his swords. Dispotier blocks each strike with his scythe blades. He is able to knock both of the Cross Knight's swords away. Then he says, "Join your friends, Cross Knight."

Dispotier then grabs him and lifts him into the air. As he lets go, the Cross Knight falls to the floor.

Now turning his attention to the remaining knights, Dispotier begins to touch each of them, starting with the Bolt Knight, who had remained hidden away from the other knights. When she sees Dispotier, she says, "How are you able to do this?"

He chuckles and responds, "That is my secret. But, for now, join your friends." Then Dispotier touches her, causing her to fall to her knees. Then he begins to go after the Beast Knight and Love Knight, and, like before, with just a touch, the Knights fall to the ground.

Now there were only two knights remaining: the Hope knight and the Faith Knight. The Hope Knight says, "What are we going to do?"

The Faith Knight says, "I'm not sure, but I've got your back."

As Dispotier walks toward them, the remaining knights are disappearing. Dispotier sees this and he says, "If you think moving them from here will save them, then you don't understand my power."

The Faith Knight then stands in front of Dispotier and says, "That may be true, but you don't understand our power either, and I won't let you touch her."

This brings a big chuckle to Dispotier. "How touching!" he says. "You really think you can stop me, when the rest of your friends failed?"

"I don't know if I can stop you," the Faith Knight says, "but like my friends, I'm willing to try."

Dispotier then grips the shoulders of the Faith Knight, who falls to the ground and disappears. The Hope Knight stands there with her swords drawn, wondering what she will be able to do against Dispotier. He comments, "It's kind of ironic, isn't?"

She replies, "What do you mean?"

Dispotier then chuckles again and explains, "You don't get it, do you? Right now, with the exception of you, all of your friends are trapped and without hope. But don't worry, you will be joining them soon. Although the ironic part is that soon you, the Hope Knight, will be without hope."

Now it's her turn to chuckle. She says, "You know what? You're right. I am the Hope Knight, and I won't give up no matter what happens."

With that, the Hope Knight launches an attack against Dispotier, who blocks her attacks. As he does, he notices that her attacks are different from that of the other knights. Before he can ponder it any further, one of her strikes connects and actually wounds him.

Looking at the wound, he says, "It's not possible. How could you wound me?"

She chuckles and says, "I'm not sure, but when I'm done, I'll do more than just wound you."

Enraged, Dispotier launches his own attack on her. As she blocks his attacks, Dispotier waits for the moment when he can touch her. When he finally does, his hands start to burn. As she turns, Dispotier notices that she hasn't fallen under his power. He says, "How can this be? No one has ever resisted my touch before. How is it possible that you can resist it."

The Hope Knight is just as puzzled by this as Dispotier, and she replies, "I'm not sure either, but since you can't, I'm going to make you pay for what you did to my friends."

Before she can attack again, Dispotier vanishes. As she looks around, she notices that she's alone and ports back to the base with her BOD Bot.

BACK AT THE BASE, the Hope Knight goes to the lab and finds Manuel and Justice looking over the fallen knights. She goes to Justice and asks, "How are they?"

Manuel replies, "Physically they're fine, but apart from that, it looks like they're full of despair. With each passing minute, they are sinking deeper and deeper into it."

Sally shakes her head and says, "Is there any way to free them from it?"

"To be honest," replies Manuel, "I'm not sure what can be done. All I know is that Dispotier must be stopped, and the knights must be freed from this as soon as possible."

Sally says, "If I was able to hurt Dispotier, then there's a way to free them. There just has to be." She then goes to a corner and begins to pace back and forth, while she waits on Manuel and Justice to find a way to free her friends.

Justice then notices something. "Look at her," she says to Manuel. "Doesn't something seem different?"

Manuel looks at Sally and notices an aura about her. Then he says to Justice, "Go to her. I'll keep an eye on the knights here."

Walking over to Sally, Justice asks, "Are you okay?"

Shrugging her shoulders, Sally says, "Not really! But I can't give up hope. I just can't."

Justice says, "There's an ancient text that reads, '*Now hope that is seen is not hope. For who hopes for what he sees?*'"[11] A bit puzzled, Sally looks at her. "I wish I knew what you meant by that, Justice," she says. Looking at her, Justice takes her hand and says, "That's just it, Sally. You need to discover what that means for yourself, and not for anyone else."

Just then, Sally remembers when she first came to live with her Aunt Deborah. She had thought her life was over because her parents had passed away. She remembers crying for hours that first day. When Aunt Deborah came to her room, she knelt down and held her niece, and the two cried together.

After what seemed like hours, Aunt Deborah spoke: "I know it's not going to be easy, but I want you to know that I will always be here for you, and no matter what, I want you to promise me that you won't ever give up hope. I know things are going to be rough for a bit, but as long as we have hope, we'll make it through."

Although Sally didn't say anything then, she had agreed with Aunt Deborah, and although they had their ups and downs, she had never forgotten the promise she made in her heart to her Aunt that day. As she remembers this now, she stands and she hears the words *Herald of Hope armor, engage*. Suddenly her armor starts to transform. A white robe with a hood forms over her armor, that goes down to her knees. Then, in her hand, is a halberd, which has a spear on one end and a double-sided axe on the other. On her feet, appear white boots that go to the top of her thighs.

Once the transformation is complete, Sally feels different. Justice walks over to her and says, "It looks like you unlocked your new armor, Sally."

Sally goes to a nearby wall that acts as a mirror. As she looks at herself in her new armor, she says, "I guess I did. I think I know how to help the others, but it might be risky."

Justice looks at her and says, "We haven't much time. So, what's your plan?"

CHAPTER 19

BEYOND ALL HOPE:
HOUR OF HOPE

DISPOTIER IS BACK ABOARD BRYKAR'S SHIP, tending to his wound and wondering how the Hope Knight was able to escape his power. But, before he can ponder the matter further, Brykar finds him. Looking at his wound, he says, "Is there something you would like to tell me, Dispotier? Like why you are here rather than out there dealing with the knights?"

Dispotier replies, "Commander Brykar, eleven of the twelve knights are under my power. However, the reason I'm back here is that when I touched the last knight, for some reason she was not affected like the others and was also able to wound me. Even though the wound is minor, it puzzles me that up until now, no one has ever been able to wound me."

As Dispotier speaks, Brykar notices that he mentioned that eleven of twelve knights were under his power, so Brykar asks, "Did I hear you correctly? Did you just say that eleven of twelve knights were under your power?"

"That's correct, Commander Brykar," Dispotier says, "however, I will make sure that this last knight is dealt with, and I will see to it personally."

Chuckling, Brykar says, "Very well, Dispotier! Just make sure this last knight is dealt with. Do you understand me?"

Bowing before Brykar, Dispotier replies, "As you wish, Commander Brykar."

WHILE DISPOTIER FORMULATES A PLAN to deal with the Hope Knight, Brykar makes his way to the revival chamber, where his fallen warriors are being revived and enhanced for his specific purpose. As he checks on their status, he looks at Leo Untaros. Knowing that he cannot hear anything from inside, Brykar says, "I don't know how, but you failed, and it appears that the Light Knight is alive and well. However, I will make sure you do not fail me a second time. In fact, none of you will."

WITH THAT, BRYKAR LEAVES and heads to his chamber. As he enters, Brykar notices that General Sadoom is trying to contact him. He activates the video communication link, and General Sadoom says, "Brykar, what is the status on your plan?"

Kneeling before General Sadoom, Brykar lifts his head and says, "Everything is going according to plan, General Sadoom. Soon my fallen warriors will be revived, and after they are, it will seal their fates once and for all."

General Sadoom then turns around with his back to Brykar and says, "Brykar, if the knights defeated your warriors before, how do you expect to defeat the knights this time around?"

Lifting his head, Brykar chuckles and answers, "That's just it, General Sadoom. I expect them to fail, and when they do, that is when we will have the knights. I will see to their destruction personally."

MEANWHILE, MANUEL FINISHES LAYING THE KNIGHTS next to each other. Once he is finished, he says, "It's done, Sally. Now, what do we do?"

As Sally looks at the other knights, she pauses, then says, "Since Dispotier infused them with despair, the only way to free them is to infuse them with hope."

"How do you plan to do that?" Manuel asks.

Sally shakes her head and says, "I wish I knew." Just then she has an idea. "Then again," she says, "maybe there is a way."

"What do you mean?" Justice asks.

"Since my powers are based on hope, maybe that's the key to freeing them," Sally says, as she walks toward each of them. Gripping her halberd, she begins to focus her power through it. This causes the spear part to glow, and as it does, she goes to each of the knights, touching them on the left shoulder, then the right.

After she does this for a brief moment, the knights' bodies begin to glow for a brief moment. Sally then says, "Now all we can do is wait. In the meantime, it's time for me to go and have a talk with Dispotier."

Manuel asks her, "Are you sure this is a wise decision?"

Sally sighs, then says, "Not really, but it's not like we have much of a choice. If I stay here and do nothing, who knows what he'll do. At least, with me being out there, maybe I can hold him off until the others can recover."

"As much as I disagree with this idea," Manuel replies, "I agree that we aren't left with many options. The only thing I'll say is this: be careful out there. He'll be more dangerous now that he knows his powers can't affect you the way they affected the others."

Smiling, Sally says, "Honestly, I'm counting on it, but my new armor should even the odds a bit. Still, before I can face Dispotier, we need to find him. Manuel, could you begin scanning the area for Dispotier?"

Walking toward the computer, Manuel begins using the scanners to scan for Dispotier.

AT THE SAME TIME, SALLY HEADS TO THE HANGER where her BOD Bot, Hope Hunter, is kept. She is lost in thought, reflecting on the fact that she's not a fighter like Tasha or Maggie. Nor is she brave like Jessica or Britney. Nor is she strong like Janet. Yet, despite all of this, Sally knows she must be a fighter, courageous and strong.

When Sally reaches the hanger, the scanners have located Dispotier, causing the alarms in the base to go off. Looking at Hope Hunter, she says, "Well, it looks like it's time for round two. Are you ready, Hunter?" He responds, "Always! Now, let's kick this creep into next week."

With that, Sally gets into Hope Hunter and races to face Dispotier once again.

AT THAT VERY MOMENT, DISPOTIER ARRIVES at the same place where he faced the knights last time. As he gets off his scythecycle, he attempts to tap into the connection he has with the knights. Doing so, he notices that something is blocking him from them. Before he can even wonder what this is and why, the Hope Knight arrives.

With his back to her, Dispotier says, "I was wondering how long it would take you to find me."

"As you can see," the Hope Knight replies, "not long, Dispotier. In fact, I was waiting for you to show your face so that I can send you back to whatever hole you crawled out of."

This causes Dispotier to chuckle. With his back still turned to the Hope Knight, he says, "That's some brave talk considering you are all alone. Besides, I've learned something since our last encounter. Even though my powers can't affect you like it did your friends, you will fall by my hand."

Sally now has Hope Hunter switch to its BOD Bot battle mode and says, "Just because the other knights aren't here doesn't mean I'm alone, as you can see, Dispotier. Also, you aren't the only one who's learned something since our last encounter. Like you, I've learned about my powers, the power of hope. As long as I have hope, there's nothing you can do to hurt me."

Now Dispotier turns around. As he sees her in her new armor, he says, "Ahhhh, so, like the others, you've unlocked your secondary armor. It will do you no good—as you will soon see."

Puzzled as to what Dispotier is getting at, Sally asks, "What are you talking about, Dispotier?"

Pausing, he realizes that she must have had a hand in blocking the connection he had with the knights. Then he says, "What I mean is this: the connection I had with the knights has been blocked, and I know you had something to do with that. However, the despair your fellow knights have been consumed with will soon leave them as nothing more than lifeless shells."

Shaking her head, the Hope Knight says, "Do you really think I would go to the trouble of blocking your connection and just let your poison consume them? If so you're an even bigger fool than I thought."

Dispotier again chuckles. "You dare call me a fool, child," he says. "I will show you how foolish you are to challenge my power."

With that, he grabs the scythe blades on his cycle and his scythe shield, and in an instant, he leaps at her, launching his assault against her.

As his attack is about to hit her, the Hope Knight leaps back, drawing her Halberd of Hope, in order to block his attack. Although Dispotier is frustrated, he chuckles and says, "Impressive, child! I see you've gotten stronger since last time. Still, it will not be enough to stop me. I will enjoy destroying you."

Looking up at Dispotier, she says, "The only one getting destroyed here is you."

Looking intently at her, Dispotier replies, "You are stronger than I first thought, child, but you are still no match for my power. Now, let me show you what I can do."

As Dispotier charges toward her, Hope Hunter says, "Just say the word, and I'll crush this creep."

Sally chuckles and says, "Not yet, Hunter! Besides, I need to take this armor for a spin. Otherwise I got all dressed up for nothing."

Although the Hope Knight stands ready to block his attack, he leaps over her and strikes Hope Hunter, sending him flying to the ground. Turning to Dispotier she shouts, "Leave him alone! This fight is between you and me."

Dispotier chuckles at that and replies, "No, it's not, and before this day is done, I will make sure to destroy you and your precious hope."

With that he makes a second attack on Hope Hunter. The Hope Knight uses her halberd to stop the attack. Chuckling again, Dispotier says, "Gotcha!" And he strikes her, knocking her to the ground.

Before she can get up, Dispotier uses his scythe shield and has the blades extend. Using it, he pins the Hope Knight to the ground. Then, he starts walking confidently toward Hope Hunter.

Struggling to break free of his scythe shield, the Hope Knight shouts, "I said, Leave him alone."

Dispotier pauses and then answers, "No, once I've completely destroyed him, I will then deal with you. For now, watch as your protector is destroyed before your eyes, child. And understand that I will not be beaten."

While the Hope Knight tries to free herself, the scythes from the shield dig deeper into the ground, keeping her pinned tight. She says, "It doesn't matter how strong you are. As long as I live and breathe, I will destroy you."

Pausing for just a moment, Dispotier turns to her and says, "Go ahead and cling to your foolish hope. In the meantime, I will destroy your protector, and you will have no choice but to watch as I reduce him to scrap metal. And know that before I destroy you, I will destroy everything and everyone that you care about, while all you can do is watch."

Pinned to the ground, the Hope Knight thinks about Hope Hunter and about her friends who are counting on her. As Dispotier reaches Hope Hunter, he lifts his scythe blades to strike. Just then, Hope Hunter turns, blocks the attack with one of his Hatchets of Hope, and says, "If you think I'm going down that easily, you've got another think coming."

Now with the other hatchet, he swings at Dispotier. Dispotier successfully dodges the strike and says, "This might be more fun than I first thought. I will enjoy taking you apart."

Hope Hunter stands to his feet and begins to attack. Dispotier blocks this attack. The Hope Knight watches, relieved. She continues to search for a way to free herself.

Dispotier continues to dodge Hope Hunter's attacks. He glances to the Hope Knight and smiles as he dodges the next attack. Now he strikes Hope Hunter, slicing first the left arm, then the right. He says, "I told you today you will watch your hope die."

MEANWHILE, BACK IN THE KNIGHTS' BASE, Manuel and Justice watch as the Hope Knight and her BOD Bot face off against Dispotier. Justice turns to Manuel and says, "At this rate, they won't last much longer. Is there anything we can do to help?"

Manuel shakes his head negatively and responds, "Unfortunately, no."

Justice asks, "What about the other BOD Bots? Couldn't they help?"

Again Manuel shakes his head and replies, "I've already checked. Whatever Dispotier did to the knights is also interfering with their BOD Bots, leaving them currently inactive."

Justice looks at him and says, "So, you're telling me we're going to sit here and do nothing?"

Manuel sighs and replies, "Of course not, but you and I both know there are limits to what we can do. Still, I agree we need to do something. I'm just not exactly sure what we can do."

Suddenly, without warning, golden cocoons form around the knights. When Justice and Manuel see this, she asks, "What's going on?"

Manuel pauses for a moment and then says, "I have a feeling that this is a result of what the Hope Knight did earlier. I know right now it's hard, but the only way she's going to prevail is if we don't lose hope."

Justice then asks, "Are we at least able to port Hope Hunter back here, so he can be repaired?"

Manuel nods and enters the command. As Dispotier strikes out at the BOD Bot, it is ported to the base, leaving Dispotier puzzled as to what just happened.

BEFORE THE HOPE KNIGHT CAN START TO WONDER what just happened, Justice appears to her and says, "Don't be alarmed! Manuel ported your BOD Bot back to the base before Dispotier could finish what he started."

"That's a relief!" the Hope Knight responds. "Now to just get out of this thing and finish off Dispotier."

With that, Justice disappears.

AS JUSTICE RETURNS TO BASE, Manuel asks, "Should I ask where you just went?"

Justice giggles and replies, "That depends. Are you going to ask a question you already know the answer to?"

"Never mind," Manuel says. "I've already started the repair process on Hope Hunter. he should be as good as new in a few hours."

Justice then asks, "Manuel, could you explain to me why we are limited in helping them again?"

Before Manuel can say anything, the knights begin to glow, and before Manuel or Justice can examine what is happening, they receive a psychic message.

Manuel says, "We're being summoned, Justice. Let's go."

As they walk through the base, Justice asks, "Do you know why we are being summoned?"

Manuel shakes his head and says, "I have no idea, but we'll find out soon enough."

When they reach the entrance to the secret chamber, Manuel touches a panel, and the entrance to the secret chamber appears, allowing both of them to enter. As they enter, the entrance closes behind them.

WHILE MANUEL AND JUSTICE ARE IN THE SECRET CHAMBER, the Hope Knight struggles to get free as Dispotier walks menacingly toward her. With each step, he gets closer. He begins to taunt the Hope Knight. "I don't know what happened to your protector, but it won't matter. Once I destroy you, any hope you have will be destroyed with you."

Looking toward him, she forces a smile and replies, "If you think by destroying me, you destroy all hope, you are sadly mistaken. You see, I've learned something very interesting about hope."

Dispotier indulges her a moment and asks, "What is that?"

She chuckles now as she answers him, "Hope is like a seed. It starts off small, but then it grows and can become as huge as a tree."

Once she says that, a burst of energy flows from her body, causing Dispotier's scythe shield fly away from her. Seeing this, he shouts, "How is this possible? There's no way you should have been able to break the grip of my scythe shield."

As she gets to her feet and takes up her halberd, the Hope Knight replies, "Well, I did. Now, shall we continue this dance?"

Dispotier chuckles this time. "Yes," he says, "let's finish this dance. And when we're done, I will mount your corpse on my wall as a symbol of the day hope dies."

Now Dispotier and the Hope Knight both charge at each other. As they are about to clash, Dispotier leaps over her and races to grab his scythe shield. Looking at his scythe shield, he notices that the blades are still good. He places it on his arm, and the blades begin to spin. Now he charges at the Hope Knight again. This time, just as the two are about to clash, the Hope Knight strikes from below with the spear end of her halberd. This knocks his scythe shield up and away from her. Now her arm comes down to strike Dispotier with the axe part of her halberd. He leaps back, gripping his scythe blades. Extending his arm, he strikes back at the Hope Knight, but she uses the axe part of her halberd to block his counter attack.

Looking at her, Dispotier steps back, then begins to chuckle. "Although you are strong, Hope Knight," he says, "it is clear that even your power has its limits."

Holding her ground, the Hope Knight replies, "What are you talking about?"

Pointing at her, Dispotier shouts, "You may not be shaking out of despair, but our exchanges have taken their toll on your body. It has become clear to me that I can continue this much longer than you can."

Although she hates to admit it, the Hope Knight is starting to feel the fatigue from this fight. As she looks at Dispotier, she shouts, "That maybe so, but I will continue to fight you with everything I have."

Puzzled as to why she still has hope, Dispotier says, "Before I end your existence, tell me what hope do you have of defeating me? Fatigue has started to claim your body, your friends are nowhere to be found, and I've disassembled your protector, so how do you expect to defeat me?"

Realizing that he has a point, Sally knows that giving up hope would be the easy route, but right now help isn't coming anytime soon. Still, she grips her halberd and says, "You're right. This battle has tired me out. You nearly destroyed my BOD Bot, and my friends are unable to help me at the moment. But the reason I still have hope is that so many people are depending on me, and I have no intention of letting them down—now or ever. I know I'm not the strongest fighter on our team. And even though they aren't here with me in body, I know their spirits are. If I'm going to meet my end here and now, I'm making sure I take you with me."

Again Dispotier chuckles and, with his scythe blades in hand, he cuts through the air, sending a dark energy blast toward the Hope Knight, knocking her backward. She tries desperately to hold her ground.

Standing there, he looks at her. He watches her body shake from even more fatigue, and he says, "Those were pretty words, Hope Knight, but that's all they are—empty words. The time has come to end this and you."

As Sally grips her halberd even tighter, she falls to one knee. She sees Dispotier walking toward her, and as she remembers the oath. She begins to recite it: "*As days of darkness near, and people run in fear, …*"

Dispotier watches her grip on the halberd, knowing that soon he will bring an end to her. With her gone, there will be no one to stop him or the Psystructs ever again.

Stabbing her halberd into the ground as she tries to stand, Sally continues saying, "*From they who prey on the weak, and silence those who speak …*"

As he begins to make his way toward her, Dispotier begins to swing his scythe blades, knowing that very soon she will become his latest trophy. The Hope Knight struggles to get to her feet, all the while continuing to say, "*We will take to the sky with courage and battle cry …*"

Before she can finish the oath, she falls to her knees. Just then Dispotier reaches her. He says, "Any final words, Hope Knight?"

As he lifts his scythe blades to strike, she shouts, "*To protect the world from loss, I am a Knight of the Cross!*" Suddenly, a surge of energy surrounds her, and she knocks Dispotier backward. The Hope Knight stands to her feet. Shocked, Dispotier shouts "How is this possible? You were on your knees moments ago."

Turning to him, the Hope Knight says, "This is the true power of hope, and it's hope that has renewed my body."

With that, the Hope Knight takes her halberd in hand and, using the axe part of it, she swings it from left to right. Dispotier blocks it with his scythe shield, only to have it shatter and fall to pieces before him. Then, with a flick of her wrist, the Hope Knight strikes him with the spear part of her halberd. It slices through his body, and as he stumbles backward, she bring her halberd over head and, with the axe part, slices through him again, causing his body to split into four pieces.

Standing over Dispotier, she knows that the battle is over, and she ports back to the base.

As the Hope Knight vanishes from sight, the Psydrones gather around Dispotier gathering up his remains to take back to Brykar.

ONCE SHE IS BACK AT THE BASE, Sally notices cocoons where the other knights were lying before. Before she can ask anything, the cocoons dissolve, and each of the knights begins to awaken. One-by-one they stand, and each of them looks at the others. Seeing Sally standing there, Joseph says, "Sally, would you mind filling us in on what happened to us?"

Sally chuckles, then says, "Well, you were all paralyzed once Dispotier touched you, but he wasn't able to paralyze me."

Before she can say anything else, Tasha says, "Wait a minute! Are you telling us that you not only fought Dispotier alone, but you actually beat him?"

Now Sally giggles and then replies, "Yep! Pretty much!"

Each of the knights are surprised by this. As they look at Sally, Max is the first to notice her new armor. He says, "Nice armor! I guess a lot happened while we were out."

She looks at all of them and says, "Pretty much! But we can talk about all that later. Right now I need to rest. This fight took a lot out of me."

Before Sally can go to her quarters to rest, Manuel and Justice walk into the lab where the knights are gathered. As they see Sally, Manuel says, "I take it this means you beat Dispotier?"

When Sally nods her head, Manuel continues, "Well done! By the way, Hope Hunter's repairs will be complete in the next few hours."

Knowing they all missed a lot while they were paralyzed, Des asks, "Manuel, can you fill us in on what happened to us?"

"When you all went to battle Dispotier," Manuel explains, "he was able to paralyze each of you with a touch of despair, leaving your bodies nearly lifeless. All ... with the exception of Sally, who, as you can see, unlocked her secondary armor. However, she didn't unlock her new armor until after she forced Dispotier to return to Brykar. And once she did, she used her powers to infuse each of you with hope, so that while she faced Dispotier again, each of you might recover.

"After that, Hope Hunter was badly damaged by Dispotier, cocoons formed around each of you, and beyond that, I'm not sure what else happened, as there were other matters Justice and I had to attend to."

Joseph and Des look at each other. Then Joseph asks, "Manuel, I don't mean to be rude, but what other matters did you need to tend to when Sally was on her own out there? I mean, seriously, what are you guys hiding from us?"

JUSTICE LOOKS AT MANUEL, and he goes to the computer and says, "As you already know, we were sent here to earth with the armors you now wear. And you know that there were three psythonians that made the armors as well. However, what you do not know is that it was the psythonians that created the Psystructs, and Justice and I are not only two of the three last psythonians. We also created the Psystructs."

Shocked by this, Brad shouts, "You're just telling us this now?"

Joseph looks at Brad and says, "I know you're angry, Brad, but I think there's a lot more we need to know before we lose it. Please continue, Manuel."

Manuel continues, "We did not want to keep this from you. However, we were not allowed to say anything until now. You see, although we are two of the three last psythonians, we are immortals. Not only are we responsible for the creation of the Psystructs; we are responsible for the creation of countless worlds that the Psystructs conquered."

Sensing their thoughts, Manuel then says, "I know what you all are thinking. If we created the Psystructs, why can't we stop them? The reason is this: when we created the psythonians and the countless worlds, we gave them what you know as 'free will' and vowed to never take it away. Although the day the Psystructs were born was the day the psythonians we gave life to perished."

Joseph then asks, "What do you mean, Manuel?"

Taking a breath, Manuel says, "You see, the psythonians were a peaceful people until the day a young psythonian scientist lost his family and, in trying to save them, created the tech that gave birth to the Psystructs. Although the tech didn't save his family, he found it had other uses, and it quickly corrupted his heart and mind. Shortly after developing the tech, he began abducting psythonians, turning them into Psydrones. Those who were enticed by the power became willing subjects and generals. When we learned of this, we immediately began the creation of the armors you now possess. Still, it took time because we needed to be certain that the power used for your armor would not corrupt you the way the tech did with the psythonian scientist."

When Manuel finishes speaking, Joseph says, "Now it's starting to make sense. Still, you should have told us this sooner. All right, everyone. Go and relax for the next six hours, and then meet me in the Training Room." Each of the knights nods in agreement.

BACK IN BRYKAR'S SHIP, the Psydrones return with the remains of Dispotier and place them in the recovery tube. As the tube closes, the machinery inside immediately begins to reconstruct Dispotier.

Brykar also arrives. As he looks at Dispotier, he says, "Although I didn't expect you to defeat the Hope Knight, her powers are still quite impressive. Still, you have served your purpose well, Dispotier." And Brykar leaves for his command chamber.

ENTERING HIS CHAMBER, BRYKAR NOTICES that General Sadoom is trying to contact him. As he establishes the connection, Brykar kneels and says, "I'm here, General Sadoom. What do you need of me?"

Noticing Brykar's mood, General Sadoom chuckles and asks, "You seem to be in a better mood than normal. Would you care to explain why?"

Brykar lifts his head and responds, "Yes, General Sadoom. As you know, my newest warrior, Dispotier, engaged the knights. He paralyzed all of them but one, and that remaining knight he engaged in battle, nearly destroying her.

Yet, like many of the warriors I have sent after these "knights," he also failed, but everything is still according to plan."

Puzzled by this contradiction, General Sadoom says, "Are you telling me that your latest warrior was defeated by these knights, and you aren't one bit bothered by it?"

Brykar says, "That is correct, General Sadoom."

Now General Sadoom gets more serious. "Brykar," he says, "do understand what will happen if you fail to destroy these knights?"

"I know," Brykar replies, "I understand what will happen to me, General Sadoom, if I fail, and that is why I've started modifying my warriors so that when they next face the knights — whether they defeat the knights or not — the end result will be their destruction."

Not impressed, General Sadoom says, "Brykar, as you know, we do not tolerate failure. However, since you seem so sure of your plan, I will allow you to continue. Just don't make me regret this decision, or the normal punishment will seem like a walk in the park compared to what I have in mind for you. Do I make myself clear?"

Lifting his head once more to General Sadoom, Brykar replies, "I understand, General, and I will not fail you."

As the communication link ends, Brykar stands to his feet and says to himself, "With each battle, these knights grow stronger. Still, once my plan is complete, they will be but a distant memory, and these earthlings will never know how much danger they were truly in. ... Although it might be time to check on how my modifications are coming."

As Brykar uses the computer in his chamber to check the status of his fallen warriors, he realizes that there are only two remaining warriors. This means that once these are defeated, that will leave him to have to face the knights himself. With that, he begins to look at the images of the knights. As he comes to the Cross Knight, he says, "Yes, this will be perfect. Once I destroy his team, I will destroy him. And once that is done, this very world will belong to the Psystructs."

Agent Wallace is looking through files of perspective candidates to join their ARC team when Agent Daniels walks in. She asks, "So, what have you been up to, Agent Wallace?"

Turning to her, he replies, "Looking through personnel files, trying to find five new team members to join our team. Each of these candidates is more than qualified. The trick is how to narrow them down to the five who will be the most effective and work well with us as a team."

Sitting beside him, Agent Daniels looks at the files. She says, "That is difficult, but not impossible. Still, there should be a way to narrow it down. Let's look at what we know about the knight's based on their forms. They look to be similar to our male and female, and there are twelve of them, right? Which means we need six males and six females in total."

As she says this, Agent Wallace starts separating the male personnel files from the female personnel files. As he does this, he begins to notice that for their team, they need three males and two females, and there are only three males in the personnel files who stand out above the others.

Next, turning his attention to the female personnel files, he knows they need two females as well, and he chooses the two who stand out the most to him. As he gathers the files, he turns to Agent Daniels and says, "Thanks, believe it or not that really helped."

Shaking her head, Agent Daniels replies "I didn't do much, but either way, you're welcome."

Agent Wallace says, "Hey, Daniels, I'm going to get some food in a few minutes. Would you care to join me?"

Surprised at his invitation, she replies, "Agent Wallace, are you trying to ask me out on a date?"

Unknown to either of them, at that very moment, Agent Saunders is listening just outside the doorway, and before Agent Wallace can confirm or deny that he is asking Daniels out, Agent Saunders walks in with her head down. She says, "Agent Wallace, there's something I need to discuss with you right…" She pauses as she see Agent Daniels. Acting as if she hasn't heard anything, she asks, "Am I interrupting something, Agent Wallace?"

Before Agent Wallace can respond, Agent Daniels says, "I've gotta go anyway, but we'll continue this conversation later. See ya."

As Agent Daniels walks out, Agent Wallace looks at Agent Saunders and asks, "What is it, Agent Saunders?"

Looking at him, she says, "Agent Martin wanted to know about the progress in selecting the new recruits to join our team."

Standing up from his chair, Agent Wallace says, "Yeah, I just got done selecting them. In fact, why don't you take someone with you and go gather them."

She says, "Yes sir, would you care to join me?" Thinking about it for a moment, he realizes that his opportunity with Daniels is gone for now, so he replies, "All right, Saunders. Meet me in the hanger in ten minutes."

She responds, "Yes, sir. I'll see you in ten minutes."

As she leaves the room and heads to the hanger, she runs into Agent Daniels. She says, "Sorry for interrupting you two earlier, I…"

Agent Daniels then replies, "Don't feed me that garbage! Or did you forget who I am and what I can do?"

A bit puzzled about this, Saunders asks, "What do you mean, Agent Daniels?"

Agent Daniels pulls up security footage of her the first time she interrupted them, then the incident just now, and says, "I don't know what your deal is with Agent Wallace, but I want you to know that I respect him, and am not sure how I feel about him otherwise, but it's clear that he likes me. So, I advise you to either tell him how you feel or back off and see what happens. If not, I won't be responsible for what happens to you. Are we clear?"

Agent Saunders replies, "Yes, Agent Daniels, we're clear." And, with that, the two female agents go their separate ways.

Meanwhile as Deborah's shift ends, she leaves the restaurant to go to her car and finds Melanie there waiting for her. She asks, "Is everything okay, Melanie?"

Melanie smiles and says, "Everything is as normal as can be. I just thought about what we talked about earlier and thought maybe you could use a bit of a break. Besides, I have David and Laura I can talk to about my concerns with our kids. But I noticed you don't really have anyone, and I thought maybe you could use a friend to vent to."

Deborah chuckles and replies, "Is it that obvious?"

Melanie chuckles and says, "Not really! I just tend to be observant of people and things around me. So, how about it?"

Deborah says, "I don't really want to go anywhere, but I would definitely enjoy the company. So, could we relax at my place while talking over pizza and a movie?"

Melanie smiles and says, "That's fine! I'll order it now so there isn't a lot of wait time. So, what would you like on your pizza?"

Thinking for a moment, Deborah responds, "I'll have mine with chicken and black olives."

Melanie chuckles again and says, "That's interesting, cause that's one of my favorites as well."

The two women get in their cars. As they drive toward Deborah's house, Melanie places the order. About twenty minutes later, the two arrive at Deborah's home. As they enter, Deborah says, "I'm going to go upstairs and get comfortable. Here's some money for when the pizza guy comes."

Melanie puts the money back in her hand and says, "This one's on me. Just hurry back cause there is a lot we need to talk about."

While Deborah is upstairs getting changed, she is surprised by Melanie's offer and is also glad because it has been hard to raise Sally on her own especially after the death of her brother and sister-in-law, Sally's parents. Still, she wouldn't trade Sally for anything. She still misses her a great deal. Hopefully she can find out more information about Sally from her talk with Melanie.

She changes into a baggy T-shirt and pajama pants and is heading back downstairs when the doorbell rings. She notices Melanie as she shuts the door. She turns to see Deborah and says, "Perfect timing! Pizza's here!"

Deborah chuckles. "I've got some juice in the fridge," she says. "Get it set up in the living room, and I'll bring the drinks and some plates."

A few minutes later Deborah comes in with a tray that has a pitcher of orange juice, two glasses and two plates. As the two get settled in the living room, Melanie says, "What are you in the mood to watch?"

Deborah snickers and replies, "Honestly, I want to watch my eyelids, but I want to say that I'm touched by your concern for me in regard to Sally. Although something tells me you have more information than you were willing or able to share at the restaurant."

It's Melanie's turn to be surprised at how quickly Deborah picks up on things. She responds, "To be honest, there isn't much news to tell. The only thing I can say is that whoever is after them is very dangerous and went so far as having someone or something try to impersonate me. Still, I figured that maybe you could use a friend."

Deborah reaches for a slice of pizza. As she takes a bite, she forgets how hot the pizza is and slightly burns the roof of her mouth. "Too hot! Too hot!" she protests. She quickly grabs a glass, pours some juice into it and gulps it down.

Sitting there chuckling to herself, Melanie asks, "Are you okay, Deborah?"

After a few moments Deborah says, "I'm fine, but it happens every time I have pizza."

"Same here," Melanie says. "That's why I'm laughing."

Before the two can say anything else, Melanie gets a call from Linda. She asks Melanie to come over ASAP. Melanie then says, "I'm with Deborah, Sally's Aunt. Can I come by later?"

Phillips wife informs her to bring Deborah the information they have concerning the kids, she should be here as well. When the phone call ends, Melanie says "That was Linda, Max's Aunt, and she said for us to come over immediately."

Without a hesitation, Deborah says, "Give me two minutes, and I'll be ready."

Deborah then rushes upstairs and changes into a pair of jeans, then rushes back down. Grabbing her keys, she and Melanie get into Melanie's car and head for Phillip's house.

CHAPTER 20

WALK OF FAITH:
NOT BY SIGHT

AFTER LEAVING HER HOUSE, Deborah and Melanie head to Phillip's. When they get there, Linda opens the door and invites them in. Once inside, they notice that Graham is there too. Melanie asks, "Graham, what's going on?"

Graham replies, "As you know, I haven't found out much in regard to what happened to my brother and the others. However, I was able to find out more about this organization that is targeting them. From what I've found out, they're alien hunters."

Deborah then asks, "Then, why are they after our kids? Your brother?"

Graham answers, "I was wondering the same thing ... until a piece of the wreckage came into my possession. After running some tests, I discovered that what caused the bus explosion was some kind of energy blast."

Melanie looks at Graham and asks, "Are you trying to tell me that some kind of alien weapon blew up their bus?"

Graham looks at each of them and then replies, "Exactly! In fact, I believe the reason these alien hunters are after them is that they want to know whatever they know. However, it doesn't mean that once they get the info, they will necessarily let them go."

Deborah shakes her head and says, "This is crazy! Are you expecting me to believe that aliens were responsible for the bus blowing up? And now Sally and the others are wanted because of their connection to it?"

Graham takes a deep breath and tries to explain, "Listen, when I first discovered this, I was just as surprised and found it just as hard to believe as you all do. However, after numerous tests and research concerning this whole incident, the only thing I can figure out is that whatever caused this explosion was not normal. These alien hunters are after them, which has forced them to go into hiding, and which is why they haven't contacted us."

Melanie now asks, "Is there any way we can contact them?"

Graham shakes his head and says, "Not without these guys being able to track them. Although, I might be able to create a communications device that would allow us to communicate with them. The only problem is: even if I can create it, I have no way to let them know, so we can give it to them to communicate with us."

Phillip then says, "Graham, I know it's a long shot, but I think it would be best if you start working on those communicators. I'll talk to Tasha's grandfather and see if he can find a way to get them to the kids."

Graham looks at Phillip and then replies, "All right. I'll get started on the devices to communicate with my brother and the others."

As the adults all nod in agreement, Melanie asks, "Graham, I thought we had agreed not to meet or contact each other over the phone?"

Looking at her, he says, "After whatever those alien hunters used to impersonate you, I've been scanning the area and have found no type of surveillance tech nearby. That's why I figured it would be safe for us to meet. Besides, if we weren't supposed to be meeting with each other, what were you doing at Deborah's house?"

"Okay, point taken!" Melanie admits. "Still, going forward, we all need to be careful. Who knows what lengths that organization will go to if they are hunting our loved ones."

AGENTS WALLACE AND SAUNDERS ARE ABOARD one of ARC's flying transports, headed to recruit the first of their new teammates. His name is Andre Marks, and he is known for his pinpoint accuracy, expertise with any and all explosive devices. As Agent Wallace pilots the transport, Agent Saunders asks, "So, where are we going to find this first guy?"

Handing her the file that is sitting next to him, Agent Wallace says, "If you look closely, you'll see that after every mission he returns to his grandmother's place. It's located in Brooklyn, New York. I know that he just completed a mission yesterday, so I'm betting that he's on his way there now."

She looks at him and says, "Okay, so how are we going to get him to join us?"

Agent Wallace replies, "I'm going to let you figure that out. All we need to know is in that file, and we have about six hours before we touch down. So, I suggest you start studying the file and figure out how to recruit him?"

Thinking for a moment, Agent Saunders responds, "What if we just tell him that we are fellow ARC agents and would like him to join us?"

Shaking his head, Agent Wallace says, "I wish it were that simple. You see, each of these ARC agents, while having special skills, are also loners, men and women who are usually sent on suicide missions. The fact that they've been working alone, with no one to answer to, may make it difficult for them to want to be subject to someone else."

Agent Saunders replies, "All right, I'll start studying his file and have an idea ready in three hours."

Surprised by this, Agent Wallace replies, "We have a six-hour flight. There's no need to rush it."

Turning to him, she says, "Learning about him from his profile in three hours isn't rushing it for me. I've learned to study people in such a way that I can learn about them from pretty much anything in a short time. Also, from the looks of this personnel file, there's not a lot that is said about the type of missions he's been on. But, from this personality profile attached, I should be able to get enough insight on him so that I can persuade him to join us immediately."

Chuckling, Agent Wallace says, "All right, then get on it, and, by the way, if he doesn't join us immediately, your buying dinner, and I'm really hungry."

"I have a better idea," she says, turning to him. "How about we have him meet us at a restaurant nearby so that we can recruit him. This way, while we talk, you can sit and stuff your face."

Nodding his approval, Agent Wallace increases the speed of the transport, as they head for Brooklyn, New York.

WHILE AGENT WALLACE AND SAUNDERS ARE OUT RECRUITING their new teammates, Brykar is in his command chamber, going over the modifications that are being made to his fallen warriors. Once he is done with that, he goes to the chamber which holds his two remaining warriors. As he enters, he opens the chamber closest to him. Inside is a creature unlike any other. It has the head of a king cobra, the body of a man and is covered in scales, with a snake-like tail. He moves and then slowly emerges, waking from a long sleep. He kneels before Brykar and says, "I'm at your sssservice, Commander Brykar. What is it you would assssk of me?"

Brykar chuckles as he remembers that although this new warrior appears to be loyal, his kind is not known for their loyalty, but rather for their treachery. Looking at him, Brykar says, "Skip the pleasantries, Sir Pentous, and rise. I have need of your skills, abilities."

Rising to his feet, Sir Pentous asks, "Sssso, what do you need me to do, Commander Brykar?"

Brykar then turns and says, "There is a group of heroes who have become a thorn in my side, and I need them to be dealt with."

Sir Pentous replies, "It will be my pleasssure, Commander Brykar."

With his back to the creature, Brykar says, "In the hanger, you will find weapons and a workshop, should you want to modify any weapons you choose. Do not fail me, Sir Pentous."

With that said, Brykar leaves.

SIR PENTOUS MAKES HIS WAY to the hanger. As he looks over the available weapons and armors, he notices an armor from his home world. It has a snake head on each shoulder and a snake emblem on the chest piece. After putting on the armor, he grabs his rattlesnake staff. Now he needs a vehicle.

As he looks at the magnacycles, he chooses one, and using his rattlesnake staff, he causes it to transform so that it looks like a snake. Once the transformation is complete, Sir Pentous goes to the computer to review past encounters with the knights. As he does this, he notices that each of his predecessors either used might or negative emotions to defeat or capture the knights. This gives Sir Pentous an interesting idea. He then walks over to the workshop, grabs a jar and a sponge-like object, and uses it to capture a large amount of his venom. He then takes the venom and squeezes it into the jar and begins working on altering its properties so that rather than poisoning the knights, this new breed of venom would trap them in their fantasies.

As Sir Pentous puts his venom in the machine, to alter its properties, he notices a wrist-mounted launcher with thirteen pellets. He examines the pellets and notices that each of them could easily hold his new venom, so that on contact, the knights would be infected, trapped within their own pleasures and desires. He watches as his venom and the chemicals begin to mix. He is now chuckling to himself as he thinks to himself, "Once I'm done with the knights, I'll use this last one on Brykar and take his place among the Psystructs."

AS THE KNIGHTS RELAX, Des goes to Joseph and says, "Hey, Joseph, do you have a minute?"

Joseph turns and says, "Sure, Des. What's up?"

Des pauses for a moment and then replies, "As you know, when we fought Nosvorat, he had to use his stare to bring out the negative emotions in each knight ... except for Max. As much as I hate to say it, I think now would be the perfect time to discuss this with him, so that there's nothing hindering us going forward."

Joseph looks at Des and responds, "So how do you want to handle this, Des?"

Des shakes his head and says, "That's just it. We all know that before we became knights, you and Max were the best of friends. But now, the fact that you are the leader changes the dynamics quite a bit."

Joseph asks, "How so?"

Des chuckles as he says, "Simple! Before you and I would hang out on occasions, but were merely associates. Now, however, you and I have gotten closer as teammates and friends due to my technical expertise."

Joseph thinks to himself a moment, then says, "You know what, you're right. I guess I should be the one to talk to Max about it."

Before anything else can be said, Max walks into the room and joins the two of them. "Talk to Max about what?" he asks, with a bit of sarcasm in his voice.

When Des tries to excuse himself, Max shouts, "Don't you dare move, Des! You we're so quick to talk about me behind my back. Now you're going to stay as Joseph tells me whatever it is you two we're talking about to my face."

Joseph sighs and says. "All right, Max, during the battle with Nosvorat, Des discovered that in order to get control of us, he had to use his gaze ... with the exception of you. For some reason, he was able to tap into the negative energy you were already showing."

Max folds his arms and replies, "So, does this mean I'm still part of the team or benched?"

Joseph shakes his head and responds, "No, it doesn't mean either one, bro. If I've done anything to hurt you, or even neglected you, I'm sorry. Also, what this means is that we can't give the Psystructs any advantage. So, if you do have negative feelings toward me or the rest of the team, let's sort it out because we need to be united, not divided."

Max pauses for a moment and then says, "I understand what you're saying, but I can't talk about it right now. I do accept your apology, and I'm sorry for being such a jerk earlier."

Max now turns to Des and says, "Forgive me for lashing out at you, Des."

Chuckling for just a moment, Des replies, "It's okay. All is forgiven. Although I should have seen this coming."

Joseph now turns to Max and Des and says, "Listen, I know we weren't good friends before, but now we're teammates, and now we need to remember that no matter what, we aren't just a team; we are a family."

The three laugh for a moment, then Max replies, "I know, and you're right. Just give me sometime to sort through what I'm feeling."

Joseph nods, and as he does, Max leave the room and heads toward his quarters.

AS MAX WALKS TOWARD HIS CHAMBER, Sally turns the corner, and the two meet. She can tell that something is bothering him and asks, "A penny for your thoughts, Max?"

At first, he wants to tell her it's none of her business, but instead he says, "I just have a lot of stuff on my mind?"

Tilting her head and smiling, Sally replies, "Well, if you want to talk about it, I'm here for you." She then begins to walk away from him. Max, left standing there alone, turns and says, "Hey, Sally, is your offer to talk still open?"

Turning back to him, she smiles and reponds, "Always! So where do you want to go and talk?"

Max thinks for a moment and says, "How about we walk to the hanger? It's along enough walk that we can have a good talk, and if we are needed, we'll be able to respond quickly."

As the two knights start walking toward the hanger, Sally asks, "So, what's going on, Max? What has you bothered?"

Max says, "Well, I walked in on Joseph and Des talking about me, and they informed me that Nosvorat was able to feed off my negative emotions without having to use his gaze. So now I've got to deal with it, or I'll just be a handicap to you guys."

Sally replies, "I see, so tell me what are you really upset about?"

Max chuckles and says, "You should ask what am I *not* upset about? I mean, honestly speaking, I guess I'm bothered by Joseph getting closer with Des and ..."

Looking at him, she says, "It's okay. You can tell me?"

Max stops now, and as she turns to look at him, he says ".... and I'm jealous that each of the others has found someone. I don't want to be someone's second or last pick, when the person I like is my first pick."

Sally frowns and asks, "So, who is it that your really like?"

Max shakes his head and replies, "Do you really want to know?"

She looks at him and says, "Yes, I do! I'll keep your secret safe."

Again Max shakes his head. Then, leaning in close to her, he whispers, "You are my first choice, Sally. Always have been and always will be." Before Sally can respond to him, the alarms go off, and Des informs everyone that Brykar's newest warrior has surfaced.

Max asks, "Can we finish this conversation later?"

Sally smiles and replies tenderly, "Definitely! But right now, let's head to the lab and see what we're dealing with."

ONE BY ONE, EACH OF THE KNIGHTS ENTERS THE LAB. Once all the knights are in, Joseph asks, "What are we looking at, Des?"

As Des uses the computer to pull up an image of Brykar's newest warrior, the knights see Sir Pentous. Joseph chuckles and says, "I guess Brykar's not pulling his punches, since he's sending a snake after us."

Max speaks up, "No kidding, so what's the plan?"

Joseph thinks for a moment, then asks, "Des, I know we don't have much info on this creature, but could you scan and see what we're dealing with?"

Typing something on the computer keyboard, Des replies, "Let's see what I can find."

Using the computer to scan Sir Pentous, he is able to notice a couple of key things. "According to the scans," he says, "it looks like there are two or three main things we need to worry about. The first is his tail. We don't know what it can do. The second thing is his staff. We don't know the effect it can have on us. Finally, the third thing is the possibility of his venom, which, if he does possess it, can have various effects."

While Joseph thinks about what can be done, Max asks, "Hey, Des, how were you able to find out all that when we usually don't know much about Brykar's warriors?"

Lightly chuckling, Des says, "You're right, Max. Usually we don't know much. But in this case, whoever this warrior is, he's not being subtle by any means. My assessment was made based on the images of what the scans showed when he was located."

Then Max asks, "How do you know if he even has venom?"

Turning to all the knights, Des replies, "I don't, but to assume he doesn't would be really stupid. Most of Brykar's warriors have special skills and abilities, and I feel his venom might be just that."

Brad then chimes in, "Hey, Des, I think it's great you got this information, but does anyone have an idea about how to deal with this guy? Or are we just going to walk into another of Brykar's traps?"

Eric shakes his head and replies, "Brad is right. Each time we go out to face one of Brykar's warriors, they find some way to trap us, leaving one of us to fight them off by ourselves. So, what's the plan?"

Joseph then says, "Enough! Trap or no trap, we have to face this guy. You're all right. We need a plan, and the only thing I can come up with at the moment is for us to surround him. This way he won't be able to get the drop on us so easily."

Tasha then asks, "Should we activate our secondary armors now or in the field?"

Joseph replies, "It would be best to activate them in the field, when we have a better idea of what this guy can do?"

Britney asks, "Why not activate them now?"

Joseph replies, "Even though your armors are strong, if we go in before knowing what we're dealing with, we could lose the advantage the armors would give. So, for right now, we'll go in with our primary armor, our weapons, and our BOD Bots. Now, everyone to the hanger, and let's find out who we're dealing with." Each of the knights nods in agreement, and Des ports them all to the hanger.

AS THE KNIGHTS GET IN THEIR BOD BOTS and race out of the hanger, Joseph establishes a telepathic link with Max and Des. He says, "Max, when we surround this warrior of Brykar's, I want you to hang back, just in case my plan fails."

Max replies, "Seriously? So after all that talk earlier, now you're benching me?"

Des chimes in, "Max, he's right. We have no idea what this guy can do, and it would be reckless for all of us to go at him."

Joseph then says, "Max, I meant what I said earlier. You're not off the team or being benched. However, I'm not a hundred percent sure that my plan will work, and so I refuse to put all of us at risk. With exception of you, Janet and myself, the others have their secondary armor, which should help even things out."

Reluctantly, Max responds, "Fine! I'll hang back, but you better not let anything happen to ..."

Before anything else can be said, Des picks up Sir Pentous on his scanners and says over their BOD Bot comm system, "Look alive, everyone! We're nearly on top of this new warrior of Brykar's.

ONCE THE KNIGHTS REACH SIR PENTOUS, they circle around him with their BOD Bots ... with the exception of Max. As they get out, Sir Pentous stops his serpentcycle and says, "Well, if it isssn't the knightsss! It'sss a pleasssure to finally meet you." He gets off his serpentcycle, takes his rattlesnake staff in hand, points it toward the Cross Knight and says, "My name is Sssir Pentousss, and today I will end all of you."

The Cross Knight steps forward and responds, "In your dreams, Sir Pentous."

Sir Pentous chuckles and says, "No not in my dreamsss, in yoursss actually."

Suddenly Sir Pentous charges at the Cross Knight, and as he does, the Cross Knight tells everyone telepathically, "Hang back! Let's see what he can do."

As Sir Pentous strikes, the Cross Knight draws his swords, blocking the attack. Sir Pentous uses his tail to knock the Cross Knight off his feet. When he leaps backward to avoid it, Sir Pentous fires a pellet at the Cross Knight, causing him to be frozen in place.

When the other knights see this, the Fire Knight shouts, "What did you do to him, you sickening snake?"

Turning to the Fire Knight, Sir Pentous replies, "You will sssoon find out, Fire Knight. That isss ... if you have the courage to ssstrike me."

The Fire Knight materializes his flame blades and charges at Sir Pentous before anyone can stop him.

As the Fire Knight charges toward Sir Pentous, the Earth Knight notices that the creature isn't even attempting to dodge the attack. So, as the Fire Knight is about to strike, the Earth Knight shouts, "Fire Knight, disengage! Now!" But the Fire Knight doesn't listen. He cuts Sir Pentous in half. His body lies there split in two. Then all the knights watch as Sir Pentous's body begins to move and regenerate so that instead of only facing one enemy, they now have to face two.

The Shadow Knight shakes his head and says, "This is just great! Now we've got two snakes to deal with. Any ideas about how to deal with this, guys?"

Looking at the Shadow Knight, the Bolt Knight says, "Not a clue! But we need to figure something out fast!"

Before the knights can come up with a plan, Sir Pentous and his double charge the Shadow and Bolt Knights. As the two knights block the attacks with their sword, Sir Pentous and his double grab their blades, cuting off four fingers of each of their hands. The fingers regenerate, and each severed finger becomes another copy of Sir Pentous. The new doubles of Sir Pentous begin to attack the knights, while the original Sir Pentous slips away, so that while the knights are distracted, he can use his new venom on them.

He next targets both the Bolt and Shadow Knights, while their backs are turned, hitting them each with a pellet and causing them to be frozen in place, just like the Cross Knight. While the remaining knights face Sir Pentous' doubles, the Faith Knight establishes a telepathic connection with the other knights. He says, "We've got to get out of here. Whatever he used on the Cross Knight he used on the Shadow and Bolt Knights, and he's going to do the same to the rest of us." Before the other knights can respond or even disengage, Sir Pentous targets the Fire, Wind, Aqua and Earth Knights, freezing them in place like the others.

Struggling to fight off Sir Pentous's doubles, the Light Knight uses the telepathic connection he has with the remaining knights to say, "Cover your eyes and grab the others!" With that. he fires a blinding flash of light that temporarily blinds Sir Pentous and his doubles, allowing the knights the time they need to escape with their frozen teammates.

AFTER ESCAPING, THE REMAINING KNIGHTS ARE ON THEIR WAY back to their base in their BOD Bots. Light Knight, with concern in his voice, asks Max, "Hey, Bro, why weren't you with us when we circled Sir Pentous as we planned?"

Sighing before responding, Max says, "It wasn't my idea. Joseph told me to hang back in case his plan went south quickly, and reluctantly I did. Right now, we've got even bigger problems to deal with."

"He's right," the Beast Knight chimes in, "we can deal with who did or didn't do what later. Right now we have to figure out what exactly he did to the others and how we can undo it."

Using the communicator in his BOD Bot, the Faith Knight contacts Manuel. "Prepare the lab," he says, "we've got a situation we need to deal with right away." Cutting the communication without waiting for a response, the Faith Knight, with the other remaining knights, speed toward their base.

JUSTICE MEETS THEM IN THE HANGER and asks, "What's wrong?" Then, as she sees them exiting their BOD Bots with the frozen knights, she asks, "What's happened to them?"

Looking at her, the Faith Knight replies, "We're not sure, but we need to find out quick." They all make their way to the lab with the frozen knights.

MANUEL WATCHES AS THEY ENTER THE LAB. Then he asks, "I take it this is the situation you were referring to?"

Turning to Manuel, the Faith Knight responds, "Yes, could you use the computer to figure out what's wrong with them?"

Moving quickly to the computer, Manuel says, "I believe I can. Justice, could you examine the knights and see if we can get a sample of what was used on them?"

As Justice walks toward the knights, she uses what's called an egnop to collect drops of the venom that still remain on each of them. As she brings it to Manuel, he has her place one of these samples in the computer's chemical analyzer. Once it is inside, Manuel begins to runs a scan to see exactly what they're dealing with.

While the computer works to analyze the chemical, Manuel turns to the knights and asks, "What exactly happened out there?"

All of the knights are silent for a moment. Then Faith Knight sighs and says, "We all went out as planned. Before we got there, Des and Joseph told, me to hang back in case this plan went south. As Joseph faced Brykar's newest warrior, whose name is Sir Pentous, he was hit with a pellet, which left him frozen. Then, each time a part of Sir Pentous was cut off, a copy of him formed. He and his doubles then went after the Shadow and Bolt knights, and using the same pellets, he froze them. He then used their weapon to create even more doubles and continued to pick us off ... until John finally fired a blinding flash. That was what allowed us to escape."

After pausing for a moment to think, Manuel is about to speak when the computer alerts them that the analysis is done. Manuel looks at the computer and says, "According to this, whatever hit them isn't natural."

The Light Knight asks, "What do you mean by not natural?"

Turning to face the knights, Manuel replies, "Meaning that whatever Sir Pentous used on them was created in a lab."

John says, "So that means that only Sir Pentous knows how to save them."

Now Sally asks, "Hey, Tasha, do you think your powers could save them, the way you saved John?"

Transforming into her secondary armor, Tasha gets ready to use her healing powers on them. Manuel says, "Hold on! Before you try that, my young friends ... ." He is now scanning the afflicted knights' vitals. He finds that they are normal ... with the exception of a large amount of endorphins are being released throughout their nervous system. "They may not be in any current danger," he says, "but if we don't find a way to reverse this, the release of these endorphins will have a similar effect to what is commonly called 'a drug overdose.'"

"What does that mean?" John asks.

"It means," Tasha offers, "that because they're not really injured, my powers might not work on them."

Frustrated with this situation, Max shouts and storms off before anyone can stop him. Seeing him go, Manuel says, "Let him go for now! Right now we need to focus on saving the others before it's too late."

WITHOUT THE KNOWLEDGE OF THE OTHERS, Sally follows Max. When she catches up to him, she sees that he's on his knees, pounding the ground in frustration. She rushes to him and asks, "Are you okay, Max?"

Without looking up, he replies, "No! I'm *not* okay! Joseph trusted me to be the backup in case his plan failed. And not only did it fail, but I failed to be the proper backup."

Remaining where she is, Sally says "Max, you can't blame yourself. We were all there."

Sighing, Max replies, "That's just it! I wasn't there with you guys! I did what Joseph asked, and I still wasn't able to be the hero that you guys needed me to be."

With her hands behind her back, Sally says, "Believe it or not, I get how you feel. I didn't think I could beat Dispotier. But I knew everyone was counting on me and that as long as I had breathe I couldn't give up. Now is not the time to doubt yourself or your value to this team."

"That's just it," Max replies. "I'm supposed to be the Faith Knight, and that feels like the one thing I don't have."

Realizing that Max needs some time to think things over, Sally concludes, "Max, I'm not going to argue with you, but I want you to know you are not only important to this team. You are important to me."

Before he can respond, she's gone, and he is left alone to wonder what he can do. He is reminded of a time when he felt like this before and thinks of something his aunt said. It was just after his parents had died and his aunt and uncle had taken him in. He doubted that things would ever be normal again. He remembers sitting on their porch with his aunt sitting next to him. She had tried to comfort him by saying, "I know it may not seem like it now, but every-thing will be okay."

Not sure of exactly what she was getting at, he just sat there. She added, "It's at times like this that you need to have faith. Do you know what faith is?" Still clueless as to what she was talking about, he remained silent. She continued, "Well, I'll tell you. 'Now faith is the assurance of things hoped for, the conviction of things not seen.'[12] What this means is: even when you can't see the light at the end of the tunnel, faith helps you to remember that there is light even when it is the darkest. Faith helps us to carry on during the toughest of times. No matter what happens, 'we walk by faith, not by sight.'"[13]

At that moment, Max realizes that despite how things look, he can no lon-ger go on doubting himself. Just as his aunt told him years before, "We walk by faith, not by sight." As he stands to his feet, a sudden surge of power infuses him, and he hears himself shout, "Faith Fighter armor, engage." With that, his armor begins to transform into what looks like a sleeveless kung fu uniform. It has interwoven buttons on the front. On his hands are gloves that cover the tops, leaving the fingers exposed. And finally, in his hands appear his Battle Batons. Once the transformation is complete, Max make his way back to the lab.

AS HE APPROACHES THE LAB, MAX HEARS MANUEL and the others talk-ing. John is saying, "All right, so since we know Sir Pentous had to make this stuff, it makes sense that he would know how to reverse it. The trick is to figure out how to do it without getting caught ourselves."

Max walks in and says, "Leave that to me! I have an idea for how to get what we need to free the others."

Chapter 21

Walk of Faith
The Fight of Faith

MANUEL AND THE OTHER KNIGHTS TURN to see Max in his new armor. John chuckles and says, "Whoa! Looks like somebody got an upgrade."

Sally giggles and says, "Hey there, hot stuff."

As the rest of the knights chuckle for a moment, Tasha asks, "So what's your plan, Max?"

Looking at all of them, he says, "First, I'm going to have a chat with Sir Pentous and get him to tell me exactly what he's done to the others. Then, we need to get one of those pellets so we can use it to make an antidote."

Janet then asks, "Well, what are we supposed to do in the meantime?"

Looking at each of the knights in turn, he replies, "That's just it. Sir Pentous used his doubles to distract you before, while the original used the pellets to freeze the others. So, this time, I'm taking on the original, while you guys keep the others busy, so I can snag a pellet to save our friends."

"Good plan!" Tasha says. "But how do we beat something that can regenerate anytime we cut it?"

Turning to her, Max responds, "There's an old saying: 'If you want to kill a snake, cut off its head.' In this case, if we want to stop him or his doubles, what we need to do is crush his skull."

Listening to this plan, Manuel he says, "That actually might work. I was reviewing the battle. I did a scan of Sir Pentous' skeletal system, which is quite interesting, considering the fact that this bones are small ... except for the skull.

The rest of his body is made up of cartilage and muscle, which is why he's able to regenerate so quickly."

Max then asks, "Before we head out, what special abilities do each of your secondary armors have?"

Janet shakes her head and says, "I don't have a secondary armor yet."

Sally replies, "I'm still learning about my armor, but so far, I know it restores my resolve."

Max nods and asks, "Who else?"

Tasha then replies, "My armor can heal, along with allowing me to communicate with animals."

Thinking for a moment, Max asks, "Could you use your armor to communicate with an animal nearby, so that we can keep an eye on Sir Pentous?"

"I believe so," she answers, looking at Max.

Max looks at John, and John begins to chuckle. "My armor's secondary power," he says, "allows me to move at blinding speed."

"Perfect," Max says. "While I distract Sir Pentous, do you think you would be able to grab the pellets from him, so we could make an antidote?"

"That shouldn't be too hard," John replies, "but how do we know he won't use a fake to fool us?"

"Not sure," Max answers, "but either way, we have to try. And once you get the pellets, I need you to bring them back here, so we can save the others."

"I'm on it!" John replies, and the other knights nod their agreement to Max's plan.

Then Janet asks, "Not that we don't like the change, Max, but do you mind telling us what happened to you?"

Pausing for a moment, Max replies, "I'll explain that to all of you later. Right now, we have to work on saving the others and stopping Sir Pentous."

A bit puzzled, Tasha chimes in, "May I ask why you have to tell us later?"

Turning to her, Max replies, "Because it's something you all need to hear, and I only want to have to say it once."

BRYKAR CONTACTS SIR PENTOUS AND ASKS, "Sir Pentous, what is your status?"

Opening the communication channel, Sir Pentous answers, "Greetingsss, Commander Brykar. Usssing my new venom, ssseven of the twelve knightsss have been paralyzed."

"What happened to the others?" Brykar asks.

"I'm not sssure, Commander Brykar," Pentous offers. "One of the knightsss used a flasssh of light to blind usss and essscape. I have my doublesss, ss-searching for them now."

As Brykar listens to Sir Pentous, he notices that the creature mentioned a new venom. Interested, he asks, "What did you mean by a 'new venom'?" Realizing that he hadn't told Brykar about the new venom, Sir Pentous explains, "Before I engaged the knightsss, I created a new venom that would paralyze them in a dreamlike ssstate of whatever pleasssurable fantasiesss their heartsss desssire. Alssso, the beauty of it isss that there isss no cure, and sssoon the venom ssshall claim their livesss."

Pleased with this, Brykar responds, "Well done, Sir Pentous! Keep me posted on your progress."

But even as he cuts the communication link, Brykar knows that this creature is up to something. As he goes to the hanger's security cameras, he is saying to himself, "All right, you snake, what are you up to?"

Reviewing the security footage, he has it zoom in on the pellets that Sir Pentous has made and notices that there are thirteen pellets, and there are only twelve knights. He then begins searching the security footage to see what exactly was used in creating this new venom Sir Pentous spoke of. When he sees what was done, he chuckles to himself and says to no one in particular, "You think you are clever, don't you, Sir Pentous? Well, let's see how clever you are and if you survive the next encounter with the knights."

BRYKAR WALKS FROM HIS COMMAND CHAMBER to where his fallen warriors are being held to check on their status. He notices that they are all revived and enhanced except for Despotier, who was only recently placed in one of the revival chambers. Although he knows they cannot hear him, he says, "Soon, my warriors ... Soon you will have another shot at the knights ... And this time, when you face them, no matter what happens, the knights will meet their end."

BRYKAR NOW MAKES HIS WAY toward his own personal lab. As he goes in, he grabs a vial and begins to work on it. He is thinking to himself, "Sir Pentous is not the only one who has a way with chemicals."

BACK IN THE KNIGHTS' BASE, John and Tasha activate their secondary forms, while Max and Sally are in the bay where their BOD Bots are stored. Max and Sally are talking. He says to her, "I know we have a lot to talk about, and I want you to know that what you said meant a lot to me." He then takes her by the hand and gives her a gentle kiss on the cheek. Then he adds, "That's just so you are clear on how I feel."

Janet walks in and says, "That makes it clear for everyone how you feel about her, Max."

A little embarrassed, Max says, "Thanks, Janet. So what brings you down here?"

Chuckling to herself, Janet replies, "Well, I think I have an idea that may give us a bit of an advantage over Sir Pentous, and I figured we could use every advantage we can get."

Max responds, "What's your idea?"

"If memory serves me correctly," she explains, "Des equipped each BOD Bot with something I believe is called a 'sentient mode' that would allow them to work without one of us being there. My idea is this: if we activate that sentient mode on the BOD Bot of the other knights, it'll give us more of a fighting chance against Sir Pentous."

Max thinks to himself for a moment, then says, "Good idea! Let's see if that's possible." He then goes to Faithlane Fighter and, as he gets inside, he says, "Faithlane, I have a question for you. Are we able to activate the BOD sentient mode on the BOD Bots that belong to the other knights?"

Faithlane Fighter responds, "Let me scan the program and find out?"

Scanning through the sentient mode program, Faithlane Fighter then says, "According to this, the only ones who can activate sentient mode on BOD Bots that aren't their own is Des and Joseph."

Max grunts in disappointment. As he gets out, he says, "This is just great!"

Janet asks, "What's the problem?"

Max says, "The only one who can activate the sentient mode in someone else's BOD Bot is Des. Still, you had a good idea about using the BOD Bots. We may not be able to use Joseph's or the others' BOD Bots, but we can use our own, and that might give us an edge."

Sally asks, "What do you mean, Max?"

Turning to her, Max says, "If I have John come back here after we get those pellets Sir Pentous is using, we'll be down one knight. So, if we activate our BOD Bots sentient mode, they'll be able to function regardless of what's going on."

Janet chuckles and says, "Wow! That *is* a good idea."

Before anything else can be said, both Tasha and John arrive. Tasha says, "I've found Sir Pentous. Are we ready?"

Max then replies, "We're ready. Let's move!"

With that, the knights get in their BOD Bots and race off to deal with Sir Pentous.

AS THE KNIGHTS RACE TO DEAL WITH SIR PENTOUS, Faithlane notices that there's something bothering Max. He asks, "What's on your mind, my friend?"

Shaking his head, Max says, "I'm just nervous. Usually I let Joseph and the others handle the plans, and I'm starting to understand how Joseph feels."

Faithlane replies, "That may be true, my friend, but as you can see from your friends, the change is a welcome one."

Max says, "Thanks, Faithlane." He then opens up the communication channel between the BOD Bots and says, "Okay, is everyone clear on the plan?"

Janet responds first, "While you face Sir Pentous, Sally, Tasha, myself and the BOD Bots will face Sir Pentous' doubles."

John then chimes in, "And when Sir Pentous gets ready to fire his pellets, I'll speed in and grab them and head back to the base."

Noticing that they're coming up on Sir Pentous' location, Max says, "All right, everyone. We're nearing Sir Pentous' location. Everyone take your positions."

Tasha, Sally, and Janet go in one direction, while John and Max go in another, as they all prepare to face Sir Pentous and his doubles.

BEFORE MAX AND JOHN EXIT THEIR BOD BOTS, John says, "BOD Bot sentient mode, activate."

Following the plan, Max does the same. As the two knights now exit their BOD Bots, Max says, "Faithlane, I'm counting on you to keep her … I mean, keep the girls safe while I deal with this snake."

The BOD Bots and John have a chuckle. Faithlane says, "I understand. I will keep them safe."

Both BOD Bots speed off to join the remaining female knights, and John looks at his friend and says, "It's okay, buddy, we get it. And you're right. We have a job to do, so let's focus on that. Still, it's hard when you're in a new relationship."

Turning to his friend, Max replies, "Thanks for that, bro. Now we need to take our position so that we can free the others."

AS MAX HEADS OFF to face the original Sir Pentous, Manuel contacts him telepathically and says, "Forgive the intrusion, my young friend, but I wanted to let you know that we've been analyzing the sample of the venom we took from the knights and are beginning work on the antidote. I will keep in touch and let you know our progress."

Max replies, "All right, thanks for the heads up, Manuel."

A few moments later, Max reaches a ledge that allows him to see Sir Prentous and his doubles, as well as the other knights who are hidden from Sir Pentous' view. He leaps from the ledge, landing before Sir Pentous, and as he does, he shouts, "It's over, Sir Pentous! Now you're going to tell me what you did to my friends and how to reverse it."

Sir Pentous replies, "Ohhhh, really? And why ssshould I do that?"

Max replies, "Simple, because if you don't, I'm turning you into a snake-skin belt."

While the Faith Knight stands before him, Sir Pentous says, "If you think you can defeat me, young knight, then go ahead and try. However, I want you to know that there isss no antidote."

Watching the Faith Knight closely, Sir Pentous realizes he's up to something. He asks, "Where are your friendsss?"

Moving closer to Sir Pentous, the Faith Knight replies, "That's for me to know and you to find out."

Sir Pentous has his doubles circle the Faith Knight, and as they do this, the Faith Knight chuckles, for he knows what Sir Pentous is up to. He says, "Are you seriously using the same move we used against you? If so, you're in for a surprise."

Taken aback for a moment, Sir Pentous replies, "Why isss that, Faith Knight?"

Faith Knight again chuckles and says, "Simple, if I can already tell what you're planning and have barely moved, don't you think we have a plan to counter this?"

Not wanting to waste more time with idle chatter, Sir Pentous has his doubles move closer to the Faith Knight. Then, to his surprise, the remaining knights and their BOD Bots charge in, forcing Sir Pentous' doubles to face them rather than the Faith Knight.

As Sir Pentous' doubles engage the knights, Sir Pentous says, "Clever move, Faith Knight! However, even with thisss, it will not be enough to ssstop me."

Looking directly at Sir Pentous, Max says, "Maybe so, but mark my words. I will save my friends and take you down with me, you sickening snake."

Chuckling at this threat, Sir Pentous replies, "Go ahead and try, but I assss-sure you that no matter what you do, you won't find a cure. It isss foolisssh to think you can sssave your friendsss."

Just waiting for the Faith Knight to make a move, Sir Pentous is ready to hit him with his pellets. Then the Faith Knight asks, "Tell me, how are you so sure we won't find an antidote?"

Thinking to himself for a moment, Sir Pentous decides to respond to the Faith Knight. He says, "Ssssimple, I usssed my venom when making thisss new batch. Becaussse it came from my venom, I am immune to itsss propertiesss and therefore do not require an antidote. Sssstill, this will be a sssecret you take with you to your grave."

Suddenly, Sir Pentous raises his arm to fire a pellet at the Faith Knight. The Faith Knight just stands there, and Sir Pentous notices that he's not moving. So he fires a pellet at him. As the pellet speeds toward the Faith Knight, it sud-denly disappears, never hitting him. Shocked, Sir Pentous shouts, "What'sss going on here?"

Holding his position, the Faith Knight asks, "What's the matter? You can't hit a stationary target?"

With that, Sir Pentous is more than annoyed and decides to fire all his remaining pellets at the Faith Knight. They all speed toward him, but just as before, none of them hit the knight they were targeting. Now, furious that he has no more pellets to shoot, Sir Pentous shouts, "How isss thisss posssible? You ssshould not be able to move."

Chuckling to himself, the Faith Knight replies, "If you must know, the reason I'm not frozen and why your pellets never hit me is that I had the Light Knight use his speed to intercept the pellets. Each time you fired a pellet, he intercepted it, and now he's already back at our base where an antidote is being created. The funny thing is we couldn't have done it without you, Sir Pentous. Thank you!"

Angered by this, Sir Pentous charges at the Faith Knight with his rattle-snake staff in hand. As he reaches the Faith Knight, he strikes, only to have the Faith Knight dodge. But as the Faith Knight dodges, Sir Pentous uses his tail to grab the knight by the leg and slam him to the ground. Before the knight can get up, Sir Pentous then begins to wrap his tail around the knight's hand. He swings him in the air several times, and then, when he lets go, the Faith Knight hits the ground hard and doesn't move.

AS THE LIGHT KNIGHT ENTERS THE BASE and heads to the lab, Manuel hands him a container, saying, "Put the pellets in here."

The Light Knight does this, and Manuel begins to use the computer to create an antidote.

The Light Knight says, "I know the plan was for me to wait for the antidote to be made, but I have a bad feeling that the others need my help. How much time do they have?"

Manuel replies, "I'm not sure. This is why I decided to work on the antidote when I did, so that we can save them in time." Manuel then uses the computer to allow the Light Knight to see the battle.

While the others are holding their own, the Light Knight sees that the Faith Knight is down. He says, "Looks like I was right. I've got to get out there."

Before the Light Knight can speed off to help the others, telepathically the Faith Knight says, "Don't worry about me. I'm fine. I need you to stay there until the antidote is ready."

Shaking his head, the Light Knight replies, "Are you crazy? I'm not going to stand by and let him kill you!"

Knowing that his friend is right, the Faith Knight says, "Have Manuel look at my vitals?"

Turning to Manuel, the Light Knight asks, "Could you pull up the Faith Knights' vitals?"

When the vitals are pulled up, Manuel and the Light Knight both notice that they are normal. The Light Knight telepathically asks the Faith Knight, "If your vitals are normal, why are you on the ground?"

The Faith Knight says, "If I'm going to stop Sir Pentous, I need to know how he fights. So, for the time being, I'm letting him think he has the upper hand."

Shaking his head in disagreement, the Light Knight replies, "Still, it's too risky."

Manuel then turns to the Light Knight and says, "According to the computer, it will take an hour to synthesize the antidote. And ... there's still no way to know if it will even work once completed."

Frustrated at this news, the Light Knight replies, "That's just great! So while I'm stuck here, the others are fighting for their lives."

Justice then walks into the lab. After Manuel explains the situation, she looks at the Light Knight and says, "I know how you feel, but as frustrating as it is, you must remain calm."

She then turns to the computer monitor and says, "As you can see, the others are holding their own. Despite the appearance of it, the Faith Knight is not currently in any danger."

Tightening his fists, the Light Knight replies, "Fine! I'll stay here. But that doesn't mean I have to like the idea of not being able to join them."

Manuel then looks at the Light Knight and says, "We're going to do everything we can. For the time being, we have to wait and be patient."

AT THAT VERY MOMENT, SIR PENTOUS IS WALKING toward the Faith Knight. When he reaches him, he uses his rattlesnake staff to turn the knight on his back. As he does this, the Faith Knight turns the movement into a roll, and this allows him to stand. Then he says to Sir Pentous, "Please tell me that isn't all you've got. I've been hit harder by pillows."

Again, Sir Pentous charges at the knight with his staff in hand. The knight grabs his Battle Batons so that as Sir Pentous strikes with his staff in hand, the Faith Knight blocks the attack. Now Sir Pentous again uses his tail to grab the Faith Knight. But this time the Faith Knight dodges the tail, causing Sir Pentous to stumble. In that moment, the Faith Knight begins to hit Sir Pentous with a barrage of strikes to the body, using his Battle Batons. He is able to knock Sir Pentous back a bit, and then the remaining knights and BOD Bots join the battle. Seeing this, Sir Pentous says, "What'sss happened to my doublesss?"

The Faith Knight replies, "We've beaten them, and you're next."

Sir Pentous then spins so that his tail can extend, knocking the Faith Knight to the ground. Suddenly the bodies of his doubles are all pulled to him. As they reach him, he begins to swallow them one by one. After the last one is swallowed, Sir Pentous grows to be fifteen feet tall. Now he says to the knights, "Let'sss sssee how well you ssstand againssst me now knightsss."

As the knights look in wonder at Sir Pentous, the Beast Knight says, "This is just great! Now what do we do?"

The Faith Knight replies telepathically to all the other knights, "I have a plan. Do you think you guys can keep him in one place for a minute and a half?"

Janet replies, "Sure! But what are you planning?"

He responds, "I'm going to fly into the sky and drop so that the speed and force should be enough to crush his skull and end this fight."

The Hope Knight says, "Go! We'll keep him busy."

With that, the Faith Knight activates his wings and flies into the sky. As he does, Sir Pentous says, "Looksss like the Faith Knight isss ssscared after all. Sssstill, I have the rest of you to play with."

While the Faith Knight soars high into the sky, the other knights begin to surround Sir Pentous. He begins to swipe at them, as if they were mere mice. While they dodge his attacks, he says, "What'ssss wrong? Are you afraid I'm going to ssscratch you?"

The Beast Knight replies, "Does it look like we're scared of you, you overgrown snake."

The Love Knight adds, "Seriously, I've dealt with bigger snakes in the woods."

Even the Hope Knight chimes in, "The only thing scary about you is your breath."

Sir Pentous continues to swipe at the remaining female knights, and they continue to taunt him relentlessly. Unknown to Sir Pentous, the Faith Knight is already at five thousand feet and climbing. As Sir Pentous continues to attack the female knights, he grows angrier with each strike that misses. He then begins to use his tail and catches the Hope Knight, causing her to stumble. As he goes to strike her, her BOD Bot, Hope Hunter, switches into battle mode and blocks the attack. When he turns to make sure she's okay, Sir Pentous uses his tail to strike Hope Hunter. As the tail is about to connect with Hope Hunter,

Faithlane switches into his battle mode and grabs Sir Pentous' tail before he can strike the Hope Knight's BOD Bot.

The Love Knight uses their telepathic link to contact to Faith Knight and asks, "How much more time do you need? I'm not sure how long we can keep him in one spot"

Having reached the altitude he needs, the Faith Knight replies, "Keep him busy for another minute and a half. I'm dropping now."

"Shaking her head, she responds, "I don't even think we have that."

With that, the Faith Knight disengages his wings and free falls with both hands forward, like an arrow. As he does, he begins to speak the oath, "*As days of darkness near, and people run in fear, from they who prey on the weak, and silence those who speak ...*"

The other knights continue to keep Sir Pentous occupied so that he doesn't suspect their plan. However, he starts to hear something and suddenly realizes what they have been doing. He starts to move from that spot, but as he does, Hope Hunter blocks his way. Sir Pentous tries to push past him, but Hope Hunter moves and successfully pushes Sir Pentous back where he was.

Before Sir Pentous can try another escape route, Faithlane and Hope Hunter hold him down, causing him to struggle under their combined grip. As they hold him there, the Faith Knight flips his body so that now his heel will strike Sir Pentous. As he does this, he continues to speak their oath: "*We will take to the sky with courage and battle cry. To protect the world from loss, I am a Knight of the Cross!*"

The two BOD Bots are starting to lose their hold on Sir Pentous, but the Faith Knight informs them that he's almost there. Sir Pentous breaks free of their grip, but Faithlane lands a punch to Sir Pentous' body, forcing him back in position just in time for the Faith Knight to strike him in the head with his heel. The impact crushes Sir Pentous' skull, causing the snake-like warrior to fall to the ground lifeless. Unfazed, the Faith Knight leaps to the ground to join his friends.

ONCE THE KNIGHTS ARE SURE SIR PENTOUS IS DEAD, they head back to their base in their BOD Bots. Over their comm system Janet says, "I still can't believe that worked, but could you do us a favor and the next time you want to play hero, don't cut it so close?"

As each of them chuckles at this statement, Max replies, "All right. Next time I'll let you play the hero. How about that?"

Now it's Janet's turn to chuckle, and she responds, "That's fine with me, and when I do it, it won't be one of these last-ditch efforts."

SOON THE KNIGHTS ENTER THEIR BASE. They all immediately head to the lab, where Manuel, Justice and John greet them.

As they enter, Max notices that their faces are saddened and asks, "What's wrong?"

Manuel replies, "We were able to synthesize an antidote, but we only have enough for six of the knights, and there are seven of them frozen."

Janet replies, "So, we won't be able to save them all?"

John looks at them and says, "That's the gist of it. So we thought it best to let Max make the decision."

The knights look to Max, who asks, "How are we giving them the antidote?"

Manuel says, "Through the same means, a pellet."

Turning to Manuel, he says, "Let me see one of those pellets." Taking one of the pellets in his hand, he closes his fist on it and then says, "Now we have seven." When he opens his hand, there are now two pellets where there had been only one before. The other knights see this and are amazed,

Max says, "Let's free the others because there's still a lot to discuss."

Manuel and Justice use the antidote on the knights. As they start to awaken, Joseph asks, "What happened to us?"

Des chimes in, "Yeah, why do I feel like I haven't moved for hours?"

Max chuckles and says, "Well, that's because you haven't moved for hours. Give yourselves a few minutes to recover. There's something I have to say to all of you."

A few moments later, as all the knight are gathered in the lab, Max begins. "First," he says, "I want to say I'm sorry about my attitude as of late, and I know there are a lot of questions, especially about how I unlocked my secondary armor. The answer to how I unlocked my armor came from me having to deal with questions Joseph and Des had asked me before they got caught by Sir Pentous' venom, along with the fact that I felt responsible for you being caught by Sir Pentous' venom.

"You see, since we became knights, I have struggled with doubt about my place on the team and about myself. It was only when I faced it and realized why I had been chosen as the Faith Knight that I was able to overcome the doubt in my heart. This experience unlocked new power that allowed us to defeat Sir Pentous, but it also gave me the confidence and clarity to lead and plan when it was needed."

Joseph grabs Max's shoulder and says, "It's okay, but I knew having you stay back was the right choice." Des and the other knights nod in agreement.

Max turns to Joseph, asking, "So what do we do now?"

Joseph replies, "I think we all need to go rest for a while and meet in the Training Room first thing in the morning." The other knights agree.

AS THE KNIGHTS GO THEIR SEPARATE WAYS, Max walks toward the hanger bay. Sensing that someone is following him, he says, "Are you ready to finish that conversation we started, Sally?"

Stepping out as he says her name, she asks, "How did you know it was me?"

Chuckling, Max says, "I walked this way because I was hoping you would come looking for me."

She smiles at him and asks, "So I was always your first choice?"

Taking her in his arms, he says, "You were always my first and *only* choice."

With that, the two knight hold each other in a warm embrace.

BRYKAR IS IN HIS COMMAND CHAMBER, watching as his Psydrones bring the lifeless body of Sir Pentous back into the base. He has them take it to the room where his other fallen warriors are recovering. Noticing that the body will no longer fit, he inputs a command code that causes the chamber to enlarge, and the body is placed inside. Once Sir Pentous's body is inside, the chamber immediately begins to work at reviving him. As it does, Brykar thinks to himself, "I can't say I'm surprised at this outcome. Still, each of them will have a use for me, one the knights will not see coming. Either way, this works out for me, because if they hadn't defeated him, I would have crushed that snake myself ... should he have tried to challenge me."

Just then Brykar is contacted by General Sadoom. As Brykar opens the holographic communication channel, he kneels. General Sadoom says, "Brykar, what is your status?"

Looking up at him, Brykar replies, "Everything is going according to plan. My latest warrior, Sir Pentous, has been defeated by the knights, but not before he paralyzed seven of them, which puts them at a disadvantage for our next strike. Had he defeated the knights, I would have been forced to destroy him myself."

General Sadoom asks, "Are you sure there's no way for them to be freed of the paralysis? Also, why would you have had to destroy your own warrior?"

Again Brykar looks at General Sadoom, then replies, "Sir Pentous informed me that there was no cure for this particular venom, as it was something he had just developed. And, because of his immunity to it, there was no need to create an antidote. Still, even if they are able to free the paralyzed knights, it doesn't change what I have in store for them. Also, the reason I would have had to destroy Pentous if he had defeated the knights is because I believe he planned to use that same venom on me."

General Sadoom turns his back to Brykar and then says, "That makes sense, but as you know, there are only so many times we will tolerate failure. Still, since your overall plan is going as expected, I will allow you to continue. However, if you fail, what you already know will happen to you will be increased by tenfold. Are we clear?"

Brykar bows his head and replies, "I understand, General Sadoom. I will not fail you."

With that, the communication ends. Standing there, Brykar begins to chuckle to himself. "Enjoy your victory, knights, for soon I will destroy you ... and this world."

WHILE BRYKAR CONTINUES TO PLOT against the knights, Agents Wallace and Saunders arrive at the restaurant where they plan to meet Agent Marks. As they enter, Agent Saunders puts her tablet away and says, "I received a message from Agent Marks. He's agreed to meet with us and should be here in fifteen minutes."

Agent Wallace replies, "Good! Shall we sit down and eat?"

She nods in agreement, and as they are seated, Agent Wallace looks over the menu. The waiter comes and asks, "Could I start you both off with something to drink?"

Agent Wallace replies, "I'll take a water."

Agent Saunders says, "I'll take a water as well."

The waiter nods and heads off to get the drinks. When he returns with the two waters, he asks, "Could I start you off with an appetizer or do you need a few more minutes?"

Putting his menu down, Agent Wallace responds, "I'll take two orders of chicken strips to start with."

Turning to Agent Saunders, the waiter asks, "Is there anything you would like, miss?"

She puts her menu down and replies, "I'll have mozzarella sticks to start with."

The waiter heads off to the kitchen. A few minutes later, Agent Marks comes in wearing a black muscle shirt with a basic pair of blue jeans. Walking toward them, it's clear that he's muscular without being ripped. As he moves toward them, Agent Saunders stands to greet him. When she reaches out her hand, he looks at her and says, "Forgive me for not shaking your hand, but I'd like to know what this is about."

Agent Saunders replies, "Have a seat. We'll explain everything."

Pulling out a chair to sit in front of them, Agent Marks looks at them and says, "Okay, I'm listening. Why am I here?"

Before she can begin, the waiter comes to the table and places their appetizers down. He turns to Agent Marks and asks, "May I get you something to drink, sir?"

Looking at the waiter, Agent Marks replies, "Get me a lemonade mixed with sweet tea, and I'll take some chicken strips and mozzarella sticks to go."

After the waiter leaves, Agent Saunders asks, "I thought you weren't staying?"

He looks at her and says, "I'm not, but I'm hungry, which is why I'm taking the meal to go. Now, make this quick, cause once he comes back with my food, I'm gone."

Agent Saunders says, "My name is Agent Saunders, and this is Agent Wallace, and we've got an interesting opportunity for you. We already know that all of the missions you've been on are classified, along with being what are considered 'suicide missions,' and currently your success rate is at one hundred percent."

Raising his eyebrows, Agent Marks replies, "I don't know how you've gotten that information …"

Before he can say anything else, Agent Saunders says, "First, calm down. We're here to recruit you, and we were given this information from Agent Martin, who recommended you."

Hearing Agent Martin's name, Agent Marks responds, "All right, I'm in. So what am I being recruited for?"

Chuckling, Agent Saunders says, "First, let's eat, and we'll explain everything."

SINCE MELANIE, DEBORAH AND GRAHAM LEFT their home, Phillip and Linda have tried to act as if everything is normal. Phillip now sits in his chair and picks up a book to read, to calm his nerves. His wife comes in and asks, "Do you think Max and the other's are okay?"

He chuckles for a moment before answering, "I don't know, but this is one of those times when, like you always say, 'We have to have faith.'"

As he says this, she laughs to herself at the irony of it, then asks, "Of all the times to listen to me, why do you listen to me now?"

He puts the book down and says, "First, despite how it looks, I've always listened to you. So has Max. And because we're doing everything we can to find out what is going on, we already know that the people who are after them are very dangerous. Which means that as much as I hate it, we have to act as if things are normal so we can stay safe. Besides, between you and me, we've done everything we can to prepare Max for his life as an adult. So we have to have faith that he and his classmates are fine."

Standing there, she realizes that her husband is right. As frightened as they are, they know they have to trust that Max and the others are okay. With that, she smiles at him.

He asks, "What's that for?"

Walking toward him, she asks, "Can I get a hug?"

Standing up, Phillip embraces her. As he hugs his wife, she looks at him and says, "Thank you for being strong … even when I'm not." And suddenly she begins to sob in his arms. He holds her tight, knowing this whole affair has been just as hard for her as it has for him. The only thing that helps him through it is the fact that he's able to contribute something to the effort of finding out what is going on and why.

He lifts her head up, wipes her tears and says, "I can't imagine how hard this is for you, but I do have an idea."

Looking at him, she asks, "What's your idea?"

Pausing for a moment, he replies, "Well, I think what will help you is to find out what you can do to help with finding out what happened to Max and the others."

She looks at him, puzzled for a moment, then asks, "Isn't that just going to make things worse?"

Smiling at her, he says, "Maybe, but I believe that by contributing in some way, it will help take your mind off your concern for Max. And, as you do this, it might help in finding out what's going on faster."

As they continue to hold each other, she kisses her husband on the cheek and nods in agreement to his idea. Then she leaves the room, shutting the door behind her. Sitting down once more, Phillip picks up his book and begins reading. As he does, he says to himself, "Hold on, Max! We're going to find you!"

CHAPTER 22

LOVE'S POWER: THE LURE OF LUST

DANA, JANET'S AUNT, IS WORRIED about her niece and the others with her. As she is driving home, she notices that she's low on gas, so she pulls into a nearby station. She grabs her debit card and keys, gets our and goes to the pump. Even as she begins the process of paying for and pumping the gas, she is looking around the gas station, making sure that she is aware of her surroundings and also to protect herself should someone try to get the jump on her for any particular reason. When she's done putting gas in the car, she puts the nozzle back in its place, gets in the car and locks the door. Then she notices that her phone is ringing. She answers it and notices that it's Phillips wife. "Dana," the caller says, "I know its late, but could you come by for a couple of hours?"

Switching from the call on her screen to her phone's calendar, she looks to see what she has scheduled for the next morning. Seeing that she doesn't have anything scheduled, she replies to Phillips wife, "Sure, I can come over for a bit. Is everything okay?"

"Everything is fine, Dana," the caller assures her. "It's just that my husband gave me an idea, and I could really use your help in getting it started, even if it's just planning what I'm going to do."

"All right," Dana replies, "I can be there in about thirty minutes. Is that okay?"

"That's perfect," Phillips wife says. "See you soon. Call me when you get here."

"Okay," Dana says. "See you soon." As she starts the car, she looks out of her side and rearview mirrors before beginning the drive to Phillip's house. She decides to turn on the radio, and, as she does, she hears an announcement asking for any information on Janet and her classmates. Hearing this, she becomes frustrated and hits the steering wheel. While driving, she realizes this is not the time to get frustrated. Still, as she drives on to Phillips house, she has to wonder what his wife is up to.

She reaches Phillip's house, parks the car and calls Linda, telling her that she's outside. Dana then gets out of the car and walks to the door of Phillip's house. His wife opens the door, Dana walks in, and they greet each other with a friendly hug. The two ladies then walk to the kitchen. Linda asks, "Dana, would you like some coffee or tea?"

Thinking for a moment, Dana replies, "I'll take some tea, please."

Linda puts a pot of water on the stove to make tea, then moves to sit across from Dana.

Dana asks, "Have there been any updates on what's going on with Janet and the others?"

"Not much," Linda replies. "The only information we have right now is that whatever caused the explosion was not something normal and that the kids are being targeted by a group of alien hunters. We're hunting information on whether this was an alien attack or not."

Dana chuckles and responds, "So, the people looking for the kids think this was an alien attack? That's ridiculous!"

"At first," Linda responds, "I thought the same thing, but the point is, if this group believes it, then it makes them very dangerous. Also, Graham is working on creating communicators so that we will be able to talk to the kids without having to worry about the signal being traced."

Thinking for a moment, Dana responds, "Wow! That's a lot of information. I'm glad I came by. So, what's this plan you have?"

Linda begins by saying, "Like you, I've been worried about the kids, and my husband suggested that I come up with a way to contribute to finding them. So, after thinking about it for a bit, I realized that maybe if I set up a bakery stand outside, I might be able to find information faster, especially since I don't look like a threat or that I'm even paying attention to the conversation. But ... in order to do this, I need your help."

As Dana listens to the idea, she smiles and says, "I like it, and I'll be glad to help." With that, the two begin to plan how to open up a bakery stand outside Phillip's house.

BACK IN NEW YORK Agents Wallace, Saunders and Marks have just reached the airport and are on their way to board their transport ship, when Marks asks, "So, where exactly are we headed?"

Wallace replies, "We'll discuss that on the transport."

Marks nods in agreement, but once they board the transport ship, he looks around and says, "Very impressive! Now, where are we off to?"

Wallace and Saunders take their seats. Wallace says, "Have a seat, and Saunders will fill you in."

Marks takes a seat behind Saunders. As he straps himself in, she reviews the next file and says, "Okay, it looks like our next stop is in Mustang, Oklahoma. Our next recruit is a woman named Alexis Styles, and according to her file, she's a stealth operative who is a master of disguise. In addition to this, she has a vast knowledge of pressure points, which allows her to silence targets and threats quickly and with precision."

Marks chuckles and says, "She sounds like a fun little number."

"Chill out, Marks!" Saunders says, "We're recruiting her for our team, not for whatever *you* have in mind."

Marks chuckles again and says, "Easy, Saunders. First off, I was only joking, and I'm not trying to hook up with anybody. I just thought she would be a good partner to have on some of the missions I've been on. Especially since the missions I'm sent on are more the smash-and-grab type."

Wallace interrupts by saying, "All right, I'm plotting a course for Mustang, Oklahoma. Everyone hang on." With that, the transport lifts off the ground and speeds into the sky. Since the course is set, Agent Wallace turns to Saunders and says, "We'll be there in three hours. Learn what you can about her so we can recruit her." She nods and begins to study the file.

Marks asks, "Agent Wallace, how many people are currently on your team?"

Maintaining his position, with his back turned to Marks, Wallace says, "With you, we now have eight members and are on our way to recruit a ninth member now."

Thinking to himself, Marks asks, "If you already have a team of seven and still need to recruit more, you guys must be dealing with something major."

With his eyes forward, Wallace replies, "Yes, it is, and once we have all the recruits, we'll explain the purpose, why we have gathered you all. Until then, sit back and enjoy the ride, Marks."

Marks pushes his seat back. He has known that the ARC Team has always been a shadow organization. Now he is starting to understand just how big an organization it actually is.

AS THE ARC TEAM GROWS, Brykar walks the chamber where his last and deadliest warrior remains stored. As he releases her, she walks slowly toward him. She looks very similar to a human female, with the exception that her hair is black with white stripes, and her face and body are blood red. She is clothed with a black and white gown that has thigh-high slits, one on each side. She stretches and asks, "What can I do for you, Commander Brykar?"

He replies, "I have a pest problem that is increasing, Jezabeel, and I need you to deal with it."

She scoffs for a moment, then says, "Commander Brykar, if you have a pest problem, should you have called an exterminator rather than waste my talents?"

Stepping toward her, Brykar replies, "You witch, I didn't release you to handle some trivial task. Simply put, there is a group of heroes who call themselves knights, and they have become a problem, a problem that all of my previous warriors have failed in dealing with. Which is why I am left with no choice but to have you deal with it."

She says, "Very well, Commander Brykar, so is there any particular way you want me to dispose of them?"

Thinking for a moment, he responds, "No, just get rid of them however you like. But ... bring their leader to me. Is that clear?"

Smiling, Jezabeel replies, "Understood, Commander Brykar."

With that, Brykar says, "In the cargo bay, you will find weapons, armor, vehicles and a lab for you to use to prepare yourself for dealing with these knights." Brykar then turns and leaves Jezabeel, who heads for the cargo bay.

AS SHE REACHES THE AREA where the armors are located, Jezabeel notices a psychromium chestplate with a cloak. When she puts it on, it automatically adjusts to fit her body. Once the process is complete, she begins to examine the cloak. She notices that although it moves like a cloth, it can also work as a shield.

Next, she looks at the weapons and notices a wand that can transform into any weapon of her choice. She says to herself, "This will be perfect!"

Turning her attention to the magnacycles in the cargo bay, she picks one, and using her powers, she waves her hand and has the cycle take the shape of what looks like a high-speed forward-facing motorcycle that is blood red.

With that completed, she goes to the monitors and begins to review the last few battles with the knights. As she does, a thought comes to her mind about a similar group she once dealt with. And so she begins to devise her plan of how to deal with these knights.

THE KNIGHTS ARE ENJOYING their down time. Sally enters the recreation area, where the other girls are huddled up, talking with Janet about her feelings for Joseph. As Sally enters, Janet says, "Sally, thank goodness. Could you please tell them to stop pestering me about whether I have feelings for Joseph or not."

Sally giggles and replies, "Now, why should I do that?"

Frustrated, Janet shouts, "Seriously, Sally? Are you going to do this now?"

Joining them, Sally asks, "Who here thinks Janet has feeling for Joseph ... raise your hand, and then say why."

With that each of the girls raises her hand, causing Sally to giggle. The other girls start laughing, and Sally says, "Since each of us raised our hands, each of us will give a brief reason why we feel Janet has feelings for Joseph. Britney, you go first."

Surprised at this, Britney says, "To be honest, the only reason I know is because I remember the day you dumped Brad and how mad you were at the fact that he continuously taunted Joseph. In fact, if I recall, that day he had tripped Joseph. As he got up, it looked like Joseph had had enough of Brad's taunting and was about to strike back. But as Joseph got to his feet, you stepped in front of him and slapped Brad in front of everyone. The next thing anybody saw was you walking off and then hearing that you and Brad were done."

Janet tries to explain herself but Sally stops her. "Janet," she says, "when we needed advice, you were there, and even though you aren't asking for advice, all we want is to help you the way you helped us. So, please just listen to us for a few moments, okay? Jessica, it's your turn."

Smiling, Jessica says, "If I remember correctly, after the bus was blown up, you stuck close to Joseph after we got separated. Not to mention the fact that when we got these powers, you were the first girl to accept them. Whether you realize it or not, I believe your feelings for Joseph really do influence a lot of your decisions."

Sally looks at Maggie, who then says, "The reason I know you have feelings for Joseph is that when I thought you were jealous of me and Brad, but you said, 'Brad couldn't keep me,' I realized that your heart already belonged to someone else."

Pointing at Tasha, Sally says, "Your turn, Tasha."

Tasha pauses a moment before saying, "The reason I feel you have feelings for Joseph is that you two have a lot in common while being so different. I mean, you are strong and confident, and Joseph is strong and confident as well. When it comes to how different you two are, you are definitely bolder than most, while Joseph is more cautious, which is why he always restrained himself."

Now Sally giggles and says, "I guess it's my turn now."

The other girls move closer to Janet. Sally looks at Janet and says, "The reason I know is not only because of our last talk, but also because I've seen what you have always seen in Joseph. Not that I want him, but I see why you care so much about him. It's because he has a character that inspired all of us, whether we realized it or not. Even though we have different preferences as far as guys go, you fell for his character, which is who he is."

Janet sighs, but before she can say anything, the alarm goes off, letting the knights know that one of Brykar's warriors has appeared. Janet says, "Thanks, girls, but we're going to have to finish this later. Let's get to the lab."

AS THE KNIGHTS REACH THE LAB, they find Des and Joseph already there. Janet asks, "What's Brykar throwing at us this time?"

Des replies, "Look at the screen and see." He then pulls up the image of Jezabeel on her blood bike.

Maggie asks, "Who's she supposed to be, a reject from a horror show?"

Sally quickly replies, "Yeah, talk about a bad hair day!"

Brad turns to Joseph and says, "Whoever she is, we need to stop her, right, bro?" Joseph nods in agreement.

Eric notices this and asks, "What's wrong, Joseph?"

Thinking for a moment, Joseph replies, "I'm not sure, but there's something strange about this newest warrior of Brykar's, so we need to be on our guard."

"So what's the plan?" John asks.

Tasha responds, "Right now, the only plan we've got is to confront her and find out what she wants and what she can do."

Eric says, "I agree, we need to confront her, but if we've learned anything, we can't just charge in blind."

Britney asks, "So, how do we confront her without knowing what she can do?"

Max says, "Des can you do a scan of her, to see if there's anything that stands out aside from her appearance?"

Jessica asks, "What are we supposed to be looking for, Max?"

Max responds, "I'm not sure, but with each of Brykar's warriors, there was some kind of signature that give away part of what they can do. We just need to find it."

As Des begins to scan Jezabeel, Janet notices her wand and says, "Hey, Des, can you zoom in on that stick on her leg?"

Zooming in on the area Janet described, Joseph says, "It looks like some kind of wand."

Max then says, "That's it."

"What do you mean?" Sally asks.

Turning to the knight, he says, "Between her hair, the wand and the fact that she and her cycle are both red, my best guess would be that her powers are based on magic, which means we need to keep her from using her hands and also her mouth to cast any kind of spell."

Brad says, "Okay, now that we have a plan, can we go?"

Shaking his head, Eric replies, "We just found a weakness. We don't have a plan yet, Brad."

Max responds, "Actually, we do. Everyone remembers the strategy we used with Sir Pentous. If we modify it so, rather than it being a circle, if we make it a triangle, we should be able to bind her hands and gag her so that she can't cast any spells."

"Now that sound like a plan," Sally says.

Joseph speaks up, "All right then, Sally, Tasha, Jessica and Maggie, you'll be the tip of the triangle. Janet and Britney, I want you both on a cliff overlooking everything, just in case something goes wrong. The rest of us will form the sides of this triangle, and hopefully we'll be able to get the drop on her for once. Now, everyone to the hanger!"

Without another word, the knights race to the hanger, each of them gets in their BOD Bot and races toward Jezabeel's location.

AFTER THE KNIGHTS EXIT THEIR BASE to face Jezabeel, the Cross Knight, using the com system, says, "Bolt and Love Knights, take your positions. The rest of us are going to see just exactly what we're dealing with."

Before the Love and Bolt Knight can break away from the group, the Earth Knight notices that Jezabeel is headed toward them. "Heads up, guys," he says, "whoever this is just changed directions and is headed straight for us."

The Cross Knight replies, "Bolt and Love Knights, find a nearby vantage point and head there now. Everyone take your positions. We have to buy them some time."

As the two knights head to find a nearby vantage, Jezabeel approaches their position fast, forcing the remaining knights to scatter and begin taking their positions, as they had planned earlier. Upon seeing the knights scatter, Jezabeel stops and gets off her bloodbike. As she does this, the knights stop as well and exit their BOD Bots. Looking at the Cross Knight, Jezabeel says, "I take it you are the knights Brykar told me about? It's a pleasure to meet to you. My name is Jezabeel, and today I will be the one who destroys you."

Stepping forward, the Cross Knight replies, "You're not the first one to make that claim, and the others all failed. What makes you different from them?"

Chuckling, she looks at him and says, "Please don't compare me to those brutes. But, if you want to know what makes me different, I'll gladly show you."

At that moment the Bolt and Love Knights use their telepathic link to let the others know that they are in position, while the Shadow Knight nods to the female knights behind Jezabeel. As they rush her, she disappears in a puff of smoke, causing the knights to miss their opportunity.

Laughing, she says, "Did you really think you were going to capture me that easily?"

Shaking his head, the Cross Knight replies, "We weren't trying to capture you, but we weren't going to just rush into a trap either. Knights, attack!"

With that, the knights draw their swords and charge at Jezabeel, who has her wand become a sword and readies herself to block their attacks. First the Fire and Wind Knights launch a simultaneous attack that Jezabeel, blocks with her blade. Then, with the palm of her hand, she touches the Fire Knight and then the Wind Knight, knocking them backward.

Next the Water and Earth Knights attack from two different directions, but Jezabeel blocks them with ease. Then, like before, she touches the two knights, and this sends them flying backward.

Continuing their attack, the Shadow, Light, Beast, Faith and Hope Knights all attack from different directions. As they do, Jezabeel blocks each attack, with only a touch, and sends them all flying backward.

Finally, the Cross Knight attacks. As she blocks his attack, she tries to touch him, but he dodges her touch. She says, "Impressive! I see why Brykar wants the pleasure of dealing with you personally. Still, it will take more than dodging my touch to defeat me."

The two then continue to battle with neither one landing a successful strike. Jezabeel then has her wand transform into a spear. As the Cross Knight attacks, she blocks him with the blade of her spear, then knocks him to the ground with the other end. She has the spear pointing at the Cross Knight when she remembers what Brykar told her. She says, "You are all pathetic, and to think Brykar wanted me to execute you. I've had enough of this game. Prepare yourselves, knights, for the next time we meet I will destroy you all." With that, she disappears, along with her bloodbike.

As the knights gather themselves, the Cross Knight, using their telepathic link, says, "Everyone back to the base."

ONCE THE KNIGHTS REACH THEIR BASE and are inside, Joseph asks the others, "What was that all about?"

Max replies, "I'm not sure. She had us beat, but made a show of the fact that we couldn't beat her. Although…"

"Although, what?" Eric asks.

Looking at Eric, Max says, "Faith Fighter armor engage," but nothing happens. As the knights look at each other, wondering what's going on, he says, "Just as I thought. When she touched us, she did something that prevents us from unlocking our secondary armor."

"Oh, great!" Brad says. "How are we supposed to beat her now?"

The Shadow Knight replies, "That's a good question, although she didn't touch all of us."

John asks, "What did she mean by, 'I see why Brykar wants the pleasure of dealing with you personally?'"

Max says, "Even though we've been the ones to defeat each of Brykar's warriors, it stands to reason that Brykar wants to make Joseph suffer because he's our leader."

AT THAT MOMENT, each of the knights Jezabeel touched begins to hear her voice in their head, as she says, "Come to me, knights, and I will give you what you most desire."

Without warning, the knights (with the exception of Joseph, Britney and Janet) begin to get in their BOD Bots and exit the hanger. As the three remaining knights watch this, they're puzzled. Britney asks, "Where are they headed?"

Joseph replies, "I don't know, but we need to find out. Let's head to the lab."

WHEN THE THREE KNIGHTS GET TO THE LAB, Manuel asks, "What's wrong, my friends?"

Janet replies, "We were going over what happened when the others fought Jezabeel, and suddenly they got in their BOD Bots and left the hanger."

Thinking for a moment, Manuel says, "That is definitely a problem."

Now Joseph goes to the console. As he tries to find the others, Janet is surprised at how he is able to use the computer. She asks, "Hey, Joseph, I thought only Des was able to use the computer like that?"

Chuckling for a moment, Joseph replies, "Normally that would be true, but one of the things I've been doing in my spare time is learning how to use the computer in the lab and access some of its base functions. One of them being the tracking device that Des placed in the BOD Bots."

Britney says, "So, where are they headed?"

Within seconds, the computer shows that the knights are traveling to where they fought Jezabeel. Joseph then has the computer pull up video of the area to the north of them, and they find Jezabeel waiting for the knights. Shaking his head Joseph replies, "I know where they're headed, and we need to get to them—Now!"

AS THEY RACE FROM THE LAB TO THEIR BOD BOTS, Janet asks, "What's wrong?"

Joseph replies, "According to the computer, the others are heading toward where Jezabeel is, and we need to cut them off immediately."

Britney asks, "So, what's the plan?"

Joseph replies, "Britney, you and I will cut them off and see if we can get them to turn around. Janet, do you think you can hold off Jezabeel?"

Looking at him, she says, "I'll give it my all."

REACHING THEIR BOD BOTS, the remaining knights get in and leave the hanger. Joseph, over their com system, says, "Janet, I'm sending you the coordinates of where Jezabeel is located. Britney, I've found a route that should allow us to cut of the other knights and keep them from reaching her."

Britney says, "Hey, Joseph, I have a question. How are we supposed to get them to turn around?"

Joseph responds, "I'm not exactly sure, but I have a feeling it won't be by gentle means."

Britney replies, "Are you saying we're going to have to fight them?"

Janet chimes in, "Why would you guys have to fight them?"

Joseph replies, "I'm hoping I'm wrong, but something tells me that whatever she did to them might mean we'll have an even bigger fight on our hands than normal."

THE KNIGHTS SOON REACH A POINT where they need to split up. As they do, Joseph says to Janet, "Be careful out there. There's no telling what else she can do."

With that, the knights split up. Janet heads toward where Jezabeel is, and Joseph and,Britney go to cut the others off from reaching Jezabeel.

RACING TO FACE JEZABEEL, Janet heads to the coordinates that Joseph has given her. As she does Heart Burner asks, "Is there a problem, Janet, my dear?"

Janet chuckles and says, "I'm not sure. I guess it's just the fact that Joseph asked me to face Jezabeel, even though he's never asked me to do anything like this before."

Puzzled by this, Heart Burner replies, "Doesn't him asking you to do this show that he trusts you?"

Shaking her head, Janet says, "Him trusting me isn't the problem. I guess I just want to know whether he loves me or not."

Pausing for a moment, Heart Burner asks, "Janet, if I may, I think the real question you need to answer is this—Do you love Joseph? If so, you have to face it. Otherwise you'll just be lying to yourself."

Before anything else can be discussed, they reach Jezabeel's location, and Janet says, "Heart Burner, activate your comm system so that Joseph and Britney can know how to deal with the others."

JEZABEEL SEES THE LOVE KNIGHT WALKING TOWARD HER and says, "Well, if it isn't the Love Knight! This is quite the surprise! I wasn't expecting you!"

Now standing before Jezabeel, the Love Knight replies, "Sorry to disappoint you. So, who were you expecting, Jezabeel?"

Snickering, she answers, "I take it you already know the answer to that question, Love Knight. But, if you really must know, I'm waiting for your friends, at least the ones that I touched anyway."

Taking a fighting stance, the Love Knight replies, "What did you do to them, you witch?"

Jezabeel says, "Seriously, Love Knight, do you think name calling is the way to defeat me? If so, then there's no way you will win this fight. Still, there's no harm in you knowing that when I touched them, I created what you humans would call a soul-tie, so that when I call to them, it will draw them to me, and they will do as I command."

Drawing her sword, the Love Knight shouts, "Tell me how to free them, now!"

Laughing at the Love Knight, Jezabeel replies, "That's just it! There is no way to free them from my power. In creating the soul-tie, I tapped into the lust deep inside of them, so that what they do while under my command is of their own choice. As you will see, there's nothing that can overcome the power of lust."

Pausing a moment, the Love Knight stands and replies, "That's what you think, you witch. With every ounce of me, I won't rest until my friends are free!"

Just then Justice appears to the Love Knight in a flash. Janet remembers when she was young, and she stepped in to help a classmate who was being bullied. In doing so, she not only got injured, but her classmate was angry that she had stepped in. When she got home, she told her aunt about what happened, and her aunt had said to her, "I know it's not easy, but what you did was out of love, and I'm proud of you for that. No matter what, I want you to remember two things about love. First, 'love builds up,'[14] and second, 'Love always protects, always trusts, always hopes, always perseveres.'"[15]

The Love Knight now starts to chuckle to herself, as she remembers this and suddenly shouts, "Life of Love armor, engage." Just as with the knights before her, she is now enveloped in a light, and her armor begins to change. First, her chestplate changes so that a vest in the shape of a heart is now over her armor, along with a pleated skirt with hearts on it. On her arms, appear gloves that have a heart where her elbows are. On her legs appear thigh-high boots with a heart at the top of them. And, finally, in her hand, appears the laser longsword of love, which is able to increase or decrease in length and width.

When the transformation is complete, Jezabeel is shocked and says, "What just happened?"

The Love Knight says, "Two things. First, lust isn't as powerful as you think it is, and second, love does conquer all, as I am about to show you by putting you down for good, you witch."

LOVE'S POWER:
THE LIFE OF LOVE

AFTER UNLOCKING HER SECONDARY ARMOR, the Love Knight faces Jezabeel, who says, "If you think that armor is enough to defeat me, you are sadly mistaken, and I'm going to show you why." With that Jezabeel, vanishes in a puff of smoke and then appears behind the Love Knight. The Love Knight has her sword drawn and sees Jezabeel in its reflection, so that when she strikes, the Love Knight is able to dodge and then counter her attack.

As she does this Jezabeel, chuckles and says, "That was quite impressive. I see that you're stronger than you let on. Still, it will not be enough to defeat me."

The Love Knight responds, "If that impressed you, you haven't seen what else I can do." With that, the Love Knight charges at Jezabeel, who vanishes. As she does, the Love Knight immediately turns around and, with the handle of her longsword, strikes where Jezabeel's stomach would be. As she reappears, she is hit by the knight's longsword and knocked backwards.

Surprised by this, Jezabeel shouts, "No one has ever been able to dodge those strikes, and you have done so twice. Tell me how are you able to do that?"

Chuckling, the Love Knight responds, "Awwww, what's the matter? Upset you've lost your edge?"

Jezabeel then says, "That's not my only trick. Still, let's see how you deal with this." Jezabeel starts to appear and disappear suddenly at various points, looking for her moment to strike the Love Knight from behind. As she strikes, the Love Knight blocks the frontal attack. Then, as Jezabeel disappears, the Love Knight turns and moves backward a few feet so that when Jezabeel re-appears the Love Knight is behind her back. When she reappears, the Love Knight kicks her in the back, so that she goes flying to the ground.

Slowly standing up, Jezabeel says, "I don't know how you are doing this, but I see it's time to use more than my base moves with you. So, let me show you how hopeless this fight will be for you."

Pausing for a brief moment, Jezabeel disappears. The Love Knight starts to move, but as she does, she notices that her body is moving much slower than before. When Jezabeel reappears, she is barely able to block the attack. Seizing the opportunity, Jezabeel begin to disappear and reappear behind the Love Knight, who continues to barely block each attack.

Then Jezabeel says to the Love Knight, "As you've already noticed, you are moving slower than before, and that's thanks to the spell I cast just before disappearing. It makes the molecules around a target so heavy that they can barely move. You're doing better than most, but in the end your body will give out, and then I will destroy you."

Standing there, the Love Knight knows Jezabeel is right. Even with her new powers, the gravity is going to get her eventually. She says, "Wait! Are you saying you can cast a spell without speaking?"

Chuckling now, Jezabeel says, "Of course! It's one of the many abilities I've been given since working with the Psystructs long ago. Although knowing that secret won't do you any good since it will die with you."

Seeing that the Love Knight can now barely stand, Jezabeel reaches out her hand, and suddenly the Love Knight is several feet off the ground and is struggling as if she's being choked. Jezabeel begins to laugh at her attempts, but she fails to notice that the Love Knight is gripping her longsword with both hands as it quickly extends. As her longsword speeds toward Jezabeel, the Love Knight continues to struggle. When Jezabeel sees the sword, she grabs her cloak and blocks the blade, as the Love Knight drops to her feet, while she tries to catch her breath.

WHILE THE LOVE KNIGHT FACES JEZABEEL, the Cross and Bolt Knights are getting into position. The Bolt Knight activates her secondary armor, and as the other knights approach, they have their BOD Bots transform into their battle form with the knights inside. The Fire Knight says, "Out of the way, Cross Knight. This doesn't concern you."

Stepping forward, the Cross Knight replies, "That's where you're wrong. I know you all heard a voice promising you something, but I can assure you that what you heard was a lie and that if you continue on this path, it will mean your destruction."

The Earth Knight then chimes in, "Listen, we don't want to fight, but what we heard is definitely something that needs to be investigated. What if what we heard is true?"

Shaking his head, the Cross Knight responds, "That's just it! We've already found where the voice came from, and you are all walking into a trap. If you don't turn around now, who knows what will happen?"

Before any of the other knights can respond, the voice that is calling to them begins saying, "He's lying. He just doesn't want you to be happy. He wants you be as miserable as he is."

The Shadow Knight shouts, "The voice is right. You just want us to miserable like you are Cross Knight, but no more. I'm taking you down now!"

As the Shadow Knight charges at the Cross Knight, he suddenly stops. Trying to move, he notices that all of his controls have gone dead. "What just happened?" he asks.

Stepping forward, the Bolt Knight replies "Sorry hun, but he's right. I used one of my lighting arrows to short-circuit your BOD Bot's power core. Now, unless the rest of you want to be trapped in your BOD Bots like the Shadow Knight, I suggest that you stand down and listen to reason."

Next, the Light Knight asks, "How can you be so sure that you're right?"

Knowing that the knights are starting to listen, the Cross Knight says, "As soon as you all left the base, I checked the coordinates you were heading to and found that it was the same area where we faced Jezabeel."

Stepping forward, the Beast Knight says, "That still doesn't prove anything."

Turning to his BOD Bot, the Cross Knight says, "Cross Cutter, play back the recording."

Cross Cutter replies, "As you wish, my friend."

With that, Cross Cutter begins to play the conversation that the Love Knight had with Jezabeel. The other knights hear the Love Knight asking, "What did you do to them, you witch?" and Jezabeel answering, "Seriously, Love Knight do you think name calling is the way to defeat me? If so, then there's no way you will win this fight. Still, there's no harm in you knowing that when I touched them, I created what you humans would call a soul-tie, so that when I call to them, it will draw them to me, and they will do as I command."

As the recording stops, the Cross Knight says, "Don't you see that this is a trap? Or do you still think I'm lying to you?"

Each of the knights struggles within themselves, as they realize the Cross Knight is right, and yet the desire is slowly overtaking them, to the point that if there is even the slightest chance that it might be true, they are willing to fight to get it.

THE LOVE KNIGHT IS STILL RECOVERING from having been choked by Jezabeel. As Jezabeel watches the knight struggle for breath, she says, "That was impressive, using your sword to distract me so that I would release you. But, it still won't be enough to save you — as you will soon see."

Pausing for a moment, as she did before, this time Jezabeel, using her soul-tie to the knights, calls to them,, "Come quickly! I'm being attacked and won't be able to hold out much longer! Please help me!"

AS THE STRUGGLING KNIGHTS HEAR THIS, they switch their BOD Bots into vehicle mode and port to the coordinates they were given (with the exception of the Shadow Knight who ports only himself.)

Puzzled, the Bolt Knight asks, "What was that all about?"

"I'm not sure," the Cross Knight says, "but I have a feeling the Love Knight is in trouble. We've got to get to her — and now!"

With that, the two knights get in their BOD Bots. The Cross Knight has the Shadow Knight's BOD Bot ported back to the base, while they port to help the Love Knight.

SECONDS LATER, THE KNIGHTS APPEAR. When they see Jezabeel, they do not see her as they first met her. They see her as a being of pure energy that looks like a rainbow of colors. Using this illusion, she releases the Love Knight from the spell she used on her earlier, which had taken its toll on her body. As she points toward the Love Knight, they see Jezabeel, and she asks them, "Please protect me from her. I was waiting for you when she attacked me, and she is determined to kill me."

The Fire Knight has his BOD Bot transform into battle mode. Then he steps forward and shouts, "I won't let you harm her, Jezabeel. Now, take this, you witch!"

Pointing both hands forward, he begins firing on what he sees as Jezabeel, not realizing it is actually the Love Knight. Soon, the other knights do the same. As the Love Knight sees the barrage of attacks coming at her, she uses what strength she has left to leap to the side, avoiding the first wave of attacks.

Getting to her feet, the Love Knight realizes that she can't dodge another attack. This time, as the knights fire another barrage of attacks at her, the Cross Knight leaps in front of her and holds out his hand in front of him to create a shield that blocks the barrage of attacks by the other knights. When the knights see this, they don't see the Cross Knight, but Brykar himself. Before the Cross Knight can say anything, the knights launch a third barrage of attacks. This time the Cross Knight grabs the Love Knight and ports her and her BOD Bot away from where the blast would have hit.

THINKING THEY HAVE CHASED OFF BRYKAR, the knights turn to the being whom they don't realize is Jezabeel. As they make sure she's okay, she says, "I'm fine, my children. Now, tell me! What it is you desire?"

Before the knights can reveal their desires, the Bolt Knight fires a barrage of lightning arrows toward them from high up on a cliff. Jezabeel, using her powers to mask her appearance, says, "If you don't stop them, soon I won't be able to give you what you desire."

Turning to where the blasts came from, the Earth Knight begins to scan the area. As he does, the Bolt Knight ducks behind a rock in order to avoid the Earth Knight's scanners. Continuing to scan the area, the Earth Knight is able to find the Love and Cross Knights, but because of the soul-tie Jezabeel has with them, they see them as Jezabeel and Brykar. The Earth Knight says, "I've got their location. Let's finish this."

AS THE TWO KNIGHTS ARE BEING HUNTED BY THEIR FRIENDS, the Cross Knight carrying the Love Knight asks, "Are you okay?"

She replies, "I've seen better days, but why are they attacking us all of a sudden?"

The Cross Knight says, "I'm not sure, but I won't let them hurt you, and I won't let her hurt them. I just wish we had time to come up with a plan."

Suddenly, using their telepathic link, the Bolt Knight, tells them of her location and where they can hide. As they head there, the knights are in hot pursuit. The Cross Knight puts the Love Knight down and says, "Go to the Bolt Knight's location. I'll hold them off."

Pausing for a moment, the Love Knight replies, "No, if you're staying, I'm staying too."

Turning to her, he says, "I said, 'Get off here! That's an order. I've already lost too much. I can't...' "

Looking at him, she asks, "You can't what?"

Shrugging his shoulders, he responds, "It doesn't matter. Just get out here—now!"

Without a second thought, he charges toward the knights, and as the Love Knight stands to her feet, she realizes she hasn't fully recovered from being choked by Jezabeel. She falls to her knees, thinking to herself, "I know he's only trying to protect me, but whatever she's done to them is causing them to use lethal force. There's got to be a way to free them."

Again the Love Knight stands to her feet. She feels her arms and legs shaking from the fatigue of the gravity spell and from being choked, but she ports to where Jezabeel is.

Seeing that the Love Knight is barely able to stand, Jezabeel laughs, "What are you going to do? You can barely stand, let alone fight?"

Slowly standing straight up, the Love Knight says, "You're right! I can barely stand. Yet, with every breath in my body, I won't quit until my friends are free and you are put down for good. If you remember, I said love was stronger than lust, and here's the proof. Even after everything you did, I'm still here and standing. If you could have destroyed me by now, you would have, but you can't."

When Jezabeel hears this, she becomes enraged and shouts, "You insolent child, I could destroy you at any time, but I've chosen to make you suffer for all your talk of love and its power (which you have yet to show me). But, if you are in such a hurry to die, I shall grant your wish."

Jezabeel then has her sword become a spear, and she walks toward the Love Knight, who takes up a fighting stance and begins to speak their oath, "*As days of darkness near, and people run in fear.*"

Jezabeel begins to lick her lips, as he taps the pole part of the spear in her hand, imagining it piercing the Love Knight. She will mount her head on top of it.

Unnoticed by Jezabeel, the Love Knight continues to speak the oath, "*From they who prey on the weak, and silence those who speak ... .*"

With each step, Jezabeel gets closer, and as she does, she can now hear the Love Knight saying something, even though it is yet unclear what she is saying.

The Love Knight continues, "*We will take to the sky with courage and battle cry.*"

Before the Love Knight can finish, Jezabeel hits her with the pole part of her spear, knocking her over. As she stands over the Love Knight, she chuckles and says, "Any last words, Love Knight?"

Looking up at Jezabeel, the Love Knight nods, then replies with a shout, "TO PROTECT THE WORLD FROM LOSS, I AM A KNIGHT OF THE CROSS!" Without warning, a beam of energy envelops the Love Knight, knocking Jezabeel to the ground. This time, when the Love Knight stands to her feet, the fatigue and soreness in her body are gone. She points her longsword toward Jezabeel and says, "It's over! Now free my friends."

Jezabeel stands to her feet and then begins to disappear like she did before. As she reappears to strike the Love Knight, not only does the Love Knight avoid her attacks, but she grabs her by the arms and throws her to the ground. Again Jezabeel stands, and, like before, tries to use the gravity spell that is not known to the Love Knight. To her surprise, the Love Knight is unaffected by the spell, and she shouts, "How are you doing this? How are you able to even fight after all I put you through?"

Smiling at her, the Love Knight replies, "What you see right now is the power of true love. You see, it would be easy not to love my friends for what they're doing, but the truth is whether they're good or bad, they're my friends and family. I love them with all my heart. This is why I won't quit. Either free them and keep what little life you have left, or continue to fight in vain. It's your choice."

Jezabeel then gets on her knees and has her spear become a wand once more. As she looks up at the Love Knight, she has the wand become a dagger. As she lunges toward the Love Knight, the Love Knight grips her laser long-sword with one hand and swings it effortlessly, cutting Jezabeel in half with a diagonal slice.

As Jezabeel falls to the ground, the Love Knight looks on. Then she says, "I really didn't want to do that, but you left me with no choice. Now, it's time to end this madness." The Love Knight then ports away.

WHILE THE LOVE KNIGHT HAS BEEN FIGHTING Jezabeel, the Cross Knight has continued to lure the other knights away, in hopes of trying to figure out how to free them. Before he can get any further, the knights encircle him. The Faith Knight says, "It's over, Brykar! We won't let you harm another living being ever again."

Hearing this, Joseph realizes what's going on, and before he can even do or say anything, the Love Knight appears in front of him. When they see her, the Hope Knight and the Faith Knight ask, "What's the deal? Why are you protecting Brykar?"

Shaking her head slowly, she says, "See for yourselves the truth, and it shall set you free."

With that, an energy wave extends from her, breaking the soul-ties, and each of the knights sees what the others who were not under Jezabeel's powers saw.

As the illusion ends, the Love Knight can see that they're all having a lot of regret. She says, "It's been a long day, and I don't know about you, but I could definitely use a good long rest."

AS THE ENERGY LEAVES HER, the Love Knight collapses into the Cross Knight's arms. He looks at the other knights and says, "She's right! We can talk about this later. Right now, we need to get back to the base. I'll wait for her BOD Bot, while you all head back." The other knights nod in agreement.

The Shadow Knight asks, "Cross Knight, since my BOD Bot is going to need repairs, can I get a lift from you?"

Chuckling for a moment, he shakes his head and says, "No, you can't."

Puzzled by this response, the Shadow Knight asks, "Why not?"

Pointing to the Bolt Knight behind him, the Cross Knight says, "Turn around, because I think your ride is here already?"

As he turns to see the Bolt Knight, she smiles and asks, "Sorry about your BOD Bot, Hun. Can I make up for it by giving you a lift?"

Showing his embarrassment a bit, the Shadow Knight replies "Sure! I'm sorry about being such a jerk."

Turning to the Cross Knight, he asks, "What happened to my BOD Bot? We can't just leave him out here."

The Bolt Knight says, "He's fine. The Cross Knight ported him back to the base after you all disappeared on us, and that's when we followed you."

AS THE TWO KNIGHTS GET IN THE BOD BOT, the Cross Knight holds the Love Knight and his BOD Bot scans for hers to see what its ETA is. As she stirs, she sees the Cross Knight above her and asks, "What happened? The last thing I remember was telling everyone that we, including myself, needed to rest."

Chuckling, the Cross Knight replies, "After you said that, you collapsed in my arms, and I told the others to head back. I was going to wait here with you while we waited for Heart Burner. I hope you don't mind."

Snuggling up close to him, she says, "Of course I don't mind. In fact, I'm glad you did."

Before anything else can be discussed, Heart Burner arrives, and the Cross Knight puts her into it. "I'll see you back at base," he says.

SPEEDING OFF, HEART BURNER NOTICES something different. He asks, "You seem very pleased right now, my dear. Would you care to share with me?"

Leaning back, she replies, "Well, you were right. I had to admit that I do love him. Being in his arms just now felt perfect. The only thing I have to do now is tell him how I feel and trust that he feels the same way."

AS THE KNIGHTS RETURN to their base, Brykar stands in his command chamber, having watched Jezabeel's defeat. He shakes his head and says, "It shouldn't surprise me that she failed, but what *does* surprise me is the amount of power those knights posses. Still, even with that power, they won't be prepared for what I have in store for them."

Brykar then has the Psydrones go to gather the remains of Jezabeel and has her body placed in the revival chamber with the other warriors. Before Brykar can leave his chamber, he notices that General Sadoom is trying to contact him. As he establishes the video link, Brykar kneels, and General Sadoom asks, "What news do you have to report, Brykar?"

Looking up at the holographic image of General Sadoom, Brykar replies, "As expected, my last remaining warrior, Jezabeel, has been defeated by the knights. In the process, I have learned enough about them and their powers that I can now begin the final stage of my plan."

General Sadoom is silent for a few moments, then says, "For your sake, Brykar, I hope their defeats are worth it, because if you fail, rather than your punishment being tenfold, it will now be a hundredfold. Are we clear?"

For a brief moment Brykar is shocked that they would ever go that far, but if his final plan is successful, the knights will be no more, and the Earth will be theirs. But, if the knights should defeat him, it will mean his death as well. Again he looks up at General Sadoom and replies, "I understand, General, and I assure you that this final plan will end with either their destruction or mine."

"As you know," General Sadoom adds, "I detest failure on any level. Still, since things are going according to your plan, I can justify showing you this…" He holds up an orb.

Seeing it, Brykar asks, "Is that what I think it is, General?"

Nodding, General Sadoom replies, "Yes, it is! And if you destroy these knights, this shall be yours. With it, you will increase your powers exponentially. So, remember that this is your last chance, and if you fail, you will have wished the knights had destroyed you. Is that clear?"

Pausing for a brief moment, Brykar looks up and responds meekly, "Yes, General Sadoom. I will not fail you."

With that, the transmission ends and Brykar heads to the revival chamber where the rest of his fallen warriors are being kept.

BRYKAR ARRIVES AT THE REVIVAL CHAMBER just as the Psydrones return with Jezabeel's remains to place them in the revival tube. As Brykar has the process begin, he looks at each of his fallen warriors. Knowing that they cannot hear him, he says, "Each of you has failed me, but soon you will have one last opportunity to redeem yourselves. Mark my words, when next you face the knights, it will be their end — one way or another."

BACK AT THE KNIGHTS' BASE, the knights have arrived (except for Joseph, who now enters the hanger bay). As he exits Cross Cutter, he makes his way to the lab, where the others are waiting for him. Walking slowly, he thinks about this last battle and realizes that this must end. In order to do that, he must end Brykar, but in order to do that, he must either act alone or risk his friends' lives.

ONCE JOSEPH REACHES THE LAB, Brad starts to say something, but Joseph stops him. "I want all of you to know this," he says. "Regardless of what happens in the field, we know there are risks, and I know you all would not willingly attack me or anyone else for no reason at all. So, there's no need for an apology. In fact, I figured out what happened just before Janet showed up. Even if I would have said something, there's no guarantee it would have worked, considering what Jezabeel did to you all. I'm not mad at any of you, and I can see all of you feel conflicted for it, but today has given me a lot to think about. First thing in the morning, we all need to be in the Training Room and training like never before. Is that understood?"

Each of the knights nods in agreement, and Joseph continues, "Good, if anyone needs me, I'll be in the library." With that, he leaves the room.

Brad speaks up, "I know he said he's not upset with us, but if I didn't know any better, I would say he's upset."

Des shrugs his shoulders and says, "Actually, Brad, I agree with you. What do you think, Max?"

Pausing a moment, Max responds, "Like you, I think Brad is right. Even though Joseph said he's not upset with us, clearly something is bothering him."

John chimes in, "So what should we do?"

Sally then walks up to the guys. She is giggling as she says, "I have an idea about what might be bothering him."

Max looks at her and says, "Well, spill it!"

With the exception of Janet, each of the female knights now takes the hands of the male knight they've fallen for. They say, "Look around. Do you notice something now?"

Each of the male knights then notices that Janet is by herself. Joseph is not here either, and as it hits them. Britney laughs, "Wow! You guys are dense. But I will say *this,* when Janet fell into his arms, I could tell he started to hold her a little closer than normal, and when I told them where I was, he purposely left her, so he could lead you all away. If I had to make a guess, I don't think he's mad at you guys, but he is upset that we almost lost Janet. What do you all think?"

Maggie nods in agreement. "That definitely makes the most sense out of everything," she says.

Jessica and the others look at Janet. Then Jessica says, "I think the best thing to do to help Joseph is to give him and Janet time to talk. What do you think of that, Janet?"

She walks past them without a word, then says, "I'll think about it?"

Each of the knights in unison shout, "Janet, are you serious?"

Laughing for a moment, she replies, "Wow! You're all too easy. I'll talk to him because there's a lot I need to tell him anyway. But I want you all to know the only way I was able to unlock my armor was when I realized that love is honesty and I had to face the truth about how I feel about Joseph, and the truth is I love him. Now he needs to know that."

WHILE JANET MAKES HER WAY TO THE LIBRARY, she hesitates for a moment, realizing that this issue needs to be addressed. When she enters, Joseph is surprised to see her. Standing to his feet, he walks toward her. Before she can say anything, he asks, "Is everything okay, Janet? Are *you* okay?"

Pausing for a moment, she smiles at him, then responds, "I'm fine, but there's a lot I have to talk to you about, and I just need you to listen until I'm done. Okay?"

Joseph pulls the chair he was sitting in closer. As he sits down, Janet takes a deep breath, says, "Joseph," she begins, "this isn't easy for me to say, but I have to say it. When we first accepted these powers, I really wasn't sure about doing it until you stepped forward. Even before getting these powers, your character and restraint always impressed me, which is the main reason I broke it off with Brad, especially after how he treated *you.* I want you to know I'm not mad at the others or even you. If you want to know why I could or should be mad with you, I mean, really, I could barely walk, and you leave me by myself, after I had the stuffing kicked out of me."

A little embarrassed, Joseph says nothing, so Janet continues, "Joseph, what I'm trying to say is: each day since we accepted these powers I've tried to deny my feelings. In doing so, I've been lying to myself and, after today, I can't do that anymore."

A bit puzzled, Joseph asks, "What exactly are you trying to say, Janet?"

She shakes her head and shouts, "I'm trying to tell you that I love you, Joseph! I always have, and I always will!"

Without realizing it, Janet starts to back away, but Joseph stands, pulls her to him and asks, "Why are you backing away?"

As they look into each others eyes, she can hardly speak. Then, taking his hand and caressing her cheek, he whispers in her ear, "I love you too, Janet. I just never realized how much until I almost lost you, which is why I left you there. I know that's no excuse. I just couldn't bear the thought of losing you."

Before either of them can realize it, their lips meet, and the two share a gentle lover's kiss. Although it lasts but a moment, when it ends, the two knights look at each other in wonder.

Finally Janet speaks, "Now that we've gotten *that* out of the way, the others could tell something was bothering you when you came back because of how you addressed everyone. So, what was really bothering you?"

Joseph chuckles and replies, "Like I said, I wasn't mad at them. I was actually upset with myself for not being able to protect you better, and I was mad because we almost lost you. I mean, if I had been any later, you might not have been able to avoid that second barrage. I didn't know until then how much I truly cared about you."

Holding him close, she says, "I understand, and so do our nosey little eavesdroppers."

Turning to the screen above them, she says, "Turn on the screen, Des. I know you can see and hear us from the lab."

Just then the screen turns on, and Des asks, "How did you know what we were up to, Janet?"

Chuckling a bit, she says, "Simple! Because I know your girls, and I know they would want the play by play of this."

Sally chuckles and says, "Don't blame them, Janet. I was the one who put them all up to it."

As all of the knights begin to chuckle, Joseph says, "I'm sorry if I was rude earlier. It wasn't directed at you guys, but without realizing it, I took it out on you guys, and I'm sorry. Can you forgive me?"

Each of the knights accepts the apology, and Janet replies, "See, I told you they would understand."

This time Joseph chuckles. "True," he says, "I guess they'll understand that for eavesdropping on us each of them has to do an extra two hours at one level higher than what we start at in the morning."

Shaking their heads, the knights begin to grumble lightly, then they all nod in agreement. They know they deserve it.

AS THE KNIGHTS RELAX AND PREPARE for the next day, Agents Wallace, Saunders and Marks have spent the last several hours waiting for Alexis Styles to arrive at a small coffee shop in Mustang. As the time she agreed to meet with them approaches, they notice several people have come in who could possibly be her but they are all gone now. Unnoticed by any of the ARC Team is an older woman who sits with her back to them. Saunders looks at her watch and says, "Well, she said she would be here by now, but I don't see her. Do either of you?"

Agent Wallace responds "This is your operation. You need to make sure you double and triple check everything."

Looking around, Agent Marks replies, "I know I'm new on the team, but have you all noticed everyone is gone except for that older lady and us?"

Turning to her, Agent Saunders asks, "Are you waiting for someone ma'am?"

The older woman turns to her and in an instant reveals herself to be the person they are looking for, the woman known as Alexis Styles. "For a specialized ops team," she says, "you sure are slow. So what's this all about?"

Agent Saunders replies, "My name is Agent Saunders, and this is Agent Wallace, our team leader, and the one who noticed you is our newest member, Agent Marks. Now, the reason we asked you to meet us here is that you were recommended by Agent Martin and because we are facing a situation that calls for us to increase the members of our team."

Pausing for a moment, Agent Styles asks, "Okay, so why exactly should I be part of your team when I'm perfectly happy with what I'm doing now?"

Agent Saunders knows the gambit she's playing, says, "I know you spent years to perfect what you do, and if you were to join us we could help advance what you do beyond anything you could ever imagine. So are you interested?"

Thinking for a moment, Agent Styles, replies "Thank you, but I'm not interested. You all have a good day."

As she walks toward the door, Agent Saunders stands, gets in front of her, and asks, "Why aren't you interested?"

Agent Styles looks at her and says, "Simple! I spent years on the tech I use to do what I do, and this is the most advanced tech money can buy. So, how can you have something like that? It's either a lie or requires a clearance that's above your pay grade."

As Wallace and Marks hear this, they both chuckle, and Agent Saunders says, "I can assure you the tech is true, and it's very experimental. If you need further assurance, I can get in contact with Agent Martin."

Agent Styles again looks at Agent Saunders, pauses, then replies, "All right, Saunders, I'll join your team, but if this doesn't work, I'm out."

Nodding her agreement, the agents make their way from the cafe to where their transport is.

JANET'S AUNT DANA AND LINDA HAVE BEEN WORKING on how to start a bakery stand outside Phillip's home. Dana has been looking at what licenses and other documents are need for them to get started. Linda has been working on the structural items, such as the name of the business, how the stand will look, and the menu of items she'll have available. As each of the women work on their parts, Phillip enters the kitchen where they are working. He is in his uniform. When he sees Dana, he says, "Hey Dana, I didn't know you were here?"

Chuckling she replies, "Sorry, it was your wife's idea, and it was late last night."

Phillip shakes his head and says, "It's fine! So, what have you two been up to?"

Walking over to Linda, Phillip gives her a hug and kiss, and she says, "Well, I thought about what you said and decided to put my energy forward and make a bakery stand in front of the house. What do you think?"

Thinking for a moment, Phillip replies "I think it's an awesome idea. So what have you gotten so far?"

Looking at him, his wife says, "Well, I've got the name and the design of the stand, and I'm working on the menu now."

Dana then chimes in, "While she's been doing that, I've been making a list of what licenses are needed and how much they each cost. This way we can see how cost effective it will be to do this."

Phillip makes a cup of coffee, then replies, "Well, I've got to get to work. You ladies keep up the good work. See you later, Hun." With that, Phillip again kisses his wife and then heads out to work.

When they hear the door close, Dana chuckles and says, "Wow! I haven't seen you two like that in a while. Since when did Phillip start becoming so lovey dovey with you?"

Turning to her friend, Linda replies, "Well, it started several months before the kids went missing. Phillip and I started going to counseling, and as we continued to go, we both made small changes. Before we knew it, we were a lot more affectionate with each other. After the kids went missing, we continued with what we were doing as a way of dealing with the crisis."

Now Dana looks at her watch, smiles and says, "That's fantastic! I need to get some rest as I have appointments tomorrow that I need to get ready for."

Linda replies, "I'm sorry. I didn't mean to keep you."

"It's fine!" Dana says, chuckling. "The appointments I have are simple things like grocery shopping, things like that."

Pausing for a moment, Linda replies, "Why don't you take the guest room and sleep in there for a couple of hours? I'll get some clothes for you to change into while you sleep. This way, you don't have to drive all the way home just to get some sleep."

Hugging her friend, Dana replies, "Thanks, I think I'll do that. Besides, we've been up most of the night, and as much as I want the comfort of my own bed, I might not even make it there safely."

The two ladies then walk upstairs, and Linda shows Dana the guest room, while she goes to her own room and comes back with a change of clothes for Dana and some towels. Again Dana hugs her friend and goes in the room to lie down. As she does, she soon drifts off to sleep.

CHAPTER 24

CROSS OF CREATION: VISIONS

IT HAS NOW BEEN TWO WEEKS since Dana and Linda started working on the bakery stand, and the two have come a long way in a short amount of time. While out getting the needed licenses, Dana runs into Melanie, who says, "Hey Dana, how's it going?"

Dana hugs her and replies, "I'm doing well. I've actually working with Phillips wife to create a bakery stand in front of their home so she can keep her ear to the ground in the event someone is monitoring us. What are you doing here?"

"I came here," Melanie answers, "because there are some documents I needed to file for a business Joseph's father and I thought about. I started working on getting it ready, but I'm not sure if I have everything right so far."

Dana chuckles and says, "I have a couple of hours. Would you like me to help you look them over, to make sure everything is correct?"

Relieved, Melanie smiles and says, "Thanks, how about I buy you lunch as my way of saying thanks?"

Thinking for a moment Dana asks, "Are you up for Italian or Spanish food this afternoon?"

Both of them begin to laugh. Melanie replies, "Whatever you want is fine with me."

Dana says, "All right! There's this Spanish place I've been wanting to try for a while. Just haven't found the time."

Soon the two women are at the restaurant and as they sit at the table, Dana is going over the document and notices something, Melanie asks, "Is something wrong?"

Dana looks at her, replies "It's nothing major, all the property documents are still good, but some of the permits need to be updated, which is a pretty easy fix."

Pulling out her notebook Dana writes down a couple of websites where Melanie would be able to get the updated permits, as he passes her the paper she asks, "So how have you been since the kids went missing?"

Melanie starts to lightly laugh, says "Forgive me Dana, I'm laughing cause that's usually my line."

Dana then asks "What do you mean by that?"

Pausing a moment, Melanie replies "Well usually when I run into any of the parents, I'm the one to ask them about how they're doing, you're the first to ask me and beat me to the punch. So that's why I was laughing. Although I am worried about them, both Brad and Joseph are very capable young men, are able to handle themselves pretty well. Still I'm more worried they'll kill each other before anyone else does."

A bit puzzled, Dana asks "Why is that?"

Taking a breath Melanie says, "Very few people know this, but Brad and Joseph are brothers by marriage not by blood, because I have tried my best to be there for Joseph since his father disappeared, Brad has always been a bit jealous of Joseph and as much as I've tried to stop it Joseph had told me to stop, let me know he'll find a way to deal with it."

Dana then asks, "Isn't that a bit dangerous?"

Chuckling a bit Melanie says, "If it had been anyone else I would be concerned, but Joseph's father had trained Joseph to have remarkable self control, so I can trust that if he's going to handle it, it will be in a way that will bring peace to the issue."

Just then the waiter brings their food and the two women begin to eat their meal.

AT THAT MOMENT THE MEMBERS OF THE ARC TEAM are gathered in their base welcoming their new team members. The first of these new members is Andre Marks, a master of precision and ballistics. The next agent is Alexis

Styles, a master of disguise and stealth. The third and forth agents are Damien and Claudia Stalks, also known as the DC Twins because they never accept solo missions. Damien is an expert tracker, while Claudia is an expert trapper and interrogator. The last of the new agents is Michael Angini, an expert mechanic who has designed several different ARC vehicles, including the transport used to recruit him and the others.

Having been recruited by Agents Wallace and Saunders, the new recruits are about to find out the exact reason for their being chosen and the purpose of being added to the ARC Team. With the original team behind them, Agent Martin stands and says, "Welcome to the ARC Team. As you are already aware, we are a group that is to locate and capture aliens or tech that would appear in nature to be alien. As some of you may have heard, a few months ago a school bus carrying a group of high school seniors was destroyed by a blast of unknown origin. There were only twelve survivors of this incident. Oddly, their whereabouts are currently unknown, and as far as the media is concerned, they are still wanted fugitives. However, we have come into contact with two warring alien groups, one that calls themselves knights and the other that calls themselves Psystructs. From our intel, we have learned that the knights are attacking the Psystructs and will not stop, even if it means human casualties. Due to this fact, we have received equipment from the Psystructs so that we may defend Earth against these alien warriors. While we are working on developing weapons and armor for you, we expect you and the other ARC Team members to undergo extreme training so that when you face the knights, you will be fully prepared. Based on what we know of them and their powers, each of you will be given a knight to study, so that when the time comes to deal with them, each of you will be able to not simply defeat them, but if need be, to put them down—and hard! Is that clear?"

Without waiting for a response, Agent Martin continues, "Also, if Agent Rivera asks you for anything, I don't care what it is, you will give her what she needs and without question. If not, the consequences will be severe."

With that, Agent Martin leaves the room and motions for Agent Wallace to follow him.

AS AGENT WALLACE MEETS WITH AGENT MARTIN, Martin turns to him and says, "Agent Wallace, I know there will be challenges with this new team, but I'm sure you are more than capable of handling them. However, I do want to advise you that the team must come first, and although we have data on most of the knights, I want you to be aware that we have very limited data on their leader, the Cross Knight. Since this is the case, your task will be to prepare to take him on. Without him, the others may quickly fold. Is that clear?"

Agent Wallace replies, "Yes, Agent Martin. I understand completely."

Turning to the door, Agent Martin leaves and Agent Wallace goes to rejoin his team.

AS THE ARC TEAM BEGINS TO PREPARE to face the knights, the knights have been in extensive training so that if Brykar should attack, they will be prepared. While the knights rest from their most recent training session, Joseph heads to the lab. As he enters, he sees Des and asks, "Hey, Des, are you able to pinpoint the exact location of Brykar's base?"

Thinking for a moment, Des replies, "Yes, I believe so. May I ask why you want that information?"

Joseph says, "Brykar's been too quiet. I have a feeling he's up to something. I thought if we knew where he is, we might be able to find out what he's up to."

Turning to the computer, Des begins to use all the data from their previous battles with Brykar's warriors to pinpoint the location of his base. Just as Des is about to give Joseph the information, Brad and Max come in. Brad asks, "Hey, guys, what have you got there?"

Before Joseph can see the coordinates, Brad grabs the paper. Looking at Des, he again asks, "Des, what is this?"

Puzzled, Des replies, "That should be the approximate area where Brykar's base is located."

Max asks, "What do we need that for?"

Des then looks at Joseph and then responds, "Joseph asked for it, because Brykar's been too quiet lately, and he wanted to do some recon, find out what he's been up to."

Brad scoffs and says, "Sorry to tell you this, Des, but Joseph lied to you. He's right. Brykar's been too quiet, but that's not the reason he wants the coordinates. It isn't to do recon, is it Joseph?"

Joseph steps forward and replies, "Stand down, Brad. This is none of your concern."

Just then the rest of the knights enter the lab. Eric asks, "What's going on here? What's your problem this time, Brad?"

Laughing for a moment, Brad replies, "Ohhh, nothing Eric, just trying to keep our beloved leader from going on a potential suicide run is all."

John then chimes in, "What are you getting at, Brad?"

Holding up the paper with the coordinates, Brad replies, "Joseph asked Des to find the coordinates to Brykar's base. As Des printed them out, Max and I walked in. When I asked about it, Joseph told me to stand down, without answering my question. So, are you or are not planning to use the coordinates to face Brykar on a suicide mission?"

Before Joseph can respond, Max says, "Enough, Brad! You've made your point."

Turning to his friend, Max pauses before saying, "I doubt there's anything we can do to stop you, but before you consider this, would you at least hear from each of us why this bothers us. Agreed?"

Joseph nods in agreement, and Max turns to the other knights and asks, "All right, who wants to go first?"

The knights look at each other. John steps forward and says, "I'll go first. The reason this bothers me is mainly because this is not your style. Granted, we don't usually have a plan because we don't know everything we're up against, but still you make sure we go in with at least *some* kind of plan."

As John steps back, Tasha steps forward. Thinking for a moment, she adds, "Joseph, of all of us, you have the most character, and because of that it makes this plan seem out of character for you."

Next is Sally. She steps forward and says, "Joseph, it may not seem like it, but I've watched you both in school and here. What I've learned is that you have a heart bigger than most, and whether any of us likes to admit it or not, you brought us together as a team. Even more, we became a family."

Now it's Eric turn. "Joseph," he says, "I know, as the leader, there are burdens you have to shoulder, but you don't have to do this alone. As you know, it took me a bit to understand my role as a protector for the team, and last time I checked, you are still part of this team. Sometimes we all need protection, especially from ourselves."

Britney is the next to step forward. As she does, she looks at the others, then at Joseph and says, "I'm not like the others, having a good reason for you not to do this. I don't, but all I can say is that just as each of our lives is important, so is yours, and don't throw it away because you feel you need to protect us."

Maggie is the next to step forward. "Joseph," she says, "I understand you are concerned and even scared for us, but if you are going to do this, don't do it out of fear because of what may or may not happen to *us*. As I learned with Phobia fighter, there are things that scare me, but courage is facing what you fear the most. Right now that is what you need to do."

Now, Jessica steps forward and says, "Joseph, everyone's made a really good point about why you shouldn't go. All I can say is that we've all been through too much for you just to make a decision like this for us. You didn't make the choice for us when we accepted the powers, so you taking the choice from us now is really selfish."

As the other knights listen to Jessica, they're a bit surprised at what she is saying. At the same time, they each agree with her. Des turns toward Joseph as he stands. He says, "Joseph, before all this, you and I were barely friends, but even then I knew there was something different about you. Still the odds of you surviving this are minimal at best, and there's no telling if you'll even survive long enough to make it to Brykar, considering we don't know what he has aboard his ship."

Max then steps forward. Placing his hand on Joseph's shoulder, he says, "Bro, I understand you have to face Brykar alone, but you don't have to assault his base by yourself. Honestly, now would be the perfect time to strike. However, it would be best to do it as a team rather than a solo mission. Still, the choice is yours."

Janet steps up next. As she approaches Joseph, she slaps him across the face, causing the other knights to turn away for a moment. Then, with tears in her eyes, she says, "I just admitted to loving you, and just as when you left me, now you want to leave us all, because you don't want us to get hurt or die? Joseph, I love you because you are strong and brave, but if you go through with this, you will hurt me more than Brykar or his warriors ever could."

Finally Brad steps forward to speak. "It's no secret," he says, "that I didn't like the fact that you were chosen to be leader, but you were the right choice. I just got used to the idea of having a brother, and now that I've gotten past my feelings of jealousy, you want to take away the only family I have left right now. I mean …"

Before Brad can say anything else, he realizes what he has said, and then continues, "Joseph, is the reason you want to do this because of what happened to your dad? If it is, you need to realize that your dad wouldn't leave you. It is true that he disappeared, but I know he wouldn't leave you, and neither will I. So, if you insists on going on this suicide mission, then I'm going too."

For a moment, Joseph just looks at each of them. Then he says, "I'm sorry for any hurt I've caused you guys. And, Brad, you're right. It is because of me losing my dad that I couldn't bear the thought of losing any of you."

Without warning, a light suddenly envelopes Joseph, Brad and the other knights hear him say, "Cross of Creation armor, engage." Then Joseph's armor begins to change. Over his armor appears what looks like a navy blue robe with white trim. Its cuffs stop at his forearm. Then they see what looks like a monocle. In Joseph's hand, appears a blue cane with a cross at the top of it. Once the transformation is complete, the other knights are puzzled at the fact that Joseph's secondary armor is now unlocked.

BRYKAR MAKES HIS WAY TO THE CHAMBER where his fallen warriors are recovering. As he enters, he notices that they are all ready to be released. He then goes to the console and places his hand on it, so that the reanimation process can begin for his fallen warriors. Power then begins to flow from the console to each of the eleven warriors, causing them to stir in the tubes they are in. Within a few minutes, all of Brykar's warriors are alive, looking at each other and wondering what is going on.

Deadly Double is the first to speak. He asks, "Commander Brykar, what's going on?"

The Scientific Samurai also speaks up. "Not that I don't appreciate the opportunity to serve you, Commander," he says, "but why have we been revived and enhanced when you said there would be no second chances?"

Before any of the other warriors can say a word, Brykar replies, "Enough! Although it is true that you are getting a second chance to face the knights in battle, I only need you to keep them busy, while I face their leader, the Cross Knight. If you should manage to defeat them, then you will have redeemed yourselves. If not, what happens to you is of no consequence to me. You all have one thing in common: each of you failed to destroy these knights. Still, because of your failures, I was able to gather the data that will allow me to destroy them once and for all. Now, each of you is to face the knight who defeated you. As I said before, you are to keep them occupied. Do not concern yourselves with defeating them, for where you have failed I will succeed."

As his warriors begin to murmur and complain, Brykar shouts, "What are you waiting for? You have your orders. Now go and deal with these knight as I have instructed." With that being said, each of the warriors leaves the base.

Now Brykar notices that General Sadoom is trying to contact him. As he establishes the link, General Sadoom says, "What do you have to report, Brykar?"

Kneeling before the projection of General Sadoom, Brykar replies, "I've just sent my eleven warriors to face the knights. This shall start the final phase of my plan."

General Sadoom then asks, "Which is what exactly?"

Brykar says, "As you know, I revived and modified each of these warriors. However, what they don't realize is that they have been infused with psyer, which, as you know, encases whatever it touches in a gel-like form that then paralyzes them. My plan is this: as I go to face their leader, my warriors will engage the knights. As they each fight the knights, a sensor has been placed on my warriors, so that as they get close enough, their bodies will self-destruct, coating each of the knights in psyer. Once they are encased, they will be moved to the ship."

Thinking for a moment, General Sadoom says, "Very good, but what about their leader? Won't he try to save them?"

Brykar chuckles at this and says, "I'm counting on it. When he does come to save them, I will destroy them before his very eyes. Then, while he is distracted by their deaths, I will destroy him. Without the knights, this planet shall be ours."

"Very well," General Sadoom says, "continue with your plan, but keep me updated, Brykar."

As the communication ends, Brykar leaves the ship and goes to an area away from his warriors, where he can face the Cross Knight alone.

THE OTHER KNIGHT ARE STILL PUZZLED by how Joseph has managed to unlock his armor. Des is scanning the armor, and as he does so, he says, "This is very interesting."

Joseph asks, "What do you mean, Des?"

Pausing a moment, Des replies, "Well, according to the scan, you did unlock your armor and it's abilities. However, there's still a large portion of your powers that remain locked. On top of that, I was also looking at each of our armors and discovered that although we unlocked their powers, like Joseph, there's still a lot of untapped power that we aren't able to access."

Eric then asks, "Why is that, Des?"

Turning to the other knights Des says, "I'm not exactly sure, but it is something we definitely need to look into."

BEFORE THE KNIGHTS CAN HAVE ANY FURTHER DISCUSSION on this subject, the alarms in the base begin to go off. Des looks at the screen and says, "Guys, we might have a problem here."

Jessica goes to his side and also views the screen. Then she says, "There's no *might* about this! We definitely have a problem."

Des then pulls up what he's seeing on one of the monitors in the lab, and the other knights are shocked at what they see. Brad shouts, "There's no way!"

"Yeah, but there they are," Des adds. "Each of the warriors we defeated is back, and it looks like they have all been upgraded."

Joseph says, "At least we know why Brykar's been so quiet."

Just then Des notices a signature that is different from the others. As he zooms in on it, he finds Brykar by himself. "Speaking of the devil," he says, "the man himself is also out and about."

John asks, "Okay, so what's the plan?"

Looking at the team, Joseph replies "There's eleven of them, twelve of us, and more than likely each of these warriors isn't exactly thrilled they got beat the way they did. So the best bet we have is for each of you to face the warriors you defeated, especially since you all have a better idea of how they fight."

Brad then asks, "While we're doing that, what will you be doing?"

Pointing to the screen, Joseph replies, "I'm going to face Brykar and see if we can end this once and for all."

Janet asks, "Is that a wise idea considering that up to this point we really haven't seen how he fights?"

Joseph ponders this for a moment, then turns and says, "Honestly, it's not the best idea, but right now to do anything else would put us at even greater risk."

Brad says, "Listen, we all agreed that sooner or later Joseph would have to face Brykar. We just didn't want him doing a suicide run. To be honest, this might just be our best shot at ending this."

Eric then adds, "I don't normally agree with Brad, but it is possible that we can end this. Still…"

"What is it, Eric?" Britney asks.

Max nods and replies, "What Eric is getting at is that even if we defeat Brykar, it doesn't mean we'll be able to return to our normal lives."

Sally asks, "Why's that, Max?"

As the knights look at Max, he says, "Even if we defeat Brykar, the ARC Team still has a wanted poster on our human identities, which means we would have to figure out how to get rid of that as well before we can return to our normal lives."

Joseph steps forward and says, "All right, everyone, let's deal with Brykar and his warriors. Then we can worry about how to return to our normal lives."

With that, the knights race to the hanger, each of them gets into their BOD Bot, and they leave the hanger, racing to where their opponents are waiting for them.

WHILE THE OTHER KNIGHTS SPEED TOWARD THEIR OPPONENTS, the Cross Knight splits off from them and heads toward Brykar's location. When he arrives, the Cross Knight exits his BOD Bot and looks around, wondering where Brykar is. Then he hears Brykar saying, "Welcome, Cross Knight! I've been expecting you."

Turning to Brykar, the Cross Knight shouts, "What do you want, Brykar?"

Brykar chuckles and says, "What I want is to fulfill the desires of my commander and to destroy anyone who gets in my way. You, young knight, are in my way."

Stepping forward, the Cross Knight replies, "You want me, Brykar? Come and get me."

Before Brykar can attack, he notices the Cross Knight's new armor. "I see that like your friends, you've unlocked a new armor," he says. "Still, it will not be enough to defeat me."

"We'll see about that!" the Cross Knight replies.

Brykar again chuckles, then draws his swords, saying, "If you are in such a rush to die, Cross Knight, I'll be glad to help you out." With that, Brykar leaps down, attacking the Cross Knight, who successfully dodges his first attack and has his Cross Blades appear.

The Cross Knight then leaps forward, attacking Brykar, who blocks his attacks with ease. "Is that truly the best you've got, Cross Knight?" says Brykar. "If it is, then you have no hope against me. Still, I've been looking forward to this. Now, die Cross Knight."

Charging at the Cross Knight, Brykar attacks with both of his blades in order to make the Cross Knight move backward. Instead, the Cross Knight uses his cross blades to block the attack, and as he does, he takes an angle which catches Brykar off guard.

As Joseph and Brykar turn to face each other, Brykar says, "You surprise me, Cross Knight. I see now that among all of you knights you truly do possess the most skill."

Holding both of his blades, the Cross Knight replies, "Compliments won't save you, Brykar."

This makes Brykar laugh. "I wasn't complimenting you," he says, "but merely stating that you have the most skill of the knights. However, it's still not enough to defeat me."

Again Brykar charges at the Cross Knight, who uses his blades to block the attack, taking an angle as before. Brykar turns to attack with his swords before the Cross Knight can block them, but instead, the Cross Knight is again able to take an angle that effectively blocks Brykar's attack.

The two warriors continues to clash, and with each clash, Brykar learns more about the Cross Knight. Then, suddenly, Brykar notices a blinking square on the back of his hand. He leaps backward and says, "Believe it or not, I've enjoyed this little sparring match, Cross Knight. But I have other matters that I need to attend to."

"What do you mean by that, Brykar?" the Cross Knight asks.

Chuckling, Brykar answers, "Simple, by now my upgraded warriors have captured your friends, and they are being brought to my ship. If you want to rescue them, come to these coordinates."

When Brykar throws what looks like a magnetic card to him, the Cross Knight shouts, "There's no way my friends could be defeated by your warriors, even if they were upgraded."

This causes Brykar to snicker. "Foolish human," he says. "I never expected my warriors to defeat your friends, but I did expect them to get close enough. And when they did, my warriors were equipped with a device that was set so that when your friends got close enough, they would be trapped and then transported to my ship." And before the Cross Knight can say anything else, Brykar vanishes.

AFTER BRYKAR VANISHES, the Cross Knight grabs the magnetic card and races to where Cross Cutter is waiting. As he get in, he asks, "Cutter, can you tell me the status of the other knights?"

Cutter begins to scan the area and is able to see the BOD Bots, but not the knights. Joseph has Cutter open a link to the other BOD Bots, and then he says, "BOD Bot sentient mode, engage—authorization, Cross Knight."

With that, the other BOD Bots switch to sentient mode, and the Cross Knight says, "All BOD Bots, return to base."

Each of the BOD Bots acknowledges the order and makes their way back to the base. Once they arrive at the hanger, all the BOD Bots begin to talk at once. Joseph says, "All of you, hold on! Rather than *tell* me, can each of you *show* me what happened to the other knights?"

Each of the BOD Bots nods in agreement, and one-by-one, they each show the Cross Knight how the other knights were captured. When he sees the Love Knight captured, he hits the wall.

Manuel arrives in the hanger and asks, "What's wrong, my young friend?"

Clearly frustrated, Joseph replies, "The other knights have been captured, just as it happened in my vision, and Brykar has given me the coordinates and dared me to come and rescue them."

'Pausing a moment, Manuel asks "Are you going to face him?"

The Cross Knight turns and says, "I have to."

Manuel then says, "Before you go, let me share something with you."

Puzzled, the Cross Knight asks, "What is it, Manuel?"

Placing a hand on his shoulder, Manuel replies, "As you know, we are Psythonians, and we have psychic abilities. One of these abilities is what you humans would call prophecy or visions. We are taught not to fear these visions. Rather, we are taught ignore our feelings and face these visions with courage. I know and understand why this vision bothers you. However, in order to save your friends, you must face it. Only then will you be able to unlock the power to stop Brykar and the Psystructs."

Looking at Manuel, Joseph asks, "Why are you telling me this now?"

Manuel sighs and says, "Up until now, I've not been permitted to say much, but what I have said I've said to help you."

Justice then arrives. Manuel looks to her and says, "Justice, it's time!"

Justice nods. Then she walks behind Joseph. Manuel says, "Joseph, in the fight with Phobia Fighter, there was a reason you couldn't remember how you broke free, and the reason is that we had hidden it. In that prison, you discovered a secret of the armor that you were not meant to know at the time."

A little annoyed, Joseph asks, "Then, why tell me now?"

Placing both hands on the Cross Knight's shoulder, Manuel says, "Because now is the time for you to know the secret, so that you can stop Brykar and save your friends."

Placing her hand on the back of the Cross Knight's head, Justice removes the psychic barrier that prevents the Cross Knight from remembering the armor he unlocked. As he remembers it, he asks, "With this armor, will I be able to actually stop Brykar?"

Manuel shakes his head and says, "I'm not sure. The trance Phobia Fighter had you in was in part the vision and the other part was the fear within your own heart. So there's no way to know whether that armor was real or part or part of your own mind. What you need to decide now is whether you are you going to face Brykar and this vision with fear or face it with the courage that you showed the day you received your powers? We'll give you some time to think about it."

Both Justice and Manuel leave the Cross Knight for the moment.

STANDING THERE ALL ALONE, the Cross Knight knows the decision he must make. He must face Brykar, and at this moment he must choose *how* he will face Brykar. Angry and also frightened for the lives of his friends, the Cross Knight stands before the BOD Bots and begins to think about each time he has used his powers. Suddenly and without warning, the cane of creation begins to glow, and as it does, his mind is taken to another world. There standing before him is a figure similar to Manuel and Justice.

As Joseph looks around, he sees a world teeming with life. The figure before him says, "Joseph Masters, also known as the Cross Knight, welcome to Croxia, also known as the planet of the Cross. My name is Padros, and I have brought you here because I know the choice before you."

Looking at Padros, Joseph notices that he looks similar to Manuel. He asks, "What do you mean?"

Padros replies, "I know you have a lot of questions, especially about your powers. I have brought you here so that you may know the reason why your powers are as strong as they are. There's not enough time to answer all of your questions. Just know that the twelve planets were chosen because each of them represents a part of creation. Here, however, the power of Croxia is the power to unite. If you are united, nothing will stand in your way."

Full of questions, the Cross Knight asks, "How is unity going to defeat Brykar?"

Padros chuckles and says, "When the time is right, you will know. Now, you must return and make your decision."

THE CROSS KNIGHT CLOSES HIS EYES for but a moment, and when they open, he finds himself back in the hanger. He looks at the cane of creation and thinks about what Padros has said. He knows that he must face Brykar, not with just what he's learned on his own, but also with everything he has learned from his friends.

Suddenly Joseph realizes what Padros was getting at. He turns to the BOD Bots and says, "I need all of you to stay here and wait for my signal. I'm going to face Brykar and save the others."

The Cross Knight now makes his way to the lab, where Manuel and Justice are. When they see the Cross Knight, Manuel asks, "Is everything okay, my young friend?"

Justice also looks at him and says, "Something seems different."

Looking at both of them, Joseph replies, "I'm fine, and I know what I have to do."

In unison the two asks, "And what is that?"

The Cross Knight chuckles and replies, "I'm facing Brykar and getting our friends back—no matter the cost."

CHAPTER 25

CROSS OF CREATION:
DESTINY REVEALED

WALKING TOWARD THE COMPUTER, Joseph shows Manuel what Brykar left behind. "Brykar gave me this before disappearing," he says. "He said it has coordinates on it, but I have no idea how to access it. Do you?"

Manuel looks at it, and recognizes it. "Yes," he says, "I do. This is called magcor." Taking the magcor in hand, Manuel walks to the computer and places the magcor on a panel that begins to scan it almost immediately. In a matter of seconds, a set of coordinates appear.

Joseph goes to where Des has placed the paper with the coordinates he found and notices that the coordinates are a match.

Manuel turns to Joseph and says, "I know there's nothing I can say to stop you from going after Brykar and the others, but at least take the BOD Bots with you."

Turning to Manuel and Justice, Joseph says, "That's just it. I plan to take them with me, but not initially."

Manuel and Justice look at each other and then at Joseph. Manuel asks, "What do you have in mind, my young friend?"

Joseph looks at them and says, "What I mean, Manuel, is that I'm going to port in first and set a timer. After I'm in, I'll have the BOD Bots port in and hopefully surprise Brykar, thus gaining the upper hand. Still, if there's one thing that can be certain it is that nothing is ever really fool proof. But we just have to rescue the others before it's too late."

Using the console, Joseph enters the coordinates and sets the timer for five minutes after he's in. He then turns to Manuel and Justice and says, "The coordinates are set. All you need to do now is port me there and wait for the timer to go off. Then send the BOD Bots after me."

Slowly Manuel walks toward the console. Looking at Joseph, he asks, "Are you ready, my young friend?"

Chuckling, Joseph says, "As ready as I'll ever be."

Manuel then presses the button that will port Joseph to Brykar's ship, and in an instant the Cross Knight is gone, leaving Manuel and Justice in the lab to wonder what will happen to the knights and if they will even make it out alive.

SUDDENLY, WITHOUT WARNING, THERE IS A SURGE OF ENERGY that damages the lab controls. As Manuel examines them, Justice asks "What just happened?"

Shaking his head, Manuel says, "It looks like the magcor that Brykar gave the Cross Knight also had a built-in fail-safe."

"What kind of fail-safe?" Justice asks.

Looking at the damage done, Manuel replies, "It looks like the magcor was designed to make this a one-way trip. We still have the coordinates, we just can't port anyone or anything there. So, as it stands, the Cross Knight is on his own."

THE CROSS KNIGHT FINDS HIMSELF ABOARD BRYKAR'S SHIP. He looks around, but is not exactly sure where he is. All he can tell is that he's in some kind of corridor. As he begins to walk down it, Brykar watches him from his command chamber.

As Brykar goes to meet the Cross Knight, he opens a communication channel between himself and General Sadoom. As the connection is established, General Sadoom asks, "What do you have to report, Brykar?"

Brykar says, "So far everything is going according to plan. Most of the knights have been captured and are aboard my ship. The Cross Knight has just arrived to free them, and before facing me, he will have to face all eleven of my warriors."

Chuckling, General Sadoom says, "Very good, Brykar. Although before you face the Cross Knight, I want you to establish a live feed so that I can see the destruction of this knight for myself."

With that, Brykar presses a button on his console that establishes the link General Sadoom is requesting, and Brykar says, "The link is established. Until I destroy the Cross Knight, this will be my last report."

Ending the communication, Brykar informs his warriors to go to the arena that has been especially constructed for this battle. "When the Cross Knight arrives," he says, "you are not to engage until I give the command. I'm on my way and will be there shortly."

AS BRYKAR MAKES HIS WAY TO THE ARENA, using the ship's surveillance cameras, he watches as the Cross Knight walks along the corridor. He unlocks every door along the way and activates the panels on the floor to let the Cross Knight know which way to go.

Moments later, Brykar arrives in the arena and has the captured knights placed behind where he will stand. His eleven warriors stand in a circle on the arena floor.

Once everything is in place Brykar activates a switch on his arm, and suddenly the Cross Knight is transported to the arena. As he looks around, he see Brykar and his friends high above Brykar. He also sees the eleven warriors around Brykar. Annoyed, he shouts, "I thought this was supposed to be between you and me, Brykar."

Brykar chuckles and says, "I said if you want to rescue your friends to come to the coordinates I gave you, but I never said it would be a fair fight. Now, my warriors, redeem yourselves and destroy the Cross Knight."

As Brykar's warriors begin to surround the Cross Knight, he draws his Cross Blades and says, "All right! If you want to play it that way, Brykar, I'll take them out and then I'm coming for you."

Again Brykar chuckles and says, "It's your funeral, Cross Knight!"

Seeing that Brykar's warriors are moving closer, the Cross Knight has only a few moments to figure out a way to defeat them. Each of them snickers and chuckles as they approach.

Deadly Double charges at the Cross Knight, while the Scientific Samurai approaches the Cross Knight from behind. The two warriors close in on the Cross Knight, who slides to the left and trips Deadly Double. Before he can react, the Cross Knight grabs him and throws him toward the Scientific Samurai, knocking them both to the ground. Dazed, the two warriors look at each other. Now Deadly double says, "Please tell me that did not just happen?"

The Scientific Samurai replies, "Well it did. Apparently the Cross Knight is far stronger than we first anticipated. Still, he's no match for all of us."

Rising in unison, both Deadly Double and the Scientific Samurai charge at the Cross Knight. He also charges at them. As the Cross Knight reaches them, he leaps and soars over them. When he lands, he turns toward both warriors and crosses his arms, causing energy to build in both arms. Pointing his arms toward the two aggressors, he fires an energy blast that hits them, knocking them both to the floor and toward their fellow warriors.

Now the Scientific Samurai and Deadly Double are furious that the Cross Knight has made them look like fools. Deadly Double transforms himself to look like the Scientific Samurai, then begins to create doubles so that instead of just two Samurai, there are now twelve. Not intimidated, the Cross Knight chuckles and says, "If you think that's enough to stop me, you're dead wrong. Now, let me show you *my* trick."

Suddenly, the Cross Knight begins to use his cross clones, so that instead of one of him, there are twelve Cross Knights, and each of the knights begins to surround each of the Scientific Samurai. In unison they shout, "This changes nothing! We are not scared of you!"

Also in unison, the Cross Knights chuckle and say, "You don't have to be scared of me for me to beat you down. It's time to end this."

With that, each of the Cross Knights crosses his arms, and energy begins to build in their chest plates. Then, as they uncross their arms, each knight forms a cross with his body, and in unison they shout, "Cross beam blast." This allows the energy that has built up to be focused in powerful beams that vaporize all versions of the Scientific Samurai. All that is left in their place is a dust cloud and a small patch of ashes.

WHEN THE DUST CLOUD CLEARS, Brykar and his remaining warriors notice that there are now only ten of the Cross Knight clones. All of the clones of the Scientific Samurai, the Deadly Double and the original Scientific Samurai have been reduced to ashes. Looking at them, Brykar says, "Impressive, Cross Knight! But if you wish to save your friends, you will have to do better than that."

Again in unison, the Cross Knights shout, "We intend to, Brykar."

NEXT, THE PHOBIA FIGHTER, THE SEDUCTIVE SIREN, THE ELEMENTAL Enforcer and Brillander step forward, and four of the Cross Knights step forward as well. First, Phobia Fighter walks toward them in an attempt to imprison them in their own fears. As one of the four Cross Knights see this, he charges at Phobia Fighter, and as he does this, he crosses his arms across his chest. Then, like before, the Cross Knight leaps over Phobia Fighter, who turns to face him, and shouts, "Cross Beam blast!" The resulting blast reduces Phobia Fighter to a pile of ashes. Brykar and his remaining warriors watch as the Cross Knight that has destroyed Phobia Fighter begins to fade.

NOW THE SEDUCTIVE SIREN BEGINS TO USE HER VOICE to put all of the remaining Cross Knights under her power. But one of the Cross Knights creates a barrier over each of the other knights, protecting them from her power. Shocked by this, she says, "How is this possible? I thought only the Aqua Knight was immune to my powers."

One of the Cross Knights replies, "That's where you're wrong, Siren. We know what you can do and what you are capable of and now that we know, we can counter your surprises immediately."

With that, Brillander begins to throw crystals from his hands, forcing all the Cross Knights to scatter. Then he nods toward the Elemental Enforcer, who charges at one of the Cross Knights in order to absorb his powers. As he does this, another of the Cross Knights uses his sword to deflect the crystals being fired so that they hit the Elemental Enforcer's gauntlets, destroying them, so that he can no longer absorb the Cross Knight's powers.

As each of these warriors becomes frustrated, the Elemental Enforcer shouts, "How is it possible? You never showed this level of skill before, so how is possible that you are able to do this now?"

In unison, all the Cross Knights reply, "That's our little secret."

The three Cross Knights then draw their cross blades and charge at the Seductive Siren, the Elemental Enforcer and Brillander. As they charge at them, their blades are being charged with energy.

Standing her ground, the Seductive Siren is the first to try to block the attack with her sonic spear. As she does, the Cross Knight's blade slices through her spear and next through her, reducing her to a pile of ash.

The Elemental Enforcer is the next to attempt to block the attack. As he does, the Cross Knight slices through his swords, then slices through him, also reducing him to ash.

Brillander uses his powers to create a crystal shield to block the Cross Knight's strike. However, even his shield is unable to block the strike that reduces him and his shield to ashes.

With only five warriors remaining, Brykar watches as the Cross Knight's doubles fade, so that now there are only six. It is at this moment that Brykar realizes the secret of why the Cross Knight is able to fight as he does.

NEXT NOSVORAT, LEO UNTAROS, DISPOTIER, SIR PENTOUS and Jezabeel all step forward at once to face the Cross Knight and his doubles. As they do so, one of the Cross Knights charges in with his blade. Sir Pentous steps in front of the others, to act as a shield. Before the Cross Knight reaches him, he leaps, revealing that one of the Cross Knights is behind him. He fires his Cross Beam Blast, vaporizing Sir Pentous and, like the others, leaving him in a pile of ashes.

Brykar's remaining warriors are frustrated at how the Cross Knight has been able to do so much damage. Before they can do anything else, Brykar shouts, "Impressive, earthling! But I know your secret and how you've been able to best my warriors thus far."

The remaining warriors look at Brykar. Leo Untaros says, "Tell us what his secret is, Commander Brykar?"

Looking at each of his warriors, Brykar replies, "No, just as I figured out what his secret is, so can each of you. All you have to do is observe carefully."

With that, Leo Untaros, roars and says, "Forget it! I will crush you myself!" Using his chain blade, he has it go to entrap one of the Cross Knights, but as it does, another Cross Knight focuses energy into his cross blades and charges in. As he does so, he cuts Leo Untaros's chain blade to pieces. Then another Cross Knight speeds past Leo Untaros and slices him with a charged energy blade, so that like the others he's now nothing more than a pile of ashes.

Like before, with the defeat of one of Brykar's warriors, another Cross Knight vanishes.

WITH ONLY THREE WARRIORS REMAINING, Brykar is somewhat amused at the fact that his warriors are so concerned with self-preservation that they cannot see what is happening. Just as Brykar has been watching the battle, so has one of the Cross Knights.

STEPPING FORWARD NOW, Dispotier says, "Enough of this! The rest of you may fear for your lives, but the only one who ever defeated me is trapped, and now this knight will be trapped as well." Walking toward the Cross Knights, Dispotier chuckles, then shouts, "It's time to die, Cross Knights!" He then vanishes, as he has done before with the other knights.

When he reappears and touches one of the Cross Knights on the shoulder from behind, he finds that his hand is burning. The Cross Knight he touched turns to him and says, "Not today, Dispotier!" Turning toward Dispotier in one swift motion, the Cross Knight slices Dispotier. As his blade points toward the sky, the Cross Knight charges it with energy so that as he brings it down, he slices Dispotier once more. With this slice, Dispotier is now reduced to ashes.

WITH ONLY TWO CROSS KNIGHTS REMAINING, Jezabeel uses her magic to create a flash of light, making herself look like the Love Knight and making Nosvorat look like her. As the Cross Knights look, they see the Love Knight standing before them. She walks toward them, noting that they are shocked to see her. She says, "It's okay! I was able to get free. Now, let's finish off Jezabeel and get out of here."

As she gets closer with each step, one of the two Cross Knights says, "Stop! If you are who you say you are, then say my name!"

Chuckling, she says, "Your name is the Cross Knight, of course."

The Cross Knight bows his head, Then he looks at her and shouts, "Wrong answer, witch!"

In an instant, he charges his blade and starts moving toward her. "What are you talking about?" she says. "It's me?"

Ignoring her pleas, this Cross Knight says, "No! You're not her! And you will never be her!"

Then, with one motion, this Cross Knight uses his blade and reduces Jezabeel to ashes. As her spell ends, the Cross Knight turns to see Nosvorat, but not Jezabeel.

NOTICING THAT HE'S THE LAST ONE LEFT, Nosvorat uses a sonic blast to try to destroy the remaining Cross Knight's balance, but it has no effect. The last Cross Knight walks toward him with his blade charged. Nosvorat turns to fly away, but before he can, the Cross Knight uses his blade to send a blast of energy and reduces him to ashes like the others.

Watching as the final Cross Knight disappears, Brykar says, "I must say this was rather enjoyable, Cross Knight. I knew, after having been defeated once, they would be defeated again, but, still, it will not be enough to defeat me—as you will now see."

Leaping down to where the ashes of his fallen warriors lie, Brykar watches as the Cross Knight he was watching also leaps down. Looking at him, Brykar says, "Are your friends really that important that you would throw you life away so quickly?"

Without any hesitation, the Cross Knight answers, "They are! And if you think you can take me out, let's see you try."

Brykar draws his swords and walks toward the Cross Knight. Suddenly there are twelve Cross Knights, including the one in front of him. Brykar says, "I find it interesting that you were able to maintain your doubles for so long while not losing any power. But still, even with a hundred of you, there's no way you could ever defeat me. Now, let me show you why." Brykar now draws both of his swords, and as he connects them, they form a new sword. "This is my Breaker Blade," he says, "and it will be what breaks you today, Cross Knight." Using his Breaker Blade, Brykar swings, sending out a wave, knocking all of the Cross Knights down and forcing the Cross Knight to have to return.

As the Cross Knight starts to rise, he pauses a moment and notices that the scene before him is the same as the vision he has seen countless times before. This time, however, he knows this is no vision and that he must stop Brykar and save his friends.

Looking at the Cross Knight, Brykar says, "If you think you're strong enough to defeat me, then stand and fight!"

As the Cross Knight gets to his feet, he notices that the BOD Bots haven't arrived yet, which must mean that something has gone wrong. Standing to his feet, he shouts, "Cross of Creation armor, engage!" In seconds, the Cross Knight's armor transforms into his secondary armor. He takes the Cane of

Creation in his hands and replies, "Yes, let's finish this, Brykar." With that, the two warriors charge at each other.

The Cross Knight uses his cane to block and deflect Brykar's Breaker Blade. Brykar chuckles and says, "You are much stronger than I first thought. Still, it will not be enough to defeat me."

Also chuckling, the Cross Knight replies, "We'll just see about that, Brykar."

The two warriors continue to clash, with neither one backing down. Then Brykar leaps to where the other knights are. As the Cross Knight watches, he knows that no matter what, this will not be the end.

Looking at the Cross Knight, Brykar says, "Say farewell to your friends!" And with that, using his Breaker Blade, he destroys the knights trapped in the psyer and shatters them into crystal-like pieces on the floor.

As the Cross Knight watches helplessly, he shouts, "YOU WILL PAY FOR THAT, BRYKAR! DO YOU HEAR ME? YOU WILL PAY!"

At this point, Brykar knows the Cross Knight will be vulnerable. As he watches the Cross Knight charge toward him, Brykar uses his blade and cuts the Cross Knight's side and throws him to the floor. As the Cross Knight lies there, Brykar leaps down and says, "It's over, Cross Knight! For all your talk, for all that you have done, you have failed. Your friends are gone, and you are wounded and beneath my feet. I've watched you and your friends defeat my warriors time and time again, and now I shall make you suffer for the humiliation that you have caused me."

Brykar watches as the Cross Knight turns to try to crawl away. Grabbing him by the ankle, Brykar pulls him back and slams him to the floor again. Brykar is surprised that the Cross Knight's cane is still in his hand. He begins to chuckle to himself.

The Cross Knight now feels his life slipping away, and he whispers to himself, "I'm sorry, everyone! I failed you!"

Brykar grabs the Cross Knight again and throws him into a wall. As he falls to the ground, the Cross Knight continues to whisper to himself, "*As days of darkness near, and people run in fear ...*"

Brykar makes his way toward him and then throws him again, this time into another wall. But even as the Cross Knight falls to the floor, he is able to hold tightly to the Cane of Creation, and he continues to whisper, *"From they who prey on the weak, and silence those who speak..."*

This time, as Brykar walks toward him, he uses his blade and stabs it through the stomach of the Cross Knight. Severely weakened, the Cross Knight is still holding the cane. He whispers, *"We will take to the sky with courage and battle cry..."*

Noticing that the Cross Knight is whispering something, Brykar chuckles. "Some last words, Cross Knight?" he asks.

Looking directly at Brykar, the Cross Knight nods. Then, summoning all of his remaining strength, he shouts "TO PROTECT THE WORLD FROM LOSS, I AM A KNIGHT OF THE CROSS! RESURRECTION POWER, ENGAGE" Suddenly a surge of energy fills the Cross Knight. He knocks Brykar back and shatters his Breaker Blade.

Watching with awe as energy fills the Cross Knight, Brykar now sees the Cross Knight stand to his feet. He notices that the energy that rescued the Cross Knight has now filled the room. It moves to where the pieces of his friend are lying. As the pieces are gathered, Brykar watches as the knights are reformed to the way they were before he destroyed them.

Shocked, he shouts, "How can this be?"

As the Cross Knight stands to his feet, the energy that now fills the room breaks the psyer and frees the once-trapped knights. Then, raising the Cane of Creation in his hand, the Cross Knight shouts, "To light the night, Armors unite! Apostolic Armor, engage! " In an instant, each of the knights becomes a ball of energy. As they gather to the Cross Knight, the light becomes brighter and brighter. The Cross Knight's armor begins to change, and instead of just one knight, now there are twelve.

When the transformation is complete, Brykar sees that there are now twelve knights as there were before. "You've tried this trick," he says, "and it won't work on me."

The Cross Knight chuckles and says, "This is no trick, Brykar! These are not my clones. These are my friends, the knights you thought you had destroyed."

Angry, Brykar shouts, "How is this possible? There's no way they could be alive!"

The Cross Knight points the Cane of Creation at Brykar and replies, "You thought power was simply to destroy, but there is a greater power, a power that can restore, and it's the power of Creation. Now, it's time I end this."

As the Cross Knight walks toward Brykar, Brykar charges at him. Using the Cane of Creation, he blocks each strike with ease. Again using the Cane of Creation, he taps Brykar on the side of his head, knocking him back with a force that sends him flying into the wall.

Brykar tries to get up and is shocked that, for the first time in a long time, he is actually hurt. He says, "I will not be defeated like this! I will destroy you! Do you hear me?"

The Cross Knight shakes his head and replies, "No, you won't! You will never harm another person after today."

Again Brykar attacks. Channeling his energy, he begins firing what looks like thousands of blades at the Cross Knight, but the Cross Knight deflects each one with ease. When the barrage is over, Brykar watches as the Cross Knight continues to approach. When the Cross Knight reaches Brykar, he tries to strike the Cross Knight. Not only is his attack blocked, but the Cross Knight's block sends Brykar flying into another wall.

The Cross Knight watches as Brykar gets up and walks toward him. When he reaches him, Brykar looks up and tries to stab the Cross Knight with his wrist blades. The Cross Knight blocks the blades, causing them to shatter.

While Brykar is on his knees, he says, "This is not the end! I will find a way to make you pay! I will kill you for this!"

Again the Cross Knight looks at him and replies, "No, you won't!" With that, the Cross Knight points at Brykar with the Cane of Creation in his hand and fires a blast that vaporizes him, just as it did his warriors.

MEANWHILE, AT THE BASE OF THE ARC TEAM, Agent Wallace has had Agent Saunders working on compiling all the information known about the knights from the video footage and other gathered intel. As Agent Wallace enters, he asks, "How's it going with gathering that information I asked you for?"

"I knew this would be a challenge," she answers, "but I never expected for it to be *this* challenging."

A bit puzzled by this answer, Agent Wallace asks, "What do you mean by that, Agent Saunders?"

She sighs and replies, "What I mean is that there's not really a lot to go on in regard to these knights. All we really know is about their power sets. Even then, from what I'm noticing, five of them are elemental warriors, and the others are powers that are really hard to pin down. If we were dealing with humans, it would be a lot easier, but we have no way of knowing what kind of beings we're even dealing with."

Sitting down next o her, Agent Wallace says, "Well, do the best you can. We need that intel as soon as possible so we can deal with them."

At that moment, Agent Daniels walks in and tosses a flash drive to Agent Saunders, telling her, "I was going through the surveillance files of the most recent battles between the knights and the Psystructs and was able to gather a bit more on the knights. I figured this might help you out."

"Thanks!" Agent Saunders says.

Agent Daniels turns and walks out. As she exits, Agent Saunders inserts the drive into the computer and discovers that it contains a lot more about the fighting styles of the knights. She says, "This is awesome! With this, I should be able to have the info we need in a few hours."

Agent Wallace stands and replies, "Perfect! I'll leave you to it. I've got some other things that I need to check on." And with that, Agent Wallace leaves the room.

As Agent Saunders looks at the info and works on the files, Agent Rivera comes in. She says, "How's the data collection coming, Agent Saunders?"

Saunders shakes her head, knowing that Agent Rivera always has an ulterior motive with everything she does. She replies, "What do you want, Agent Rivera?"

Taking her glasses off and wiping them, Agent Rivera answers, "I'd like you to make a copy of the info your gathering so that I can use it to enhance the armors I'm working on. I know you have a lot on your plate, but it would really help me to make sure we're prepared."

Thinking for a moment, Agent Saunders asks, "Is that it?"

Putting her glasses back, on Agent Rivera replies, "That's pretty much it."

Tilting her head to the side, Agent Saunders says, "As soon as I'm done, I'll take care of it, so that you'll have what you need."

Pivoting on her feet, Agent Rivera turns to the door and leaves Agent Saunders to complete her task.

GRAHAM HAS JUST FINISHED TESTING the communication devices he has created. They look like normal smartphones, with one unique feature, and that feature will allow him and the other parents to communicate with his brother and his friends without being traced. He then contacts Melanie via text: "Gather everyone together. I've got the devices we need to communicate to the others. We just need to figure out a way to get one to them."

After a few minutes, Melanie replies: "All right. I'll work on it. We should be ready to meet in a few hours."

Graham looks at the communication devices. He desperately hopes they will be the key to finally reach his brother and find out what exactly is going on.

Just then there's a knock on the door, and Graham's mom enters. She asks, "How's it going with the communication devices, so that we can speak with your brother and the others?"

He smiles and says, "They're ready. We just need to find a way to get one to them. Melanie says we should be able to meet in a few hours."

Smiling at her son's success, she replies, "That's good to hear. I can't wait to hear from him and know if they're okay."

Graham bows his head and replies, "Same here. I mean, even though, in theory, the adjustments I made should work, there's no real way to know until we fully implement the system."

Looking at her son she asks, "What is it exactly that you did to those phones?"

Taking a breath, Graham replies, "Well, first I put a scrambling chip inside the phones and then created an app to activate it. Once the app is active, calls between the phones will be constantly bounced so that it will be hard to pin down any exact location."

His mother shakes her head and says, "Sometimes it's hard to believe you and Desmond are my sons. I'm so proud of both of you."

Before anything else can be said, both of them receive a text from Melanie which says, "Everyone will meet at my house in two hours to discuss his device and how they can talk to the kids."

Graham looks at his mother and says, "Now, the hard part: how to get these to Des and the others."

始まりの終わり

CHAPTER 26

THE END OF THE BEGINNING

TWO HOURS LATER, THE PARENTS ARE ALL GATHERED at Melanie's house. As everyone gets settled, she says, "Welcome everyone! As you know, Graham has been working on a device that should allow us to communicate with the others and finally find out what is going on. We all have a lot more questions than answers. Right now, the main question we have to answer is this: how to get one of these communicators to the kids so we can know that they are okay."

Each of them thinks for a moment. Phillip asks, "This might be a long shot, but what about going to where the bus was destroyed and seeing if we can leave it there."

David replies, "Even if we did that, who knows how long the battery will last or if it will fry in that dessert heat."

Now Graham stands up and says, "Those are all valid points, but the main concern here is being able to reach them without drawing any unwanted attention. I think going to that area would be the best place to try to get the communicator to them, but I agree: we can't just leave it lying around. So, this is what I propose. I'll drive out there with the communicator and see if maybe they're hiding somewhere in the dessert."

Shaking his head, David responds, "I don't like this, but I don't think we're really left with any other option."

Deborah then asks, "Won't that area be watched for anything suspicious?"

Graham replies, "Normally it would, but I have been noticing that the parents of the students who died have been going there frequently to mourn the loss of their children. So, traffic there is actually pretty common now. Still, that's why I'll be the one to go, and my jeep will be able to handle the terrain should I go off-road."

A bit stumped, Phillip asks, "What do you mean by 'off-road'?"

Looking at them all, Graham replies, "What I mean is there are a lot of dirt roads around that area, so my jeep would probably be the best vehicle to handle them. Besides, most if not all of you have day jobs, whereas I'm on a break currently and can make it out there quickly."

None of the parents like Graham's idea, but they also know that at this point in time it may be the best option they have. Melanie then speaks up, "Graham, none of us likes the idea of you going alone, ... which is why I'm going with you. This way, if anything happens, someone will be with you to watch your back."

Before anyone can object to her idea, Melanie adds, "I know me going out there is probably not the best idea, but I have two children missing, and nothing and no one is going to change my mind." With that, everyone in the room nods their agreement, and Graham begins making a list of the items they will need to make the trip.

THE ARC TEAM IS CURRENTLY MEETING in Agent Rivera's lab. Agent Saunders has finished compiling her analysis of the knights powers and abilities, and she hands a stack of papers containing the info on all twelve knight to Agent Rivera. Agent Stanton asks, "Why is she getting a stack on all twelve knights?"

Turning to him, Agent Saunders replies, "Because she's developing the weaponry so that we can fight the knights and so you will be able to take them out."

Turning to the files before her, she looks at each of them and says, "Now comes the hard part, which is to distribute the files to each of you so that you can study a particular knight and learn their weaknesses."

Pausing a moment, Agent Saunders looks at Agent Marks, then hands him the file on the Fire Knight.

Next, she hands the file on the Earth Knight to Agent Stanton.

After that, she hands the file on the Wind Knight to Agent Rivera, who looks at her and says, "I already have this information."

Agent Saunders replies, "I know you do, but the reason you have it was not for studying their weaknesses. This time it is, and it's a formality that must take place."

Looking at Agent Daniels, she hands her the file on the Aqua Knight. Then she hands Agent Ryan the file on the Bolt Knight.

She looks around at the remaining agents, then passes the file on the Shadow Knight to Agent Miles, the file on the Light Knight to Agent Damien and the file on the Beast Knight to Agent Claudia.

With four files remaining, she passes the file on the Hope Knight to Agent Styles and the file on the Faith Knight to Agent Michael. This leaves the final two files. Agent Saunders takes the file on the Love Knight, who, to them, is known as the Lust Knight, and gives Agent Wallace the file on the Cross Knight.

Now that all of the files have been distributed, Agent Saunders gives the floor to Agent Wallace. He says, "All right. You all have your assignments. Now, I recommend that each of you get started so that as soon as we face these knights, we can take them down. I want each and every one of you to be in top form. I don't want any slip-ups. Is that clear?" All the agents nod in agreement, and with that they dismiss.

Agent Saunders goes to Agent Daniels and says, "Hey, Daniels, I never got a chance to thank you for the drive you gave me. It really helped. I just have one question: why did you give it to me?"

Shaking her head, Agent Daniels tells her, "As much as I can't stand how you've been acting, the fact is it's in my own best interest to help you. Besides, we all need to go into this as prepared as possible."

Surprised by this, Agent Saunders replies, "Well, I know it may not seem like much, but I want to say thanks for the assist. Now, let's get started on our training." The two agents go off in different directions to train.

THE KNIGHTS ARE STILL ABOARD BRYKAR'S SHIP. As the Cross Knight stands over the remains of Brykar, the other knights gather around him. The Fire Knight asks, "What exactly happened? The last thing I remember is being trapped, watching you fight Brykar ... and then nothing."

Stepping forward, the Earth Knight replies, "I agree. This makes no logical sense. How are we even still alive?"

Looking at his friends, the Cross Knight says, "I know you all have a lot of questions, as do I, but right now let's see what we can learn from this ship. Then we can figure out what just happened. Does everyone agree?"

Each of the knights nods their agreement, and they make their way out of the arena.

THE LIGHT KNIGHT ASKS, "So, where exactly are we headed?"

Pausing a moment, the Cross Knight says, "That's a good question. Earth Knight, can you pinpoint where exactly Brykar's main computer is?"

Thinking for a moment, he replies, "That shouldn't be too difficult." Walking over to the nearest computer panel, the Earth Knight places his hand on the panel. Searching through the base archives, he finds a map of the base and uploads it to his helmet. He tells the others, "I've got a map, so let's find out what secrets Brykar was hiding."

AS THE KNIGHTS MAKE THEIR WAY THROUGH Brykar's base, the Earth Knight notices one room that looks like a central command station. He says, "I think I may have found where Brykar's central computer might be, but I have no way to be a hundred percent sure."

The Cross Knight replies, "We still need to check it out. Something tells me this is not the end."

As they are making their way through the base to what they believe to be Brykar's main control room, the Shadow Knight asks, "Has anyone noticed that since the Cross Knight defeated Brykar, we haven't seen even one Psydrone?"

Pausing a moment, the Bolt Knight replies, "That's a good point. Why does this place seem so deserted?"

Before anything else can be said, they come across several Psydrones that are motionless. As the Earth Knight approaches, he touches one of them, and it falls to the floor with a loud thud. As the other knights watch this, he says, "Just as I thought."

Shaking her head, the Aqua Knight asks, "What is it?"

The Earth Knight replies, "Without Brykar or his warriors, the Psydrones are just lifeless husks."

Chuckling, the Wind Knight says, "Could you say that in English please?"

Turning to address the rest of the knights, the Earth Knight replies, "Simply put, the Psydrones are powered by psychic abilities, and without Brykar or his warriors, they're nothing more than statues."

MOMENTS LATER THEY MAKE IT to what they believe to be Brykar's central command station. As they enter, the lights come on, and they see what appears to be some sort of chair and a computer system. The Earth Knight goes to check it out and notices that the tech is similar to their own base and that someone is trying to contact Brykar.

The Earth Knight sees a magcor next to him. After scanning it to be sure what it is and what it can do, he uses it to start downloading the data from the main computer. Then he opens the communication channel to receive the message.

As the link is established, they see General Sadoom, who then says, "Welcome, Knights of the Cross! My name is General Sadoom, and I was the one who sent Brykar to your planet. Now I see that this is something I must handle myself."

Stepping toward the Cross Knight asks, "What do you mean, Sadoom?" General Sadoom chuckles as he replies, "What I mean is that I will be making my way to Earth, and I will make sure to end you. It will take me and my team three months to arrive. You have until then to say goodbye to your loved ones because once we reach your planet, we will destroy you. Also, I've activated this ship's self-destruct system, which gives all of you just two of your earth minutes to escape." With that, the communication ends, and a countdown timer appears.

The Cross Knight says, "We need to get out of here—NOW!"

The Earth Knight turns to the Cross Knight and says, "I just need a little bit of time to finish this download."

The Shadow Knight shouts, "We don't have time for that!"

The Cross Knight responds, "Everyone, port out of here—NOW! I'll stay with the Earth Knight until the download is finished."

Nodding in agreement, the other knights port out of Brykar's ship one by one.

WHILE THE TIMER COUNTS DOWN, the Cross Knight asks, "How much longer on the download?"

The Earth Knight replies, "About one more minute."

Looking at the timer, the Cross Knight replies, "Good, cause that's all we've got."

As the timers for the download and the self-destruct race against each other, the two knights begin to feel Brykar's base shaking more and more as the countdown gets closer to the end.

With seconds remaining, the download finishes, and the countdown timer also reaches its end. The two knights hear explosions going off throughout the base. The Earth Knight grabs the magcor. Just as the explosions reach where they are, the two knights port from the base, and Brykar's ship is consumed by the explosions.

BACK IN THE KNIGHT'S BASE, the Cross Knight arrives safely in the lab with others. Manuel and Justice are there, but there is no sign of the Earth Knight. Looking at Manuel, the Cross Knight says, "Where's the Earth Knight?"

The Shadow Knight replies, "I thought he was with you?"

Turning to the other knights, he says, "He was. We ported out together. Manuel, is it possible the explosion affected where he ported to?"

Manuel thinks for a moment and then replies, "That's very possible. I'll conduct a scan to see if we can find him."

While Manuel does that, the Cross Knight says, "Okay, until Manuel finds the Earth Knight, we need to focus on this new development."

Justice asks, "What do you mean?"

Looking at Justice, the Light Knight replies, "While we were searching Brykar's ship, someone named Sadoom said he is on his way here and will be here in three months to destroy us."

Pausing a moment, Manuel asks, "Did you just say 'Sadoom' as in General Sadoom?"

Looking at Manuel, the Cross Knight asks, "I take it you've heard of him."

Nodding his head, Manuel replies, "Yes, I have, and if he's on his way, you all need to be prepared, for he is far stronger than Brykar or his warriors."

Manuel now turns his attention back to the console and resumes the search for the Earth Knight. The Cross Knight gathers the other knights and says, "I know you all have concerns, but right now we need to focus and train, not just our bodies, but our minds, so that when General Sadoom gets here, we'll stand a fighting chance. If there's anything I've learned today it is that as strong as the Psystructs are, they're not invincible. As long as we remember the lessons that allowed us to access our secondary armors, our powers will grow. Now, I want all of you to go and relax until we can find the Earth Knight."

Slowly each of the knights nods in agreement and leaves the lab, with the exception of the Aqua Knight and the Cross Knight. The Cross Knight asks, "Is everything okay, Jessica? Why aren't you going to relax?"

She chuckles as she responds, "You should already know that until we find the Earth Knight I can't relax. By staying here, at least I can help with the search. Besides, shouldn't you be taking your own advice."

The two knights both begin to chuckle, and the Cross Knight replies, "Okay, point taken. I just hope we find him soon."

Then the Aqua Knight asks, "By the way, you mentioned that you would explain later how we were all brought back."

Both Manuel and Justice are listening. Justice asks, "What do you mean by brought back?"

The Cross Knight responds by saying, "Do you remember how I said in my vision I watched all the knights die?"

Justice nods and the Cross Knight continues, "Well, Brykar destroyed the psyer that had the knights trapped, and he stabbed me through the stomach. As I recited the oath, I felt a strange surge of energy and shouted, "Resurrection power, engage!" The next thing I knew the other knights and I were restored, and the armor I had unlocked in Phobia Fighter's vision enabled me to defeat Brykar."

As Manuel hears this, he tells the Cross Knight, "Once we find the Earth Knight, I will explain what exactly happened."

Suddenly Manuel gets a location on the Earth Knight and chuckles as he says, "Guess where I found him."

"Where?" The Cross Knight asks

"According to the scans," Manuel answers, "he's actually in your home ... where your mother is."

AT THAT MOMENT, THE EARTH KNIGHT STARTS TO AWAKEN. He notices where he is and thinks to himself, "How did I get *here*?"

Standing to his feet, he notices the magcor next to him. When he grabs it, he reverts to his human form and makes his way downstairs. There he sees everyone, including his brother Graham and his mom. For the briefest of moments, Des is overjoyed, but he knows he can't stay. As he gets ready to go back upstairs, Graham notices him. He taps Melanie and says, "Follow me—now!" The two head quickly up the stairs.

As Des enters an upstairs room, he attempts to port, but is unable to. Just then, Graham and Melanie enter the room. Graham grabs his brother and hugs him. "I knew it was you," he says, "I knew it."

Melanie also tears up.

As the brothers separate, she says, "Hey Des, it's good to see you."

Looking at her, he says, "It's good to be seen."

Taking a deep breath, Melanie asks, "Des, I know it may sound rude, but are Brad and Joseph okay?"

Knowing why she has asked this, he replies, "Yeah! They're both fine ... and they're getting along."

Overjoyed that both of her sons are okay, Melanie starts to cry.

Graham eyes the communicators. He picks up one, gives it to Des and says, "Hey, Bro, I developed two of these so that we'll have a way to communicate with you guys that can't be tracked."

Looking at the device, Des responds, "This is fantastic! But where I'm at, I have gear that will improve on this exponentially. Could you give me both of them, and I'll send one of them back to you?"

Graham grabs the other one and gives it to his brother. Then he says, "I know you had nothing to do with the buses blowing up, but what actually happened?"

Des sighs and then replies, "I'll tell you both, but you aren't going to believe it. You see, the day the buses blew up, both Brad and Joseph were about to fight, and the rest of us were just going to watch. Then we heard the explosion. At that point, we looked to see what was going on and saw that the buses had been destroyed by an alien craft."

Looking at him in shock, Graham says, "Are you talking little green men aliens?"

Chuckling a moment, Des replies, "No, they were not like that. But these things would give movie monsters nightmares. After that, those aliens came after us, and luckily we were able to beat them. But, shortly after that, we were taken to a secret base, where we were given powers in order to protect the Earth ... which is why we weren't able to contact you."

Taken aback by this statement, Melanie asks, "If that's the case, why are you here?"

Looking at both of them, Des replies, "That just it! I don't know how I got here! But I have to get back — and soon. Just know that we're all okay and we're safe."

Suddenly the Cross Knight appears, causing Graham and Melanie to jump. As Graham sees him, he asks, "Who or what is that?"

Shaking his head, the Cross Knight reverts to his human form of Joseph. When Melanie sees him, she runs to him and hugs him, and he hugs her back. He says, "It's okay, mom. Brad and I are okay. I hate to do this, but I only came to get Des. Now we have to go. Just know we're okay."

With that, Joseph steps back and, placing a hand on Des, he ports both of them back to their base. Melanie and Graham are left looking at each other. She says, "They're never going to believe *this*."

WHEN JOSEPH AND DES RETURN TO THE BASE, the Aqua Knight reverts to her human form of Jessica and hugs Des tight. Joseph chuckles as the others rush to the lab. Seeing that the other knights are there, Joseph says, "Okay, Manuel. Now that we're all here, what is it that you wanted to explain to us?"

Manuel then stand before the knights and says, "As you know, each of your armors comes from a different planet, but what you do *not* know is that the final planet was a planet of unity. Being such a planet, it's power was based on creation. You see, only through the power of unity could the power of creation be unlocked. Apparently, during the battle with Brykar, the Cross Knight was able to unlock it, which allowed him to use what's known as 'Resurrection Power,' which was a well-kept secret of Croxia."

"Awesome!" Brad says. "Now we can't die!"

Before anything else can be said, Manuel replies, "Hold on, my young friend. Although it's true that the Cross Knight accessed this ability, it's not something that can easily be done. I would advise you not to push your luck since we're not sure how often it can be used."

Walking over to the computer, Des begins a scan of himself. Joseph asks, "What's wrong, Des?"

Des turns to his friend and responds, "I'm bothered by the fact that I couldn't port back, and I want to know why."

Moving next to him, Jessica asks, "So, what have you found out?"

Studying the screen, Des replies, "According to this, when I tried to port, there was a negative charge from the explosion that temporarily disabled my ability to port. But, if that's the case, then Joseph's ability to port should have been affected too."

Then he says, "Wait a minute!" Using the computer, he adds the fact that he had the magcor. Now he shouts, "Of course! That's why I couldn't port back!"

Puzzled, Joseph asks, "What did you find, Des?"

Tossing the magcor from his pocket, he says, "That's what caused the problem."

Still a bit baffled, Joseph asks, "How did a magcor disable your port system?"

Looking at all of them, Des replies, "Normally the magcors are harmless. However, when used with porting technology, the port process causes a small feedback loop, blocking the ability to port for some time."

Turning to Manuel, Joseph asks, "Is that why the BOD Bots weren't able to follow after me." Manuel nods, and Joseph continues, "Well, now that we're all back, I think everyone should take tonight off, and tomorrow we'll begin training. We've got a long road ahead."

GENERAL SADOOM HAS GATHERED ELEVEN of his most powerful warriors and has them aboard his ship. He now turns to the other nine generals and says, "With Brykar defeated, I shall now have go to destroy these humans myself." The other generals, hidden around him in shadow, all nod their agreement.

Before General Sadoom gets on his ship, he goes to where his chamber was and grabs the orb that he had shown Brykar. With the orb in hand, he now boards a craft very similar to the one Brykar commanded. As the ship's engines start, the psystruct General makes his way to his command post and he sits down. He has the Psydrones that are with him plot a course for Earth.

Soon General Sadoom's aid, known as Vagros walks in. He looks like a mix between a human butler and a robot. He says, "General Sadoom, I know this is protocol, but are you sure it was wise to give the knights three month's time to prepare for our arrival?"

Standing to his feet, General Sadoom replies, "Given the situation, I would have given them less time. However, due to our current position, even at max power it will take three months for us to get to Earth. So, Vagros, it was not only simply because of protocol that I had to give them three months; it was also because of necessity. Now, Vagros, pull up the video of the final battle between the knights and Brykar so that I may study it and them."

As Vagros gets everything ready, he begins to watch the video of their final battle with Brykar.

A FEW HOURS LATER, THE SHIP for General Sadoom and his warriors is ready. As they board it, Sadoom takes his seat. When the hanger doors open and the ship begins it journey to earth, General Sadoom says, "It's time to light the knights!"

ENDNOTES

1. Genesis 4:6-7
2. Proverbs 11:2
3. Proverbs 29:2
4. 1 Corinthians 3:18
5. Proverbs 14:15
6. Psalm 18:14
7. Romans 7:15
8. John 1:5
9. Ibid
10. Matthew 10:16
11. Romans 8:24
12. Hebrews 11:1
13. 2 Corinthians 5:7
14. 1 Corinthians 8:1
15. 1 Corinthians 13:7

AUTHOR CONTACT

You may contact the author by email at:

knightsofthecrossbook@gmail.com.

www.ingramcontent.com/pod-product-compliance
Lightning Source LLC
Chambersburg PA
CBHW031958060726
47497CB00015B/290